Love In Lansing
BOOK THREE

A Calling *for* Phoebe

JENIFER CARLL-TONG

philo se
PUBLISHING

WOULD YOU LIKE A FREE BOOK?

~

Have you read Book 2 in the Love in Lansing series? Would you like to stay up to date with all the latest news and upcoming releases? Sign up for Jenifer's newsletter and receive *Avoiding Esther* as a free ebook download! Visit https://goo.gl/Qur2sU today!

DEDICATION

In memory of Janet Yvonne Rock...
Beloved aunt, confidante, cheerleader and friend. I wish you could be
here to celebrate the book that you so ardently encouraged me to write.
I miss you every single day.

"I thank my God every time I remember you." ~ Philippians 1:3

MEETING THE CONSTABLE

"*N*ext stop – Lansing!"

The landscape flew by, just like it had so many times before, but Phoebe didn't notice. How many times had she taken this trip? Too many to count, but this time was different. This time, she was coming home for good.

Here she was, a Bible College graduate, bound for home to begin the rest of her life. She only wished she knew what the *rest of her life* looked like.

"Lansing!" shouted the conductor, startling Phoebe. She was so lost in her own musings that she hadn't realized how close she was to home. She finally looked out her window at the scenery that she'd been ignoring. Farmland stretched out, like an ocean of tilled dirt, touching the sky where the Earth seemingly dropped off and the sky took over. There was little to differentiate this land from the countless miles that she had already passed, except for the occasional oak standing in the middle of a field, left untouched by the farmer, his crops just encircling these massive trees - as if giving respect to their impressive elder.

Phoebe then looked at the ground closer to the train. At this speed, the vegetation close to the tracks was nothing more than a blur. Phoebe couldn't help but think that it was exactly the opposite in life. "God only allows us to see clearly what is right in front of us," she thought to herself, "but beyond today and tomorrow, the future is all a blur."

The train chugged as it slowed its pace. A woman across the aisle rose and began to gather her things, but Phoebe knew better; she had taken this train far too many times to fall for the deceivingly slow pace the train was now making, though the temptation to stand and stretch one's legs was difficult to resist. She kept her seat and watched as the train jerked to its final stop, sending the woman, valise in hand, careening backward. Had it not been for the gentleman in the seat behind her jumping to her aid, she would have surely fallen flat on her backside.

The rest of the scene played out as Phoebe could have predicted: the woman thanked the gentleman, he said something in return - which caused her to blush, and then the real flirting began. It took everything in Phoebe's whole being to not roll her eyes at the display. She had never been one to participate in such ridiculous activities as fawning and flirting. But, maybe, she should have tried. Maybe she could have spent a little more time trying to impress the men she attended school with. Maybe she should have attempted the practice of flirtation like her sisters were always encouraging her to do.

Maybe then...

"Oh, what does it even matter," Phoebe muttered. She exhaled deeply. God could have provided, but he'd chosen not to. There was no use dwelling on what wasn't meant to be.

Phoebe turned her attention to gathering her things and then headed for the exit. The sun shone bright as she departed the train, and she had to squint to see around. Her hazy perception of her surroundings reminded her of her earlier observation.

'Well,' she thought, 'I may not be able to see all of what's ahead, but with God's help, I can handle whatever lies directly in front of me.'

With a new-found resolve, Phoebe squared her shoulders, lifted her chin and took her first step into her future. Unfortunately, that first step got caught somewhere in her skirts. She flew, unable to slow her descent, and would have landed in a very unladylike manner on the train station platform had God not intervened and landed her into the arms of a Michigan State Constable.

The officer's uniform scratched where it touched her soft skin, his firm arms and chest instantly removing the fear that had only seconds ago engulfed her, replacing it with an admittedly delightful yet unfamiliar feeling of warmth.

"Oh, my!" was all she was able to sputter. The constable had saved her from a nasty fall, for which she was very grateful, but the fact that he still held her in his arms - strong, warm arms - was beginning to make Phoebe...she wasn't sure what. She only knew she was eager to stand on her own two feet. And quickly. "I'm so sorry..."

"No apologies necessary. Are you alright, Phoebe?"

Shocked that this brawny officer not only knew her Christian name but also addressed her by it, Phoebe scrutinized the face of her savior. Beneath the khaki Montana campaign hat were two of the brightest blue eyes Phoebe had ever seen. She searched his face, still at a loss. He certainly knew who she was.

Her confusion seemed to delight the officer.

"What's the matter, Pheebs? Don't you recognize me?"

Her eyes grew wide as suddenly Phoebe did recognize the man whose arms held her.

"Will Caffey?" she gasped.

"Oh, good. I was beginning to think that you had forgotten all about me," he said, smiling down at her.

Forgotten? Will Caffey? How could she forget the boy who had teased her relentlessly her entire childhood? The adolescent that chased her around the playground every day at school. The teenager that had captured her behind the church and...

She longed to slap the mischievous grin off his face. If she'd had any difficulty connecting the little boy of her memories with the handsome, and now very grown up, man of today, that smirk erased all doubt. This was the same obnoxious Will Caffey she had always known.

"Put me down, sir." She struggled to free herself. "People are beginning to stare!"

"Sir?" Will chuckled, setting her on her feet in an upright, balanced position.

She straightened her skirt, gathered her things, then looked up at him.

"Thank you for saving me from a vicious fall. For that, I am very grateful." She looked frantically for her father, wishing to escape the embarrassment of the situation as quickly as possible. "But your prolonged embrace... that was unnecessary and has only delayed me further. So, Mr. Caffey, thank you, but good day."

"Sir? Mr. Caffey?" Will chuckled again. "Well, I guess if we are being formal, then the name is Constable Caffey now, *ma'am*," he replied with exaggerated gallantry, tipping his hat and bowing to her.

"I stand corrected," she said, picking up her valise. "Let me try again. Goodbye...*Constable* Caffey." She turned to leave.

"C'mon, Pheebs. You aren't still mad about that kiss, are you?"

Phoebe stood frozen. "Kiss? I have no idea what you are talking about," she lied.

"So, you are still sore."

She whirled to face him. "Sore? Mad? Why would I be upset about having a kiss roguishly stolen from me when I was still a child? I couldn't care less!"

"Oh, that's apparent."

"What's apparent is that you haven't changed...not one bit. You are still the most annoying boy I have ever known. I've wasted enough of my time with the likes of you. Good day, *Constable*!"

She turned and strode toward the depot, anxious to find her father. All she wished was to be home and the last thing she wanted was any more banter with the likes of Will Caffey.

"I wouldn't dismiss me so quickly if I were you," she heard him yell after her.

"Oh," Phoebe called over her shoulder. "And why is that?"

"Because it's a long walk home from here."

2

THE ALBRIGHTS

*P*hoebe was fuming as Will loaded her trunks into her father's car, but Will didn't mind. Even in anger, she was the most beautiful woman he had ever seen.

"Are these all the bags you have?" He asked incredulously.

"It was Bible College, not finishing school, constable. I didn't have a need for many things."

"Fair enough." Will cranked the car and jumped into the driver's seat, thankful for the engine's roar which would hopefully conceal the hammering of his heart. It had been so long since he had seen Phoebe, let alone sat this near to her. He was going to have a hard time keeping his eyes on the road.

They traveled in silence for some time, save for the tapping of Phoebe's left foot.

"I was surprised to hear that you were coming home," Will said, trying to break the silence. He knew Phoebe and he had a lot of ground to cover, a lot of lost time to make up for. "I expected you to be off on some sort of adventure. Evangelistic work or something." Will always loved to see her face light up whenever she spoke about her plans to serve God.

But even her favorite topic of conversation wasn't tempting

7

enough to draw her into conversation with Will, and she sat in the car, staring straight ahead. Will tried another tactic.

"Furthermore, I find it hard to believe that no man at that Bible College of yours was wise enough to snatch you up before graduation. What's the matter? You too opinionated for them or something?"

This tactic worked to get Phoebe talking, but not exactly in the way he had intended.

"My opinions and my personal life are not your concern, constable," she spat at him. "I don't see a ring on your finger. Shall we discuss why you haven't been 'snatched up', as you say? It certainly couldn't be your lack of charm."

Will chuckled, enjoying the wit he had missed for so long. "Or maybe it was your sharp tongue that kept them away. Can't imagine many preachers looking for that in a wife."

Phoebe gasped. "How dare...I would thank you very much to not talk to me the rest of the trip! Your rudeness is exasperating."

Will nodded his head, but continued to chuckle. He remembered well her reaction to his teasing, but he couldn't resist goading her. It was too much fun.

But as the silence wore on, he couldn't help stealing glances her way. Her face was flushed, which was normal when he teased her, but something was different.

And then he saw it. A single tear escaped the corner of her eye. It lasted a mere second before she swiftly wiped it away, but it was definitely a tear.

He had gone too far.

PHOEBE FELT blood rushing to her face, though she wasn't sure if it was due to anger or humiliation, because Will had come so close to the truth.

Most every girl in Phoebe's graduating class had either already married or was engaged to be married. And, truth be told, most men didn't give Phoebe a second glance. It wasn't that she wasn't beautiful. It was her personality. Try as she might, Phoebe could not conform to the standards most ministry-minded men looked for in a wife. Quiet, demur, sweet. Those were three words others did not use to describe the pretty brunette. Stubborn, sassy, opinionated – those were much more fitting.

However, she did have many good qualities – qualities that could be very useful in ministry. And it was her heart's desire to be in ministry. She had been praying since her first day of Bible College that there would be a man that saw her through God's eyes – that could see what God saw and loved about her. But that had not happened, and Will's words were a painful reminder.

Despite her best efforts, tears brimmed on her lashes. She turned her head, hoping he couldn't see the effect his words had on her.

A few minutes later, the car pulled up to the parsonage of Lansing First Church, home of Phoebe's parents, Reverend and Mrs. Albright. Just the sight of the spring tulips and daffodils blooming in front of the white foursquare home made her heart ache, reminding her of just how long it had been since she had been home.

She was so anxious to see her parents and sisters, but not more anxious than she was to be rid of her escort. When the car came to a stop, Phoebe jumped out unassisted and went to retrieve her cases. Will was out just as quickly.

"Let me get those," he said.

"I am completely capable of getting my own belongings," Phoebe answered, even as she struggled to pull even one bag from the back of the car.

Will laid his hand on hers and said gently, "Please. Allow me."

Phoebe was so taken aback by his change of demeanor that she stepped aside without further argument. Without any struggle, he had all her cases and bags removed and in his arms.

"After you," he said.

Will's transformation from rogue to gentleman had Phoebe feeling as if she were being played with, and she didn't appreciate it. But, her time in his presence was nearing its end, so she said nothing.

"Phoebe!"

Phoebe turned toward the house just as the front door flung open. Her younger sister Sarah flew down the porch steps.

"I'm so glad you're home! Momma, Daddy, she's home... she's home!"

Sarah coiled her arms around Phoebe's waist and buried her head against Phoebe's shoulder.

"My word, Sarah," Phoebe said as she returned her sister's embrace. She laid her head on top of Sarah's blonde curls. "When did you get so tall? It's only been six months since I've seen you last. You've grown a foot!"

Sarah lifted her green eyes toward Phoebe. "It won't be long, and I'll be taller than you."

Phoebe nodded and smiled. Sarah, who in every physical way mirrored their mother and older sister, would most likely tower over Phoebe who favored their father's mother, with her diminutive stature and dark hair.

Sarah stepped back and grabbed Phoebe's hand. She spoke excitedly as she pulled Phoebe into the house. "How was your train ride? Did you sit next to any handsome men? How long are you staying? Please say that you're home for good!"

"Good grief, child! How is she supposed to answer if you keep asking questions?"

Mrs. Albright wiped her hands on her apron as she approached. She opened her arms and Phoebe gladly accommodated her. She snuggled into her mother's shoulder the same way that Sarah had done to her only moments earlier. If Phoebe ever bemoaned her lack of height, moments like this made her appreciate the fact that she would always fit into her mother's embrace like this.

"Welcome home, dear," Mrs. Albright whispered against the top of her head. "It's been too long."

"Yes, it has," Phoebe whispered back, squeezing her mother a little tighter.

"I hope you have one of those for me as well," a familiar voice boomed from behind Mrs. Albright.

Phoebe lifted her head and saw her father, his large frame filling the doorway of the parlor. He stood rather sheepishly, his hands in his pockets, watching her. His dark head dipped and he raised an eyebrow at her, something he had done many times to signify that he was waiting for something. When they were children, the look usually meant he was waiting for one of them to confess to a wrongdoing. But today, Phoebe knew he wanted something much better.

She nearly skipped as she threw herself into her father's arms, giggling as he lifted her off the ground as easily as he had when she was a child. His meaty arms had always been a place of love, of safety for the Albright sisters, and now, as an adult, Phoebe realized they always would be. This was home, and it felt good to be home. Here was happiness.

But that happiness was short lived.

"Good grief, Will," Phoebe heard her mother say. "Put those heavy cases down."

In all the excitement, Phoebe had forgotten that Will Caffey was still there.

"Will, my boy, thank you for the trouble of getting our girl home," her father chimed in.

"It was no trouble at all, sir. Miss Albright was a joy to be with," Will said, his face beaming with another mischievous smile.

"The pleasure was all yours," smirked Phoebe. No one but Will seemed to notice her harsh words. However, rather than inflicting injury, as she had hoped, he seemed more amused than ever. When she scowled at him, he just raised his eyebrows in some sort of innocent gesture, which Phoebe found absurd. There had never been anything innocent about Will Caffey. She crossed her arms and glared at him.

Will cleared his throat and bit his bottom lip as if trying to keep from smiling. "Well, I must be going," he said, finally.

"Oh, can't you stay for a little? You only just got here," Mrs. Albright implored.

Phoebe turned to her mother. Was she mad? Why would she want to prolong this man's visit?

Will's soft chuckle brought Phoebe's attention back to him. He stared straight at her but spoke to her mother. "Sorry, I can't ma'am. I have to report to headquarters shortly."

Relief flooded Phoebe and she felt her shoulders, for the first time since landing in the rogue's arms, begin to relax. That relief, however, was short-lived.

"But I'm free for supper," Will said, turning to smile at her mother.

Mrs. Albright clasped her hands. "Dinner it is! We look forward to it."

With that, Will tipped his hat to her mother and sister, winked at Phoebe, and turned to leave.

Phoebe was still trying to process what had just happened when her mother grabbed her by the elbow.

"You should walk him to the door, dear."

"Gladly," Phoebe said through clenched teeth.

Phoebe rushed after him, the speed of her gait growing at the same rate as her anger, but Will moved quickly as well. He was already on the front porch when she caught up with him.

"What kind of person invites himself over for supper?"

He appeared to think about it for a moment. "A hungry one," he answered with a crooked grin.

Will continued his departure, but when he reached the bottom stair, he stopped, as if he had forgotten something, then turned back to her. He climbed halfway up the stairs.

Phoebe was certain that if he took one more step and put himself within reach, she might just punch him in that cocky smirk of his. But even as she considered this, a couple strolled past the parsonage and nodded a greeting as they passed. She crossed her arms and said a prayer for strength.

To her relief, Will stopped just out of her reach. "I am sorry about today, Pheebs. Really, I am," he said. He looked at her with such earnestness that she almost believed him. "I feel that I pushed you too far, and I shouldn't have teased you so much. But," he said, looking away slightly and smiling before returning his gaze to hers, "I couldn't help myself. It's just so much fun watching you blush."

And with that, he skipped down the stairs again and was off, whistling some aggravating tune that left Phoebe wondering how she would keep from assaulting the man at dinner that evening.

3

UNPACKING THE TRUTH

"*And* then he said, 'Darling, you have the prettiest hair I have ever seen.' Hmph! As if that's the first time I've heard that!"

It hadn't taken Phoebe long to calm down from her encounter with Will Caffey, and she had her little sister's nonstop chatter to thank for that.

"Well, you do have beautiful hair, Sarah," Phoebe said, tugging on one of the blonde curls. Phoebe had always been jealous of her sisters, with their mother's fair complexions and beautiful green eyes.

"That's what every boy says. I'm just sick of hearing it."

"Every boy! My goodness, Sarah. You sound like a veritable harlot!"

Sarah laughed. She plopped down on Phoebe's bed and hugged one of her pillows.

"I'm not a harlot just because lots of boys think I'm pretty. I don't pay them much heed, anyway. I'm waiting for a mature man. One that thinks I'm more than just pretty hair."

"I'm glad to hear that," Phoebe answered, folding another of her blouses and placing it in the dresser. She was only half unpacked, and she had already heard all the latest town happenings from her thirteen-year-old sister - who was courting who, who had gotten married, who had just come home from war. It was enough to make a person's head spin, if they were actually listening, which Phoebe wasn't. That is why she didn't immediately notice when her conversation turned to Will Caffey.

"...and when he asked father if he could pick you up at the train station, I about died! I couldn't think of anything more romantic! The beautiful girl goes off to college, returns home a woman and is swept off her feet by her childhood love..."

"Wait one minute! Will Caffey is *not* my childhood love. And his retrieval of me from the train station was anything but romantic."

"Still, it must'a been nice to have a man as handsome as Will greet you at the station."

"Will? Handsome? I hadn't noticed. I'll have to take your word for it," she replied as she threw another blouse in the drawer a little harder than she had intended.

Phoebe didn't understand why everyone in her family seemed so enamored with Will Caffey. They had known him his entire life, knew all about his propensity for teasing Phoebe. It wasn't like her whole family didn't all already know what a cad he was. And to think, Father had given Will permission to pick her up...

Phoebe stopped unpacking. "Wait a minute. Sarah, did you say that Will *asked* father if he could pick me up, not the other way around? I mean, are you certain Father wasn't busy and had to enlist Will's assistance?"

"Of course, I'm sure —"

"That seems a bit ridiculous. How can you be certain?"

"I was right outside the parlor listening the whole time Will was in with Daddy."

"Sarah! That's horrible! You can't listen in on Father's

conversations. He's a pastor. What if it had been a personal matter?"

"Oh bother, I don't do it often - only when it's a handsome gentleman caller."

Phoebe rolled her eyes. Her sister was incorrigible, but her mind was already well past Sarah's antics.

'Why would Will want to meet me at the station?' she thought to herself. They hadn't seen each other in years, before Phoebe went off to Bible College and Will went off to the Great War. No letters were ever exchanged between the two, not even the correspondence of childhood friendship, let alone ...

"...just so handsome, what with those wide shoulders, that thick black hair and rugged profile, and those eyes! Oh, those eyes! I think they are green..."

"They're blue," Phoebe corrected without thinking.

"Aha! So, you have noticed him! How else would you know what color his eyes were?" Sarah plopped onto the bed, looking triumphantly at her older sister.

Phoebe sighed. "If you must know, I fell stepping off the train this morning and Will caught me. It put my eyes directly in line with his eyes. That is how I know."

Sarah threw herself back on the bed, jostling Phoebe's belongings. "Oh my gosh! It's all just so romantic!"

Phoebe tried not to be annoyed and to remember what it was like to be thirteen like Sarah, but in all honesty, she could not remember ever being as starry-eyed as her little sister. Phoebe never cared much for the attention of teenage boys, nor the company of girls that did. It all seemed so futile to her, fiddling around with romantic matters years before marriage was possible. It was a waste of time that was better suited for doing the Lord's work. That's why the stolen kiss had been such a shock.

It was the summer before Phoebe's last year of high school, and the church was having its annual Sunday School picnic.

Everyone was milling around, eating, talking, and just enjoying a beautiful day. When elementary aged children began a game of Blind Man's Bluff, many of the teenagers Phoebe's age joined in as well.

Will ran up to her. "C'mon, Pheebs. Play with us!"

"Will Caffey, that's not my name!"

"Awe, come now, you know it's my pet name for you."

Phoebe sighed. It was true; he had called her that since they were quite small. She never knew why, but it always bothered her.

Sarah, only a child then, came running up as well. "Please, Phoebe! Please come play! Everyone else is."

It had always been difficult for her to deny her sister anything, and before she knew it, she was right there in the middle of the game of tag.

Phoebe laughed as the children each took a turn as the blind man. Sarah especially enjoyed her turn in the blindfold. She caught several children but could not correctly identify any of them. That didn't seem to damper her spirits, though - she laughed and giggled with every step. Just as Phoebe was becoming convinced that Sarah was lengthening her turn by not identifying anyone on purpose, she caught Phoebe and promptly identified her.

"Phoebe!" Sarah exclaimed.

Shocked, but giggling, Phoebe took the blindfold from her sister and dutifully slipped it on.

She had forgotten how much fun it was to play this game - the challenge of sensing the location of the other children using only your flailing arms, the thrill of uncertainty as you lunge forward, not knowing what might lie in your path. She had also forgotten how confusing it was. She felt a tree – was it the large oak or one of the smaller ones to the east of the building? She felt gravel underfoot but had no idea where there was gravel on this side of the property. And where were all the children?

Phoebe kept flailing, feeling the air, searching for another person. She walked a little further - still no one. She was about to give up and pull off the blindfold when she bumped into something – *someone*.

"Got you!" she squealed. *'Now, the identification,'* she thought. Without the use of her eyes, she would have to rely on her other senses. She could tell that the person wasn't a small child. Her hand reached out and encountered a broad chest and shoulders. This was definitely a man, not a woman. She began to feel his face. It was clean-shaven. Maybe a boy her age? She felt his hair. It was thick, maybe wavy.

'This part is much harder than it looks,' she thought.

Just when she was about to concede defeat, she felt his arms slip around her waist. Before she had a chance to react, his lips were on hers. She knew she should protest, push him away, but she had never been kissed before and the shock of it happening was magnified by the new sensation of the act itself. His lips moved on hers and her stomach flipped. Then, as quickly as it had started, it was over. He removed her blindfold. It took a moment for Phoebe's eyes to readjust to daylight, but when they did, they were focused on two blue orbs sparkling with mischief - Will Caffey. He ran backwards three steps, eyes twinkling, twirling the blindfold and smiling as if he had just accomplished something. Then yelling, "She found me. I'm it," he ran off to rejoin the others at the front of the church.

"Phoebe? Phoebe, are you listening to me?"

"Sorry," Phoebe responded, snapping back to the present and picking up another article of clothing, "I guess I wasn't. What were you saying?"

"I was asking what you'll be wearing tonight, when Will comes for supper?"

"What's wrong with what I'm wearing now?"

Sarah wrinkled her nose. "You traveled home in that dress."

"And what of it? Honestly, Sarah, I have no intention of putting on airs for the likes of Will Caffey."

"But surely, you'll want to at least freshen up, Will Caffey or not."

"That's a wonderful idea," Phoebe decided, as she ushered her sister to the door. "So, you had better give me some time to right myself after the long day I've had."

"All I am saying is that someone as pretty as you should realize it and start using it to her advantage."

She pushed her sister through the door and shut it firmly behind her then examined her reflection in the newfound quiet of the room. It had been a long day, and Sarah was right - she could use some freshening up. She browsed through her wardrobe of freshly unpacked clothes. She pulled out an especially drab skirt, one common to deaconesses.

The plainer the better, she thought. *Wouldn't want Will Caffey thinking I was dressing to impress him."*

Though she knew she was attractive, she was not vain. She didn't have Sarah and Esther's curly blonde locks or their pretty green eyes. She favored her father, not her mother, in looks. Her hair was brown, a very dark brown, just like her eyes. But she was not unpleasant to look at. She had always considered her beauty a gift from God, a gift that someday the man God intended for her to marry would appreciate. It had been a long time since she had considered her beauty, and what it might mean to a man. For all of her adult life, she had been focused on her studies. But she wondered now, had she been too focused? Had she been so intent on preparing herself for God's work that she had missed out on the pleasures inherent to being a woman?

As she stared in the mirror, something in the wardrobe caught her eye. She turned, pushed the freshly unpacked dresses out of the way and pulled a frock from the back - a beautiful blue dress that her friend Anna had made for her to wear to her high school graduation. She had forgotten all about it. The skirt of the dress was a little longer and fuller than current fashion, but it was still a beautiful garment. She held it in front of her and looked once again in the mirror.

'It might be a little too fancy,' she thought. *'But all of my other clothes are so wrinkled from the trip...'*

Phoebe turned and hung the deaconess skirt back in the closet.

~

WHEN PHOEBE HAD FINISHED UNPACKING and freshening up, she found only her father in the house, quietly reading his Bible and sipping a bottle of Vernor's Ginger Ale in the parlor.

Phoebe's father was unconventional for a pastor, and not only for his fashion sense. He always wore a fine suit like other men his age, but rather than a fedora or a bowler hat, as was the fashion, the Reverend Albright preferred a Stetson, an uncommon hat in Michigan. His unique style only amplified his unique personality.

He hadn't always been a man of God. He was apt to say, "But for the Grace of God and the love of a good woman" he might have died. But his sordid past gave him an understanding and an empathy for 'sinners' that other ministers did not possess, and made him approachable to all kinds of people, not just members of his congregation.

Reverend Albright was loved and respected by everyone in the community, including Phoebe, and that respect was what made her nervous about the conversation she was about to have with him.

"Hello, Daddy."

He looked up and smiled. "Well, there you are, my dear. Don't you look lovely. Prepared to receive our dinner guest, I see."

Phoebe felt her cheeks grow warm and instantly regretted her decision to wear the blue dress. "It's just an old garment, really. Where is mother?"

"She and your sister went to visit Mrs. Knapp. She's been under the weather and your mother wanted to take her some soup and fresh cut flowers. Don't worry. The roast is in the oven and she'll be back in plenty of time to finish up the meal."

Phoebe was glad they had the house to themselves. She stood there a moment, wanting to speak, but not knowing how to start.

"What's the matter, darlin'? Something wrong?"

She sat in her mother's chair across from her father. She took a calming breath, then began. "Daddy, why didn't you send word that Will Caffey was picking me up at the train station?"

Reverend Albright sat his Bible on the table beside his chair. "Well, I didn't think it would matter. Was it a problem, Phoebe?"

"Yes. It was. A very big problem," she started. "I know you are unaware of this, but I find Will Caffey to be one of the most disagreeable men I've ever met."

Her father's eyebrows shot up. "Disagreeable? Will? I'm not sure I've ever heard anyone use that word to describe the boy."

"Well, I use that word, and I have a hundred more like it to describe him."

Reverend Albright leaned forward, his face wrinkled with concern.

"What's he done that's so disagreeable?"

Phoebe paused. What could she say? She didn't dare tell her father about the kiss. He would ask if she had pushed him away, which she had not. He would wonder if she'd slapped him, but the answer to that was no as well. He would also ask her why she didn't tell him, her father, who would have taken the boy to task, but she did not have a good answer for that, either.

"I'm – I don't really want to discuss…"

"This isn't because of that kiss he stole from ya, is it?"

Phoebe gasped. "How did you know about that?"

Her father shrugged. "He told me."

Phoebe didn't think she had ever been more shocked in her life. "Will told you? When?"

"The next day. He also told me about how awful he felt for acting like such a scoundrel."

Phoebe couldn't believe what she was hearing. "Will told you? What did you say?"

"Well, we had a long talk about the sin he had committed against you, against me, against the Lord. I gave him an earful about how I had no use for a man that would do something to a woman against her will. There ain't much more in life I find more contemptible."

Contemptible. Yes, that was a word Phoebe would use to describe Will Caffey. "Yes, Daddy, I agree —"

"After chewin' him out, I gave him some time to think on what I'd said. Then he told me more."

"More? What did he say?"

"He admitted to having feelings for you. That's no excuse for his behavior, mind you, but he said that his actions were motivated more by his inability to keep his emotions in check than they were by some latent disrespect for the fairer gender. But he knew he could make no promises of a future, with the war looming and all, so even if you had given him permission, he knew it was wrong to kiss you."

Phoebe was momentarily dumbfounded. Will Caffey had feelings for her?

Her father continued. "He also said that, if he returned, he intended to court you, if I gave him permission."

This got Phoebe's attention. "Court me? What did you say?"

"I told him to see me when he returned."

She felt the familiar heat blazing a path up her neck. "Daddy! I am surprised at you, giving someone of such low morals hope that he might court me someday!"

He leaned forward in his worn, leather chair and shook a finger at her. "What Will did, coming to me, your father, and admitting his guilt, that's something that only a man with honor would do. If he'd have kept quiet, I'd never have known about the incident - until now, I reckon." He lifted a knowing eyebrow at her, then leaned back. "But that didn't matter to him. He felt he had wronged you – and me – and he intended to make it right."

"And what about making it right with me?"

"I think he plans to, eventually," her father said, smiling knowingly.

Phoebe gasped. "Daddy, I have no intention of being courted by the likes of Will Caffey!"

"Oh, Phoebe, don't be so hard on the boy. He was a bit impulsive, it's true. But there was a time when I was just as impulsive." His lip curled on one side. "I may have stolen a kiss or two from your mother before we were wed, but don't tell her - or Will, for that matter - I told you that."

"That's different..."

"Different? How? Because your mother and I ended up married? I guess only time will tell if your story will end differ-ently – or the same," he said, unsuccessfully hiding his grin behind another sip of ginger ale."

Phoebe crossed her arms. "I could never end up with a lout as disagreeable as Will Caffey. I'd rather die a spinster."

Rev. Albright shook his head and scowled at her. "Those are harsh words. And I don't appreciate the way you treated him today. Will has been through a lot, Phoebe, at home and abroad. War is hard on a man. I know, Will doesn't seem worse for the wear, but mark my words, there are scars, even if they're the kind a person can't see. And he doesn't deserve your ire. If that is the way you were taught to behave in college, then I believe you have wasted the last four years studying the wrong Bible."

His words stung. Her father was right. The way she had

treated him today was not kind, nor was it in keeping with how a woman of God should treat others, and she knew it.

"I'll try to be kinder with Will," Phoebe said. "But it isn't going to be easy."

"Nothing in life ever is, darlin'."

4

PLAYING FOR KEEPS

*W*ill stood outside the Albright home, running his fingers through his dark hair, still damp from his hurried washing. He'd had a stressful afternoon and was looking forward to an evening with his favorite family to help him forget the news he'd just been given, if only for a few hours. He'd have to face the reality of his situation eventually. But not tonight. Tonight was about reconnecting with the Albrights, one Albright in particular.

Phoebe.

Will tapped the brim of his campaign hat against the bouquet of flowers he held in his other hand and stared at the front door. Although he had apologized for his previous behavior, he hadn't waited around to find out whether or not Phoebe had accepted that apology. He couldn't - watching her stand there, arms crossed and all bulled up like she was ready to clean his clock, it took all of his willpower to not reach out and take her into his arms and kiss those pursed lips of hers. But standing here now, knowing Phoebe was on the other side of that door, he worried that he might be entering a war zone.

A slow smirk played at the corner of his mouth. He'd had

plenty of experience in war zones. This one, he would enjoy. He lifted his hand and knocked.

"I'll get it!" he heard Sarah holler.

"No, you won't!" Mrs. Albright's voice reverberated through the door. "Phoebe will."

He chuckled when Phoebe's muffled, indiscernible words were followed by an enormous sigh loud enough to hear on the porch. But any mirth he felt dissipated immediately when the door opened, and she stood before him. Though he would have sworn it impossible, she seemed to have grown more beautiful in the past few hours.

She wore a pale blue color that, against her perfect creamy skin, accentuated the heightened pink of her cheeks. Her dark, silky hair which had previously been pulled back in a tight bun, a look Will always appreciated because it gave him full view of her beautiful face, was now softly swept high upon her head.

Will cleared his throat when he realized he had been staring, mouth agape. "Good evening, Pheebs. Don't you look lovely."

"I will thank you very much to stop calling me that." She turned and stormed.

Will smiled. *War zone.*

~

"THAT, MY DEAR, WAS A DELICIOUS DINNER," Reverend Albright said, patting his protruding stomach.

"I absolutely agree," Will said, leaning back and doing his best to stick his otherwise flat stomach out. "Haven't had a meal that delicious since my ma passed."

The conversation in the room stilled. Will was grateful. He hadn't prepared himself for the torrent of emotions that washed over him at the remembrance of his mother. Having lost his father at nine years-old, Bessie Caffey became all things to her young son - spiritual guide, hardworking breadwinner, steady disciplinarian - all the while remaining the loving mother she had always been. Everything she did was done with a quiet grace, whether washing his scraped knee or baking his favorite cookies, and she always found a way to make Will feel loved. And though he knew she was in heaven with Jesus, there was a part of his heart that ached for her every single day.

"Your ma was a great woman," Reverend Albright said, breaking the silence.

"Yes, sir. She was," was all he could think to say.

"I cared very much for her."

Phoebe's gentle voice stunned his senses momentarily. She reached down and took his empty plate. "She was special to me," she said.

Will looked up at her, enraptured by her sincerity as much as by her nearness. "Thank you, Phoebe. You were special to her as well." Mrs. Caffey loved all of her Sunday School students, especially the Albright sisters, but Will knew that Phoebe held a special place in her heart. Something he and his mother had in common.

"Phoebe, why don't you and Will head on into the parlor for a game of checkers," Reverend Albright suggested.

"Oh, yes," Mrs. Albright chimed in. "You two go on. Sarah and I can see to the dishes."

"Of course," Phoebe said, handing the plates she held to her mother. "Would you like to play checkers, Officer Caffey?"

Will tried to not look shocked at her acquiescence. What happened to the spitfire that had met him at the door? "It's Will, remember?" he said, rising as well. "And I would like that very much, although I do prefer chess to checkers."

"Actually, so do I," she said as she led him into the parlor. Phoebe pulled a worn chess box from the shelf and began setting the game up on a small table in the corner.

"Do you play often?" Will asked as they began.

"Not recently," she answered. "I haven't had much idle time in the past few years to play."

"Neither have I," Will admitted. "It's nice to play again. It's nice to play with you."

Phoebe tensed slightly at his words, but all she said was, "It's your move."

Will was confused by Phoebe's change in demeanor. Her usual wit and sarcasm had been replaced with a forced civility that seemed strange on her. Many men would have welcomed the change, but not Will. He liked Phoebe just the way she was.

They played swiftly, Will capturing her rook, Phoebe taking his bishop. She was quite skilled in the game as well and made for a worthy opponent.

"Do you remember playing marbles when we were kids?" he asked.

Phoebe's hand paused on a knight and tilted her head. She nodded and scowled. "We always played keepsies. You won my favorite aggie off of me."

War Zone.

Smiling, Will unbuttoned one of his shirt pockets and pulled out a large, glass marble. Phoebe gasped and reached for it, but he yanked it out of her reach.

"Hey, now!" he laughed. "It's mine."

"I loved that aggie. It was unfair of you to take it."

"Unfair? I won it fair and square!"

"You knew that I wasn't very good at marbles, yet you insisted we play for keeps."

Will leaned closer. "With you, my dear Phoebe, I have no other intent than to play for keeps." He carefully placed the marble in the center of the board and leaned back into his chair. "Tell you what…I'll give you another chance to win this back."

She scowled at him. "What's the catch?"

"No catch. Winner of this game takes all."

"All?" She leaned back slightly. "By all, you mean the aggie?"

Will raised his own eyebrows in response. "Unless you'd like to sweeten the pot."

She rolled her eyes and crossed her arms. "I'll have you know, I'm not a novice at chess."

"Neither am I."

It was only a marble, but Will knew Phoebe well enough to know that it meant something more to her. Winning the aggie back meant redemption, vindication, and a chance to regain her pride.

A slow smile spread across her face. "Well, sir, I believe the next move is yours."

Will nodded and they returned to play. Where their conversation had been stilted before, it was non-existent now as they both focused on the board with intensity. Will played well, but Phoebe was a formidable opponent, as he knew she would be.

"You could just give me the aggie and we can call the game complete," she said after taking out his knight. "It isn't necessary for you to be completely humiliated in order for me to get it back."

Will smiled. "You should know me by now, Pheebs. I don't give up. Especially where you are concerned."

She did not respond, nor did she lift her eyes from the board. "Tell me, why'd you keep it all these years?"

"The aggie?" Will shrugged. "It's special. I don't believe much in luck, but this was a comfort to me while I was in France."

"I hardly see how something as trivial as an aggie could bring you comfort."

"It wasn't the aggie itself. It was the memory of the girl it belonged to."

She looked up then and locked eyes with him. Her mouth opened and Will thought she was about to say something but just then, Mrs. Albright spoke quite loudly to her husband across the room.

"My word, James. How many times are you going to read that letter? Is it really that interesting?"

Rev. Albright rubbed his forehead. "It's from Frank."

Mrs. Albright put down the copy of Ladies' Home Journal. "Is something wrong? Please tell me it isn't Helen."

"No, nothing like that. He's having trouble filling posts at some of his churches."

"Well, no wonder. The U.P. is desolate, void of the modern conveniences most young preachers and their brides are accustomed to."

"He says it's not all that bad. With the copper and iron mines came the railroads. Lots of small towns, and good-sized ones, have popped up all over."

"Well, what does that have to do with you?" she asked, flipping through her magazine again. She stopped suddenly. "He doesn't expect *you* to pick up and move north, does he? At our age?"

"No, no. Not at all."

"Well, what then?"

"He is inquiring about Phoebe."

At this, all heads in the room turned toward the minister.

"Me?" Phoebe asked. "Why on earth would he be asking about me?"

Reverend Albright looked at her. "He wants to know if you'd be willing to take a church."

"You must be joking!" Mrs. Albright sputtered. "Why on earth would he ever suggest such a thing? A young, single woman - pastoring a church on her own? Well, that's absolutely ridiculous..."

Mrs. Albright continued speaking, but Will heard none of it. All of his attention was focused on the woman sitting across from him and the emotions that played about her face.

"Now, Ruth, don't be so old-fashioned. There's nothing wrong with a woman pastor."

"But in the Upper Peninsula? How would she survive? How would she live?"

"I'm sure it's not as bad as you are imagining, otherwise Frank wouldn't be suggesting it."

Phoebe's gaze dropped from her parents' conversation and settled on the chess board, but it was obvious that her mind was not on the game. Her delicate forehead wrinkled above knitted brows as she bit her bottom lip. Was she honestly considering taking a church in the Upper Peninsula? Was she scared of the idea? Worried? Or was she experiencing something different? Was her heart beating as erratically as his was at that very moment?

This isn't what Will wanted for her. Phoebe deserved so much more in life than the hardships the Upper Peninsula could offer. Surely God wouldn't subject her to a life like that. Hadn't he said those exact words to God this very afternoon?

Phoebe's eyes lifted and locked with Will's.

They do not know the thoughts of the Lord, they do not understand His plan.

When Will had read that scripture in the book of Micah that morning, he had thought God was giving him a message for another reason, that God was giving him confidence to turn down the assignment he had been given. But now, staring into Phoebe's dark eyes, he realized that he was the one who did not understand God's plan. He was the one who would be gathered like sheaves on the threshing floor if he impeded the Lord's plan.

It was Will's turn to avert his gaze from Phoebe's. "Did he mention where this church is?" Will asked Reverend Albright, not looking up.

"A place called Iron Falls," Rev. Albright answered.

"I don't care what it's named, no daughter of mine..."

Mrs. Albright's rant was interrupted when the front door swung open.

"Where is that college graduate of ours?"

All eyes turned toward the entrance as Esther, the eldest Albright sister flounced into the room. She pulled Phoebe from her chair and into an embrace.

"I've missed you so much," Esther nearly squealed. "I'm so glad you're finally home!"

"So am I," said her husband John as he casually entered behind her. "Now my wife will have someone else to take her shopping. It is a truly taxing event."

Esther smiled coyly at him as she rubbed her protruding stomach. "Well, you are to blame for this ever-growing belly of mine, are you not? The least you can do is to help me replace the clothing I've outgrown."

John had no response to that, except to rub the back of his neck and clear his throat, a nervous gesture that brought Will to laugh out loud at his friend's discomfort.

John elbowed Will in the ribs. "It's your fault I married her."

"I will proudly accept the blame," Will said, slapping John on the shoulder. "I knew she was the perfect match for you."

John, a journalist at the Lansing State Journal, had been Will's best friend since they fought side-by-side in the Great War, and his marriage to Esther had only strengthened that bond. It also, Will hoped, would someday make them brother-in-laws.

"Daddy's friend wants Phoebe to pastor a church in the Upper Peninsula!" Sarah exclaimed.

In unison, Esther and John looked from Sarah to Phoebe.

"The U.P.!" exclaimed Esther. "Oh, no! You can't! You've only just come home."

John looked at Will and raised an eyebrow in question. Will stuffed his hands into his pants pockets and averted his gaze. He knew what John was wordlessly asking, but Will didn't have an answer.

"It's one thing to pray for God to protect you while you are away at college," Esther continued. "Quite another to send you off to the frozen frontier! Daddy, tell her she can't go!"

"Well, Esther, nothing's been decided." Reverend Albright rocked back and forth on his heels. "There's no need to go worrying."

No, Will thought. *I'm worrying enough for all of us.*

"I hate to interrupt," Will said, "but I must be getting back to the barracks."

John looked surprised, as did Mrs. Albright. "Oh, must you? Can't you stay a while longer?" she asked.

"No, I'm sorry. But thank you so much for dinner. You have no idea what it means to have a home-cooked meal."

"But what about our game?"

It was Will's turn to be surprised. Everyone, including Will, turned and looked at Phoebe. Her cheeks instantly flushed.

"I – I mean, there is the matter of the aggie," she managed to stammer out.

"Of course, Pheebs," Will said. They both returned to the table. He concentrated for only a moment, moved his remaining bishop, and took out her knight.

"Checkmate."

Phoebe's mouth slowly fell open as she stared at the board then lifted her eyes to stare at Will. He winked as he grabbed the aggie off the board and nodded goodnight to everyone.

"Wait, Will," Esther called out. "Phoebe will see you out."

Will grabbed his hat off the hook in the foyer and stifled a grin at the sound of Phoebe's exasperated sigh. He turned to see both Mrs. Albright and Esther feverishly whispering and wagging fingers at her. She clenched her fists at her side and strode toward Will and the door he held open for her.

～

"Thank you for coming to dinner," she said in much the same rehearsed sounding way she had all the times when, as children, her mother had made her apologize to him even though it was obvious she wasn't the least bit sorry. "And for once again stealing my aggie."

"You mean once again beating you fair and square," Will said with a wink.

She lifted an eyebrow at him. "I will admit, you are a better player than I expected, Officer Caffey."

"Officer Caffey?" Will chuckled. "Well, Miss Albright, have we returned to formalities?"

"I'm sorry," she said. "I guess seeing you in your uniform brings formality out in me."

Will leaned against the handrail. "Well, I'd gladly take it off for you."

Phoebe's eyes grew wide, and she gasped. "Why, I never... How dare you!"

It only took a moment for Will to decipher the look of shock on her face. He threw his head back and laughed heartily.

"That's not what I meant," he said, trying with great difficulty to gain control of his mirth. "All I meant was that when I'm invited for supper again, I'll be sure to wear civilian clothing."

"Oh," she whispered and averted her eyes. This disappointed him greatly. He loved looking into her eyes.

She wrapped her arms around her middle.

"Pheebs, you're shivering."

"Why must you always call me that?"

He knew he shouldn't press his luck, but he just couldn't help himself. "Because you won't allow me to call you darling...yet."

That was obviously her breaking point.

"Will Caffey, you are the most annoying man I have ever met! I tried in vain to be polite to you, but at every turn, you provoke me! I - I hope you choke on that aggie!"

She turned quickly, skirts twirling, and stormed up the

stairs. But her hands were still clutching her waist, and not her skirt. Her boot tangled in the fabric and she lost her footing. Will watched as she tried in vain to right herself, but her efforts only made matters worse, and she began to fall backwards.

Phoebe screamed. Will lunged toward her and, for the second time that day, caught Phoebe before her backside landed on the ground.

His heart thrummed hard against his chest as he held her in his arms, her large brown eyes looking up at him, wide with shock. Those eyes. How he longed to lose himself in those dark orbs. He said the first words that popped into his head.

"Why Phoebe, I do believe you are making a habit of this."

WILL'S GOODBYE

"*Naw, Pheebs, like this,*" Will said, dropping to the ground on his belly. "*Ya gotta keep your whole body flat and crawl with your arms and legs.*"

Phoebe rolled her eyes as she dropped to the ground. The last thing she wanted to do was get her dress dirty, but mama had said to play with Will outside, so she guessed she had no choice.

"*Why do we have to do it like this?*"

"*Cause, that's how they do it in the army. Keeps you safe from bullets.*"

"*There ain't no bullets in my momma's garden.*"

"*Maybe not now, but you never know. Besides, you don't know what dangers you'll face out there in the world. Someday you'll be glad I taught ya this,*" *young Will said with a wink.*

Phoebe awoke with a start. It had only been a dream, but it was more. It was a memory; one she had long ago forgotten. But it was flooding back to her now. She remembered Will's insistence that they pretend to be army soldiers, even though at the time Phoebe had no idea what that meant. She also remembered how much trouble she got into for ruining her new dress with grass stains. But what she remembered most was the infuriating wink.

The past two days had been quite uneventful for Phoebe. In fact, they had been downright boring. Without her studies to keep her busy, she found them long and tedious. She tried busying herself with helping her mother, but there wasn't much to do. She tried reading her Bible, but found her mind constantly drifting off in one of two directions.

The one direction led her thoughts to the letter. She had always assumed the Lord would provide a husband whom she could support, perhaps even work alongside with, in his ministry. Could God be calling her to minister alone? She had never considered that. And so far from home, away from her friends and family, away from her entire support system? She felt confident in her preaching skills, she had been well trained in that, but there was so much more to pastoring a church than just speaking well. How could she manage such a calling on her own?

But what if this was what God had been preparing her for all along? The thought was both frightening and curious at the same time.

When she wasn't consumed with thinking about the letter, her mind ran another path…a path that led to Will, and it irritated her.

As much as she tried to convince herself that she only thought of him because he irritated her so, her own mind betrayed her with the memory of his face, made even more handsome in the moonlight as he smiled down at her. She couldn't escape the memory of being held in his arms or the faint scent of masculinity that seemed to emanate from him as he held her close against his chest. These thoughts stirred something in her that she didn't understand, and it angered her. How could she allow her emotions to be so affected by a rascal such as Will Caffey?

As she paced the floors, her mind kept replaying the moments after she'd fallen off the stairs. She couldn't get over the way her treacherous heart raced at the sensation of being once again held tightly against his chest, even as he smirked down at her. Every time she walked past the window, she glanced out at the front stairs, and replayed the scene in her mind, sometimes with anger, other times with puzzlement.

Imagine her surprise when, on one of those occasions, she in fact did see Will. He had just dismounted and was tying his horse to a post.

Phoebe stepped onto the porch. When he saw her, Will took off his hat and grinned. He placed one foot on the bottom stair and rested his elbow on his knee.

"Good afternoon, Phoebe," he said, his lip curling.

"Good afternoon. Come to invite yourself to dinner again?"

"I wish I could. Is your father home?"

Phoebe had expected an irksome flirtation, but the serious look on Will's face gave her pause.

"Oh, I – I mean, yes. Please – come in."

Phoebe led Will to the dining room, embarrassed at the assumption that he had been looking for her. Reverend Albright sat reading, preparing his message for the following Sunday.

"William, my boy!" Her father stood up and extended his hand. "What a pleasant surprise."

"Thank you, sir," he said. "Could I have a moment of your time? There's something I'd like to discuss with you – in private, if I may?"

Both men looked at Phoebe. "Oh, of course," she replied, turning on her heels and quickly leaving the room.

In the hallway, Phoebe caught her little sister eavesdropping.

"He wants to talk to Daddy alone?" she whispered.

"Yes," Phoebe whispered back. "So that means just that, alone. Now you go on, or else I'll tell Daddy what you're doing."

"Do you think he's asking Daddy for your hand in marriage?"

"What? Don't be absurd!"

"Well, what else would he need to talk to Daddy about in private?"

"In case you haven't noticed, Sarah, our father is a minister. People come to see him all the time, and most of the time for private conversations."

"But not Will. He's never done that."

"Sarah, mind your own business. Now off with you!" Phoebe said, shooing Sarah toward the parlor.

She picked up the letter from Frank Berger off the table by her father's chair and slipped it into her pocket. As she headed for the stairs, she glanced once more toward the dining room. She knew that she shouldn't peek in, but she couldn't stop herself. Will sat with his head bowed, as did her father - they were praying together.

Phoebe quickly climbed the stairs, ashamed that she had spied in on such a private moment.

Once upstairs, she pulled the letter out of her pocket and read it. There were other pleasantries that you would expect in a post, but the main purpose of the letter was just as her father had said. There were churches that needed pastors. Rev. Berger spoke of the number of women pastors that were coming out of college and wondered if Phoebe would consider taking a church in the north.

Her mind kept spinning around the thought of leaving home and heading to the Upper Peninsula. There were so many reasons why she should not do it. She was a woman, and a single one at that. And, as Esther and her mother had pointed out, the conditions in the Upper Peninsula were much harsher than they were in Mid-Michigan. Yet, somewhere inside of her was a desire to try, even if only temporarily, until a proper pastor could be found. Surely, she could help out until then? If only she had found a husband in Bible College.

Without meaning to, her thoughts turned to Will and she

remembered the image of him praying with her father in the dining room downstairs. Was Will alright? What could have been so important that he couldn't have discussed it in front of her?

Could Will Caffey have some sort of dark secret? Phoebe laughed at the thought.

Then a worse thought came to her... what if Sarah were correct? What if Will was asking for her hand in marriage? Hadn't he been very attentive, even flirtatious since picking her up from the train station? And hadn't her father hinted as much, saying that Will had "intentions"?

Father wouldn't agree, would he? She tried to convince herself. She couldn't believe that her father would ever consent to something so sudden, but Reverend Albright seemed to have a great respect for Will. He had an honorable occupation and could support a family. And what did Phoebe have going for her? A college degree with no plan for which to use it.

"Oh my gosh!" she said out loud. "Daddy may actually wed me off to Will Caffey!"

She had to put a stop to this. Privacy or not, she had to let both her father and Will know that she was not interested in marrying him!

As she rushed down the stairs, her father was just coming out of the dining room.

"Is something the matter, darlin'?" he asked.

Embarrassed, Phoebe slowed her descent. She wanted to appear as calm and collected as possible when speaking with the two men.

"I'm fine, Daddy," she said, looking beyond the reverend. "Where's Will?"

"Gone."

"Gone?" Phoebe said. *But what of the proposal?*

"Take a walk with me?" her father asked.

Phoebe nodded her agreement, still shocked, as her father spoke to Sarah.

"Tell your mother when she gets back from the Smiths that your sister and I will be back in time for supper."

Reverend Albright led Phoebe down the porch stairs and turned right toward downtown. Phoebe had expected to turn left toward the church, as her father was apt to do.

"Where are we going?"

"There's someone I need to visit. I thought you could keep me company on the walk."

They walked in silence for a few minutes, and Phoebe wondered if she should bring up her father's conversation with Will.

"Have you thought much about Dr. Berger's letter?" he asked, interrupting her thoughts.

"A little," she admitted.

They walked again in silence.

"And?" he eventually asked.

Phoebe took a deep breath. "I don't know, really. There are a lot of reasons why it is a preposterous idea."

"But…"

"But I am trained to do the work, and there is a need that has to be filled."

Reverend Albright motioned to a bench. They sat and he turned to look at her.

"Phoebe, God doesn't *need* you to accomplish his work."

"I know that Daddy. He owns the cattle on a thousand hills."

The pastor nodded. "Then answer me this…when you think about going north, does something happen inside of you? A stirring? A desire to go, even though you don't know what that means exactly?"

"Yes," she answered honestly.

"Have you been praying about it?"

"I have."

"Do you have an answer yet?"

"I – I don't know."

"Well, then, I guess we'll just pray some more."

Reverend Albright stood and offered his arm. She accepted and they continued walking until they had reached the front gate of Esther's house.

"Why didn't you tell me we were coming here?" she asked.

"Because I didn't know myself. Just knew we needed to visit someone."

The front door opened and out stepped Will.

"We meet again, Reverend Albright," he said, smiling at the preacher. "Phoebe," he said with a nod. "Do come in. I wish I could stay and chat, but I have things to attend to. Good day," he said before rushing off.

'Strange,' she thought, but didn't have time to dwell on it before her brother-in-law was ushering her and her father into the house. Esther was seated in a chair in the parlor.

"Oh, Phoebe! I've been hoping you'd come to visit."

Phoebe blushed. In all of her boredom, she never once thought to visit her pregnant sister. "I'm sorry, Esther. I promise I won't wait so long to visit again."

"So, what's new with you?" Esther patted the seat next to her. "Have you thought anymore about the church up north?"

"Actually, Father and I were just talking about it on the walk here," Phoebe said, preparing for another dose of her sister's opinions.

"And have you decided? Oh, I think it sounds like the most exciting adventure!"

Phoebe stared at her sister in disbelief. "Adventure? You said that you would worry too much if I went. You called it the Frozen Frontier, or something like that. Now it's an adventure?"

Esther laughed and waved a hand. "Phoebe, haven't you learned by now not to listen to my rantings? I was just shocked. You know that I'm in full support of women pastors, don't you?

I think it's about time. Of course, I will miss you, but you are a strong, capable woman. And you still feel called into the ministry, don't you?"

"Well, yes, very much so."

"Well, then what's stopping you?"

Phoebe pondered that. *What was stopping her?* "It's just so far away, and the conditions would be so much more – more difficult than those to which I am accustomed."

"That's why it would be such an adventure!" her sister said excitedly. "Besides, I have faith that God will provide special protection for you. Remember, '*The Lord is good, a strong hold in the day of trouble; and he knoweth them that trust in him.*' Do you trust in Him, Phoebe?"

THAT EVENING, Esther and John joined the Albrights for supper. They were just finishing when someone knocked on the door.

"I wonder who that could be," Mrs. Albright asked, starting to rise.

"I'll see to it," John said. He returned to the dining room, followed by Will.

"Good evening, Will," said Mrs. Albright. "You are just in time for dessert and coffee."

"Thank you, ma'am, but I didn't come to interrupt your dinner. I was hoping to speak with Phoebe."

All eyes turned to Phoebe.

"Oh – oh, of course," she answered, uncomfortable with the attention.

"I thought we could go for a walk, if that is alright with you, Reverend."

"Certainly. Why don't you join us afterward for coffee?"

Will didn't answer; it was as though he was waiting for

Phoebe's response. As she pushed back her chair and started to rise, Sarah leaned over and whispered, "I told you so!"

Phoebe's stomach was in knots. She would have preferred to have avoided, rather than rejected, Will's proposal. She had never been in this situation, never having been courted by anyone. She clasped her hands to keep them from shaking.

"Don't forget your wrap this time," Will said. "It is a chilly night."

Phoebe clutched her shawl around her as they walked in silence, a silence she found very uncomfortable.

"You were right," she began. "It is chilly tonight."

"I'm sorry Phoebe, is it too cold? Would you like to go back?"

"No, no. I'm fine." She would much rather do this out of the watchful eyes of her entire family.

They walked in silence a little longer. '*He doesn't seem nervous,*' she thought. How did he appear to her, she wondered. Thoughtful? Concerned? Almost…sad?

Since Phoebe couldn't avoid the conversation, she decided to hurry it along. "You wanted to speak with me?"

"Yes. Would you like to sit?"

"I'm actually enjoying the walk."

"Then we shall continue walking."

When they reached the same bench Phoebe had shared with her father only hours earlier, Will stopped and turned to face her.

"I'm leaving," he said bluntly.

"Leaving?" Her stomach dropped.

"Yes. I finally got my orders. I leave in the morning."

"Oh," she answered. Neither of them spoke for a moment as Phoebe struggled to understand the unexpected feeling of disappointment that assailed her.

"What are you thinking?" he asked.

Phoebe couldn't explain feelings she did not understand, so

she asked another question rather than answer his. "Are you being sent very far away?"

"Yes."

Will said nothing more until they stood together on the parsonage porch. Phoebe realized that his intent had not been to propose, but to say goodbye.

"Phoebe, my post is far away from here. I don't know when, if ever, I will be able to return to Lansing. I just wanted to be able to say goodbye to you, and to let you know that I – I will miss seeing you."

She wanted to tell him that she would miss seeing him as well, but she didn't want him to misinterpret her words.

"May I write you? Once I am settled?"

"Of course, I would like that." Her own words shocked her. In truth, she would like to hear from him, but she was afraid he would think her accepting him as a suitor. If she were to accomplish God's call on her life, she could never consider a man like Will Caffey, or any other potential suitor not called to ministry. Being the wife of a Michigan State Constable was a noble thing, but it wasn't God's plan for her. If she married, she would be giving up her career.

What about Anna? a quiet voice inside asked.

Anna is different, Phoebe thought. She was able to continue her dream because her husband allowed her to continue working. Other men would not be so modern. Phoebe knew this well. She had seen it many times in Bible College - smart, dedicated women studying for the ministry right alongside of the men, until they married a farmer or an automobile worker. Then, they were resigned to the life of wife and helpmate. No, Phoebe could not consider any man other than a pastor so as to complete God's call on her life.

Will smiled, oblivious to her inner turmoil. "Please say my goodbyes to your family. I have to get back to the barracks to pack." He nodded and bounded down the stairs.

"Will?" Phoebe called. He stopped at the bottom, turned and looked at her.

"Yes Pheebs?"

"I – I don't want to mislead you. If it is your hope that I will wait for you, that – that this is the beginning of a long-distance courtship, well, then, you need to understand that I am not – I …" she trailed off. She took a deep breath and began again. "I'm not interested in putting my life on hold, or ignoring God's call on my life, for you or for any man. I'm sorry if that is a shock to you or injures you. That is not my intent."

Will smiled up at her, his eyes dancing in the gleam of the streetlights. He placed his foot on the second step then leaned his elbow on his knee, as seemed to be his habit when speaking with her.

"I wouldn't want you to put your life on hold for me, Pheebs. And I certainly don't want you to ignore God's calling. Just the opposite. I pray you find the answers to His call on your life, just like I have."

Another nod, and he turned to go.

"Will?"

He chuckled and returned to the bottom of the stairs, looking up at her. "At this rate, I'll be here in the morning for breakfast," he laughed.

"I just have one more question. Are you happy with your new post? Is it what you were hoping for?"

"I think it will be, but only time will tell," he said with his signature smirk. "I'll let you know, I promise." And then he was gone.

When Phoebe returned to the dining room, conversation ceased, and everyone looked at her.

"He is leaving. He has been given his new assignment," she said. They continued watching her, as if anticipating something more. "That is it. He asked me to say his goodbyes to everyone. He had to return to headquarters to ready himself."

She again took her seat at the table. Nobody spoke. Something felt strange, and then it occurred to her – nobody seemed surprised. She looked up at her father.

"You knew, didn't you. About Will leaving. That's why he came to see you this morning."

"Yes, that is part of the reason," her father answered.

"And you?" Her eyes zeroed in on her sister and John, who looked guiltily at one another.

"Yes. We knew," John answered. "Will came to say goodbye to me this afternoon. He asked us not to say anything to you. He wanted to tell you himself."

"Well, I don't know what all the fuss was about," Phoebe said. "Why did he feel the need to speak with me privately if everyone else already knew?"

"Well, I didn't know!" exclaimed Mrs. Albright. "This is a shock to me."

"I'm shocked as well," Sarah added. "I thought he was here tonight to propose to Phoebe."

"Don't be preposterous!" Phoebe snapped. "Men don't go around proposing to women they aren't courting!"

"Agreed," said Esther, speaking up finally. "But, to answer your question, Phoebe, I believe all the fuss was maybe Will's hope – his way of giving you one last chance to show some affection toward him."

"I have no affection for Will. I do wish him the best, but that is all."

"Well, enough of this chatter about proposals and affection. Tell us, dear. Where is Will's new posting?" asked Mrs. Albright.

"I have no idea," she said, to her own amazement. "I never asked."

"You didn't ask?"

"Oh, now mother," said Esther. "I am sure Will will write as soon as he can and tell us all about it. Now," she said, rising from her chair. "Shall we play something in the parlor? How about a game of chess, Phoebe? I'm sure I'm not as formidable of a foe as your last opponent, but I'm not terrible either."

"Not tonight," Phoebe said, standing as well. "It's been a long day and I think I will turn in early."

She said goodnight and as the rest of the family headed for either the parlor or the kitchen, Phoebe headed for the stairs. She placed her hand on the rail just as someone else placed a hand on hers.

"Don't worry," Esther began, "I don't think this is the last you have seen of Will Caffey."

6

DECORATION DAY

*I*t appeared as if the entire town had come out for the Decoration Day picnic.

Phoebe loved Decoration Day. Already, there had been a parade and a moving service at the ceremony, reminding Phoebe of the great sacrifice so many had made for their country. Seeing the Michigan State constables among them had reminded Phoebe that Will was among their number and had shamed her a bit. She regretted not respecting his position as an officer more.

But there was no time for regrets, now. Now it was time to eat. The church grounds were packed with townspeople, and tables covered in food went on for miles. Phoebe's favorite table was the one filled with desserts. There was something about a potluck that brought out the competitor in every baker. Each and every delicacy you could imagine was on display, from blackberry pie to layered cakes to pastries of all kinds. Several women stood nearby, trying to appear engaged in conversation or observation of the children playing nearby, but Phoebe knew their real intent was campaigning. They each wanted validation that their confection was superior to the others. When an

53

unsuspecting person would happen by, just to take a look at what the table had to offer, of course, the women would descend like vultures. While this often took them by surprise, Phoebe and Sarah relished it.

"Oh girls, you must certainly try my strawberry rhubarb pie. The ingredients are fresh from my garden!"

"Of course, Mrs. Talbot!"

"Have a slice of my lemon cake...it's my secret recipe!"

"If you insist, Mrs. Shaffer!"

"How about some bread pudding?"

"Certainly, Mrs. Lemont!"

Before long, the girls had plates piled high with every imaginable sweet.

They walked away, laughing and stuffing their faces.

"Phoebe? Phoebe Albright? Is that you?" came a voice from behind.

Phoebe turned, mouth full of cake, to find Stella Franklin, one of her old classmates and the last person Phoebe would want to see her stuffing an entire plate of sweets in her face, quickly approaching.

"Oh, it is you!" she exclaimed, hugging Phoebe dramatically.

"Well, Stella, this is a surprise," Phoebe responded, wiping her mouth. Of all the people who could have caught her stuffing her face in such a manner, Stella Franklin would have been at the bottom of Phoebe's list. Swallowing the remaining cake, Phoebe mustered as genuine a smile as possible for the young busybody. "I'd heard that your parents had moved to Detroit."

"Oh, they did, but I moved back home when I married Billy Bowen. Did you know that I married Billy Bowen? Oh, you probably didn't know that, with you being away at college and all. Yep, we got married last month after a whirlwind romance. It was something, Phoebe. Billy is such a romantic. I bet you never thought of Billy as a romantic, did you? Well he is, and I'll tell you..."

She spoke a million words a minute, and Phoebe's head started to spin. Stella had always been a talker, and her favorite subject had always been herself – and this conversation was no different. She went on and on about her courtship to Billy Bowen, about their wedding and their new house. She transitioned from one topic to another so quickly, that Phoebe couldn't keep up. So, when her conversation turned to a question, Phoebe wasn't prepared.

"Phoebe, dear, did you hear me?"

"I'm sorry Stella, I got distracted. What did you ask me?"

"Silly girl, I asked what you are doing now – now that you are finished with Bible College?"

Phoebe didn't know what to say. She'd had to answer this question a few times, but most people were too polite to ask. Phoebe knew people felt sorry for her, being 22 and still not married.

"Phoebe's been asked to pastor a church in the U.P.! Isn't that exciting?" Sarah exclaimed.

"A pastor? An unmarried woman? Are you serious?" Stella laughed. That's about the most ridiculous thing I have ever heard!"

"Ridiculous?" Phoebe could feel her face growing warm. "What exactly is ridiculous about it?"

"Well... everything, I suppose. I mean, the thought of you being a pastor..."

"I have the same exact schooling as all the men that graduated from Bible College, so I am certainly qualified for the position."

"You might have the schooling, but you are a woman. You went off to Bible College to marry yourself a preacher, not become one! Besides, you would never last a week in the Upper Peninsula. You are far too delicate."

"Now you listen to me, Stella Franklin, or Bowen, or whatever your name is now. Not only am I trained and capable of the work, but I am called of God, so He will provide all I need. Was David strong enough to face the giant? No, but God provided the stone, didn't he? Did Moses have the voice of a leader? No, but God provided Aaron. Was Sarah at an age to bear children? No, she wasn't, but you know how that story turned out as well, don't you? God doesn't ask for us to be strong in our own strength. All he asks is that we respond like Isaiah – 'Here I am. Send me.' So, you'll excuse me if I don't listen to your lunacy that I can't do what God is calling me to do, and instead listen to Paul when he tells us in Hebrews that God will make me perfect in every good work to do his will. Good day, Mrs. Bowen!"

Phoebe turned and stormed off leaving Stella standing, mouth agape, and Sarah chasing after her, mouth full of strawberry cake, laughing all the way.

And with that, Phoebe's decision was made.

7

GRAND TRUNK STATION

"*S*ettle yourself, dear," Mrs. Albright said, squeezing Phoebe's hand.

She looked into her mother's soft, green eyes and smiled. "Is it that obvious?"

"You're about to wear a hole in the platform with your tapping."

Phoebe stilled her foot. "It would be easier if Father weren't taking so long purchasing my ticket."

"Oh, he probably found someone to have a chat with."

Normally, her father's propensity for gabbing didn't bother Phoebe, but today was different. "But if I miss this train, I'll have to take the next. If I take the next train, I won't arrive at Indian River when the Reverend and Mrs. Cook are expecting me. They might assume I'm not coming. If they leave the station, I'll be stranded there until the next morning. If that happens—"

"Hush, now. Here he comes. And I was right...he found someone to talk to."

Phoebe turned to see her father and Sarah weaving through the crowd with two more family members close behind.

"Esther!" Phoebe said. "I told you to stay home and rest!"

"I wouldn't let you leave without seeing you off! Besides, the doctor said that I am the picture of health!"

Her brother-in-law John helped Reverend Albright carry Phoebe's trunks to the baggage car. Truth be known, she owned enough to fill three trunks, but Dr. Berger had said in his final letter that the parsonage would be outfitted with everything she needed. And, after all, she had spent the last four years with only one trunk's worth of belongings, so certainly she could make do with only two. But those two were packed to the brim and were apparently very heavy. Her father faltered a bit, but before he dropped the chest, a Michigan State Trooper who was boarding the train was there to assist him.

"Very dashing," Esther whispered, motioning toward the officer. "And handsome."

Phoebe shot her sister a look. "You're married!"

"I didn't say he was more handsome than John. That would be impossible." She winked at her. "And I suppose he's not as handsome as your constable, either."

"I don't know who you are talking about."

Esther snorted. "Don't try to deny that he reminded you of Will."

"He did not. And Will is not my constable."

Esther rolled her eyes. "Of course, he isn't."

Phoebe was irked by her sister's assumption, but not more so than she was with herself for lying. In truth, the man had reminded her of Will, though she was loath to admit it. She was also loath to admit that it wasn't the first time she had thought of him. She had expected Will to at least have written her father, if not a letter penned to her personally, but they'd heard nothing from him since he'd left Lansing, despite his promises to do otherwise. And now she was leaving.

'Serves him right,' she thought as she imagined him returning home for a visit only to discover that she wasn't there. 'I guess he should have written like he promised.'

The two men rejoined the women just as the train whistle blew.

"Well, I guess it's time to say our goodbyes," John said. He gave Phoebe a brotherly hug. "Win some souls, ya hear sis?"

Esther pulled Phoebe into her own arms. "You will write, won't you? Every week. Promise me."

"Every week," she said, her voice cracking slightly. She then turned to her little sister.

"Oh, Sarah, don't cry. You'll just make me cry as well."

"I'm going to miss you," Sarah blubbered. "What if I never see you again."

"Of course, you'll see me. Tell you what, maybe next summer you can visit me up north?"

Sarah perked up at that, although Mrs. Albright didn't seem too pleased. Her countenance didn't stay sour for long, however. She smiled at her middle child and grasped her hands.

"Phoebe, dear, I couldn't be more proud of you!" Mrs. Albright gathered her in her arms. No sorrow. No tears. Just joy. Phoebe was grateful for her mother's positivity, but she was surprised by it.

"You aren't worried anymore?" Phoebe asked.

"Oh, no dear. I know now that you'll be safe," she said, then ended with, "but I will miss you terribly."

Reverend Albright cleared his throat. "Alright, then, let's pause a moment to pray together as a family – one last time."

As they all circled and held hands, Reverend Albright led them in a prayer of thankfulness – for God's calling, His provision, and His hope for their futures. He prayed for guidance for Phoebe and for strength for her family back home in her absence. Above all, he prayed that God's will be done in all their lives.

"And Lord, we pray for Will. Continue to protect him and bless him. We thank you for the sacrifices he makes for this

State and for our family. We ask this in the matchless name of Jesus, Amen."

They finished praying and Phoebe reached for her bags, but her father grabbed them instead.

"I am fully capable of carrying – "

"I know you are," he said picking up another bag that Phoebe didn't recognize.

"Wait, that one isn't mine."

"I know," he answered matter-of-factly. "It's mine."

Realization dawned on Phoebe. Her father was going with her.

"Daddy, I know you mean well, but if I can lead a church alone, I can surely travel alone. I don't need an escort. I don't need a guide. This isn't my first train – "

"Already bought my ticket."

"I mean no disrespect, but – "

"Listen, darlin' I know you're prepared for this mission God is sending you on. I believe you can do anything God calls you to do. As your pastor, I'm proud of you and your determination. But as your father," he looked her in the eyes, "As your father, I need to make sure you get to your assignment safely. This father needs to baby his daughter one last time – before he has to finally admit that she's all grown up and doesn't need him anymore. You won't deny me that, will ya?"

"No, Daddy," she said, swallowing the lump in her throat.

"Good. Well, we had better get on board. John, you'll be sure to check in on Ruth and Sarah for me? I'll be back within the week."

Once on board, Phoebe located a window seat where she could see her family on the platform.

"Daddy?" she said as he sat down beside her.

"Yes?"

She tried to form words to express what the gesture of accompanying her meant — sure, she talked bravely to Sarah, and there had been no difficulty in loudly proclaiming her intentions once the decision had been made, but inside, secretly, Phoebe was scared to death. In the end, she could only manage a weak, "Thank you."

He patted her hand. "No, darlin'. Thank you."

Phoebe waved frantically out the window as the train pulled away. Sarah ran alongside the train, waving and hollering goodbye until she ran out of platform. Phoebe watched her until her silhouette was so small, she was unrecognizable among those around her. It was at this point, when Phoebe could no longer see her sisters or her mother, that it became real to her. Very real. There was no turning back. She was moving hundreds of miles from home, away from everyone she loved. She was moving to the Upper Peninsula – a place she had never even visited.

Try as she might, she couldn't keep tears from welling up. She glanced over at her father. His eyes were closed.

'Dear God,' she prayed silently. 'How am I to answer your call to Iron Falls if I can't make it five minutes from Lansing without breaking down?'

She began playing her father's prayer over in her mind, and it comforted her. He had prayed for guidance and for workers to help her. She remembered him asking for strength in the tough times. *Right now is one of those times, Lord.* He had also prayed that God would begin preparing the hearts of her congregation before she'd even arrived. Knowing how big God was and believing that he was already at work brought joy to her heart.

The more she thought about the prayer, the calmer she became. She laid her head back and allowed her mind to replay more of the prayer. He had asked that she listen to God's plan, even when it didn't align with her own. This made her smile. How well her father knew her! Sometimes Phoebe got so caught up in *doing* God's *work*, that she forgot to *listen* to God's *voice*.

Then she remembered the end of his prayer...he had prayed for Will. He prayed for his safety and thanked him for the sacrifices he makes...

"Daddy?"

"Hmph?" her father answered without opening his eyes.

"Your prayer for Will – you mentioned sacrifices he has made for our family. What did you mean by that?"

"Well, I guess that's a story for Will to tell, not me."

"I guess I'll never know, then."

"Hmph," he grunted and pulled his hat over his eyes.

THE FIRST LEG of the trip was exhausting. All the jerking and constant stopping gave Phoebe a headache but didn't seem to bother Reverend Albright in the least. More than once Phoebe had to elbow her father because his snoring had become so loud that others were beginning to stare.

When they finally stopped for lunch, Phoebe was elated to stretch her muscles. Most of the passengers funneled into the dining establishment in the station, but from Phoebe's experience, those restaurants were overpriced and the food underseasoned. Besides, Mrs. Albright had been so afraid they would go hungry that she had packed a basket full of enough food for the entire passenger car, and Phoebe was sure there would be some of her favorites in there.

Several outside tables were set up for passengers to use, but by the time Phoebe and her father stepped off the train, they were all taken. One table, on the very end, had only one gentleman seated at it. Reverend Albright approached him.

"Excuse me, my boy, but would you mind if my daughter and I shared your table with you?"

The young man looked up, and Phoebe saw that he was indeed that – a *young* man. He couldn't have been a day over fifteen. He smiled and Phoebe recognized him from the Grand Trunk Station.

"Yes sir, I'd be happy to share." He looked at Phoebe and blushed.

"You're from Lansing, too," she said as she sat across from the boy. "I saw you saying goodbye to your mother."

He pulled at his collar. "Yeah, my ma made quite a scene. It was embarrassing."

"I thought it was sweet," Phoebe said, remembering the older woman's loud crying. "It just shows how much she cares."

Phoebe opened their basket. Just as she thought... plenty of all her favorites: roast beef sandwiches, cold fried chicken, berries from Mrs. Albright's garden, a jar of her pickles, apple turnovers and nut tarts.

"I wonder where I can find a water pump?" Phoebe wondered out loud.

"Let me get it for ya, ma'am," said their lunch companion, grabbing the cups Phoebe held and running off.

Phoebe smiled after the boy. She turned to her father, who was frowning at the table.

"I'm feeling mighty over-blessed right about now," he said, motioning to the young man's lunch.

Phoebe's eyes followed her father's. An unwrapped piece of brown paper lay on the table, its only contents: three hard boiled eggs and two apples.

Phoebe shrugged. "Well, I guess we know why mother packed so much food – God knew who we were going to sit with all along."

Her father's face softened and looked at her doubtfully. "If he'll accept it. You don't want to bruise his pride."

The young man returned with the cups full of cold water.

"Thank you so much," Phoebe said. "Oh dear, we don't even know your name."

"It's Wendell. Wendell Jackson, ma'am."

"Well, Wendell Jackson, I am Phoebe Albright, and this is my father, Reverend James Albright."

"Pleased to meet ya both."

"Wendell, we appreciate you sharing your table," Phoebe said. "But I have another favor. You see, my mother packed far too much food, and there isn't any way we could possibly eat it all. Would you be a dear and help us eat this lunch?"

"Oh, I couldn't, ma'am. I couldn't eat your lunch."

Despite his youth, Wendell Jackson donned a manful pride far beyond his age. His shoulders, not quite the width they would reach some day, straightened and lifted, as if accustomed to bearing a weight the world could not see. His eyes spoke another story, though, one that although silent to Phoebe, tugged at something deep inside of her. That hidden story, and the gaunt appearance of the boy caused Phoebe to stand her ground. Pride, no matter how noble, would not fill a growing boy's stomach.

"But it will just go to waste. You don't want that, do you?"

His shoulders lightened a little and he laughed. "No, ma'am. Of course, I don't want that."

"Then, that's settled." Phoebe smiled and began dividing the food.

"But I…" Wendell sputtered, looking back and forth between his lunch partners, seemingly at a loss. "I didn't say –"

"So, Wendell, where ya headed?" Reverend Albright asked, ending the conversation.

Still appearing a little stunned, Wendell picked up the sandwich Phoebe placed before him. "The Upper Peninsula, sir, to a town called Iron Falls."

"Hey, you don't say! That's where Miss Albright here is headed as well."

The young man's face lit up. "Really? That's great!" He began to blush again. "I mean, well – " he stammered a bit. "Well, you must be meetin' your husband up there?"

"No, Wendell. I'm not married."

He looked confused. "Then why ya headin' up there? Most girls wouldn't be caught dead going to the U.P."

Phoebe suppressed a laugh. "I'm the new pastor of Iron Falls."

His brow furrowed as he looked at her. "Are you teasin' me?"

"No, I promise you I am very serious."

He thought for another moment, nodded his head, and smiled.

"Well, I think that's great. My Ma would have made a great preacher, you know. She's always lecturing to me from the Bible. You excited?"

She thought for a moment. "Yes, very much so," she said honestly. *'And nervous,'* she thought silently.

"Well, I'm excited, too. Not only have I made a friend in my new town, but I've already met the pastor!"

Both Phoebe and her father laughed.

"So why are you headed to the Upper Peninsula, son?" asked Reverend Albright.

"Got me a job in the mines, sir. The pay is pretty good, and the housing is free, so it's not a bad job."

Phoebe was shocked. "Work? Why, you can't be old enough to work in a mine!"

Her words seemed to wound the boy and his shoulders lifted again. "I'm sixteen… but I'll be seventeen in November."

"Well, that sounds like right honorable work," her father interjected, giving Phoebe a reproachful look she was all too familiar with. This wasn't the first time he'd had to save her from her own mouth.

"Yes, it does," Phoebe agreed. "Your mother must be very proud."

"She is, but she wishes I weren't moving so far away. She's worried about me…thinks I'm too young."

"I'll let you in on a little secret, Wendell," Reverend Albright said.

"No matter how old you get, your mother will never stop worrying about you." He patted Phoebe's hand. "It's part of being a parent."

"If it would make you feel any better, sir, I would be happy to keep an eye out for Miss Albright, you know, and help her whenever she needs it. I could help if she had chores or things a man needs to do."

"That is very sweet, Wendell, but I can take care of my own chores."

"Well, you'll need help around the church, isn't that right? I would be happy to be a helper in that way, if I could."

Helper – around the church. God was already answering their prayers and she wasn't even halfway to Iron Falls yet!

"Yes, yes I will need help around the church! And I would be honored if you were willing to volunteer."

"Well, then, I guess that makes me your first parishioner!" he said with a smile.

They finished their lunch and packed up their belongings.

"We are stopping in Indian Lake for the night. Where are you stopping?" the reverend asked Wendell.

"Oh, I'm not stopping until I get to Iron Falls."

"Really? That will be one long day for you."

"Yes sir, but the woman at the company's boarding house, a Mrs. Smith, she's waitin' up for me. And it's within walking distance of the train station. It'll be late, but it won't cost me anything to sleep there."

Phoebe looked down in the basket she carried. "Wendell, take this basket with you. You can eat the rest for your supper."

"But won't you and the reverend get hungry?"

"Goodness, no. Mrs. Cook, whom we are staying with this evening, will provide us with supper tonight, and will pack us a lunch to take tomorrow, so this food will just go to waste if you don't take it."

Wendell hesitated when she thrust the basket toward him.

Reverend Albright chuckled. "You might as well give up the fight, son, because she has made up her mind."

"But your basket..."

"Just return it to me later this week. We'll need to catch up on your first days in the U.P. anyway, won't we?"

"Now, you see, that's something that an old man preacher like myself just can't do," Reverend Albright said as they watched their new friend make his way to his car.

"What's that?"

"Convince a young man to not only share my lunch, but to also volunteer at a church he has never seen," he said, turning to her. "Do you know how long it took me to find someone to count the offering at church? Five weeks! It took me five weeks to find one person to do one little job in an established church full of members. You've only one member and he just volunteered to do whatever needs to be done. Seems to me that you are going to make a fine pastor." He placed his hat on his head and walked back to the train.

Laughing, Phoebe followed right behind, elated that God was already showing his presence in this adventure.

THE WIND WHIPPED stray hairs in her face, but Phoebe didn't notice. She was far more concerned with keeping the rolled brim hat atop her head that her sister had convinced her to wear. She sighed. Esther was far more interested in fashion than Phoebe ever cared to be. Had she chosen the simple deaconess bonnet as was her custom, it would be securely tied around her chin and she wouldn't be struggling with the Lake Huron breezes right now. But, at her sister's urging, she had relented. Phoebe was no longer a deaconess, Esther pointed out. She was a pastor, and she had to start acting, and dressing, like it if she expected people to see her as such. She just wished there was a uniform for pastors.

Another strong breeze swept up from the Mackinac Straits and onto the upper deck of the Chief Wawatam. She supposed she should go below where most of the other passengers were, but she just couldn't bring herself to. A bent hat and a tousled pompadour was a small sacrifice in exchange for the magnificent view from the deck.

It had been a shock boarding the Wawatam. Phoebe hadn't thought at all about how she would cross the Mackinac Straits to arrive in the Upper Peninsula, but she certainly didn't expect it to be on a ship that transported not only the train passengers, but the entire train as well. It was a little frightening, she had to admit, to trust one boat with so much weight, but the vessel seemed well built and all the passengers, including a few with their motor vehicles, seemed at ease with the situation. Who was she to question the mode of transportation?

The wind died down and Phoebe took the opportunity to release her grip on her hat and adjust the collar that refused to stay down in the wind. But just as quickly as it had died down, the lake breeze swirled up once more and Phoebe was helpless to reach her hat in time. In an instant, the rolled brim hat, along with all the pins that tried in vain to hold it onto her head, ripped out of her hair and flew behind her.

She gasped and turned, ready to run after the frustrating accessory, but to her shock, the hat wasn't halfway across the deck. It was only a few, short feet away where it had hit a man in the face.

"Oh, my!" she gasped, reaching for her hat. "I'm so sorry! I – I..."

Phoebe stopped short when the man pulled the hat away and she found herself face to face with one of the most handsome men she had ever seen.

Warm, brown eyes smiled down on her. "As lovely as I find

your hat," he said with a chuckle, "I really don't believe it matches my suit."

Phoebe could feel her cheeks grow warm as the man stared at her. "No, I don't suppose it does." She stood there, half wanting to find a place to hide for the remainder of the trip, half wanting to hear the handsome man chuckle again. She liked how it sounded.

Phoebe reached for her hat, but the gentleman pulled it just out of reach.

"Sir, if you please?"

"You may have your hat, for a price."

Phoebe arched one eyebrow. She didn't like being toyed with. "A price? How about a hand-shaped mark across your cheek?"

He threw his head back and laughed heartily. "You wound me, madam. The only price I ask…is your name." His laugh sounded even better than the chuckle and Phoebe found herself considerably less inclined toward violence.

Her shoulders relaxed. "Of course. My name is Albright. Phoebe Albright."

It was the man's turn to arch a brow. "*Mrs.* Albright."

So, that was his real question. "No, sir. *Miss* Albright."

A large, straight smile spread across the handsome face as he handed her hat to her. "I am very pleased to meet you, *Miss* Phoebe Albright. I am Gregory Parker."

"A pleasure." She twisted her hat in her hands, uncomfortable with the man's attentions, no matter how pleasant his attentions were. She searched for what to do or say to end, or extend, the conversation, because she wasn't sure which would please her more.

Mr. Parker nodded toward her head. "That must have hurt."

Phoebe scowled in confusion, then her hand flew to her hair. With no mirror at hand, she could only assume how terrible her hair must look. She had no other option but to slam her hat back into place and pray she hadn't worsened the situation. "Oh, I must look a fright!"

"On the contrary. You're beautiful."

Her heart stopped beating. How brazen of this man, a stranger, to pay her such a compliment! She found herself at a loss for words.

"She gets that from her mother."

Phoebe turned to find her father standing behind her.

"Father, may I introduce Mr. Gregory Parker. Mr. Parker, this is my father, Reverend James Albright."

"Reverend? What a coincidence. I'm an evangelist, myself."

Evangelist? He's a pastor? Phoebe thought excitedly. Her heart began beating rapidly.

Her father unbuttoned his jacket and stuffed his hands in his pants' pockets. "Parker, you say? Never heard of an evangelist by that name."

"Well, that makes two of us, because I've never heard of a pastor by the name of Albright."

"Humph," her father grunted. "Well, now you've heard of two of them."

"Excuse me, sir?"

"My girl, here. Didn't she tell you? She's a pastor as well."

The man chuckled again, but this time, Phoebe didn't find it so alluring.

"And what is so comical, sir?" she asked.

Gregory Parker regained his composure quickly. "Not the fact that you are a pastor, madam, for I assure you that I find that most interesting. I only laugh at your father believing that we had had enough time to discuss each other's personal lives so in depth in just the few moments I've been graced with your presence. That is all."

"Oh," she said, ashamed she had assumed the worst in the man.

Mr. Parker continued. "I'm an evangelist in the U.P., which is most likely why you've never heard of me."

"Have you ever traveled through a town called Iron Falls?"

"Why, yes. Many, many times. Miserable place, Iron Falls. Why do you ask?"

Phoebe swallowed hard. "That's where I'm to pastor."

Gregory Parker's smile widened. "Well, the town will surely brighten with the addition of a pastor so fair. And," he said with a wink, "the town is on my circuit. That means we will be seeing each other again."

She wasn't certain if it was the chill of the wind or the promise of his words that caused her hair to stand on end. Maybe both.

"Well, I'm sure Miss Albright will be far too busy to worry about entertaining any evangelists for some time," her father said. He grabbed her hand and placed it on his arm. "Come, now, darlin'. We best be getting down below. We'll be docking in St. Ignace soon."

"I look forward to our next meeting, Miss Albright." Gregory flashed a bright smile and nodded at her.

"As do I," she said as her father whisked her below deck.

8

INVESTIGATION

*W*ill unfolded the letter he'd received from John and read it again.

By the time you receive this, Phoebe should have arrived at her new residence. To say that Esther and I are concerned about her welfare would be an understatement, as I am sure you can understand. But we all know Phoebe. She is stubborn and strong-willed and would not be swayed. Not that any of us tried, mind you. Any opposition from us would only have pushed her to make the decision faster. We only wished she wasn't moving so far away from friends and family.

Will sighed. He refolded the letter and stuffed it back into his pocket. Yes, he did understand John and Esther's concerns, more than anyone. And he also knew better than anyone that once Phoebe had made up her mind about something, there would be no deterring her. But unlike the others, Will had peace about her decision. Will had never met a woman with more faith than Phoebe Albright. If she trusted God's calling, so did Will, whether it made sense to him or not.

God's calling. How many times had Will questioned God's calling in his own life since he left Lansing? More than he could count. But, even though a posting in Lansing or even

Detroit might have meant more prestige and more creature comforts, Will knew that wasn't what God had called him to. And Phoebe receiving the letter from the U.P. only confirmed that for him; there was no use staying in Lansing if Phoebe wasn't there.

"Look who decided to show up."

The caustic greeting came from one of the main reasons for Will's doubts about his calling - Jesse Moore. Although not the only officer whose feathers seemed ruffled by Will's arrival at the post, he was the most vocal.

Will looked Jesse straight in the eyes. "I got here as soon as I heard. Maybe next time, you'll follow procedure and inform your superior officer before heading out to investigate a crime."

Jesse did little to disguise the smirk that played on the corner of his mouth. "Guess I forgot."

"You haven't missed much, Sergeant," Frank Little, a more congenial officer interrupted. "Mr. Lambecker isn't giving us much to go on."

Will nodded. "Understandable."

Eugene Lambecker, the owner of the property, was well-known around the community as a moonshiner, even if the force had been unable to prove it. But, with his barn burned to the ground, it was hard to hide the charred remains of the still underneath the now missing floorboards.

Will moved in that direction, and Officer Little fell into step beside him. "Tell me what you do know."

"Seems the fire started on the Northeast side of the barn and spread from there. Makes sense that someone would enter from the woods, where there's the most coverage."

Will stopped. "Someone? Northeast side? Are you saying this wasn't an accident involving the still?"

"No, sir. It was a deliberate act."

"Did Lambecker say who would have done this?"

"Nope. Like I said, he isn't talking at all."

Will shook his head. "Great. Sounds like we have a feud of some sort on our hands. A neighboring still owner, perhaps?"

"That is what Lambecker did say. He said it wasn't another moonshiner. He was adamant."

Will shook his head. "We can't help him if he won't talk. We have nothing to go on."

"I know. That's what I've been telling him."

"Alright, well, let's get a wagon out here to collect all this," Will said, motioning to the soot-blackened still.

"Is that your idea of helping the man?" Jesse Moore said from behind them. "Taking away his livelihood?"

Will scowled. "Do you have a problem fulfilling your duties, soldier? If so, speak up now and I will have another officer take your place."

Jesse's eyes darkened. "No, sir. I have no problem."

"Good. Then do as I said."

Will walked away. He refused to engage in public with Moore, but he didn't think it would take much to convince him to engage in a private altercation. Jesse Moore was taller and older than Will, but Will had no doubt he could take him in a fair fight. It wasn't how he wanted to operate as the commanding officer of his post, but if Moore continued to defy him in front of the other officers, he might just have to set Jesse Moore straight.

But Moore's words had hit a sore spot: hunting down every bathtub gin maker in the county was the last thing he wanted to do as a member of the Michigan State Constabulary, but it seemed all he did at his new post. When prohibition had first passed, most people ignored home brewers, who were mostly immigrant families just trying to continue life the way they had always known it, maintaining cherished recipes and traditions from "the old country." But opportunists soon moved in, lured by the cheap cost of doing business and the high demand for product. In an attempt to produce liquor quickly and cheaply, many had resorted to all sorts of unsavory practices, including the use of ridiculous - and unsanitary - ingredients, such as bleach, rubbing alcohol, and paint thinner. Will had even heard of manure and urine being used in the distillation process. These shoddy practices led to toxic alcohol, unfortunately only identifiable by the damage it caused - usually blindness and sometimes death. News of several miner deaths due to bad booze near Watson, a town just an hour away, had just come across Will's desk last week. Finding home stills and dismantling them was now a priority.

"Ignore him. He's just mad because he thought he was a shoo-in for C.O."

Will looked up to find Thomas Rogers, another State Constable, leaning against a nearby tree.

"Vandercook had other plans - sent you in," Rogers continued. "So, you can't really blame him. Jesse's not a bad guy. He'll get over it."

"Why didn't the force promote from within?" Will asked the question that had been plaguing him for weeks.

Rogers laughed. "Because they know how little they pay us and how well the blind pigs and bootleggers pay to look the other way. They must figure if you can't be sure who's on your side, send in a ringer."

"Someone who hasn't been tainted."

Rogers nodded. "Yet."

Will cocked his head. "I don't think you know me well enough to judge my character with the word 'yet.'"

Thomas Rogers slapped Will on the shoulder. "I'm just messin' with ya, Sarge." He grew serious and nodded toward the men dismantling the still. "But I do know those men, and I guarantee you...not a single one of them is in cahoots with the wets."

Will hoped Rogers was right. He hoped none of the men serving under him were involved with bootleggers, but just in case, he decided to keep a close eye on Jesse Moore.

9

IRON FALLS/WELCOMING COMMITTEE

The sound of steel grinding against steel reverberated inside the railcar as the train finally came to a halt at the Iron Falls depot. The small, splintered platform was empty and nobody in the car moved. Apparently, Phoebe and her father would be the only passengers disembarking.

"Go on ahead, darlin'. I'll get our bags."

It was not a bright day, but the overcast sky seemed to fit the mood of the town. Gray – that was the color of this town. Worn wood siding covered the little train depot, but it was apparent by the few specks of paint still clinging to the crevices that the building had been white at some point in its history. That was more than she could say for the small buildings on either side.

"Mrs. Albright?"

Phoebe turned to find four women making their way toward her.

"Sorry our husbands weren't able to greet the train," said the smallest of the four women. She extended her hand. "But they haven't returned from the mine yet."

"That's quite alright. I'm just so grateful someone is here to show me the way." Phoebe took her hand. "I'm Phoebe Albright."

"We're so glad you're here, Mrs. Albright!" the woman continued. "Is your husband grabbing your bags?"

Phoebe was momentarily dumbfounded. Before she could recover, her father walked up.

"Good afternoon, ladies! I'm Reverend Albright."

The women looked a little confused.

"Oh, I see," said a second woman, older and a bit more severe looking than the rest. She gave the other women a knowing look.

Realization hit Phoebe. "No! Oh, no," Phoebe interrupted. "I mean, yes, this is Reverend Albright, but this is my father, not my husband."

Reverend Albright chuckled. "I've been mistaken for a lot of things, but never Phoebe's husband!"

The women laughed a little, apparently relieved that their new pastor wasn't a cradle robber, then turned their attention to Phoebe's father. "So, you are our new pastor?"

Rev. Albright scowled as his eyes darted quickly back and forth between all the women, including his daughter.

"I - I, that is, uh..."

Phoebe took a deep breath. "I'm afraid there has been some confusion. I am your new pastor, not my father."

The women looked at one another. It was several moments before the short woman spoke. "Ya aren't what we expected..." she began.

"That's certainly true!" said the second. "Not only have they sent us a woman, but an unmarried one at that? Well, I never!"

"What's more upsetting," Phoebe asked, "that you have been sent an unmarried pastor or that I am a woman? If I were an unmarried man, would you be as upset?"

The older woman's eyes narrowed. "Maybe things are different in that big city you came from, but up here in Iron Falls — "

"I have the same training and education as any man coming out of Bible College, of that I can assure you."

The short woman stepped between them. "I'm sure you are quite qualified. We've been praying that God would not only send us a new pastor, but that He'd send the right one." She turned and looked at the group. "He knows what He is doing, doesn't He?"

The youngest of the group nodded her head in agreement. The other two said nothing.

"Well, I'm not happy," said the second woman. "Pardon my bluntness, Miss Albright, but I am afraid that you have no idea what you have gotten yourself into. Iron Falls is no place for fancy city girls. We are a common bunch of people with no need of your genteel foolishness."

"Mrs. Smith!"

"I don't care! We are all thinking it. I'm just the only one not too polite to say it."

"I'm not thinking it," said the youngest woman. "I think we could use a bit more gentility around Iron Falls. Besides, I think a woman pastor is a grand idea."

"Of course, you would, Mary," Mrs. Smith said over her shoulder but keeping her eyes on Phoebe. "Our former pastor would visit my boarding house on a regular basis - trying to keep those young men on the proper spiritual track. Will you be able to do that, Miss Albright? Do you think a house full of young, single men will respect you at all? Let alone respect you as a preacher?"

"Probably not," Phoebe said.

All four of the women lifted eyebrows at her answer.

Phoebe squared her shoulders. "If I am unable to get the respect I deserve as pastor from the women of the greeting committee, then my hope of garnering respect from anyone in this town doesn't seem very likely."

Mrs. Smith gasped, and the others dropped their eyes.

"You ask me, Mrs. Smith, if I think I will be respected. And my answer is – probably not, at least not at first. But in my experience, respect is an honor that is earned, not passed out according to one's gender. God has called me to be the pastor of Iron Falls, and until He says otherwise, I will answer His call to the best of my ability. Now, if you don't mind, it has been a long couple of days, and I would like to get settled. If you would be so kind as to point me in the direction of the parsonage, I will go there now."

The youngest woman, who had been addressed as 'Mary,' was the first to answer.

"Welcome to Iron Falls, Pastor Albright." She hooked her arm in Phoebe's and led her away from the train.

Phoebe glanced back at her father, who was following along with their bags, smiling. She wondered what he'd thought of the confrontation she'd just had, but Mary's constant chatter about the town's landmarks gave her little time to ponder.

"And that's where you will find me," she said, pointing to a building with a sign that read Middleton Mining Company Store. "Pay no mind to the sign - the store is no longer company owned. When Middleton pulled out of town, my husband took it over. He hired me to help run the place but ended up with a wife instead!" Mary had an infectious laugh, and Phoebe couldn't help but smile along as the woman pointed out the various buildings and shops, attaching names to them that Phoebe feared she wouldn't be able to remember.

"Up that hill, you'll find the constabulary post as well as a few other businesses, - oh, and Mrs. Smith's boarding house. And that's the livery and the blacksmith is there beside it. McDaniels owns the livery if you are interested in riding. He has horses to loan. And over there is Dr. Langley's office, but he's the doctor for a few towns around here, so he isn't always there."

"Slow down, Mary. You're going to make her head spin," chastised the first woman.

The group came to a stop in front of a church. It was much larger than Phoebe had expected, with faded white clapboard siding and tall, arched windows flanking the sides.

"Well, here is your new home away from home," said the first woman.

Home. Yes. It has that feel, Phoebe thought.

"It's lovely," Phoebe said.

"Yes, well, back when the company was still here, they donated the land to build a church. Times were pretty good then, and there were lots of people to give and to help. It can seat nearly a hundred, which makes it bigger than most churches in towns the size of Iron Falls."

They walked only a few feet, then turned toward a tiny building, some sort of log-constructed outbuilding of the church - an office, perhaps, though only very large churches tended to have offices. Mary opened the door and they walked in.

"It isn't much," said the first woman, who appeared to be a spokeswoman for the group. "But we've made sure it was nice and clean for ya."

Phoebe looked around the room. There was a table with four unmatched chairs. In the corner, there was a small stove and another taller table pushed against the wall with shelves hanging above. In the opposite corner, she saw a double bed with a tiny table next to it. Then it hit her. This was the parsonage! This is where they intended for her to live! She hadn't expected anything grand, but this was little more than a shed with a stove to warm it.

Phoebe refused to let the women see her disappointment. "Well, this is lovely as well," she said, smiling brightly.

"I'm sure it's not what you are accustomed to, but —" Mrs. Smith grumbled.

Phoebe interrupted her. "It's more than adequate. And I appreciate you taking the time to clean for me. That is a blessing."

Mary smiled. "And we have loaded the cellar with canned goods and other staples. You shouldn't go hungry."

"I should say not! We were expecting a young married couple straight from Bible College. There's enough food on hand here for two people, at least!"

"I'm happy that there is an abundance of food," Mary said. "I won't worry, knowing she has something to put in her stomach every day."

"What a blessing," Phoebe said. "This is so much more than I expected. And Mrs. Smith, don't be fooled by my small frame. I'm a hearty eater. I may be out of provisions within the month."

Mary laughed at this, but Mrs. Smith continued to frown.

"Well, if you do, please let us know," said the spokeswoman. "We have already agreed to provide you with more canned items from this year's harvest, since it is too late for you to have a garden of your own."

"That is so kind of you, Mrs. — ?"

"Oh, dear me, we never introduced ourselves! How shameful. My name is Emma Speer. My husband Thomas and I and our six children live on our small farm on the outskirts of town. This is Mrs. Smith, the matron of the town's boarding house. And this is Mrs. Wiggins," she said, introducing the only woman who had not spoken. Mrs. Wiggins smiled shyly. "She lives two doors down from me. And I believe Mary has already introduced herself."

"Not properly," said Mary. "I'm Mary Simmons."

"Well," said Mrs. Speer, "We should be getting back to our families and let you settle in."

It wasn't until that moment that Phoebe saw her trunks sitting by the door.

"Oh, my things are here!"

"Yes," said Mary as the women began to leave. "One of Mrs. Smith's new boys helped one of our constables bring them in last night. He said he met you on the train?"

"Yes – Wendell. Very nice boy. How is he doing, Mrs. Smith?"

"Today was his first day in the mine. That's all I know," she said gruffly, walking out. Mrs. Wiggins followed.

Mary hugged Phoebe. "You must come for tea. It will be so nice to have someone to chat with." She winked and then followed the other women.

Mrs. Speer was the last to leave. "If you are so inclined, my family would like to have you and your father to our home this evening for dinner. I know you are tired, but you need to eat, right?"

Phoebe turned slowly and spotted her father leaning in the corner. He gave a slight nod.

Phoebe smiled. "That would be lovely, thank you Mrs. Speer."

"Alright, then. I'll have my oldest pick you up at six," she said, closing the door behind her.

"Well, you've been awfully quiet," Phoebe said, hands on her hips.

"Didn't have anything to say," her father laughed.

"You don't think I was wrong, the way I chastised Mrs. Smith at the train station?"

"You were nicer than I would have been," he answered. "And I'm proud of the way you reacted to your new home."

"Well, that was more stubbornness than joy, I'll tell you. I wasn't letting that Mrs. Smith see my disappointment. That's all she would have needed, and she would have been off to the station to buy my return ticket."

Phoebe looked around, shaking her head. *How can a town that builds such a nice church provide such a dismal parsonage?*

"Well, I think I'll take a walk around while you unpack and

see what this town offers in the way of overnight accommodations."

Phoebe looked at the one bed in the corner.

"Oh, Daddy! I'll sleep on the floor. You don't need to..."

"No, you will not. I'm sure I can find something. Maybe that
nice Mrs. Smith has a room for me," he said, winking.

WITHOUT HER FATHER - or the judgmental eyes of the welcoming
committee - present, Phoebe finally let her true feelings for her
new home settle into her soul. It was horrible. The cabin, the
furnishings, everything. How could Dr. Berger have ever
thought to call a woman into a pastorate like this?

Not only was the area small, it was so sparsely furnished that
she wondered how anyone had ever existed here, not at all what
his letter had promised.

*'You'll find a quaint cottage near the church that will be outfitted
with everything you'll need to begin your new life in the Upper Peninsula,'* he had written.

"Quaint, my foot," she muttered under her breath. A small
bed, an even smaller dresser, a table and chairs and a stove. How
was she supposed to begin a new life with so few items?

'The foxes have holes, and the birds of the air have nests...'

"But you had nowhere to lay your head, Lord." She raised her
eyes toward heaven. "Forgive me Father."

Feeling a bit better, she began unpacking her belongings into
the dresser. Thankfully, she had packed lightly; the few items
she'd brought barely fit into the bureau.

She was finished unpacking everything except her books.
With no bookshelf, she had no other choice but to leave them in
her trunk, as sad as that made her feel. She stepped back and
crossed her arms. Had Dr. Berger's letter been more honest, she
would have thought to pack additional items. Crocheted

runners or doilies, some lace curtains or tablecloths would have made a big difference in making the cabin feel like a home.

'We are a common bunch of people with no need of your genteel foolishness.'

Phoebe wasn't certain what was more annoying, hearing the real Mrs. Smith say those words, or the imaginary Mrs. Smith that seemed to be settling into her brain repeat them.

Phoebe frowned. Something was off about the dresser, besides its size and a few broken off drawer pulls.

'It's missing something,' she thought. But what was it...

"A mirror!" she blurted out to the empty room. How in the world would she be able to make herself presentable without a mirror?

'You have no idea what you have gotten yourself into,' Mrs. Smith's caustic words echoed in her mind. "No." Phoebe spoke the word aloud to silence the grouchy woman's voice in her head. Everything would be fine, Phoebe realized, but there was no way around it - she would have to spend some of the little money she'd brought along on some essentials.

Intending to start a list, she dug through the trunk containing her Bible study materials until she found a pencil and a piece of paper upon which she wrote the word *Mirror*. She started a list of items, beginning with a mirror.

She next turned to the kitchen, if it could be called that. Dr. Berger had said in his letter that the parsonage would be equipped with everything she needed, but the corner of the room that would serve as her kitchen contained no more than a pot belly stove and two shelves. Phoebe sat at the table and scribbled more items, then crossed her arms again and leaned back in the chair, her foot tap-tap-tapping under the table. Her list was long, but as she looked it over, there was no fat to cut. It only contained necessities. Still, Phoebe knew enough about the cost of living to know her list contained far more than she could afford.

"This is impossible."

'They that seek the Lord shall not want for any good thing.'

Her foot stopped tapping. God had called her. He was here. He would not forsake her.

She looked at the list again. Maybe there was a little fat she could cut, after all. She began scratching items off.

With her edited list in hand and her hat pinned back in place, Phoebe set off for Mary's store.

It wasn't a long walk - no distance between points of interest was in a town the size of Iron Falls. You could pretty much see everything the town had to offer in the short jaunt from the church to the store, and Phoebe decided she liked the quaintness of the little village. The store stood on the corner of Commonwealth - the same street as the church - and what appeared to be the only other street in town. Mary had already pointed out all the buildings on Commonwealth. The other street, which ran up a moderately steep hill to the north of town, seemed almost identical to the first, lined as it was with a mixture of businesses and small homes. The only difference Phoebe could see was a larger, newer looking one-story building at the end that she couldn't identify. She spotted her father in front of that building talking with another man. Even from this distance, the man's khaki uniform and campaign style hat immediately identified him as a Michigan State Trooper. Of course; this building must be the Constabulary.

Her father waved, then shook the officer's hand and headed her way.

"Going shopping?" he asked, nodding toward the piece of paper in her hand as he approached.

"Just perusing," she replied. "The parsonage has none of the necessities that Dr. Berger said that it would."

"Can I see your list?"

"Of course."

As he read the list, she looked over his shoulder at the

constable in the distance.

"Daddy?"

"Mhmm."

"Is that constable the one who delivered my trunks to the parsonage?"

"Why, yes. Yes, it is."

"Could you introduce me? I think it only proper that I thank him for his assistance."

"Oh, I'm sure you will have plenty of chances to thank him. He's a member of your congregation, you know."

Phoebe found it comforting that her church had a police officer as a member. "But couldn't you introduce me now? I would feel less awkward with you present."

"You're going to have to get over that awkwardness if you are to be the pastor here. Besides, we haven't the time now. We're going to have to hurry if we're gonna purchase your supplies and get you home before our dinner escort arrives."

Phoebe shook her head. "But I'm not ready to buy anything yet. I need to figure out what I can afford to spend, then decide what's most important..."

"Looks to me like everything on here is important."

"Well, yes, but I can't afford everything on the list. Some things will just have to wait."

"*You* can't afford 'em. Never said that I couldn't."

"Daddy, I know you and mother don't have much money. I can't expect you to — "

"Phoebe, listen. Your momma and I discussed this before I left. We have been saving up some money, and this is what we want to do with it."

"But Daddy..."

"No 'buts;" he said, ushering her toward the door. "Besides, without a few shiny, new copper pots, how will you keep up your 'fancy city girl' image. And we wouldn't want to disappoint Mrs. Smith, now would we?"

10

SETTLING IN

*a*s promised, Phoebe's father bought everything on the list. Everything, that is, except the mirror - after seeing the prices, she refused to let such an extravagance be purchased. It had been a hard-won battle, one that amused the mercantile owner Jack Simmons, Mary's husband. However, Phoebe eventually won out. And, though she hated to admit it, the nagging voice of Mrs. Smith chiding her about her 'fancy ways' and 'airs', helped Phoebe decide that a mirror was not a necessity.

At the time, it seemed like a wise choice. But, back at the parsonage, as she readied herself for dinner with the Speers, she began to doubt her decision. Phoebe had never been one to worry about fashion or beauty, but she certainly wanted to appear neat and tidy to her new congregants. Now, thanks to her own stubbornness, she had no mirror with which to check her appearance.

Still frustrated with her own shortsightedness, she carried the water she had used for washing to the back of her yard to dump it. As she turned back to the house, she noticed how the windows reflected the trees behind her yard and it gave her an idea.

She positioned the water bucket upside down on the ground under one of the windows, but it wasn't quite tall enough. She looked around her overgrown garden and discovered an old, dented washtub. She replaced the bucket with the upside-down washtub, then placed the bucket on top of that. If she stepped on this makeshift platform on her tiptoes, she could see the top half of her head reflected in the window. From this view, she was able to repin some loose hair back into her bun and smooth out her chignon until she was confident that she appeared neat but not overly fussy. Satisfied, she climbed down from her makeshift platform.

"Fancy city girl, indeed!" she said as she swung the bucket over the water pump's handle. "The only foolishness in me is letting that woman get under my skin."

She walked next door to the church. She opened the door and looked at her new sanctuary for the first time. It was plain – no, that wasn't quite right. Simple was a better word - pretty in its own way.

Mrs. Speer had said that the small church would seat a hundred. The pews appeared handcrafted - most likely by a local, Phoebe mused - from a beautiful white pine, as were the pulpit and cross that hung on the wall behind it. The walls were simply painted white, and the ceiling was just the exposed timber stained to match the pews.

Tall, thin windows flanked both sides of the sanctuary letting in beautiful, natural light. There was a quiet reverence about the place, the likes of which Phoebe had never experienced in the many churches she had visited while in college. Then again, none of those had meant to be hers.

She walked down the aisle and climbed the stairs to the platform. The pulpit was simple also, but well crafted, with a beautifully carved cross adorning the front of it. She stood behind it and looked out where her congregation would be sitting in just a few short days.

"It suits you," her father said from the back pew.

So engrossed in her own musings, she hadn't noticed her father. She descended the platform and slid into the pew next to him. "It could use a good dusting, but other than that, I think it's a pretty little church." She sat next to her father.

He didn't respond. She turned to see if he had heard her and saw tears on his weathered cheeks.

Phoebe grasped his hand. "Daddy, don't worry about me. I know it's a little church and a little town, but God is here."

"I know that, darlin'. I'm just overwhelmed by the blessings God is bestowin' on ya. When I first read that letter all those weeks ago, I thought you'd be comin' to a desolate place with a shack of a building for a church. But God has sent you to a real church building in a town full of people hungry to hear God's word. People who've been praying for a pastor. I thought you were going to have to build the congregation from the ground up, but you are beginning with at least five, maybe six, families. That's more than most new pastors have. Don't get me wrong, this is going to be hard work, but I won't worry so much knowing what I know now."

Relief washed over her. "Well, all I'm worried about now is missing our ride to dinner. We'd better get back to the parsonage before the Speer boy comes looking for us."

As they left the church, a state trooper rode by, tipping his hat as he passed them.

"Is that him?" she asked after he passed.

Her father looked up. "Hmmm? Oh, nope. Not met that one yet."

"How many constables does this little town have?"

"Well, let's see. I've counted four so far, counting that one there."

"Well, then, how will I know which one to thank?"

"My heavens, Phoebe. You have a way of finding things to worry about." He placed his arm around her shoulders. "Don't you worry. I'll talk with him tonight and let him know you are anxious to meet him."

She could feel her cheeks grow warm. "No, don't say that!"

Her father laughed heartily and, realizing that he was teasing her, she elbowed him in the ribs. "I should have known. Why would you see him tonight, anyway?"

"Did I forget to mention that's where I'm staying tonight? Made arrangements with that officer you saw me speakin' with. Said I'm welcome to one of their extra bunks as long as I'm here."

"A bunk at the constabulary? That will be so uncomfortable for you!"

"It's better than spending the night in one of their jail cells, I suppose," he chuckled. "Don't you worry none. It'll be like I'm back in the military. Besides, it'll give me a chance to scope out all those young foxes that'll be crowdin' into that church once they realize the new pastor's a beauty. I gotta put the fear of God in 'em while I'm still here, don't I?"

Phoebe groaned, knowing that although he was teasing her, her father wasn't entirely joking.

DINNER with the Speer family was just what Phoebe needed to end the whirlwind that was her first day in Iron Falls. Not only did Mrs. Speer prepare one of Phoebe's favorite meals, chicken and dumplings, but she also served one of her favorite desserts.

"Wait until you try Mama's peach cobbler!" little Helen said excitedly.

Phoebe chuckled. Of all six Speer children, the two youngest – Helen and Margaret – were the most outgoing. The two little girls talked almost incessantly; if it wasn't Helen telling Phoebe all about her mother's cooking or the chores around the house, it was Margaret telling her the names of all of the chickens, promising to introduce Phoebe to them later. In fact, they didn't leave much room for the four boys to speak, but they didn't seem to mind. Jacob, the oldest, involved himself in the conversation between Mr. Speer and Reverend Albright. The other three boys ate hungrily, listening to all the conversations at the table and spoke when spoken to.

Phoebe had so much fun listening to the girls' chatter that she heard little of the conversation between the adults. She did hear Mr. Speer explain to her father that most of the houses in town were built like theirs – a saltbox house – because the mining company that owned the town was from Boston where saltbox houses were popular. That's also why the streets had New England names...Commonwealth, Marlborough, Beacon. She also heard about the company pulling out of Iron Falls.

"Yep, lots of the men cleared out and left when Middleton pulled out, but a lot of us wanted to stay – or had nowhere else to go. This was home. So, we pooled our resources and reopened the mine."

"Really?" her father asked. "I've never heard of such a thing."

"Yep, happening all over the place. We first heard of it in Copper County, up near the Keweenaw peninsula. It was a struggle at first, getting it all organized, but running the mine ourselves has become right profitable for us. We've been able to bring some new boys in to work, like that boy you met on the train."

"Wendell? How did he do his first day?"

"Pretty good, I suppose. He's young, but he seems to have a good work ethic. I think he'll do just fine, and we'll treat him far better than we were treated when we first came to Iron Falls."

Mrs. Speer served the peach cobbler while Mr. Speer told the story of how the couple had come to live in Iron Falls. They were both children when their parents moved their families to the Upper Peninsula.

"Back then, company housing was nothing more than tents set up on the outskirts of town."

Phoebe shivered, imagining enduring even a single chilly Upper Peninsula evening in a tent.

"But as the mines began profiting, the company-owned houses started going up." The corner of Mr. Speer's lip twitched. "They got tired of losing good workers during the winter months. Can't expect a man, much less a wife if he has one, to stay around without four walls and a roof to call his own. That's when my father was promoted to Captain and was given the option of a company house or property. He chose the property and built this house right here."

"And these company houses, what happened to them when the company left?"

"Abandoned," Mr. Speer answered. "Anyone living in 'em got to keep 'em. That's why so many chose to stay and work the mine with us. The homes of those that left, well most of them still sit empty, but we're hoping as time goes on, we'll be able to bring more families in to live in 'em."

Phoebe partially listened to the girls' chatter and partially listened to the adults' discussion of how Iron Falls had changed in the past several years. They talked of the addition of the State Constabulary Post and Jack Simmons taking over the store. When the conversation turned to the previous pastor, however, Phoebe turned her complete attention to the adults.

"His salary came from the company, so when Middleton left, he started packing. We tried to convince him to stay, but the promise of living off tithes and offerings wasn't as appealing as heading south to a larger city church where a salary might be offered. We've been petitioning the district for a new pastor for a couple years now, but I think most folks thought Iron Falls would become a ghost town like Fayette and some of the other mining towns."

"Dr. Berger told us that he is having difficulty filling lots of churches here in the Upper Peninsula. Most new pastors find the idea of moving here too unpleasant."

"It can be rough, to be sure, but we band together in this little town. You can rest assured, Reverend, that this little congregation will keep an eye out for your daughter."

"Oh, I have no worries there. I believe God is already putting people into place to watch over her."

There was a lull in conversation and Phoebe took the opportunity to speak.

"I'm very sorry that your last pastor left you like that, with no replacement. I can't imagine a person called to ministry could treat his congregation so callously."

"Good riddance, I say," Mrs. Speer broke in. "That man was as crooked as a broken stick."

"Now, Emma," Mr. Speer scolded.

"If he wasn't a crook, then you tell me what happened to the bake sale money? It's no coincidence that it went missing when he did."

"Well, regardless," Mr. Speer began, "we have been given a fresh start with a fresh pastor. Something tells me things are about to turn around for our little church."

THE NIGHT HAD GROWN QUITE crisp by the time Jacob Speer dropped her off at her new home, much cooler than the July evenings she had been experiencing back home in Lansing. Even her father, who never complained about the temperature, rubbed his hands up and down his arms as the buckboard rambled down the street on its way to the constabulary.

Although the sun was just beginning to set outside, inside the log-built parsonage it was quite dark. It wasn't until the moment she stepped through the door that Phoebe realized another household item the house did not possess...a lamp.

Moving as quickly as she could in the waning daylight, she made her way next door to the church where she was certain she had seen a few lamps scattered along the back wall.

The church, having far more light filtering in from its tall windows, was far easier to navigate in the semi-darkness and it only took a moment to find a lamp with some oil and a near empty box of matches on a cluttered shelf of the pulpit. She lit the lamp and said a prayer of thankfulness for not having to spend the evening in darkness.

When she finally stepped out into the night air again, the sun had set, and the town had grown quite dark. There were no streetlights like Lansing, and since the street, which she learned from the Speers was named Commonwealth, was mostly busi-nesses that were now closed, there was no light save for the lamp she carried and the nearly full moon that was beginning to make its presence known. It was an eerie feeling, being a part of such darkness, and the feeling made her hasten her steps home.

Passing between the church yard and the beginning of the parsonage property, she heard a strange sound - the yipping of animals, not unlike the sound of puppies, echoed in the distance. But, as she took another step, she heard movement in the grass near the fence of her backyard.

It wasn't a loud sound, and at first, she tried to convince herself that it was just the wind rustling the overgrown weeds, but when the sound grew closer and the swishing of the grass grew faster, she knew that something was there, and it was making its way toward her.

Clutching the lamp tightly in one hand and her skirt in the other, Phoebe raced to the front door of the cabin.

She threw open the parsonage door and fell against it on the other side. As she did, she heard the eerie, high-pitched howl of an animal she could not identify.

Her heart continued to pound heavily in her chest, sending thumps of pain into her temples as she tried to calm her breathing. In that moment, reality hit - she was hundreds of miles from home, in a town full of strangers, surrounded by wildlife she couldn't identify... and she was alone. There was no stopping the tears, and Phoebe didn't have it in her to try any longer.

She cried for several minutes, head on the table, feeling sorry for herself, wondering how she could have made a life-changing decision like this without realizing how hard it was going to be.

She could change her mind, couldn't she? Her father was still here. There was no reason why she couldn't just return to Lansing with him.

Her family would be so happy to see her come home.

And so would Stella Bowen, Phoebe thought disdainfully. And what about Mrs. Smith? She would gloat at Phoebe's departure as well.

'Is that the only reason I'm here? To prove naysayers wrong?' Phoebe wondered. She knew that it was not.

"No," she said, pounding a fist on the table. She knew that God had called her here, called her to pastor Iron Falls. Yet, merely surviving Iron Falls was proving to be a challenge in itself. She looked at her tiny fist. It looked so small, so weak, so incapable. She opened it and clasped it with her other hand, interlocking her fingers.

'Lord,' she began praying. 'I am weak. Please help me find strength in You.'

Deciding the best thing to do was to try and get some rest, she prepared for bed. She turned down the wick of the lamp and crawled into bed.

A silver streak of moonlight peeked through the flour sack curtains that covered her front windows. Phoebe climbed out of bed and pulled a curtain back, praying that whatever she had encountered earlier would not now be prowling around her front porch. There was no wildlife there. There was nothing moving outside her home except for a man on horseback riding slowly down the street.

The pale moonlight sliced through the darkness, outlining the man's uniform and campaign hat - a Michigan State Trooper on his night rounds. She felt herself begin to relax as she let the flour sack fall back into place. She was alone, but she wasn't unprotected. God was providing.

She crawled back into bed and prayed for God's guidance, for the Speer family and for the rest of her little congregation. She prayed for God's assistance in accomplishing all that needed to be done before Sunday. Finally, as she hovered somewhere between the land of awake and the dreaming, she thanked God for the constables who kept Iron Falls safe, and she whispered a prayer for Will Caffey, wherever he was.

11

GOLDEN BOY

"*Y*ou know, you don't get paid extra when you work a double shift," Jesse Moore said.

Will hung his hat on the hook and unbuckled his holster. "It isn't always about the money," Will said in return, once again reminded of his concerns about Jesse. "Sometimes it's about doing what's right."

Jesse stared at Will for a long time. He finally nodded. "Yep, once you figure out what's actually right."

"Is that something you have difficulty doing?"

Jesse shook his head. "Nope. Just saying that what's right for you might not be what's right for me. We each gotta find our own version of right."

Thomas Rogers didn't look up from the gun he was meticulously cleaning in the corner of the office. "In my experience, most of life falls somewhere in the gray area."

"Yep, I guess I agree with that." Jesse turned back to Will. "What about you, Caffey? I bet you see the world as black and white. For you, it's good versus evil, huh?"

"Isn't that how it's been since the beginning of time?" Will asked. "Since the fall from Eden, haven't we all been living in a world of good versus evil?"

Jesse pushed away from the desk and stood. "Hmph! And I bet you think you're always on the good side." He scowled and shook his head. "I'm going out for a ride. You ain't the only one who can catch the bad guys."

Will thought momentarily about following him outside and adjusting the attitude problem he'd had since Will's first day on the job. Will had hoped that once the man had gotten to know him, he would have settled down.

"Don't mind him," Thomas said as if reading Will's mind. "It's just his bruised ego showin' through. He'll get over it and get used to the fact that the force's Golden Boy is running the show, not him."

It wasn't the first time Will had been called "Golden Boy," and he wasn't sure what to make of it. Sometimes, like now, the moniker seemed used with admiration, as if Will's reputation was something to be idolized. Other times, usually when Jesse Moore was speaking, it was said with such an air of contempt that Will felt the need to knock someone's block off.

"Rogers, doesn't it seem strange to you that we can't get a lead on who burned down the Lambecker place? Doesn't it feel like every lead we get is a wild goose chase? Like things have been cleaned up before we even get there."

Rogers pursed his lips as if contemplating the question. "I hadn't really noticed."

"You don't think there's someone inside that's leaking information, do you?"

Rogers lifted his eyebrows and laughed. "You're thinking Moore, eh? No way. He might be a little moody, but he's not the type. He's neither smart enough nor industrious enough to make the kind of connections you're talking about."

Will wasn't convinced. Something wasn't right and his gut was telling him the problem was coming from within his ranks.

Rogers put his gun away and continued. "I'm sure you've figured out by now that this work is hard. It's hard and it pays very little. Before long, every man realizes that there's more money to be had lining their pocket with bribes from the likes of Lambecker, among others. But most men decide real quick that they aren't in this for the money - they're here for a higher calling."

"You said most men."

Thomas Rogers nodded slowly. "Yes, most. Unfortunately, it's your job to figure out the rest. But I would lay my money on Jesse Moore. He's stubborn and hard to get along with at times, but he's no Benedict Arnold. You need to look elsewhere for your mole."

Will didn't like the idea that one of his own could be working against him, but he knew it could be true. Even Jesus had a betrayer. Will just hoped he could identify his Judas before it was too late.

IT IS WELL

*a*s they scrubbed the floors and wiped down the pews of her new church, Reverend Albright regaled Phoebe with stories of his evening at the constabulary.

"We talked for hours," he said, tinkering with the insides of the church's piano.

"Hours? What could you possibly talk about with complete strangers for that long?"

"Oh, you know me. I can talk with anyone. Besides, they're all war heroes. Every single one of 'em," he said. "This town's lucky to have such fine young men protecting it. What'd you do with your evening?"

Phoebe knelt next to the bucket of soapy water and told her father all about her experiences from the night before.

"Sounds like coyotes," her father mused. "They mostly hunt small animals and will likely stay clear of humans, so I wouldn't worry too much about 'em. Still, I'd stay within my fence when it's real late."

Phoebe agreed. She had a hard enough time taming the angry herd of women she encountered at the train station yesterday. She didn't think she'd be any more successful with actual wild animals.

"And, like I said, there are plenty of fine men here protecting this town. Plus, many of them are single," he added with a wink.

"What's that?" she shouted over the increased speed of the brush she was scraping across the old floorboards. "I can't hear you."

"Don't worry, darlin'. I let them know there's already someone out to win your heart."

She threw down the brush and popped her head above the pew. "Daddy! You didn't!"

"I did! Would you rather have a town full of single officers vying for your attentions?"

"Of course not, but to insinuate that Will was my beau —"

"Now, what makes you think I was talking about Will?"

She scowled at her father even as she felt heat leap into her cheeks, but her attempt at a scolding did nothing but extract a howl of laughter from the elder preacher.

"C'mon, girl, and get over here and try this thing out. I think I got all the strings righted."

Glad for the change in subject, she took a seat on the bench. "It looks like it's never been played."

"That's what worries me. Nothing worse on a piano than neglect."

Phoebe opened the fallboard and found that the keys in fact did look untouched. Was there no one in Iron Falls who played? Would she be expected to play? How would that work, her at the piano for the hymns, then scrambling to the pulpit for the sermon? Why, it'd look more like a variety show than a worship service!

Phoebe played from memory one of her favorites – *It is Well with My Soul*. As she played, her father listened intently.

"It isn't too bad, but still a little off. Play middle C."

Phoebe complied, and her father adjusted something else behind the upright.

"I never knew you could tune a piano."

"Well, as a pastor you have to learn to do all kinds of things. But you'll learn soon enough that they don't teach you everything you need to know in Bible College. Play the whole scale."

He continued working until he was satisfied each note was on key. When he finished, he had her play again and Phoebe was amazed at the difference.

"I know it was close before, but now it's perfect!" she said excitedly. She began the song again, her excitement coursing through the music as she added additional runs and fills. She became completely lost, as if the music were coming from somewhere deep within her. It was, indeed, well with her soul, whatever her lot - even if that lot was a small, poorly furnished cabin in the upper peninsula, playing piano and preaching to a tiny congregation of dubious miners' wives - her soul was God's, and God's alone.

It wasn't until she was finished that she noticed Mrs. Speer standing next to the piano.

"Oh my!" she said, shocked. "I didn't see you come in. How long have you been standing there?"

"Long enough to realize that we have a very talented pastor!" she said warmly. She handed a basket to Reverend Albright. "When Tom came home, he said the doors to the church were open and it looked like you two were hard at work. I brought you some fried chicken, baked beans, and corn bread. It isn't much, but it will fill your stomachs." She looked around the sanctuary. "I wish I would have known you were doing this today. My boys are good workers. I would have sent them over."

"Well, I'm leaving in the mornin'," Reverend Albright said. "Maybe they could help on the outside of the church? It could use some work before Sunday."

"Of course. I'll send 'em over tomorrow and you tell 'em what to do, alright Pastor Albright?"

Phoebe was thrilled. "Tomorrow will be fine, as long as it isn't an inconvenience to you?"

"It won't be. Alright, I'll leave you to your evening," Mrs. Speer said. She shook hands with Reverend Albright, then turned back to Phoebe. "Pastor, would you ever consider giving lessons to my little ones? I don't have much money, but I could pay you in eggs and milk and whatever we have around the farm that week."

Phoebe agreed happily. Whether it was the thought of fresh eggs and milk every week or the lingering scent of the fried chicken in the basket she held that made the thought of teaching those sweet children so enticing she wasn't certain, but the growl of her stomach told her she wouldn't regret it.

"Well," her father began after Mrs. Speer left. He wiped his hands on his handkerchief and chuckled. "Did you notice she called you pastor?"

Phoebe smiled. "I did. What a difference a day can make."

He nodded and wrapped his arm around her shoulder. "His mercies are new every morning." He stuffed his handkerchief back in his trouser pocket. "But I won't reach morning if I starve to death, so let's eat!"

13

CONSTABLES

*P*hoebe awoke early, just like the previous morning. She looked at her watch and realized that if she hurried, she could still catch her father at the train station. Rev. Albright, not being a fan of parting from loved ones, had insisted they say their goodbyes last night, but Phoebe was already missing her father and could not pass up the opportunity to see him one last time before he left.

Normally she would never think of leaving without pinning her hair, or at least braiding it, but not wanting to miss the train, she quickly dressed and dashed out the door. *Besides, who would be out at this hour?* she reasoned. She walked briskly up the street toward the train station, straining for sight of him in the distance. To her relief, the train was still there. She just hoped he hadn't boarded yet.

As she drew closer, she could see three State Troopers on the platform surrounding a man in a dark suit... her father.

Reverend Albright shook two of the troopers' hands, then clasped the third in a hearty embrace, and the sight of this brought her to tears. That was her father. He loved quickly and he loved whole-heartedly.

With each step she took, her pace quickened, and her vision became more and more blurred.

"Phoebe!" Reverend Albright exclaimed as she threw herself into his arms, nearly knocking the officer out of her way. She sobbed uncontrollably, not caring who saw her or what they thought.

"I know you told me not to come, but I had to, Daddy."

"Darlin', don't cry. We'll see each other soon. There'll be holidays, and you know your mother. There's no way I'll be able to keep her from you for long. I'm sure she's already planning a visit. Though, not sure she'd appreciate the free accommodations at the constabulary as much as I did."

Phoebe chuckled through her tears. "No, I can't imagine she would."

"I am so proud of you, child. And don't you worry. God has a plan, and he's already working it out. Of that, I am sure." He kissed Phoebe's forehead one last time, then boarded his train.

The last whistle blew, and the train chugged its way out of Iron Falls, taking part of Phoebe's heart with it.

When she could no longer see her father waving from his window, she took a deep breath and turned to face the officers that had been witness to her embarrassing display of emotion. But when she turned, mercifully, they had gone.

PHOEBE STOOD and stretched her back. She had spent the past few hours working on her sermon for Sunday, but it was already ten o'clock. She couldn't wait any longer for the Speer boys - she needed to get the church grounds ready to receive congregants.

When she stepped out onto her front porch, she was greeted by not only the bright, morning sun, but also the sight of a well underway clean-up production.

She circled the church and found plenty of evidence of the boys' hard work - much of the grounds around the church already cleared of brush and debris - but no sign of the boys themselves. Finally, on the far side of the building, under the shade of a silver maple, she found the three eldest Speer boys resting, melted chocolate covering their hands and faces.

"Hello, boys. How long have you been here?"

"About three hours," said Jacob, the oldest and, apparently, the spokesman.

"Three hours! I'm so sorry. I would've come out had I known you were here."

"Nothin' to be sorry 'bout, ma'am. We didn't expect to see you at all. Ma told us we weren't allowed to bother you. She also said that we weren't to let ya help us, either. Said you had preachin' to prepare for."

She knelt in the shade next to them. "What's that you're eating?"

"It's called Goldenberg's Peanut Chews. The constable gave it to us."

"Constable?"

"Yep, he rode by and asked what we were doin'. When we told him, he said to wait here. Came back with these." Jacob held up the chocolate bar. "Said you can't buy 'em in stores. They was a treat for soldiers in the Great War. He only has a few left, but he said what we was doing was so nice, he wanted to share somethin' special with us."

"Would ya like a bite of mine, Miss Albright?" Jonathan Speer asked.

"Pastor Albright, you numb-skull!" Jacob chastised his younger brother.

"Miss Albright is just fine," Phoebe said.

"It's just fine if he wants a smack from Ma."

Phoebe smiled but tried to disguise her surprise at the turnabout in Mrs. Speer. "That was very kind of that constable. Did he say what his name was?" she asked.

All three boys shrugged.

"Officer somethin'," Jacob said. "Can't remember. Sorry. But he did say he would see us in church. That part I remember."

"And he took that old bookshelf with him," Peter said without looking up from his chocolate.

"Bookshelf?" she asked. "That nasty, old one my father threw out back? I was planning to burn that with the brush."

Peter shrugged. "He said he could fix it up."

Jonathan turned his candy bar around. "I haven't eaten off this end, Pastor. Come on, you gotta try this."

Unable to turn down the sweet boy's request, Phoebe sampled the candy. It was delicious and she said as much. Jonathan seemed very pleased.

"The constable told us he shouldn't have given us any. He said we was gonna fall so in love with it that we were never gonna want to fall in love with any girl, because no girl could compare with a Goldenberg Peanut Chew."

Phoebe suppressed a chuckle. "Is that so?"

"Yeah, but we told 'im that was fine by us, because there ain't no girl out there we wanna fall in love with anyhow."

Phoebe laughed out loud at this. The boys laughed too. They apparently thought the idea of love was ridiculous.

"Pastor Albright?" The youngest of the three asked shyly. "You been sick?"

"No, Peter. I haven't. Why would you ask?"

"Because the constable asked how you were doin'. When we told him we hadn't seen ya, he kept looking at your cabin like he was all worried or somethin'."

Phoebe flushed, remembering the scene she had caused earlier that morning. "Was he here long?" She rubbed her neck to disguise the growing blush she felt creeping up it.

"He sat and had a peanut chew with us and talked a little, but he seemed to be in a hurry to get outta here. Prob'ly had some important investigatin' or arrestin' to do."

"That's probably true," Phoebe agreed. "Well," she said, standing up, "I should see what I have to fix for you young men to eat."

"We can't stay," Jacob said. "Ma told us we had to be home for lunch. We'll come back after to finish. We'll probably bring Stephen, and maybe the girls. Ma thought there wouldn't be much for them to do, but they could pull weeds and stuff. They're big enough for that."

True to their word, the boys returned with the three littlest Speers in tow. This time, however, Phoebe was waiting for them. When the boys protested, she said to let her deal with their mother. They didn't argue, but their eyes showed they were not sure who would come out the victor in that confrontation.

As they busied themselves, Phoebe was impressed by the work ethic of the children. The bigger boys tackled the heavier work of raking and chopping down thick brush, while the little ones, Stephen included, worked at pulling the weeds around the base of the building.

The little ones worked so fast even Phoebe was having trouble keeping up. But the fast-paced labor did nothing to slow down the conversation. Helen and Margaret let not a moment pass without filling it with words.

While some may have found the constant chatter annoying, Phoebe enjoyed it immensely. Growing up with two sisters meant growing up in a house full of chatter and the Speer children filled an emptiness Phoebe hadn't realized her heart possessed before that moment.

Phoebe enjoyed the morning filled with not only the quirky banter of the Speer children, but she also enjoyed the weed pulling. Who would have guessed a day of labor would have turned into such a treasure hunt.

"What's that?" Helen asked, pointing out a delicate, purple bloom.

"Columbine," Phoebe said. "And that other purple flower is a coneflower."

"Did you know you could eat those?" Margaret asked. "Momma uses them to make tea when we're sick."

"I did know that," Phoebe said.

"You sure know a lot about flowers," Stephen pointed out.

"My mother has one of the most beautiful gardens in all of Lansing," Phoebe said. "She loves being able to bless others, especially those who are ill, with bouquets of fresh cut flowers. She says flowers are the best cure for any ailment."

Peter came around to the back of the church, carrying another load to add to the burn pile. "The constable was here again. He said when we finish to go get an iced cream at the store and he'll pay for it!"

"He's here?" Phoebe asked, standing and hurrying around to the front of the church.

"He was. Rode off already, though," he called after her.

The children finished their work and waited for Phoebe's approval. She ceremoniously walked around the building, tapping her finger on her chin in a serious manner. They followed, watching and waiting for a response. When they reached the front of the building again, Phoebe clasped her hands behind her back and lifted her eyebrows.

"Well," she began without smiling, "it appears to me that we have a church ready for Sunday Service." She smiled at the children. "Who's ready for a trip to Simmons' Store?"

The six children cheered in agreement.

Obviously having been warned of the children's impending visit, Mary called to them as they entered the store. "How are the church workers doing today?"

As the children perused the selection of candies and sweets, Phoebe spoke with Mary.

"Peter said that one of the constables offered to pay for their treat today. Do you know his name?"

"I didn't get his name, but I'm sure Jack knows, because he's the same handsome officer who borrowed our wagon to deliver your trunks." Mary winked, then continued. "Unfortunately, Jack went to Marquette for supplies. I can ask when he returns."

"That's not necessary," Phoebe said, feeling the heat rising in her cheeks.

After the ice cream, Phoebe walked the children home. Mrs. Speer invited her to stay for dinner and she accepted heartily. She really wasn't that hungry, but she looked forward to spending some time with Mrs. Speer.

"It's a blessing to have that piano tuned," the kind older woman said, "but after hearing you play, I worry you'll be disappointed with our simple worship. Mrs. Daniels, although not as talented as you, is a fairly decent pianist herself. And I have led the singing in the past. But it is your right to change anything you want, so if you would rather…"

"Oh, no," Phoebe interrupted. "I am so pleased to hear that there is someone to play and someone to lead. I wasn't sure what I was going to do on Sunday. I am so grateful, truly!"

Phoebe left the Speer farm that evening floating on air. She hadn't realized how worried she had been about the music until God provided for that need and the weight was lifted from her. Now, if He would just provide a finishing paragraph for her sermon.

14

SAFE IN THE ARMS

The Sunday morning sunrise cast bright streaks across the town of Iron Falls, beckoning the inhabitants to rise and meet it, like little orange fingers reaching through the gaps in their curtains. But one member of the tiny town had been awake for hours and was ready to face her first Sunday as pastor.

Phoebe thought she had conquered her public speaking jitters - she had preached many times in her Bible College classes in front of her professors and her peers - but her stomach was so knotted that she hadn't been able to choke down any breakfast. So, at the first sign of light, and when she hoped all coyotes had retired for the day, she left the parsonage and made her way to the church.

She wasn't sure how long she knelt at the altar, but when she finally lifted her head from prayer, the room was no longer dimly lit but fully illuminated by the full sun gleaming through the tall windows. She rose and turned to find a couple standing at the back of the church.

"Good morning!" She approached them with her hand held out. "I'm Pastor Albright."

"Of course, you are," answered the man. "You have your father's eyes."

Phoebe stopped mid-stride.

"Oh, Frank – you've shocked the poor girl."

"My apologies, dear. We should have introduced ourselves. Of course, you wouldn't recognize us – it's been so long, and you were quite little. I'm Frank Berger, and this is my wife Helen."

"Dr. Berger!" Phoebe exclaimed, relieved. "I didn't know you were coming."

"Well, you have to be commissioned into your new assignment, do you not?"

Phoebe hadn't thought about that and had little time to do so now, because even as she greeted him, members of the congregation began arriving for service.

"You'll have to excuse me," she said to Rev. Berger. Taking a position at the door, Phoebe began shaking hands to greet the people as she had seen her father do every Sunday of her life.

When Mrs. Speer finally came to tell her it was time to begin, she was completely unprepared mentally. She had been so busy greeting that she hadn't paid attention to the time, nor had she noticed exactly how many people had actually filed through the doors.

It wasn't until she was seated on the platform that she realized just how crowded the church actually was. It was packed full, with many men standing in the back and around the sides. She took a deep breath and willed her stomach to stop flipping.

The first hymn *Safe in the Arms of Jesus* began, and Phoebe forced herself to take another deep breath. Mrs. Speer had a beautiful voice and Phoebe found listening to her quite calming. She closed her eyes. Why was she so nervous? Had not God promised "He which hath begun a good work in you will perform it until the day of Jesus Christ?"

'Be confident. Be confident,' she thought, clinging to the

promise in Philippians 1:6. Not because she had anything to boast about, of course, but because God had begun this work, and he was going to see it through.

The doors opened and Phoebe's attention was drawn to the back of the sanctuary. A Michigan State Trooper entered, removed his hat, and found a spot to stand in the back of the room in front of one of the windows. The morning sun that poured in behind him made it difficult to make out any discernible features, but the uniform was unmistakable.

The rest of the service was a dreamlike blur. Rev. Berger stood up first and gave a very flattering introduction for Phoebe, much of which was based on her father's bragging and very little on Rev. Berger's actual knowledge of her. She just hoped that the congregation did not expect her to have super-human abilities as his introduction might have led them to believe. He then prayed over Phoebe before descending the platform, leaving Phoebe alone to look at her congregation.

Somehow, by the grace of God, she made it through her sermon. And it must have been agreeable to most because she made eye contact with many smiling faces. There were also some unhappy faces among the crowd, but she chose not to allow her gaze to linger on those for long - there would be time in later sermons to accept the challenge of coaxing a smile from a challenging personality. Before she knew it, Phoebe was praying the closing prayer and Mrs. Speer began the benediction song.

Phoebe stepped off the platform just as the constable slipped out the door. Not wanting to delay her expression of gratitude any longer, she quickly followed him out.

"Constable?" she called after him.

The officer turned back to the stairs leading to the church.

"Yes ma'am?" He took off his khaki campaign hat, revealing a well-trimmed head of sand-colored hair.

"I'm so glad to have finally met you. I've been trying to track you down for the past week." Phoebe smiled.

"Ma'am? You were trying to find me?"

"Well, yes, to thank you. You are the State Trooper who brought my trunks to the parsonage, aren't you?"

The officer climbed closer to her on the stairs and Phoebe couldn't help but notice how handsome he was. He rather reminded her of her brother-in-law John, not only because of his hair color, but he also shared the same blue-grey eyes.

"No, I'm sorry. That wasn't me. But I sure wish that I had been the one to have earned your appreciation," he said, the corners of his eyes crinkling as he smiled.

Phoebe frowned. "Oh, I was told that a State Trooper from my congregation had assisted in their transport."

"Well, this is my first time in this church, so I don't think I would be considered a member. I met your father and was impressed by him, so I decided to visit your church today."

"Oh, I see. Well, I hope I didn't disappoint you. My father has very impressive shoes to fill."

"Not at all. I enjoyed it very much."

"Then I hope to see you next Sunday as well, Officer..."

"It's James, ma'am. Lance James, and I wish that were possible, but I leave tomorrow for a new post. I was only here for the past few weeks training with some other new men."

"I see. Well, I hope you enjoy your new post, Officer James."

"So do I, but I doubt the view will be as beautiful," he said, smiling roguishly.

Phoebe pretended not to understand his meaning and wished him a good day. The officer was nearly back to his horse when Phoebe stopped him.

"Officer James, were you the officer who brought chocolate to the children working at the church this week?"

He turned and acted as if thinking about it.

"If I say yes, will it earn another smile from you?"

"Only if it's the truth."

"Then, alas, I must depart without a smile because that also was another officer. Would you like me to investigate and find the correct man?"

"No, no. That isn't necessary," she said. "But thank you for the offer."

He tipped his hat and rode away. Phoebe was pleased that this officer was being transferred. She would have difficulty concentrating on her sermons if that State Trooper were present every Sunday.

She could hear the final song ending and the door opened for the first of her congregation to exit. She shook hands and thanked everyone for coming – or at least she attempted to thank everyone. There were quite a few in attendance that passed by without so much as making eye contact, including Mrs. Smith.

But among the naysayers were also many smiling faces. Some were faces that she already knew: Mary and Jack Simmons, Wendell, and the Speer family, especially the children, were all a welcome sight.

"I had no idea the congregation was so large," she whispered to Mary as she passed.

"I don't believe it is," she whispered back. "I think many of them just came for the show."

"The show?"

"Yes, to watch you fail. That didn't happen, so I'm not certain most of them will return next week."

People actually came to church with the expectation that I would fail? Phoebe realized she was going to have to work hard to win over the little town of Iron Falls.

WITH A NEWFOUND DETERMINATION, Phoebe rose the next morning ready to win over her naysayers. She had spent Sunday evening baking cookies and had decided that Mrs. Smith would be her first convert. The timing of her visit was important - she wanted to arrive after the boarders had left for the mines, but not so late as to be interrupting any other plans Mrs. Smith may have for the day.

She didn't want to wear something pretty for fear that Mrs. Smith would have cause to complain about Phoebe's big city ways, so after a hurried breakfast, Phoebe dressed in one of her more modest skirts and a simple blouse. She was about to braid her hair but thought twice about the youthful style, which might not help her to appear mature enough for her position. No, a braid would not do on the day she was to visit Mrs. Smith.

She went to the backyard and positioned her tub and bucket in an attempt to utilize the reflection of the windows as she had the day she'd first dined with the Speers, but soon discovered that the sun was not in the proper location to create a mirror-effect on her back windows. It had been late afternoon when she'd first used this trick. She wondered if the sun were reflecting on any of her other windows. With the bucket in one hand and tub in the other, she circled her parsonage, but she only had windows on the north and south sides of her home. She needed an east-facing window. She turned toward the church. The windows were large enough, but a little higher off the ground than her own. She wasn't sure she would be able to see into them, but it was worth trying.

When she arrived at the east side of the building, she realized immediately that the windows were much higher than she thought. However, if she positioned the tub a bit farther back than before, instead of closer to the window, she would be able to see herself. Closer would have been more ideal, but she would take whatever reflection she could get.

The ground around the church was more uneven than in her

backyard and Phoebe had difficulty finding a spot level enough that was also the right angle. She finally found a spot that she believed would work and placed her makeshift platform in place. It worked, but her distance from the building made it difficult to see herself well enough to do a good job. She moved the tub a little closer, hoping to get a better view. From this vantage point, she needed to stand on her toes and stretch as far as she could.

It was not the easiest of tasks, but she was able to do a half-way decent job on her hair. It was only a simple chignon at the base of her neck, not some pompadour like Esther always insisted on, so smoothing the stray hairs that always seemed to curl around her face was more of a concern than creating a pretty silhouette.

The sun was completely above the horizon at this point and she began to fret that her pampering had delayed her too much. She hurriedly pinned the last stray strand into place, but in her haste, she lost her balance a little. She felt the bucket beneath her wobble, but only the slightest bit, but she threw out her arms to steady herself. Her sudden movement only made things worse. The washtub tilted drastically, and the bucket slipped completely out from under her.

Phoebe screamed as she fell backward, helpless to stop what was happening, but just when she thought she would hit the ground, she found herself safe in the arms of a man wearing a familiar looking khaki uniform. In shock, she inhaled sharply and looked up into the face of the man who had caught her - the man who had saved her from utter humiliation, or worse.

Two sapphire blue eyes – eyes that she had come to know very well.

They crinkled at the corners. "Hello Pheebs."

15

THE SARGENT AND THE EVANGELIST

$\mathcal{T}$he white clapboard siding of the church looked gray this morning under the unusually cloudy August morning. Will dismounted and as he tied his horse, the normally placid gelding pulled against the hitching post, ears turned back.

"Woah, boy," Will said, patting the chestnut Morgan's neck. "What's the matter, Tolly? You nervous about something?"

Will chuckled. Not because he was talking to his horse. He did that often. He chuckled because it was Will, not the horse, who was worried. It had been almost a week since he had first made himself known to Phoebe, and it hadn't gone well. Since that fateful day outside the church, she had avoided him at every turn, completely shunning him from her life. But today was Sunday. She couldn't very well ban him from church. At least he hoped she couldn't.

So, here he stood, excited and anxious all at the same time, with no idea how she would react to his presence. However, he knew that if he didn't start working his way back into her life, he might never find a way into her heart.

Sun broke through the clouds and reflected off the tall

windows of the church, reminding him of that early Monday morning. He smiled at the memory of her atop that rickety contraption. His Phoebe certainly had a resourcefulness that most women lacked, if not the gracefulness to accompany it.

She also had quite the temper.

"What are you doing here?" she had asked immediately after recognizing him.

Will set her back down on her feet and shrugged his shoulders. "This is my new post."

"Your new post? But – when did you arrive?"

"A little over two months ago."

She stood there staring at him, cheeks flushed, tiny wisps of hair blowing across her forehead. Her perfect lips parted, but no words came out.

The desire to kiss her was strong, but instead, he just said, "Phoebe, you are going to catch flies with your mouth hanging open like that."

As soon as the words left his lips, he knew he had made a mistake. Her mouth slowly closed, and the color of her cheeks increased to a bright red.

"So, you are telling me that you have been here the whole time?" she asked through gritted teeth. "You knew this was your post and you never said a word? Is that why you never wrote to tell us where you were? Do you know how worried I – we all were?"

"I wrote your father, and I wrote John."

"My father knew? How long has he known?" she asked, turning from him. But before Will had a chance to answer, she whipped back around. "That morning! When you came to see my father...you told him then. That's why you came to my parent's house?"

"Yes," he said.

"And when I saw you at John and Esther's, you told them also?"

"I spoke with John, yes. I can only assume he told Esther. I didn't ask him not to. The only person I asked him not to tell was you."

"Well, of course you did!" she said, her voice rising to meet the color of her cheeks. "Why would anyone tell me, the only person that this information would affect?"

As angry as she was, he knew she didn't want the whole town to see her like this. "Phoebe, please calm down. People are going to hear you."

His assumption was right, because she turned toward the parsonage and motioned for him to follow, which he did dutifully. She kept quiet, but only until he had closed the door behind them.

"How dare you! How dare you deceive me like this?" she screamed.

"Phoebe, I never lied to you."

"You omitted the truth. That is the same as lying."

"When did I omit the truth?"

"That night – when you asked me to take a walk with you. You had every opportunity to tell me then that you'd been stationed in Iron Falls, but you didn't!"

"I wanted to tell you, Pheebs…"

"Don't call me that!" she interrupted.

"Phoebe," he began again, "I really wanted to tell you. I wanted so badly to tell you. I had spent every waking hour since that dinner with your family praying that God would show me what was best for you. Like Gideon, I laid a fleece before Him. I told him that if you asked me where I was going, that I would tell you. I also said that if you showed me any sign of tenderness, if you gave me any hope that you had any feelings for me, then I would tell you. But you did neither, so I had my answer."

"And His answer was to deceive me?"

"His answer was to go to Iron Falls, not knowing what decision you would make, and trust Him to take care of the rest. It isn't for me to question God when he answers my prayers, Phoebe. It is only for me to honor His will."

His heart wrenched at the look of pain that contorted her face. "No wonder everyone's attitude changed. Esther, my mother – all that talk about God providing protection for me. They were talking about you!"

"Yes, that's probably true, though I can't speak for them."

"Apparently, they can't speak for themselves, either, since everyone was so tight-lipped about the whole matter!" She paced the floor, arms crossed around her waist, shaking her head. "I cannot believe that no one, not a single person who claims to love me, thought that I could do this on my own. How weak they must all think me." Her voice cracked as those last words caught in her throat.

"No, Phoebe, oh no. That isn't how it is at all," he said. "I will admit that my being here has probably helped to lessen your mother's worry, but that doesn't mean that anyone thought you too weak for the task." He reached for her elbow, but she yanked it away.

"Don't touch me! Don't ever touch me!" she yelled, tears falling freely down her face. "No matter what any of you think, I am capable, and I don't need your coddling."

She walked to the door and opened it. "You need to leave," she stated without looking at him.

"Please, Phoebe. Don't do this."

"Go! I want you to leave and I don't want you bothering me ever again. Stay away from me. I don't need your help, or your protection, or whatever it is you planned on doing. You can just fall off a cliff for all I care. I just want you out of my life forever!"

She stared straight ahead, refusing to look at him. He had made a mess of this, and he knew it. He also knew her well enough to know that if he pushed her any further right now, she might never forgive him.

Slowly, he put on his hat and walked through the door. Phoebe wasted no time slamming it behind him, and the sound was the loneliest sound he had ever heard.

That lonely feeling had become his closest companion this past week. His heart ached. Before she had known he was here, he had enjoyed watching her from afar, seeing the way she settled into her new home, building relationships with the people around her. He had felt a sense of pride watching her, a sense of hope that God was fulfilling His will for both of them. However, having her close but not being able to talk to her no longer held the same hope it had the previous week. Now, it felt lonely. This isn't how it was supposed to have happened. How had he screwed things up so badly?

"Good morning, Officer Caffey," a woman's voice said as she walked past him on her way to the church, but he didn't really hear. He was too distracted by the image of perfection that had just opened the doors of the church and now stood greeting the townspeople. Her dark hair, pulled into a simple bun at the nape of her neck, looked like silky strands of molasses against her creamy complexion. Will liked Phoebe's hair like that, all pulled back, giving him a full view of her beautiful face, though he preferred it loose and flowing like she wore it when they were younger.

Her cheeks were a bright pink, not from rouge, Will was certain. No, he knew what caused that color; Phoebe was flustered. Never one to be comfortable as center of attention, she was handling this moment with such grace that Will's heart swelled with pride.

"She was born to do this," he whispered to himself.

His perusal lifted from her bright cheeks to the eyes he had seen in his dreams for so long. How many nights had he lain awake in a dirty French trench, imagining her eyes, the darkest of chocolates, her eyes as deep and as rich as her silky hair, her eyes...

Suddenly turned and settled right on him.

Her smile faded, as did the glow of her cheeks.

He was caught. Not that he cared - there was no use avoiding the inevitable, though it probably would have been easier to just slip into the back of the church after the music had begun.

As he joined the line of people entering the church, he was grateful; they kept Phoebe from running as she'd done all week.

He smiled as he reached the top of the stairs. "Good morning, Pastor." It was the first time he had used the title to address her and he liked how it sounded. "It's a beautiful morning."

"Is it?"

The smile that had graced her beautiful face while greeting the other parishioners remained but was not as welcoming as it had been.

"From where I stand, it is," he said with a wink.

Her smile quickly evaporated. "Perspective is everything, isn't it?"

Now he'd done it - she was angry. Why was he so bad at this? "I'm sorry. I shouldn't have –"

"Shouldn't have what, Constable? Lied? Misled? Deceived?"

Will sighed. "All of the above, I suppose." He opened the door and entered the church. This was neither the time nor the place to have this conversation.

He took a spot on a pew along the back wall.

A soldier never leaves his back exposed, even if he is in church.

The last of the parishioners found their seats and the music began. Will stood and opened the hymnal.

'Wouldn't Ma be proud of her?' he thought as he sang along, and while thoughts of his recently departed mother typically added to his pensiveness, Will's heart filled to bursting with unexpected joy as a renewed knowledge of his mother's eternal rest in glory fell upon him. A double blessing, Will considered,

that the first hymn of the morning was one of his mother's favorites, "And Can It Be, That I Should Gain."

The second song was just beginning when the door opened, and a stranger walked in. He wore fine clothes, finer than Will had ever seen in this town, and Will's curiosity was piqued.

The man took off his hat and winked at Phoebe and Will's eyes shot to her. Although she tried hard to hide it, her reaction was unmistakable to Will... a slight smile played at the corner of her lips. The hair on the back of Will's neck stood on end.

Phoebe began preaching. Will didn't miss a word, but his eyes never left the back of the stranger's head. Something wasn't right about him, and Will didn't like the fact that he was so openly casual with Phoebe.

But what if they knew each other? Could this be a suitor of hers? Perhaps a man from Bible College? Will doubted it. If there were a man in her life, he would know about it.

Wouldn't he? After all, Phoebe would certainly have told her family, and wouldn't Esther have told him immediately?

Once the service ended, Will waited until the church had emptied before leaving. Unfortunately, the stranger had the same idea.

"After you, Sarge," he said, sweeping his arm toward the door.

Will shook his head. "You first. I insist."

The man smiled and again the hair on the back of Will's neck stood at attention. It was the same feeling that had woken him in the trenches the night he'd found a snake slithering across his chest.

He'd shot that snake.

Will and the stranger exited the church and stood with Phoebe at the top of the stairs.

"Why, Miss Albright, I thought my memories were exaggerating your beauty, but you are even lovelier than my dreams have depicted you." He grabbed her hand and placed a far too long kiss upon her knuckles.

Will had a strong urge to shoot this snake.

Phoebe withdrew her hand. "This is quite the surprise, Mr. Parker. Other evangelists I know seldom get a Sunday off to visit friends."

"I'm not like most evangelists."

He stood far too close to her, in Will's opinion. Will cleared his throat and both the man named Parker and Phoebe turned, as if neither had noticed him before that moment.

Phoebe scowled. "Mr. Parker, have you met Officer Caffey? He is one of the State Troopers here in Iron Falls."

Parker smiled a sugary sweet smile back to Phoebe. "Not officially, but by his proximity to our conversation, can it be that he is more than just a police officer to you?"

Phoebe's eyes grew as large as saucers. "You are mistaken, sir! Will, I mean, Constable Caffey and I are nothing more than - than –"

"Friends," Will said, extending his hand to the stranger. "Friends since childhood."

The other man shook Will's hand. "Pleased to meet..." He turned his attention back to Phoebe, "a *friend* of Miss Albright's."

"I didn't catch your name," Will said.

"Parker."

"Do you have a first name?" Will was having difficulty disguising his annoyance.

"Sure do."

"Mind sharing it?"

Parker's eyes rotated in Will's direction, but he kept himself facing Phoebe. "What for, Sarge? You going to investigate me?"

"If I have to," Will answered honestly.

Parker's eyes flicked back to Phoebe and the sticky sweet expression returned. "I didn't realize you brought your own personal bodyguard to the Upper Peninsula. But I assure you, the only crime I'll be arrested for is stealing your affections. Shall I pose for my mugshot now?"

"He is not my bodyguard." She placed her hands on her hips. "And he has no right to harass anyone I associate with."

"Now, settle down Miss Albright. Nothing to get yourself worked up over. A little good-natured competition never hurt any man." He turned to face Will. "Gregory. That is my first name."

Will just nodded, silently memorizing as much as he could about the man's appearance. Maybe he would do a little investigating.

"I was hoping you would do me the honor of accompanying me for a stroll through town. I have an evangelism meeting this evening in Richmond, but I really would like to catch up with you before then if possible." He looked at Will. "Unless, of course, you have other plans."

"That sounds lovely," Phoebe said, placing her hand on the arm Gregory Parker offered her.

Will never knew the sting of jealousy until this moment. He didn't like this man, but even more, he didn't like that Phoebe didn't share his distaste for the fellow.

As he watched the pair walk away, Wendell Jackson climbed the stairs of the church and stood next to him.

"Do you know that man?" Will asked.

"He looks kind of familiar. Why?"

"No reason. Just curious."

Maybe it was just jealousy. Maybe it wasn't. Either way, the uneasy feeling growing in the pit of his stomach meant that Will was going to keep a very close eye on Gregory Parker.

16

BY FAITH

"Good evening, Miss Albright!"

Phoebe cringed. Of all the evenings for him to show up out of nowhere, Gregory Parker had to show up this one. She wasn't in the mood to socialize, let alone entertain the man for dinner, which she assumed was his intent. She'd pretty much had her fill of Gregory Parker last Sunday - with no restaurant in town, she'd no choice but to invite him for dinner. That dinner had lasted all afternoon, in spite of his protestations that he "must be getting along to his next church very soon."

She pasted a smile on her face and slowly turned toward the road. Gregory Parker sat in his new Buick Roadster, looking every part the Douglas Fairbanks, with his expensive suit and slicked back hair.

"Good evening, Mr. Parker," Phoebe said. "I didn't expect to see you so soon. No revivals this week?"

"Got one starting tomorrow in Gwinn. Since Iron Falls was on my way through, I thought I would stop by and visit the prettiest woman in the Upper Peninsula."

"Really? Well, then don't let me stop you from finding her."

Gregory laughed. "I see she's also the funniest."

Phoebe fought the desire to roll her eyes. Instead, she took a deep breath slowly and stepped off the porch. "I was just headed into town. Do you fancy a walk?"

"Why walk when you can ride in style?'" He jumped out and opened the passenger door.

Phoebe shook her head. "Really, Mr. Parker, wouldn't it be strange to drive such a short distance? Besides, the walk is a pleasant one."

"Only made pleasant by the company," he said. "Come on, humor me, Phoebe."

She gasped. "Mr. Parker, I really don't think it's appropriate for you to address me so informally."

His smile faded. "I'm sorry if I've offended you. I won't address you by your given name if that's what you prefer." He shut the car door. "Is that a right that you reserve for your constable?"

Phoebe felt her cheeks grow hot, but more out of indignation than embarrassment.

"You have no right –"

"Hey, Pastor…is everything alright?"

They both turned and found Wendell Jackson walking up the road.

"Oh, hello Wendell. Yes, everything is fine." She took a step back, putting distance between herself and Gregory.

"Yessir, my boy, everything is fine with your lovely minister here. I was just offering to take her for a ride."

Wendell's frown did not soften. "I came by to do some of the chores I promised I'd take care of."

"That's very kind of you, Wendell." She turned back to Gregory. "I'm very sorry, Mr. Parker, but it seems I am no longer free for our drive."

"Perfectly alright. Another time, perhaps?"

"Perhaps."

Gregory leaned in close to Phoebe. "I'm sorry for what I said earlier," he said softly. "I guess I fell victim to the green-eyed monster. 'Oh beware, my lord, of jealousy! It is the green-eyed monster which doth mock the meat it feeds on.' That's Shakespeare."

"I'm aware," she said.

"I'm praying for you, Miss Albright, that you will see that God had His hand in our meeting. That state trooper may have his sights set on you, but he'll never be able to give you the life that I can." With that, he climbed back into his Buick and sped off.

"I kind of lied," Wendell said.

Phoebe turned her attention away from the road and back to the young man. "Lied?"

"Yeah, I know Will already chopped some wood for you."

"Will?" Phoebe gasped, remembering the generous amount of immaculately stacked wood she had discovered earlier in the week after returning from a morning of calling on parishioners. "I thought you were the one who had chopped it all!"

"Nope. It was Will. I saw him this morning and he told me that he got most of it done already."

Phoebe noticed that the boy did not refer to Will as Officer Caffey but said nothing. She was too busy trying to not let the boy see how angry she was with Will for entering her back yard without permission.

"I actually just wanted to stop by and apologize for not gettin' the chores done like I promised."

"There's no need to apologize. You tried last week, remember? But you looked so exhausted that I didn't have the heart to have you labor more. I hope you don't think that I was upset in any way. Besides," she stood a little straighter and put her shoulders back. "I am completely capable of handling all my own chores."

"Oh, no ma'am. I knew you weren't upset. And I wasn't sayin' you couldn't do your own chores, only that you needn't, not with Will and me around. It's our ministry to free up your time to do pastorin', ya know?"

Wendell looked so proud of his self-proclaimed responsibil- ity, that she didn't have the heart to argue further. Besides, if she were to be honest, chopping wood was near the bottom of her list of things she'd like to spend her time doing.

"But I still feel bad," he continued. "I wanted to get to it this week, but it's been a long one."

"I can imagine. Working in the mine must be difficult?"

"Yep, it wears ya out, but I don't mind it really. They're really nice there and we only have to work Monday through Friday, which is great. I've just been choosing to work Saturdays for the extra money. But I'm not workin' this Saturday. I figured I need a break."

"I'm glad to hear that. Taking Saturday off should give you some much needed rest."

"Well, that's the other reason I wanted to come by, to let you know that's when I'll be over to finish chopping the wood."

"Wendell, that isn't much of a day off! Besides, Officer Caffey chopped enough to keep me for quite a while."

"I don't mind. It won't take long – I already looked at the pile. And I'll have plenty of time afterwards for fun - Will's gonna teach me to shoot."

"You've never shot a gun before? I thought all fathers taught their sons to shoot." In fact, some, like her father, taught their daughters as well.

"My pa died when I was nine, so he never got around to it."

This stopped Phoebe in her tracks, and she turned to look at the boy. "Just like Will," Phoebe whispered, mostly to herself.

"Yes ma'am," Wendell answered her. "He and me, we got lots in common, besides being from Lansing."

"I'm so sorry," she said earnestly. "I had no idea."

"How would ya?" he smiled. "It's alright, Pastor Albright. I'm not sad about it anymore. I miss him, mind you, but I have all good memories of my pa. He was a good man."

"Well, that's something else you have in common with Officer Caffey. His father was a good man as well."

"Did you know him?"

"Well, I was nine as well when he died, so I only knew *of* him, really. But my father knew him very well. They were best friends, in fact. I do remember his funeral, though. It's the only funeral that I ever saw my father cry during – and he was the one conducting the service."

"Was that hard for you to watch?"

"It was heart-wrenching to see my father so broken, and to see Will standing so straight and steady, his arm around his mother's waist. I couldn't stop crying, but Will didn't shed a single tear at the funeral. He was as solid as a rock for his mother," she said.

"I'm not that strong," Wendell said. "I cried like a baby at my pa's funeral."

Phoebe remembered more but didn't share it with Wendell. She remembered the dinner at her house after the funeral, and all the family and friends quietly milling around, sharing stories of Mr. Caffey. She remembered all the women gathered around Mrs. Caffey, one handing her a cup of tea, another a handkerchief, all trying to comfort her with words of condolence.

She also remembered that she couldn't find Will. She looked all through the house, on the front porch, even upstairs in the bedrooms, but he was nowhere to be found. She finally found him in her mother's garden, on his knees, hunkered down between two rose bushes, crying.

Phoebe said nothing, just knelt next to him and placed her

hand on his back. Immediately, Will wrapped his arms around her and the weight of his sorrow brought her to tears as well. They stayed like that, wrapped in each other's arms, two children crying adult-sized tears, until there were no more to fall. When they had finished, Will wiped his eyes with the back of his sleeve, Phoebe on the skirt of her dress, and they returned to the house. Neither of them had ever mentioned it again.

"Tears are not a sign of weakness, Wendell, but rather a sign of affection. Clearly your father meant a great deal to you. Of course, you cried, and I'm sure Officer Caffey did as well, whether anyone else witnessed it or not. Your strength has been proven by the life you have lived, and continue to live, since your father's passing. Continuing to make him proud of the man you are becoming, that's the true sign of strength."

Wendell smiled. "I never met Mr. Caffey, but I'm sure he's proud of Will, too."

"I'm certain that he is," she answered honestly.

"Miss Albright," Wendell began, "does that mean you believe they can see us from heaven? I mean, our loved ones that have died?"

"Yes, I do," Phoebe answered. "Do you remember the 'By Faith' scriptures found in Hebrews?"

Wendell flushed a little and looked at the ground, kicking his foot around in the dirt.

"I don't know much about the Bible, ma'am."

"Have a seat on the stairs while I grab mine."

She returned shortly and sat next to Wendell. She opened to Hebrews 11 and began reading Paul's accounting of the saints and how they exhibited their faith in God, from Abel to Rahab and all of them in between. Wendell interrupted her.

"What does this have to do with heaven, other than all these people bein' dead?"

"This doesn't mention heaven, but it's so important to the

next chapter of Hebrews. Read that first verse of chapter 12 for me Wendell."

"I'd rather you read it. I don't like to read out loud."

Phoebe paused and looked at the boy. "Alright. It says, 'Wherefore seeing we also are compassed about with so great a cloud of witnesses, let us lay aside every weight, and the sin which doth so easily beset us, and let us run with patience the race that is set before us.' Now, Wendell, after reading chapter 11, who are the cloud of witnesses that Paul is referring to in chapter 12?"

"Well, I guess all those people who had faith."

"Exactly. All those that have gone on before us. And not only can they see us, the Bible also says they are cheering us on as we race through this life. Isn't that exciting?"

Wendell's shoulders slumped and he turned away from her.

"Wendell? What's the matter?"

"I was hoping that you would tell me that my pa couldn't see me, because if he can see me, I know he ain't proud of who I've become."

"Why on earth would you say that?" Phoebe asked, shocked that this kind-hearted teenager would feel this way.

"Because my pa – he was just like all those people you read to me about. He had faith. He believed in God. But me, I – well I gave up on God when he took away my pa. And if he knows that, then I know he's disappointed in me."

Phoebe took a deep breath. She let the silence hang between them for a moment, allowing the Holy Spirit to work, not only on Wendell, but on her soul as well. She wanted her next words to be the Lord's, not her own.

"Wendell, I believe your father, if he was a man of faith, is cheering you on just like the Bible says. And until you die, he will continue to cheer for you. But I don't believe that he is cheering for you to work harder at the mine, or for you to volunteer your free time to the church. Those things are all commendable, but what he is cheering for is for you to turn from the sinful life and accept Jesus as your Savior. He is cheering for you to become a man of faith like him."

With tears brimming in his eyes, he turned to Phoebe. "How do I do that?" he asked.

She flipped the pages of her Bible to the book of Romans. "Let me show you."

COLD TRAIL

*W*ill reigned in Tolly and dismounted. Three other constables were already there. Officer Thomas Rogers stood over an older woman seated on the back porch stairs, the other two, Frank Little and Jesse Moore, leaned on their saddles, talking with the store owner Jack Simmons.

"Is it teatime already, boys?" Will asked the two loafers, more than a little annoyed.

"No, sir," Frank said, he and the other constable straightening. "Just waiting for the mortician to show up."

Will nodded to Jack. "You found the body?"

"It's Jimmy Richardson." Jack nodded in the direction of the saltbox house. "I was delivering a crock his mother ordered from Marquette. Wanted to get it to her before I opened the store this morning. Found him just like this, laid out in the middle of the front yard. His poor mother."

"Is that her?" Will asked, motioning toward the woman being interviewed.

"Yeah," Jesse Moore answered. "Said she thought he was still in bed. By the looks of it, he's been here most of the night."

Will slowly circled the body. "Do we know what happened?"

"Likely an accident. There wasn't much of a moon last night. Maybe someone was coyote hunting and he just happened to be in the wrong place at the wrong time."

Will walked around the body and crouched near his head. "Not likely. This was close range. Look at the entry wound."

Officer Moore knelt beside him as Will carefully turned the boy's head and pointed at the wound. "That wasn't caused by a shotgun."

"Yeah, you're right," Moore conceded. "That's a clean entry. Close range, I'd suspect."

Will looked back at the mother who at this point was wailing uncontrollably.

"But who'd want to kill Jimmy Richardson?" Little asked. "He's just a kid."

"He could be a little arrogant at times," Jack interjected. "But nothing more than what's typical for a kid of fourteen. I can't imagine anyone having cause to murder him."

Will removed his hat and rubbed the back of his neck. "Well, someone did, and it's our job to figure out who."

Thomas Rogers joined them near the body.

"She says Jimmy wasn't home when she went to bed. She didn't hear anything, but she admitted to taking some of her headache powder before turning in."

Will nodded. "Some of that stuff out there could put an elephant to sleep for the night. Did she say why her son was out after dark?"

"She wasn't certain, but she had suspicions that he had been going to Lambeckers at night."

"But we busted and dismantled that distillery weeks ago," Officer Little said.

Will stood. If Jim Richardson had made a habit of visiting the Lambecker place, he'd probably rubbed shoulders with a few unsavory characters. Even so, Will had to agree with the others

- Jimmy was an agreeable kid. It seemed unlikely he had made too many enemies in life.

"Well, Lambecker's is the only lead we have. Little, you and Myers stay here until the coroner arrives. I'll pay a visit —"

Before he could finish his sentence, a loud gasp directly behind him halted him.

"DEAR JESUS."

Will turned quickly. "Phoebe!" He placed himself between her and the body, blocking her view. "You shouldn't be here."

Phoebe pulled back from him. "Why not?"

"This is a crime scene, closed to the public."

"Jack is here. He's not an officer."

"He's a witness."

"Is that the only reason you are allowing him to stay, but kicking me out?"

He could see the indignation rising in her eyes. She was right, of course. It hadn't bothered him that Jack was on scene and witnessing the gore. But Will wasn't in love with Jack.

He exhaled slowly and looked straight into her eyes, willing her to understand. "I don't want you seeing this. I'm just trying to protect you."

She blinked several times then said, "I never once asked for your protection."

Her words carried a weight that, although audible to all those standing nearby, was only understood by Phoebe and Will. She was angry about him attempting to dismiss her from the crime scene, yes, but it was more. But, like it or not, he was in charge here and she was going to have to understand that.

"You have to leave."

"You aren't the boss of me, Will Caffey."

He grabbed her elbow and roughly dragged her away from the scene.

"This is not up for negotiation. Go home."

"I am the pastor of this town, and that mother needs me."

"Phoebe," he said, lowering his voice. "I know you are angry with me, but you have to trust me in this. I know what is best. It's my job."

"What is your job?"

"To protect."

Her eyebrows knit over her dark eyes as she crossed her arms. "And my job includes compassion. As the pastor, I am to comfort the people of this town in their times of need." She shoved him out of her way and headed for the crying Mrs. Richardson. She called to him over her shoulder. "And you will refer to me as pastor in the presence of others, Officer Caffey."

The stubbornness and defiance that he had always loved about her now felt like a vise around his throbbing temples. Will yanked his hat off but resisted the urge to throw it to the ground. When he did, he saw something in the dirt.

"Rogers," he called and motioned for the constable. "Does the victim's mother own a car?"

Rogers looked around but shook his head. "Not that I can see. That barn's gotta horse, but no car. Why?"

"Because these tire tracks are fresh. Somebody drove a car up here very recently."

"And you think that somebody is our murderer?"

"It's all we've got. Double check with Mrs. Richardson about a car. If she has one, check the tires. One of the tires on whatever vehicle left these tracks is near bald." He untied Tolly's reins and mounted. "I'm going to follow these."

He looked up toward where Phoebe sat with her arm wrapped around the sobbing mother, feeling a strange mixture of adoration and anger towards the beautiful brunette. "Little, Moore," he hollered.

The two junior officers stepped toward him.

"Little, grab your horse and come with me. Moore, find something to cover the body with." He reined Tolly away from the house, then immediately circled back to Jesse Moore. "And make sure the pastor gets home safely once she's finished here," he said before turning again and heading in the direction of the tire tracks, Frank Little close on his heels.

~

BACK HOME IN LANSING, a set of tire tracks wouldn't have been evidence at all, what with all the vehicle traffic around town. But in the Upper Peninsula, cars weren't as common. And although the tracks turned out to be a wild goose chase, fading to nothing within a few hundred yards of the crime scene, Will still had a hunch that whoever killed Jimmy Richardson had driven away in a car with one bald tire.

"What now?" Frank Little asked, leaning forward in his saddle.

Will tipped his hat back and looked at the sun, now centered in the sky above them. "Well, I suppose it would be a good idea to canvas the area and gather a list of the townspeople who own a vehicle."

"So, we're headed back?"

"Not quite yet." Will stared for several moments at the pine shaded road off to their left. "I think first, we ought to pay Mr. Lambecker a visit."

"Lambecker?" Frank said incredulously. "You don't think they've set up another still, do ya?"

"One way to find out."

The rundown shack was still stark looking, with its gray, splintered wood siding hanging loosely on its rickety framework, the bones of which Will doubted had ever stood perpendicular to the ground. The fact that the building had ever withstood a Michigan winter was a shock. The sloping front porch was still home to three mismatched rocking chairs and two disgustingly dirty spittoons. The only difference from

Will's first visit here was the missing copper kettle moonshine still the troopers had seized and destroyed.

Henry Lambecker stepped out of the shack, sliding his suspenders onto his shoulders as he did.

"Yer wastin' yer time, constable," he hollered toward Will. "You done took my livelihood. Nothin' left to confiscate."

"Good day to you, too, Henry. How's the job search going?" Will asked.

"Hmmph. Ain't no jobs to be had."

"That's not what I hear. Just the other day, Thomas Speer was telling me that he can't get enough workers."

"Humph. Mining's dirty business."

"Moonshining isn't all that clean," Will responded.

Lambecker spit in the general direction of one of the spittoons. "My moonshinin' business wasn't hurtin' anyone."

"I'll bet that's what that farmer in Watson thought before killing all those miners with his rotgut," Frank Little said.

"You ain't gotta be worried about me killin' anyone."

Will remembered his original mission. "Jimmy Richardson is dead." He said it matter-of-factly.

Henry Lambecker's face turned ashen. He sunk into the nearest rocker and placed his head in his hands. "He was just a kid. He didn't deserve to die."

Will and Frank looked at one another.

"Henry," Will started. "Are you trying to tell us something?"

Henry's head shook back and forth in his hands. "I told 'im to leave it alone, to mind 'is own business, but he had some sort of itchin' to solve things. I thought it might get 'im roughed up. Never thought it get 'im killed."

"So, you know who killed Jimmy?" Frank asked.

Henry looked up, as if he had forgotten Will and Frank were there. His face grew dark. "I don't know nothin'."

"That's not what it sounds like," Will said. "I never said Jimmy was murdered, but you knew. You said Jimmy was sticking his nose where it didn't belong. Where was that exactly?"

"I told you, I don't know nothin'."

"Maybe we should continue this conversation at the Constabulary post."

Henry shrugged. "Fine by me. You gotta feed yer prisoners, don't ya?" He laughed. "But beyond what I'd like on my sandwich, I ain't got nothin to tell you." Henry stood and headed for the door of the shack. He turned back to Will and said, "Before prohibition, I was considered a law-abidin' citizen. No one cared none about my still. Now I'm a criminal. Well, I'll tell you what, I'm not the real criminal. If you boys don't start doin' yer job and figure out who the real bad guys are around here, Jimmy won't be the only kid lost."

IN THE GARDEN

"Good morning, Mrs. Wiggins!" Phoebe called, crossing the street. "What are you doing?"

"Pulling weeds," she said, wiping her hands on her apron. "I've been a little negligent in my care of this garden and am paying for it in lambsquarters and crabgrass."

Phoebe looked over the fence. "I had heard that in company towns there was often a lot left open for townspeople to do additional gardening. I didn't realize that lot was across the street from the church."

"True, there are lots for those in company housing to farm on, but this isn't one of them. This property belongs to the church. It's the location of the future parsonage."

"Future parsonage? I didn't know there was to be a different parsonage."

Mrs. Wiggins laughed. "Oh, yes. You didn't think that little building you're living in was our plan all along, did you?"

"I wasn't sure," she admitted.

"Goodness, no. The plan was always to build on this site, but when the company pulled out, taking half the town and their money with it, plans were put on hold. So, we've been using it for extra gardening space. Actually, most of what is in your pantry came from this garden."

Phoebe looked around the lot, remembering what the women had said about supplying her with more goods once this year's harvest came in.

"May I help you?"

Mrs. Wiggins looked up, surprised.

"If you have time, that would be much appreciated!"

Phoebe hurried back to her house to put on an apron and grab a stool. The two women worked through the morning together, chatting as they cleaned around the plants. Mrs. Wiggins had a pleasant personality and Phoebe found her extremely easy to talk to. She learned that like Mr. Speer, Mr. Wiggins had become a partner in the mine after the Middleton Mining company pulled out. The two of them, along with a few more, oversaw the day-to-day operations of the mine. In fact, it had been Mr. Wiggins who had hired Wendell.

The sound of horse hooves interrupted their conversation. Phoebe looked up to find Will Caffey dismounting and tying his horse to a post. She rose and met him outside the gate.

"Hello Officer Caffey," she said coolly. "Is there something that you need?"

"No, ma'am," he responded without smiling. "A letter arrived for you and I told the postmaster I would deliver it."

He handed her the envelope, which she took without another word. She turned her back to him to return to the garden.

"Phoebe," Will spoke softly. "How long will you be angry with me?"

She stood frozen, shocked by the tenderness in his voice. Mrs. Wiggins was hard at work and appeared not to have heard him.

"Please. I can't take your contempt much longer."

Phoebe took a deep breath and was about to respond when

Mrs. Wiggins stood up and came toward them, carrying a basket of cabbage and her stool.

"Well, that takes care of things for the day. Thank you, Miss Albright, for your help. I'd have been here all day without you. Good day, constable," she said nodding and smiling.

Mrs. Wiggins' departure left Phoebe and Will alone on the street, a dilemma Phoebe was about to remedy. "Thank you, Officer Caffey, but if you will excuse me, I'd like to be alone to read my letter."

Without another word, Phoebe crossed the street to her parsonage. Once inside, she peeked through the curtain to see how he'd respond. To her astonishment, he was headed straight toward her house. She jumped away from the window and positioned herself in front of the door, ready to pounce when he knocked. If he was going to follow her after she had so blatantly dismissed him, then she was finished with formalities. Will Caffey was about to hear how she really felt about him.

She heard him climb the stairs, and then she heard him place something on her porch. She waited for the knock, but it never came. All she heard was the sound of his boots bounding back down the steps. When she looked back out the window again, he was riding away.

When she was certain he was out of sight, she opened her front door. Sitting off to the side, right where he had left it, was her stool.

She sat at her table and with the envelope. The name on the return address read only *Albright*, but Phoebe knew by the handwriting that it was from her father. This is the post she had been waiting for – the one in response to the letter she had sent him after discovering Will Caffey in Iron Falls. She ripped the envelope open.

The letter began with the usual pleasantries. Her father wrote about news from home, what her mother had been doing since she left, what kind of mischief Sarah was getting herself into, how Esther was feeling this late in her pregnancy. It wasn't until the second page that her father addressed the Will Caffey situation.

I received your letter today. I was expecting it, knowing that by now Will would have made his presence known. I am sorry that you have been hurt by our actions. That was never our intent. In fact, it was just the opposite. Keeping the news of Will's whereabouts was, we all felt, in your best interest. It was not in any way intended to 'manipulate' you, as you so bluntly accused.

Do you remember that conversation you and I had on the train? When we discussed the decision to move north had to be your decision and your decision alone? It couldn't be influenced by my ideas or anyone else's, otherwise you may weigh your options based on the world's thoughts and not on God's will alone. Whether you want to admit it or not, if you had known about Will's appointment, it would have clouded your judgment, maybe even swayed your decision. Of this I am certain, because I spent many hours on my knees asking God for wisdom and He made it very clear to me that I was not to tell you. I don't know why for certain; I just know I was not. So, rather than manipulate, our intention was to give you the freedom that you needed – and deserved – to make your own choice.

I'd also like to remind you that Will accepted the post weeks before you made your decision to take the church there in Iron Falls. Once you made your decision, we decided to wait to tell you that he was there, too. I will admit that it felt underhanded, acting like some random constable was delivering your baggage or that I didn't know the man who'd arranged a place for me to sleep. But everything said and done was for your benefit. I had hoped that, given a week or so, you would have enough time to discover what we already knew – all of us - that you were capable of conquering any task God asked of you, with or without Will Caffey nearby.

Still, I must admit that I'm glad Will is there. We all need help in this life, Phoebe, and I am glad that a man of God like William Caffey is there to help you, should you ever need it.

I meant what I said at the train station - God has a plan for your life, and I am so very proud of you for following Him.

All my love,

Daddy

Phoebe was in tears, but there was more to his letter.

"P.S. From one pastor to another...the next time you are angry with someone, do not respond immediately. Take a deep breath and give yourself time to pray. I am your father and love you no matter what. I can forgive unkind words and unjust accusations. But others, especially those in your congregation, may not be so forgiving. And words, once spoken (or written,) can't be erased.

P.P.S. You should know that I've received a letter from Will, as well. He fears that he's hurt you so deeply that the wound may never heal. Phoebe, my dear, you are being too harsh on that young man. Stop being so prideful and forgive him."

Phoebe laid down the letter, sick to her stomach over the harsh words that she had written to her father. He was right, of course. She had written in anger and had not taken the time to pray. In fact, in the time since she first discovered Will's presence in Iron Falls, she hadn't prayed about it at all – not once. She had, however, thought about it constantly, feeding her own anger, wallowing in her own self-pity.

When a knock came at the door, she was so startled she nearly screamed. She wiped her face, praying that it was not puffy enough to telegraph her recent crying fit to whomever was on the other side. She opened the door and was surprised to find Mary's husband, Jack Simmons, standing there holding something wrapped in paper.

"Good afternoon Pastor. I have your delivery here," he said

cheerfully, stepping into the parsonage and laying the large, flat package on the table.

"But I didn't order anything, Mr. Simmons," she argued.

"There's a note on top. Have a good day."

He was gone before Phoebe could respond. Confused, she picked up the small envelope and read the note inside.

"Please forgive me. And for goodness sake, please stop standing on buckets. You are going to break your neck. ~Will"

Thoroughly confused, she tore the paper off the package. Inside was a pretty yet puffy face, staring back at her in red-eyed wonder.

"Will Caffey," she breathed.

He had purchased her a mirror.

THE MIRROR

"*We're* ready, Sergeant."

Will looked up from his desk. "Right. Training." He stood. "I'm coming."

"Is everything alright?" Officer Little asked. "You still worried about the Richardson case?"

"Of course, that case is bothering me. A boy is dead, and we don't have a suspect." Truth be known, although he hadn't been able to shake that unsolved mystery, Will's thoughts at the moment were on a much more personal, and beautiful, matter.

"Should we bring Henry Lambecker in and try to get him to talk?"

"I don't think we'll get anywhere; Lambecker's more scared of whoever killed Jimmy than he is of us."

Frank nodded. "Ya, I got that feeling as well." He motioned toward the exiting officers. "You want us to go without ya?"

Will shook his head. "No. I could use some fresh air."

He followed the other officers out of the constabulary, but nearly plowed into Frank and the others when all seven men stopped dead in their tracks, staring at the same thing.

"You boys look like you've seen a —" but he stopped short

when he saw what, or more correctly, whom the officers were staring at. "Phoebe!"

The morning sun gleamed against the silky, dark hair that peeked from beneath the rolled brim hat she wore, but her face was shadowed enough to make it difficult to see her expression. Will had seen little but a scowl on her beautiful face the past few weeks. But her delicate hands spoke loudly - they clutched her reticule so tightly her knuckles were white. Worry gripped Will so tightly, his throat felt as constricted as the silk purse in her hands. When she lifted her gaze to him, and the morning sun illuminated her face - full of fear and apprehension - Will's knees nearly buckled beneath him.

Something was wrong.

"Wait up," he said to the other officers. "I need a moment."

"Good morning, Pastor," he said, praying that his controlled voice did not betray his worry. "This is a surprise." He took Phoebe's elbow and led her back down the road a bit.

When they stopped, she turned to face him. Her brows knit over her dark eyes creating two little creases between them. She wasn't looking at Will. She was looking over his shoulder at the other men.

"They can't hear us," he reassured her.

"No, of course not," she said softly, her eyes turning to his. She drew her bottom lip into her mouth and broke eye contact with him.

"Is everything alright?" Will asked. He knew Phoebe had a penchant for chewing her bottom lip when something was bothering her.

"Yes, yes. Everything is fine. I just wanted to – I wanted..."

She stopped and all that could be heard in the silence was the rapid beating of Will's heart. Or was that hers?

"I received the package you ordered, and..."

"The mirror? What's wrong with the mirror?"

Her head snapped up and her look of worry turned to one of confusion. "No. Nothing is wrong with the mirror."

Will's patience began to waver. He had been torn in pieces thinking Phoebe was in trouble. "So, you sought me out to discuss a mirror?"

He regretted the words the minute they left his mouth. He was happy to see her. It wasn't her fault he'd worked himself up over her visit.

"Well, yes. I do think we should discuss the mirror. You shouldn't have done that. I mean, you shouldn't have bought me a mirror. It isn't..."

"You don't like it?" Will tried to soften his tone, and he could tell she noticed. He could also tell that she wasn't quite sure how to take the change.

She cocked her head slightly and looked at him quizzically. "It's beautiful. It's just that you shouldn't have bought me such an expensive item."

Will took off his hat and ran his fingers through his hair. He wished she had chosen a more opportune time to engage him in a conversation about wall hangings and such. He looked over his shoulder at the other State Troopers. They stood staring at them, talking and laughing, most likely at Will's expense.

"I'm sorry, Pheebs, but I don't have time to waste on —"

"Time to waste? So, I'm a waste of time!"

"Stop putting words in my mouth. You are not a waste of time, but this conversation is."

"Well, I'm sorry if I am wasting your time discussing the appropriateness of your gift."

"See, that's the problem. Why discuss it? The purchase has been made. It can't be returned, and even if it could, I wouldn't allow it."

"You wouldn't allow it? So, now you're telling me what I can and cannot accept from you?"

"In this case, yes."

By this point, her cheeks, previously flushed pink with what Will attributed to embarrassment, now flamed red with what Will knew very well to be anger. The problem was, he was angry, too.

"You are the most infuriating man I have ever met! The size of your ego is astounding! I don't have the right to return a gift, just because you gave it?"

"This has nothing to do with my ego and has everything to do with your pride."

"Pride? I'm not prideful."

"Are you kidding me?" Will laughed. He had spent far too many days suffering her wrath quietly and with humility. A man can only take so much before he reaches his breaking point, and Will had just reached his. He balled his fists at his hips and leaned close to her face. "The problem here, my dear pastor, is that you don't want to swallow your pride and accept something from me, no matter how desperately you want or need it."

"That is the most ridiculous thing I have ever heard."

"Is it ridiculous? Tell me, Phoebe, if that mirror had been given to you by your father, would you have rejected it?"

"That's different. He's my father. You're —"

"What about Jack Simmons?"

Phoebe flinched as if she had been smacked. "What about Jack Simmons?"

"What if it had been a present from Jack and Mary? Or the Speers or Wiggins families? Would you be having this conversation with Emma Speer had you received the mirror from them?"

Will waited momentarily for an answer, but all he received was her eyelashes fluttering rapidly.

"We both know that you would not," he spat.

They stared at one another for several moments. Logically, Will's mind knew he was acting foolishly and that he should get a hold of his anger before he said anything more he would regret, but his heart was in control now, and it was too bruised to back down.

"I don't have to stand here and listen to your nonsense!" Phoebe finally spat back. "I didn't even come here to argue about the stupid mirror!"

"Then why are you here?" He had expected her to storm off, because that was what he was about to do.

She took a jagged breath and looked away from him. "I – I wanted to apologize."

In all the years he had known Phoebe, she had never once apologized to him. Will was stunned to silence.

Phoebe was silent as well, but Will noticed how her lips quivered slightly as they tried to form words.

"Does this mean that you have forgiven me?" His words came out so softly that he wasn't certain that they came from him. He wondered if she could hear his yearning, the aching to finally receive her forgiveness.

She lifted her eyes to his, and he saw something there he didn't quite recognize, a tenderness he'd never seen before. But almost as quickly as it appeared, it was gone.

Phoebe cleared her throat nervously. "You need to understand that I do not, by any means, agree with what happened. I still feel betrayed. But I have decided to not be angry any longer. It is time to move on. So, yes. I forgive you, if you can forgive me for all of the awful things I said to you."

"You mean you don't want me to fall off the nearest cliff?"

She blushed. "No, I don't want you to fall off any cliffs, near or far." The corner of her lip twitched. "I wouldn't mind if you tripped and skinned your knee a little, but no cliffs."

Will laughed. This was the Phoebe he knew and loved. "Well, I suppose I can accept that."

"You certainly deserve that, if not more."

A surge of energy burst through him as they laughed

together. This is why God had brought him to Iron Falls. This is why God had chosen him.

Will smiled. "I'm glad you're not angry with me anymore. I don't know how much longer I could have handled being shunned. It's not a particularly good feeling."

Her face grew solemn. "I'm so sorry, Will."

"Listen Phoebe, this whole thing started off so wrong. I want you to know that I only had your best interests at heart – and still do. I have no doubt that you can handle anything the Upper Peninsula throws at you, but I want you to know that if you need anything – anything at all – that you can come to me for help."

She once more drew in her bottom lip. "Well, there is one thing…"

"Anything," Will insisted.

"I have this new mirror that I need help hanging," she said, smiling coyly.

Will grinned. "I'll stop by later today."

They stood looking at each other, neither saying anything. Then Will saw Phoebe's eyes glance over his shoulder and an attractive pink flushed her cheeks again. Amid the argument, he had forgotten all about the waiting men.

"I'm sorry to have interrupted your duties," she said.

"I'm sorry, Phoebe. I would offer to walk you home, but we were just about to head out for some training exercises."

"That's quite alright. I'm fine walking myself."

Will tipped his hat to her and promised to see her later that afternoon. He turned to walk away.

"Will?"

He turned back. "Yes, Pheebs?"

"I would have forgiven you, eventually, whether you bought me an expensive mirror or not."

Will smiled. "I would have bought you a mirror, whether or not you ever forgave me."

20

EXPOSED

*J*ust as Mary had predicted, attendance at Phoebe's second Sunday was half that of the first Sunday, and even less than that at her third, but she wasn't deterred. In fact, she was much more relaxed in front of the smaller crowd; unlike the first Sunday when most of the service had become a blur, she felt much more focused and at ease behind the pulpit.

It helped having Wendell in the middle of the sanctuary smiling at her throughout the sermon. And though she didn't like to admit it, Will's presence seemed to be a comfort to her as well.

Besides Wendell and Will, all of the women from the greeting committee and their families were there, including Mrs. Smith, who actually gave Phoebe a slight smile and wished her a 'good day' on the way out. No one tried to skip past her at the door. Mrs. Wiggins and her family were the last to leave the little church.

"I really enjoyed your sermon this morning," said the quiet woman. Mr. Wiggins stood next to her, saying nothing and looking straight ahead. Phoebe wondered if he disapproved of her, but she chose to ignore the stern man and instead to focus on his wife's kind words.

"Thank you, Mrs. Wiggins. I'm so glad to hear that."

They left with their three children following close behind. A few parishioners were milling around outside the church involved in various conversations, including Will and Jack Simmons. When Will saw that Phoebe was finished at the door, he excused himself from the conversation and approached her.

"I enjoyed today's service immensely. Your father would be proud. It was like listening to one of his sermons."

An unfamiliar sensation ran up her spine as he hopped up the steps, closing the distance between them. He smiled at her, his blue eyes sparkling against his neatly cropped dark hair that was brushed back from his face.

He added, "But served up in a much prettier package," and gave her a wink, causing another sensation, one she was accustomed to experiencing with Will Caffey.

"Why do you have to do that?" she asked.

"Do what? Compliment you?"

"Give me a compliment that I really appreciate then ruin it by tacking a flirtation on the end."

"You misread me," he said. "Flirtation is for schoolboys. When I compliment you, I mean what I say."

"Thank you for comparing me to my father," Phoebe answered, "but please refrain from addressing my looks when others might hear you. I want to be taken seriously as the pastor of this town."

"I will try my best," Will responded. "But if you look pretty, it will be difficult for me not to think...or say it."

She was ready to argue more, but Will was already bounding down the stairs and untying his horse.

Phoebe was about to go back into the church when she noticed Wendell was now talking with Jack. When she saw that the conversation was at an end, she got his attention and motioned for him to see her.

"You need somethin', Pastor?" the boy asked.

"Yes Wendell, I could use your help inside the church."

He followed her inside.

"Oh, would you do me a favor?" she asked as she walked toward the pulpit. "There are two black books on the back row. Could you bring me the one that says Strong's Concordance, please?"

Phoebe stood at the front of the sanctuary waiting for Wendell to bring her the book. He stood there looking for some time. Finally, he picked one up and brought it to her.

"Here you go, ma'am."

Phoebe took it from him and read the cover. She held the book against her stomach and looked at him kindly. "You can't read, can you Wendell?"

The boy blushed and refused to look her in the eye.

"I can, I just forgot which book you said you wanted," he said, starting back down the aisle toward the back pew. He came back with the other book. "Here you go. Concordance."

She did not take the other book from him. "Don't lie to me."

The young man's face flushed bright red. When he said nothing and refused to look up, she put her hand on his shoulder.

"Wendell, I was just testing my theory. Neither of these books is a concordance."

Wendell shook his head slowly. "I'm sorry Pastor Albright. I'm sorry I lied to you."

"I'm not upset. I just don't know why you felt you couldn't tell me the truth. There's nothing to be ashamed of."

"But I am ashamed. You and Will are about my only friends here in town, and you are both the two smartest people I've ever met. I didn't want you to think I was too stupid to be your friend."

"Oh Wendell! Our friendship isn't based on your ability to read or not. You have been a good friend to me, and I'm sure Officer Caffey would say the same. I didn't ask because I wanted to embarrass you. I asked because I want to help you. If you will allow me, I would like to help you learn to read."

"I'm just too stupid to learn."

"Stupid? That is one word that I would never use to describe you. And I'm sure your supervisors at the mine would agree with me. You are an intelligent, hard-working young man. If you weren't, you wouldn't have been able to fool everyone into thinking you could read all this time. Now, I can't force you, but I would really like to help you learn."

Wendell was quiet. Phoebe waited patiently for him to respond. She was praying that God was working on him in her favor.

"How 'bout I come by Monday after evenin' supper?"

21

THE BOARDING HOUSE

*P*hoebe and Wendell had just sat down for his reading lesson when there was a loud banging on her door. A young man she had never met was on the other side.

"I'm sorry to bother you Pastor, but I was looking for Wendell," the young man exclaimed. He spoke to Wendell. "I need you to come back to the boarding house with me. O'Grady and Fuller are at it again, and they aren't backin' down."

"Sorry Pastor. I gotta go."

Phoebe followed closely behind the two. "What's going on?"

"There's a fight at the boarding house."

"Why doesn't someone call a constable?" she asked.

"Mrs. Smith is afraid they'll get arrested," Wendell answered. "If they get arrested, they'll get fired from the mine. Mr. Speer and the others don't want any trouble, so they don't mess around with anyone that causes problems."

Phoebe remembered her first meeting with Mrs. Smith. She rushed to the wagon with the boys.

"What are you doin', ma'am?" the other boy asked.

"I'm going with you."

"Awe, no," came his reply. "What's a woman going to do to break up a fight? You need to stay outta this."

Phoebe ignored his warning and pulled herself into the seat. "I'm not a woman," she said. "I'm the pastor."

Without a word, Wendell jumped in the back of the rig. Dumbfounded, the driver looked from Phoebe to Wendell, then back to Phoebe. He shook his head in disgust but clicked the reins and hurried the horses.

When they arrived, shouting could be heard before the door to the home was even opened. Wendell ran ahead to open the door. Inside was complete chaos. Around the perimeter of the dining room stood several cheering men, all about Wendell's age. In the middle, near the table, two young men were fighting.

As Phoebe stepped further into the room, she and Mrs. Smith caught sight of one another. The older woman, visibly upset, threw her hands in the air.

"What in the world do ya think yer gonna do?" she yelled.

Phoebe ignored her and pushed her way through the crowd. Some of the men, seeing her, stopped their chanting, though she wasn't certain if it was out of respect for her position or out of just plain shock.

"Gentlemen!" Phoebe shouted to no avail. "Men! BOYS!" She yelled at the top of her lungs, but the boys in the scuffle did not notice her at all. One threw the other into the wall, knocking a picture off and breaking the frame.

Her presence was having no effect on the scuffle and it angered her. She spun around, looking for something to help. Seeing the dining table, she climbed on a chair then on the table. She stood with one foot on the table and one on the back of the chair. Sticking two fingers in her mouth, she whistled a loud, high-pitched whistle while simultaneously kicking the chair into the grappling young men. The shock of the whistle coupled with the flying furniture was enough to separate the two boys.

They stood, breathing heavy, staring at Phoebe who towered above them on the table.

"I – BEG – YOUR – PARDON!" she screeched. "What on earth do you think you are doing?"

Both boys began speaking at once, blaming the other for the scrap. Phoebe shook her head.

"I know I asked, but I don't care. I – DO – NOT – CARE!" she yelled. She looked around the room. "Look at this place." When the boys continued to stare at her, she yelled again, "LOOK AT IT!"

The boys looked around sheepishly.

"Do you see what you've done? How you have wrecked poor, sweet Mrs. Smith's place? Why would you do this to her, the person who has opened her home to you, fed you, taken care of you? And you destroy her personal property because you choose to act like little boys rather than men? Where is your respect?"

The room remained silent, so she continued in a much calmer tone.

"Listen, like you all, I left my family behind to move to Iron Falls. I miss them terribly, but God has given me a new family. The community of Iron Falls is my new family, and it is your new family as well. Mrs. Smith has been so exceedingly kind to me since I arrived here. She reminds me of my grandmother, in some ways. Would you treat your grandmother's home the way you have just treated Mrs. Smith's home?"

She stared the boys down until each answered "No."

"Help me down," she demanded of the two. One boy picked up the chair for her. The other held her hand while she stepped down. The chair was wobbly. She frowned.

"It appears I may have damaged the chair."

"No ma'am," one of the boys said. "That chair's been rickety for weeks."

"Then why haven't one of you fixed it?" The whole room was

silent as she scanned the faces of each of them. "Honestly, boys, I just don't understand. Would you let your grandmother's chair fall apart? Of course, you wouldn't. You would fix it.

"This is your family now – each other, Mrs. Smith, me – all of Iron Falls. And family takes care of family. Every one of you boys – not just these two – needs to take some responsibility around here. When I return here next, I had better find everything in this room righted and repaired. Do I make myself clear?"

"Yes ma'am," various voices murmured throughout the room.

"Very well. Mrs. Smith," she said, addressing the matron who stood in the corner with her mouth wide open. "I will come for tea with you soon and to check on the boys. Good day to you all." She walked toward the door but turned back. "Oh, and in case you were wondering, Jesus had a lot to say about grace and forgiveness. I'll see you boys in church on Sunday. You are all in need of a little refreshing of that knowledge."

Phoebe turned to leave, nearly knocking into a state trooper who was leaning in the doorway. She looked up to find Will Caffey smiling at her. He motioned for her to proceed then followed her out.

Once outside, Phoebe's heart began racing. Now that the heat of the moment had passed, she felt weak in the knees. What had she been thinking, jumping up on that table? What must they all think of her?

Will grabbed the reins of his horse and fell into step beside her. She refused to look at him, knowing the smirk that would be plastered on his face.

"How long were you standing there?" she asked.

"Hmmm – long enough to see you kick a chair at two very surprised boys," he said with a chuckle.

She stopped then and looked at him. "Why didn't you say anything? Weren't you there to break up the fight?"

Will shrugged. "You didn't appear to need any help."

"I'm afraid I've made a fool of myself." She turned and continued walking, picking up her pace a little.

"Quite the contrary, I believe. I think you just earned the respect of about a dozen rambunctious boys."

"How could they respect a pastor that climbs on furniture?"

"I think you frightened them a little," Will chuckled again. "And fear is respect's first cousin. If they are a little scared of you, they will respect you."

Phoebe wasn't convinced, but she appreciated Will saying so, nonetheless.

Will lifted his eyes toward the sky. "It's getting late. Wait here while I check the store for messages, then I'll walk you home."

"I don't need an escort. I know the way well." Phoebe laughed.

"It's getting late."

She rolled her eyes. "I know the way. I shan't get lost."

"It isn't safe. This isn't Lansing. There is wildlife, among other things, here that you should be wary of."

Phoebe remembered her first night in Iron Falls and her close call with such wildlife but refused to let Will win this one. "I don't think I'm going straight home. I thought I might visit the Speer family before calling it a night."

"Then I'll walk you there first," he said over his shoulder. "I won't be but a minute."

"Will Caffey, I don't need you —" but he was inside the store before she could finish her sentence.

It only took a few minutes for Phoebe's anger to begin to boil. It was only a few short days ago that Will had stood with her in front of the constabulary and told her that he had confidence in her, that he believed she could handle anything the Upper Peninsula could throw her way. Yet, here he was now, saying she couldn't take an evening stroll without his supervision! It was ridiculous. She didn't need an escort around town, and she didn't need Will Caffey's permission to walk through it.

She waited another moment or so, wrestling with the decision to either stay and tell Will exactly what she thought, or with just leaving and avoiding the confrontation. She chose the latter. Even though the streets were fairly empty with most folks home having supper, she still didn't wish to have the fray on display for any onlookers.

When would Will Caffey learn that she wasn't a woman to be told what to do?

22

STUBBORN SHORTCUT

*T*he setting sun cut slits of light through the densely wooded copse that separated the main road to the livery from the upper road that led to the Speer homestead. Phoebe had lived in Iron Falls long enough to have explored most parts of this town by now, and she knew that taking the little shortcut through the trees would save her nearly a half an hour of walking than if she stayed to the road. The copse was a little steep, but nothing she couldn't handle, and had already handled several times when visiting the family. And, as Will had pointed out, it was getting late. She would need the shortcut if she were to make it there before it got too dark.

With one hand, she grabbed a fistful of her skirt and lifted it out of the way and with the other she grabbed a hold of the nearest evergreen branch. The trees were massive, but this close to the ground, where little light filtered down through the dense upper branches, the branches were sparse, poor excuses for evergreen boughs. But, empty and spindly, they were perfect handles for climbing steep inclines.

Phoebe had made it about a third of the way up the incline when she heard a noise. She stopped, listening for the sound again, but heard nothing. Deciding she had only heard herself stepping on dry, fallen needles, she continued her ascent, branch by branch, until she heard the sound again. This time it was unmistakable. The noise was not coming from her. The problem was, she wasn't certain where it was coming from. She looked left to right but saw nothing other than that the light was fading much faster than she had expected. Of course, she thought. Inside the woods would darken faster.

An eerie feeling nagged at her stomach and she decided that maybe she should wait until tomorrow to visit the Speers. She turned to follow her steps back down the hill. It was then that she saw Will at the bottom of the incline.

"Why are you following me?" she demanded.

"What do you think you're doing?" Will asked angrily, ignoring her question. He pulled himself up along the same path Phoebe had taken, only at twice the pace she had accomplished it. "It's too late for you to be out here all by yourself. I told you to wait for me outside the store."

Phoebe's pulse quickened. "You told me? You told me! Well, Constable, this may come as quite a shock to you, but I am not a child and you are not my father. You cannot tell me what to do!"

Will stopped halfway up, his face darkening. "When you act like a child, I'll treat you like one. You have no idea what kind of danger you could be facing out here. Come on, Pheebs. I'll walk you back to the parsonage."

Will turned and headed back down the hill. Phoebe stood, mouth agape, amazed at his arrogance.

He reached the bottom and turned back expectantly. "Well?"

"Well, what? I'm not a dog, Will. You can't order me around and expect me to follow your every command."

He sighed. "Phoebe, please come down here."

"No."

"I said please."

"You said it too late."

Will clenched his fists and let out an exasperated groan. "Woman! You are enough to drive a sane man crazy."

"Seems to me you've made that trip all on your own! Now, if you'll excuse me, I'll be on my way. As you have pointed out, it's getting quite late, and you are only delaying me." She turned back toward the upward path, the one she had only moments earlier decided to abandon. But anger and indignation drove her forward without another thought to the darkness or the sound that had unnerved her before.

"Phoebe."

It wasn't what he said but how he said it; he'd spoken her name, but not in a harsh, angry way. No, Will's voice was wary, and it surprised her. She turned back to him.

"What now?"

"Don't move," Will said sternly.

This was more like the Will she'd expected. "Don't tell me what to do," she snapped.

Will raised his gun and pointed it at her.

"Are you serious? I know you aren't going to shoot me."

"I said DON'T MOVE!"

Phoebe placed her fists on her hips and stepped backward. "I'll do whatever I please..." but before she could finish the argument, Will cocked the gun and pulled the trigger. Phoebe screamed as the gun fired and, from seemingly nowhere, something large crashed into the back of her legs, sending her tumbling forward down the hill.

She came to rest at the bottom near the narrow roadway and rolled over to find herself face to face with a very large, and now very dead, gray wolf.

Will ran to her and knelt. "Pheebs, are you alright? Are you hurt?"

She scrambled to her feet, shaking uncontrollably. "You... you shot at me."

"I shot at the wolf."

"But I was in front of it."

"I had a clear enough shot, but it would have been easier if you had listened," he said, grabbing her shoulders and moving her out of his way. "Next time, duck."

Phoebe sucked air. *Duck?* "Excuse me?" *Had he really just said that?*

Will turned his back to her and knelt beside the carcass of the enormous beast. He rubbed his forehead and was silent.

Looking at the wild animal, nearly a match of Will in size, caused a chill down Phoebe's back. The shock was beginning to wear off of Phoebe, and the truth of the situation finally hit her... Will had just saved her life.

"Will, I —"

He stood and threw his hat down on the dirt path. "Darn it, Pheebs. Do you understand what has happened?"

"Yes, of course I do. You've saved my life."

"Your life? I'm not talking about your life. I'm talking about his."

Phoebe looked at the animal. Its long, silvery body stretched out before her. It must have been nearly six feet across. Its mouth lay open, razor sharp teeth still protruding from the lifeless snout. It was terrifying even in death, yet Will was upset over its demise?

"Its life? This dangerous beast? You're worried about its life? What about mine? It would have ended mine had you not come along."

"Exactly. That's why you can't walk around this late by yourself. You could have been killed."

"But I wasn't."

"No, but I had to take his life to save yours," Will said, snatching his hat from the ground. "Do you know how rare wolves are? In fact, before finding him, it was believed that there weren't any left in the Upper Peninsula. And now, I may have possibly killed the last of his kind."

"Well, I'm glad. It isn't safe with beasts like that roaming the woods."

"They roam at night when sensible people are at home."

"So, now I'm not sensible? You aren't being sensible, to mourn the loss of something so vicious."

Will's jaw clenched. A low growl escaped his parted lips as he slammed his hat back on his head. In one quick movement, Will bent and lifted Phoebe. He threw her over his shoulder and turned back toward town.

"Put me down, Will Caffey," she screamed as she beat her fists on his back. "Do you hear me? I said put me down!"

Will said nothing as she continued to scream.

"Put me down, before the entire town sees me!"

"If the entire town sees you, it will be because you are making such a ruckus and drawing them out of their homes."

Phoebe looked from left to right. From her upside-down position, she could see that Will spoke the truth. No one was around. At this hour, everyone would be home with their families.

"This can go one of two ways," Will continued as he walked. "You can scream like a crazy person and alert the entire town to your present predicament, or you can calm down and I will let you walk. What do you say?"

Phoebe gritted her teeth. "I will calm down if you just put me back on my feet."

Will paused, as if trying to judge her sincerity. He finally set her back on the ground.

The minute her feet touched dirt, she lit into him again. "How dare you! You are not my keeper! You can't tell me where or when to walk, and you certainly can't go around treating me like a sack of grain when I don't..." but she didn't have time to finish before she found herself once again unceremoniously thrown over his strong shoulder.

Will had quickened his pace this time and before she could catch her breath, they were in the middle of town.

"Will," she whispered this time, more conscious of the scene they were making. "Will, please put me down."

He continued walking in silence, completely ignoring her quiet pleas. She pounded against his back in vain, but the rock-solid muscles seemed unaffected by her onslaught. She only stopped when she saw them pass by Simmons' store and head up the hill.

"Will, you can't be serious," she whispered. "Take me home, please!" But no matter how much she begged, he wasn't taking her home. He was taking her to the Constabulary.

Will threw open the door of the station. From her position, she couldn't see the occupants of the room, but she heard a boisterous conversation fade to silence as he threw open the jail cell door and dropped her roughly onto one of the cots. He locked the door and threw the keys on the desk where a young officer sat.

"Don't let her out," he barked, then stormed down a hallway and out of sight.

Phoebe's cheeks grew hot as six officers stared at her, mouths agape. They then turned and looked at each other, then back at her. Finally, five of the officers quickly followed Will down the hallway, leaving the desk officer hollering, "Hey! Don't leave me alone with her."

Phoebe bolted from the cot and grabbed the bars of the cell. "Will Caffey! You come back here right now!" she yelled. "Don't you leave me in here!" When no answer came, she screamed and shook the bars.

The poor man at the desk stared wide-eyed at her. She pushed away from the bars and began pacing back and forth in the tiny cell, muttering as many unkind words as she could muster about her captor. She occasionally shouted these insults in the direction of the hallway. After several minutes of this with no response, she decided it was time to try another tactic.

Her eyes flew to the officer at the desk. He still stared at her, but when their eyes met, he quickly found papers that needed organizing in front of him.

"Officer Little, am I correct?"

"Y-yes, ma'am," he said without looking up.

"Officer Little, could you please let me out of here?"

"No, I can't, ma'am."

"Come, now. I've calmed down. And it's getting late. I really should be getting home."

"If I let you out, the Sarge will kill me."

Sergeant. Phoebe knew enough about the force to know that the Sergeant would be the man in charge of this post.

"Well, Officer Little, why don't you introduce me to your Sergeant. Maybe he and I can work this whole thing out."

"Introduce him to ya? Are you feelin' alright, ma'am?"

Phoebe took a deep breath. She was certain that this Sergeant was the key to her release. But how could she convince this man to intercede for her.

"You want to help me, don't you?"

"Well, I —"

"I'll take it from here."

In her earnest attempt to persuade Officer Little to release her, Phoebe hadn't noticed Will return. He stood in the doorway, arms crossed, casually leaning against the jamb as if he hadn't just thrown the town's pastor in prison.

"Give us a few minutes," he said to Officer Little as he stepped into the room. "Then, I'm going to need you to help me recover a wolf carcass."

"A wolf? You kiddin'?"

"No, unfortunately not. Give me a few minutes first, though."

Officer Little left, and with him, her chance at freedom.

Phoebe was so angry she could feel her neck turning red.

He'd locked her up and called her a prisoner! This was entirely unforgivable. For the present moment, however, she knew she needed to play nice. "I'm calm now," she said through gritted teeth.

Will chuckled but said, "Alright. I'll have Rogers take you home."

"I don't need an escort," she said.

Will just shrugged. "You either walk next to Rogers, or you ride on my shoulder. Those are your only two choices."

Phoebe folded her arms. "I choose Rogers."

Will smirked. "I'm disappointed, but not surprised. But, first, you're going to listen to what I have to say."

"And what if I don't want to listen?"

Will chuckled. "Well, my dear Phoebe, you're kind of a captive audience right now, don't you think?"

She was trapped. She crossed her arms and nodded once, signaling her reluctant acquiesce.

Will took a deep breath and crossed his arms as well. "Whether you like it or not, I am here. I am here to protect everyone in this town, including its pastor. And, whether you realize it or not, I do have your best interests at heart. I always have."

As small children, Will always saw to it that Phoebe's 'interests' were taken care of, whether it was making sure she had her turn on the swings on the playground, or seating himself on the floor of the Sunday school room so she could have the last chair. It didn't matter that she would have rather waited a few minutes before swinging to let her lunch settle, or that Phoebe preferred to sit on the floor closer to the teacher. Will always refused to listen. She didn't appreciate it then. And she didn't appreciate it now. "This isn't Lansing, Will. And you can't force me to swing before you do."

He swallowed hard but said nothing. He turned back toward the hallway. "I'll send Rogers in."

"Will?"

He stopped and looked at her over his shoulder. "Yes?"

"You understand how humiliating this is, don't you?"

Will visibly flinched at the word humiliating. "I never intended to humiliate you. I just don't know how to get through to you, Phoebe."

"Just because you know me, just because you feel some sort of responsibility for me, doesn't mean you can treat me like this." She flung her arms wide and looked around the cell, then locked eyes with him. "There isn't a woman in this town, nor in this whole state, that you would have treated the way you treated me tonight."

Will was silent for a moment, then nodded slowly. "You're right, Pheebs, because there isn't another woman in this world that I care about the way that I care about you," he said simply, then turned and left the room.

23

MARQUETTE

"*C*affey?"

Will looked up quickly from his doodling. "Sir?"

"By the looks of that hole you are digging, you don't seem to be with us anymore. Got something else on your mind?"

It wasn't a reprimand, exactly, but by the tone of his voice, Will knew his commanding officer wasn't happy. He looked at his drawing. Captain Reynolds was right. He had ripped a hole completely through the paper he had been doodling on. "No, sir. I've heard every word said. Guess I was just concentrating more on the briefing than on what my pen was doing."

It was the truth, but the raised eyebrow he received from his captain told him that the man did not believe him. Understandable, Will thought, because although he had heard everything being discussed with his mind, his heart was miles away at the moment, with a certain brown-haired pastor.

"Maybe the great Will Caffey has some insight to share," another sergeant, Bob Collins, said with a smirk.

Will dropped his pen and leaned back in his chair, ignoring the caustic attitude of his peer. "Well, I agree that distillers and moonshiners are a big problem in my area, but my gut tells me we have more runners than what the force thinks."

"Runners? In the middle of the U.P.? That doesn't make any sense," Sergeant Collins said. "Why would they waste their time trekking through the snow when they can move more quickly through the water. I'm telling you; we need to focus our efforts along the shoreline."

"That does make more sense," Captain Reynolds agreed.

"I'm not disputing that water is quicker," Will said. "But what do those bootleggers do once things freeze up? They don't take a sabbatical from smuggling, do they?"

Collins laughed. "Nope. Most of them turn to driving on the ice."

"And how do you know that?"

"Because we catch 'em, that's how."

"Exactly my point. You know where to find them once winter hits, and they know it. It just stands to reason that some of those smugglers might find alternate routes to maintain their business."

"And you think Iron Falls is along one of those routes?"

"I don't know, but it could be. There are modern roadways, train stations, places to lodge and eat along the way, but there's less people than along the shoreline. If I were a smuggler bringing alcohol in from Canada and I wanted to avoid the police, it's the route I'd take."

"It's not a bad theory, but not one I'd stake extra troopers on," Sergeant Collins said.

"I'm afraid I have to agree with Collins," said Reynolds. "I can't go moving men around based on a theory. However, I think it's worth keeping an eye on. Report back next month and let us know if you see anything more concrete. Now, speaking of old mining towns, there was another problem up in Calumet..."

Will listened quietly but returned to his doodling. The rest of the briefing would be discussing worker strikes and upris- ings, problems Will didn't need to worry about at his post. The mine at Iron Falls was miner owned now and did not face the same employee discontent that larger, company owned mines faced.

In fact, until recently, Iron Falls had been a piece-of-cake post - the majority of his assignments consisting of handling coyote issues and the occasional moonshine arrest. But things had felt different around the mining town since the Henry Lambecker situation. Will found it unsettling that no arrests had been made, but his hands had been tied, as they hadn't actu- ally caught him using his still.

Then there was the matter of Jimmy Richardson. Will was plagued by the fact that they still hadn't solved that murder. And although he had no doubt there was some sort of connection between the two cases, he hadn't been able to find it.

Thomas Rogers leaned over, interrupting Will's thoughts. "Collins is a jerk. I can't stand big city folks and their smug superiority."

"You forget, I'm from Lansing," Will whispered back.

"You're the exception. You don't treat any of us country boys like we're dumb or below you. Collins lives to degrade anyone he sees as beneath him, which apparently includes you now that you're in Iron Falls."

Sergeant Bob Collins' attitude toward Will had nothing to do with the size of Iron Falls. From his first days in the Upper Peninsula, Collins made it clear that he resented Will. Will had had his pick of posts, including the much larger Marquette post. If he had chosen Marquette, Will would have been Collins' superior officer. But, as the Sergeant of Iron Falls, they were nothing more than peers. However, his choosing Iron Falls changed things for new recruits in the peninsula. New recruits, who would have previously been trained in Marquette, were now funneled through Iron Falls under Will's instruction, per

Colonel Vandercook's orders. Collins took it as an insult. He had a few more months experience than Will in the U.P., but Will was a better marksman, a skill that apparently Vandercook felt important.

"At least the runners are bringing in pure stuff," Rogers continued. "It's those home batchers that are the problem. Lost another three young boys up in Copper County who drank some bad hooch just last week."

Will didn't agree - the bootleggers that had invaded Michigan were an unsavory lot - but he didn't have time to argue because the meeting ended, giving Will something else to look forward to...returning to Phoebe.

He hadn't had a chance to make things right with Phoebe before having to head to Marquette for this meeting, and the way he had treated her weighed heavily on him. Yes, he'd been upset that she had acted foolishly, but his reaction had far less to do with anger than it did with his fear of losing her.

When he'd spotted that wolf on the ridge above her, alert and ready to pounce, Will's entire world threatened to cave in on him. He'd thought of nothing but saving her, of protecting her. He vaguely remembered yelling at her, but not what he'd said. He only remembered the world going silent as he lifted his gun and aimed. The next thing he remembered was kneeling over Phoebe's body, praying desperately to God that she was alright.

But his actions afterward were what was troubling him. Yes, he was angry. But that gave him no right to humiliate her, no matter how much pleasure he had derived from the experience. And it had been a pleasure, indeed, to carry her over his shoulder, if he were being honest.

Nevertheless, his behavior had been wrong, and he knew it. He just hoped that by the time he returned tomorrow, it wasn't too late to tell her so.

PHOEBE WAS ANGRY. But she wasn't angry at Will, at least not anymore. It didn't help that he had humiliated her by treating her like a sack of livestock feed. That had kept her angry for a good twenty-four hours - angrier than she had ever been, and she had been angry plenty of times in her life.

But now, she was angry at herself.

She had acted rashly, setting out that late in the day across the countryside. Truth be told, she had only done so to prove Will wrong. She could see that now. And if it hadn't been for the adrenalin rush that followed Will shooting at her, or at the wolf, really, she may have been able to see her error sooner.

But as loathe as she was to admit it, and she couldn't help but do so once she had calmed down and spent some time in prayer, she knew she deserved everything that Will had said, and did, following the incident with the wolf.

Overhearing the townsfolk talk about the tragedy of losing the wolf, as though it were some sort of silvery mythical creature, made Phoebe cringe inwardly. It was full size. It had probably co-existed with the people of Iron Falls its entire life without anyone the wiser. And had Phoebe not so foolishly crossed into its hunting territory, during a time most sane people would have kept from the woods, it would still be alive. Its death sat squarely on her shoulders.

Blessedly, Will and the other troopers had kept her name out of the incident, for which Phoebe was grateful. They didn't have to do that; she certainly didn't deserve the anonymity.

Nor did Will deserve her animosity. What he deserved was an apology.

The problem was, she couldn't find him to apologize. She spent the morning following the incident trying to appear casual as she strolled the streets of Iron Falls looking for him, but he was nowhere to be found.

'*Any other day, that man is everywhere I turn,*' she'd thought miserably, '*but the one day I want to find him, he's hidden away.*'

She had assumed she would see him before the day was spent, but she didn't see him at all that day, nor the next. She thought she saw him once, but it wasn't Will, just another officer, Frank Little, on patrol.

Come to think of it, although she saw no sight of Will, she realized she had seen Frank Little quite a bit over the last two days. Toward the second evening, when she once again saw Constable Little ride past her parsonage, it suddenly occurred to her that he may have a need. She was the preacher in this little town, after all. Maybe he was uncertain about approaching her, especially after their awkward first meeting during her confinement at the constabulary.

She stepped onto her porch and he immediately looked at her, as if he'd been waiting for her to come out. He rode over to where she stood.

"Is there something I can do for you ma'am?" he asked politely. Frank Little was the newest member of the Constabulary in Iron Falls, and his youth stood out to Phoebe. She thought he looked somewhat like a boy playing dress up in his father's uniform.

"I was about to ask you the same question, Constable Little. I've seen you so many times over the past couple of days that I thought you might need something from me."

"Oh, no ma'am," he answered sincerely. "It's just that with Caffey being called away on State Trooper business, I'm to make sure you're kept safe."

Phoebe frowned. "I didn't realize that Constable Caffey had been called away. Is everything alright?"

"He's safe, if that's what's worryin' ya, ma'am. As far as why he was called away, well, I'm not at liberty to say."

"Oh, of course not," she answered, more than a little embarrassed that her worry had been so evident. She cleared her throat and willed the blush to not creep up her neck. "Thank you for your concern, Constable, but it isn't necessary for you to keep an eye on me. I'm quite capable of taking care of myself. You needn't trouble yourself."

"Oh, it ain't no trouble, Miss Albright. All the troopers do this – look out for each other's girls when we go outta town."

There was no controlling the instantaneous heat that flamed her cheeks. This man thought Will was her beau. If this man, so new to the force, thought this, how many others in town believed the same?

"Well, have a good evenin', ma'am," Frank said, nodding to her and riding off before she had a chance to inform him that she was definitely and absolutely *not* Will Caffey's *girl*.

24

CHARM IS DECEPTIVE

"*W*ait up Pastor!"

Phoebe turned back toward the boarding house she had just left to find Wendell running after her.

"Is something the matter?" she asked when he had caught up with her.

"No ma'am. It's just that the days are shorter now and it will be dark soon. I didn't want you walking home alone."

Phoebe felt her cheeks grow warm as she was reminded of the last time a man warned her of walking alone at dusk. "That's sweet, Wendell, but I wouldn't want to detain you. I was planning to stop by Simmons store to pick up a few items."

"That's perfect!" he responded. "I need a few things myself. I'll go with ya – then I'll walk you home," he said firmly. He smiled easily and returned his focus on the road ahead of them. "I really enjoyed the devotions tonight."

Devotions at the boarding house were one of Phoebe's new responsibilities. After her handling of the ruckus between the boys, and the effect her words had on all the boarders, Mrs. Smith deemed it necessary for Phoebe to conduct a weekly study with her young charges. The last thing Phoebe wanted to do was to spend an entire evening once a week in a room full of single young men, but she did want to expand her ministry in Iron Falls. The look on Mrs. Smith's face that dared her to decline also helped her make the decision to comply. And, she'd reasoned, conducting the Bible study might help grow her little congregation. That, however, had not been the case.

"Thank you, Wendell. Sometimes I wonder if I'm getting through to the other boys. Besides you, Lester and Tommy are the only ones that attend church regularly."

A sheepish grin broke out across his face. "Yeah, I've been bribing them to come," he admitted.

"Bribing?" Phoebe asked in disbelief. "Surely you don't mean that you have been paying Lester and Tommy to attend church!"

"Oh, no ma'am. I've been bribing them with chores. I told them if they went to church with Granny Smith and me, then I would do their chores for that week."

"But Wendell, you shouldn't have to…"

"Whatever gets 'em in the door, Pastor. They gotta be there to hear from God. What was that scripture you preached from last Sunday – somethin' about the word of the Lord falling to Earth?"

"Isaiah 55… *For as the rain cometh down, and the snow from heaven, and returneth not thither…*"

"That's the one. As I see it, God is calling me to bring as many to him as I can, so that they can hear His word preached. They may not act like it now, but God is changing those two – Tommy and Lester. But they gotta be there to hear it, ya know? Even if they aren't excited to be there like I am, that scripture there says that the Bible comes straight from God's mouth, and it ain't gonna just go back to heaven all empty. It's gonna do the work it's meant to do. So, I keep doing their chores and they keep comin' to church. Whatever it takes. Besides, a little extra work ain't never hurt no one," he finished, shrugging his shoulders.

Phoebe looked in awe at the young man walking beside her. Although only a Christian for a matter of weeks, his servant's heart had developed beyond that of any student Phoebe had known in Bible College.

"I just feel like I'm here to make a difference for God," he continued. "I may not be able to use pretty words to preach like you or sing nice like Mrs. Speer, but I know God's got something big for me to do. And somehow I just know it has to do with them two and all the others at the boarding house."

Phoebe was about to agree but was distracted by the sight of two people who stood in front of the store.

"Look – there's Will," Wendell said.

Phoebe was already quite aware of Will's presence. She was also quite aware that he wasn't alone. He stood talking to a woman.

Even from a distance it was apparent that the woman was unabashedly flirting with Will. What Phoebe also noticed was how much Will seemed to be enjoying it. The woman said something, and Will threw his head back and laughed. He said something back to her that made her laugh as well.

Their laughter floated in the air as pleasantly as the sound of a stuck pig pierces a person's eardrums. Phoebe rolled her eyes. Why were men so drawn to such foolishness?

As she and Wendell approached, the woman reached out and rested her hand on Will's chest. Phoebe expected him to move away or brush away her hand, but he did not. Phoebe's stomach lurched.

"You go on ahead, Wendell. I am not feeling well all of a sudden," she said, rushing off toward her home. Wendell called after her, but she didn't slow.

She had only made it about halfway home when the sound of horse hooves came behind her.

"Where are you off to in such a hurry?" Will asked. He jumped down and led his horse by the reins.

'Away from you,' she wanted to yell, but instead muttered "I'm headed home. It's getting dark, you know."

She didn't look at him, but knew he was smirking at her.

"True," was all he said. He continued walking with her in silence.

"Was there something you needed, Officer Caffey?" she asked coolly.

"Why no, Pastor Albright. I just thought I would walk you home, you know, because as an officer of the law, it is my duty to protect the citizens of Iron Falls," he said, bowing ceremoniously. "Wouldn't want you getting attacked by any wolves." He chuckled, but when Phoebe's demeanor did not change, he sighed. "Is that what this is about? Well, I suppose now is as good a time as any... I know I was out of line that night. You scared me terribly, but that's no excuse for how I overreacted. Please forgive me."

"I've already forgiven you." She stopped and faced him. "And it is I who should be apologizing. I acted rashly, foolishly in fact, and in my distress, I treated you harshly. For that, I am sorry."

His eyebrows shot up over his sapphire eyes and he let out a long breath. "The words are an apology, but the tone sure doesn't feel like one. Why do I feel like there's something else going on here?"

Phoebe did not know how to respond. She had searched for him for days in order to apologize, and this is the thanks she received? She turned and walked briskly away.

"I'm sorry. I shouldn't have said that," he said as he caught up and once again fell into step next to her. "I just didn't expect you to apologize. I accept your apology."

"Good."

They continued, side-by-side, in silence.

"Alright Phoebe, what's wrong?"

"Nothing is wrong. Who said anything is wrong?" she said, her voice squeaking.

Will grabbed her elbow and turned her to face him.

"Something is obviously wrong. Listen. Wendell said you were on your way to the store until you saw me. If you had already forgiven me, then why are you in such a hurry to be rid of me?"

"I'm not. I did see you, but you were otherwise engaged in another conversation, so I didn't want to interrupt," she said flippantly.

Will threw his head back and sighed. "I see."

"You see what?"

"We were just talking, Phoebe. Nothing else."

"It's none of my business."

"Would you have me ignore every citizen of Iron Falls who is a single woman?"

"Do you allow every single woman in Iron Falls to touch your chest when they speak to you?"

As soon as she said the words, she wished she could take them back. She sounded like a jealous sweetheart, and that is the last thing she wanted Will to think her.

"I'd allow you to touch me..." he winked.

Phoebe exploded. "You are improper, sir!"

"Calm down," he chuckled. "I was just trying to lighten the conversation. Listen, I'm not sure what you think you saw, but Miss Miller was only asking me about my uniform. She must have touched my jacket at some point – I really don't remember. But that is all there was to it."

'How could a man not remember a woman touching his chest?' she wondered.

"Like I said before," she began, turning back toward her house, "it really is none of my business."

He followed her to the parsonage. She walked up the stairs and turned to face him.

"Your obligation of protection has been met, Officer Caffey.

I'm sure Miss Miller is waiting with bated breath for the handsome constable to return to her."

"Why, Miss Albright, if I didn't know any better, I'd say you were jealous."

"I am," she said, lifting her chin. "I'm jealous of her. She is on the other side of town while here I am, stuck still speaking with you."

Will laughed, infuriating Phoebe. She had meant for that to injure him, not entertain him.

Phoebe looked away, as if something in the distance were far more interesting than her current company.

"You have to admit though... she is very pretty." The softly spoken words were out of her mouth almost before the thought had had time to form in her mind.

"That is certainly true."

Phoebe's blood boiled. He was so aggravating.

"But remember, Phoebe, *'Charm is deceptive, and beauty is fleeting; but a woman who fears the Lord is to be praised.'*"

With that, he mounted his horse, wished her a good evening, and was gone.

25

THE STUFF OF DREAMS

*W*ill poked the fire iron at the spent logs to make room for fresh wood. Dreams of his days in France were becoming fewer and less vivid, but this most recent nightmare had been a doozy, and he had needed something to take his mind off the memories. He'd left the barracks over an hour ago hoping to shake the remnants of the nightmare by finding something to occupy himself. Lighting the fire in the sanctuary's stove was just the distraction he'd needed. Getting a chance to see Phoebe first thing in the morning would be an added bonus.

He heard the large door open and shut, followed by the sound of her boots hurrying down the church aisle toward him.

"Good morning," he said as he turned and straightened to his full height. He wasn't an especially tall man, but he towered over Phoebe's petite frame.

She stared open-mouthed at him for a few moments, then shook her head as if to clear it. "Um, I'm sorry," she stammered. "I didn't recognize you out of uniform.

He couldn't stop his lip-twitch from turning into a full-blown smile. "After all these years of knowing me as just plain old Will Caffey, have you become so comfortable with me as Constable Caffey that you don't recognize me in plain clothes?" He threw another log into the stove and gave her a wink. "I guess you'll have to spend more time with me socially, so you don't forget who I really am."

"What are you doing here, Officer Caffey?" she snapped at him.

The fire cracked and spit behind him, sending more heat into the room, but it suddenly felt much chillier than it had a moment before.

Her arms crossed, feet planted firmly on the oak-plank floorboards, brows furrowed over eyes turned black as the stove behind him. Yes, very chilly.

"It was cold when I rose this morning, so I thought I'd get the fire going before the Speer children arrived for their music lessons."

"And how do you know the Speer children have lessons with me?"

Because I know your every move. Not something that the independent pastor would want to hear.

"I've seen them coming and going every Thursday and heard the piano as I rode by. Didn't take much investigative work."

Her brows sunk even further above her dark eyes. It was the truth, but he suspected that she had already figured out that he kept a pretty close eye on her. How could he not? She made for a pretty subject to observe.

"I'm perfectly capable of starting my own fires, thank you," she spat at him. "The room would have been plenty warm by the time the children arrived."

"I wanted it to be warm for you."

Clenched fists flew straight down to her sides. She looked like a smokestack ready to blow. He wasn't certain what he had done to make her angry, but he sure did enjoy watching the fire ignite in her cheeks. *Gosh, she's beautiful.* "I got the fire going," he snickered, "but it sure has gotten chilly in here in the last few minutes."

"My warmth is none of your concern, neither is my social life!"

When his smile and charm did not melt her attitude, he reached for her shoulder. "Pheebs, what's the matter? What'd I do this time?"

She jerked from his touch. "How dare you suggest we see each other socially!"

"What's wrong with that?"

"Well, Mr. Caffey, it would seem that a man interested in seeing a woman socially wouldn't have called her ugly only the night before."

He didn't know whether to laugh or cry, because for the life of him he could not remember a moment in his life that he didn't think her the most beautiful woman in the world, let alone voice an opinion to the contrary.

"What are you talking about? When did I call you ugly?"

"Surely you remember your assessment of Miss Miller's beauty, then praising me for my fear of the Lord. You might as well have called me a hag who loves Jesus."

Will dropped his eyes, chuckled, and shook his head. He looked at Phoebe again, and, realizing that his reaction had only angered her more, became serious. He reached for her hand. She looked at him wide-eyed and tried to withdraw, but he held it tightly.

"I owe you an apology. In my attempt to pay you a compliment, I've insulted you. In truth, I do admire your commitment to God and your faith in His will for your life. I even admire your stubbornness because it keeps you from listening to others and their doubts. You know your calling and you answer it. To me, your relationship with God is far more beautiful than any outward appearance God could have bestowed on you. Plus, I thought you didn't care for compliments - I assumed you already knew how attractive I find you, but clearly I haven't told you nearly enough."

Will reached out and tucked a loose strand of dark hair behind her ear and she did not pull away. His eyes sought hers as he continued. "I have never, in all my life, come across another woman as beautiful as you. Your hair, the darkest of browns with eyes to match – eyes that beckon me to get lost within them – you are a vision of beauty. You bewitch me, consume my every thought, take my breath away. Honestly, Pheebs," he chuckled, "it is difficult breathing in Iron Falls because your beauty stuns me every single day."

Phoebe stood staring at him, eyes wide and lips parted slightly, as if willing words to come out of them.

What would she do if he kissed her?

Will took a step closer to her and she didn't back up. Her head tilted upward towards his. He had waited so long for this moment —

Just then, the door flew open and in walked the youngest Speer boy.

"Stephen," Phoebe said, quickly stepping backward. "I'm glad to see you're feeling better."

"Yeah, but now my sisters have got the sickness... Ma too. She just asked me to run over here and give you this." He handed her a basket filled with eggs and two mason jars of milk. "Also, I'm to tell you we won't be comin' to practice. I have to take care of the animals today for Ma."

Phoebe stared at the basket. "Oh, I couldn't accept payment if I don't give you and your sisters lessons."

"Ma said you would say that. She told me I was to give it to you anyway." He turned to Will. "Hey Constable. You got any more of those chocolates?"

Phoebe turned and looked at him, recognition settling on her face. He chuckled. "Sorry, buddy. All out. But I've got a friend sending me some more. I'll let you know when I get them."

Stephen nodded and headed back toward the door. "Bye Miss Albright, Constable."

Phoebe stood staring at him. Will wanted desperately to pick up where they had left off before Stephen's arrival, but the moment was lost. However, he wasn't ready to leave either. He gestured to the piano.

"Play with me?"

It was a simple request, but one he knew she would be unable to resist. Phoebe loved music. Like her father, it was a part of who she was.

Quietly, she settled herself onto the bench next to him. "What shall we play?"

"How about a little Bill Bailey. You know it, don't you?"

Phoebe nodded and began to play. She sang, "*Won't you come home, Bill Bailey, won't you come home...*"

Then Will joined her, "*I've moaned the whole night long. I'll do the cookin', honey, I'll pay the rent...*"

They sang the whole ditty together, Phoebe's voice blending perfectly with Will's.

The tune ended and they both laughed.

"My father taught me that song," she said when they had calmed.

"Yep, he taught it to me too."

"He did?"

Will nodded. "He did. When he was teaching me to play the guitar."

"Are you serious? I never knew my father taught you to play the guitar."

"Honestly, Phoebe, how is it that you know so little about me?"

She bit her bottom lip, reminding Will of his plans before Stephen had interrupted.

"Did my mother teach you piano as well?" she asked.

"No," he chuckled. "My mother did." He moved closer to the center of the bench, edging Phoebe over slightly, and began to play.

"I am dreaming Dear of you, day by day. Dreaming when the skies are blue, when they're gray; When the silv'ry moonlight gleams, Still I wander on in dreams, in a land of love, it seems, just with you."

Will turned to her and sang the chorus.

"Let me call you "Sweetheart," I'm in love with you. Let me hear you whisper that you love me too."

Their eyes locked and he let the chorus fade off, unable to continue. She was so close, so real, and he wanted her to know in no uncertain terms just how attracted to her he really was.

Wait on the Lord: be of good courage, and he shall strengthen thine heart.

The Psalm he had memorized as a child rang through his mind. He knew God's will for his life, but he also knew that Phoebe needed time. Time he must be willing to give her.

Will stood before he changed his mind. "Well, I'd best be getting back to the constabulary before the afternoon shift begins."

He absentmindedly stuck his hands in the pockets of his wool coat and felt paper.

"Oh, I nearly forgot. A letter came in the morning post for you. It's from Esther."

Phoebe pounced upon the envelope like a starved feral cat.

She stared at the writing on the envelope. "It says Ward, but it isn't Esther's handwriting."

Fear beat against Will's ribcage. Why was John writing to Phoebe?

Phoebe ripped open the envelope and read the contents quickly. She let out a squeal.

"The baby has arrived! It's a boy, Will. The baby is a boy!"

The worry melted away from Will's chest and was replaced

by a mixture of relief and pure joy. He laughed and whooped loudly, lifting Phoebe into his arms as he swung her around.

"There's more." She pushed away from him, seemingly unfazed by his display. She handed him the letter.

He is so beautiful, Phoebe, and very healthy. I think he looks just like his mother, but Esther insists he looks like me. We have given him the name William James – James, of course, after your father, and William after my best friend and the man who saved my life. Without Will, I wouldn't be here to rejoice over the birth of my son.

"You saved John's life?"

It was asked so quietly, almost reverently, that Will had to look at her to be certain he hadn't imagined it.

Two little lines furrowed between her eyes. "Why didn't I know that?"

Will took a deep breath and shrugged. "It was war. I don't talk about it much."

"But saving a man's life... that's something to be proud of."

"Like you saved Wendell's?"

"How do you know..."

"He told me. He pretty much told the whole town."

She shook her head. "That isn't at all the same thing. What happened with Wendell was God. I was just the vessel He used to accomplish His mission."

"Then it is exactly the same." He reached out and picked up the worn Bible she had left on the pew next to the piano. "This is the same book that guides both of our actions, Pheebs. God has called you to save souls, and he has called me to save people in another way. It's just who we are."

26

YET

"Here's that list of townsfolk you requested."

"Thank you, Roberts." Will read over the names. "Not a very long list."

"Longer than I expected it to be in a town this size."

"And you confirmed that each of these people do in fact own a car? Not just hearsay?"

"Yes, sir. I saw for myself each one."

Will nodded. "Any of them with a bald tire?"

"Lots of them. But none with just one."

Will was disappointed. Another dead end. "Good work. Don't want to go chasing down any trail that isn't necessary."

It had been several weeks since the murder of the Richardson boy, and the case was running cold. The only evidence they had was the tire tracks at the scene, and even that wasn't much of a lead.

His eyes stopped at a name on the list. "Mrs. Smith? At the boarding house? That's interesting. Lots of men who would have access to it."

"That's what I thought as well, but she says it's not been out of the barn in two years, and her story checks out. The driver's seat is covered in dust. No one's driven it in a long time."

Will rubbed his eyes with the heels of his hands. He didn't like the feeling of having a murderer so near. He had too much at stake.

"Where are Little and Moore?"

"Still over at Lambeckers lookin' for clues, though I think it's a waste of time. If there was a connection, we'd have found it by now."

"I don't know. My gut tells me otherwise." Will stood and grabbed his hat off the desk. "There's something we're missing, something or someone that we haven't thought of. I'm going for a walk."

He headed toward the Simmons' store with the goal of purchasing a cold Vernor's to clear his mind. And, if he were to be honest, with the hope of catching a glimpse of a beautiful brunette that may be out calling on members of her congregation.

The one thing he hadn't counted on when taking a post with Phoebe near was the distraction she would cause. Sure, he'd expected the usual distraction her beauty afforded, but Will had spent his entire life being distracted by her nearness. What he hadn't expected was fear. He'd known there'd be dangers in the U.P. and he knew that he had an intense need to protect Phoebe from them, but he had never imagined those dangers would include a murderer on the loose. He couldn't think about the case without thinking about her, wondering what she was doing, and if she were safe. Will had lived through war and the loss of both of his parents. Still, when he thought of what it would mean to lose Phoebe, he realized he had never really experienced fear. Not like this.

He passed Mrs. Smith's boarding house. It would be empty this time of day, but not for long. It was nearly supper time and those boys didn't miss a meal, especially on Tuesday evenings when the pretty pastor joined them for Bible study. Maybe Will should join them tonight, just to check things out. Never hurt for an officer of the law to let his presence be known. It also wouldn't hurt to make his intentions known to them either, he imagined. Not sure how he would do that without getting slugged by Phoebe, though. The thought made his lip twitch. Yep. He might just drop into that Bible study tonight.

As he approached the store, he saw Leta Miller and a group of men talking on the porch. She reached out and swatted one of them on the arm as she threw her blonde hair over her shoulder. Will suppressed a chuckle, remembering Phoebe's strong reaction to the girl. Honestly, he couldn't figure out how Phoebe would ever think he would be interested in a girl like that. But he sure did like the hope that her reaction had given him.

Leta Miller skipped down the steps and turned in the opposite direction of Will. Grateful that he wouldn't have to converse with her, he continued to cross the street. As he neared the store, he could hear the men's conversation.

"Yeah, that Leta is pretty, but she's not as pretty as that oldest Wilson girl. What's her name?"

"Elizabeth? You're crazy. She's got a crooked nose. She ain't pretty at all."

Will's hackles rose. It wasn't just the disrespectful words the men were using. It was the way they spoke. Will had been raised to respect women, all women, and he didn't take kindly to men that didn't.

"I agree with Fred. Leta is prettier, but she's as dumb as a bag of marbles."

Will had heard enough. He unclenched his fists and cleared his throat. But before he could utter a word, Phoebe stormed out of the store.

"What gives you the right to speak about those young women like that – like they are cows at the county fair, and you are the judges?"

When one of them laughed, she whipped around and focused her fury on him. "Did I say something humorous because I find nothing funny about this. Do you realize that those young women you're speaking so rudely about are some other men's future wives? And furthermore, did you ever think that your future wife is out there somewhere right now? And how would you feel if she were getting treated the way you are treating these women? Remember, until such a time as a woman is united in marriage to a man, she belongs to God – she is his special treasure. Is this how you treat God's treasures?"

"No, ma'am," the man responded, clearly chastised by either her words or her petite fury, Will wasn't certain which.

"You are acting like little boys," she exclaimed to all three of them. "Boys treat women like toys to be played with. Men honor women with their thoughts, words, and actions. You all have a choice. Will you be boys, or will you be men?"

She stormed away from the store, nearly crashing into Will as she did so. Her dark eyes locked with his and he saw the indignation shift to embarrassment as a bright blush flooded her cheeks. She pushed away from him and rushed down Commonwealth.

He stood for a moment watching her retreating form, wrestling an internal fight. A fight he knew he was losing. It had been a long time coming, but he was about to offer an apology that should have been given years ago. He followed her down the street.

She rushed through the door of the parsonage and slammed it shut before he could reach her, but he did not let that deter him from his task. He knocked on the door.

It took a moment for her to open it. He could tell that she was trying desperately to breathe normally, her cheeks aflame. *She's embarrassed,* he thought. *And beautiful.* Will cleared his throat.

"I'm sorry," he said.

She blinked at him several times, clearly confused at his apology. "You're sorry? I wasn't chastising you, Will. You had only walked up when—"

"No, you misunderstand me," he said, his eyes earnestly searching hers. "I'm sorry for – for the kiss. All those years ago. I never understood why you've always been so angry about a silly little kiss, but now I understand." His eyes dropped as he ran his fingers through the thick, dark waves atop his head. He took a deep breath and lifted his eyes once more to hers. "You didn't belong to me yet and I had no right. I was young and impetuous, and I shouldn't have done it. I want you to know that I am truly sorry that I failed to give you the respect you deserved."

Several more blinks, then she inhaled slowly, raggedly. "Thank you, Will."

Beautiful, he thought again. He turned to go before he did something foolish that would deserve another apology.

"Will?" she said, interrupting his departure. "You said that I didn't belong to you 'yet.' You understand – I still don't belong to you."

Will smiled, unable to keep his mirth at bay. "Yet." He turned and walked away, satisfied that with that one word, he had brought the flame back to her beautiful face.

27

GOD'S CALLING

"Why Wendell, this is a pleasant surprise," Phoebe said, beckoning the boy to come in.

"I'm sorry to just show up like this, ma'am, but I need your help."

"Of course, Wendell. What is it you need?"

"I need your help writing a letter."

"A letter? But Wendell, you haven't needed my help with letter writing for quite some time now. You've come so far in your lessons, I'm sure your mother..."

"This one isn't for Ma," he interrupted. He looked at Phoebe shyly. "It's for my girl."

"Oh," she said with a small smile. "I didn't realize you had a girl."

"This will explain it to ya," he said, handing her an envelope. "I've done read it, but you should too so you can help me write mine."

Phoebe read the note. It wasn't very long, and it wasn't very kind. Apparently, Wendell's 'girl' had found herself another boy – one that wasn't so 'religious.'

"Oh, Wendell. I'm so very sorry."

"Would you write what I say? I want to make sure it says exactly what's in my heart, and I'm afraid that my writin' isn't good enough yet to get my point across."

"Of course. Have you any stationery?"

Wendell blushed. "I guess I forgot that."

"No worry, I have plenty," she said, rising. She lifted the lid to the trunk that held her books and pulled out a box with her stationery. As she returned to the table, she prayed that God would give her the right words and attitude to help this young man. He was surely hurt and angry, but Phoebe remembered her letter to her father all those weeks ago, and her subsequent guilt over having written it. She wanted to help Wendell to not make the same mistake. She sat down and nodded that she was ready.

"My dear Beth. I have received your letter and I want you to know how hurt and upset I was when I first got it. But I have spent time prayin' to God and he has comforted me. I know it must have been difficult for you while I've been away, and I am glad you have found someone to love. I will be praying for you and him, praying that you two will be happy together, but most of all that you will find God and His call on your life. As much as I loved you, Beth, God loves you so much more and wants what's best for ya'. Please give my regards to your family. God Bless – Dell."

It took all of Phoebe's willpower not to throw down her pencil and hug the boy. Tears brimmed on her lashes as she looked up.

"Wendell, you are gracious far beyond your years or your experiences. You put me to shame with your demonstration of God's love through this letter. How are you able to forgive so quickly – and completely?"

"I don't exactly know," he said, shrugging his shoulders. "When I first got her letter, I was real upset. I questioned God – even doubted him. I didn't understand why - now that I had my life right with him and was doing everything I thought he wanted me to do - why he would let this happen to me. Then, He led me to Isaiah 55, to the two lines right before the ones you and me discussed the other day. You know, the ones about how His thoughts and my thoughts ain't the same, and how His thoughts are higher than mine. I guess that if God controls everything in heaven and on earth, well, then he's got control of my life, too. I can't see what he sees, so I just gotta trust him."

Wendell rose to leave. "Sorry to run, but I need to post this and get home. I've got to get to bed early. Tomorrow's my birthday!" he said with a huge smile.

"It is? Well, Happy Birthday Wendell!" she said excitedly. "What are you doing to celebrate?"

"Will's taking me deer huntin'! He found out I've never been, and since it's season, he said it was the perfect time!"

Phoebe smiled as brightly as possible for Wendell, but the mention of Will's name brought heat to her cheeks. Her interactions with the State Trooper over the past couple of weeks had been, well, confusing. The emotions that man could stir in her, from complete fury, to forgiveness, to something she wasn't able to label yet was something that unsettled her. She preferred when he only evoked frustration because she knew what to do with that emotion.

But this latest string of encounters with Will, whatever it was, only left her confused, and since she did not deal with uncertainty well, she did the only thing she knew to do. She avoided it.

But avoiding the conflicting emotions had meant avoiding Will as well, which was no easy task in a town the size of Iron Falls. To make matters worse, the more she'd tried to avoid him, the harder he'd tried to insert himself into her life. When he'd shown up for Bible study at the boarding house, Phoebe knew she had to put a stop to his relentless pursuit.

After the study, he had offered to walk her home. She'd

accepted, not only because she hadn't wished to be tossed over his shoulder again, but also because the walk would give them the time needed for her to speak with him in relative privacy.

They walked in silence for a short distance and Phoebe struggled with how to begin. To her relief, Will broke the silence.

"Something is bothering you. I can tell."

"You can? How?

"You have a special frown when you are troubled. It's different than your angry frown. When you're angry, you have two little lines between your eyebrows that crease, your jaw tightens, and your brown eyes turn almost black. Your 'something's bothering me' frown is softer – the two lines between your eyebrows aren't so pronounced and your jaw isn't clenched. I prefer your angry frown."

She felt her jaw tighten. "Why on earth would you prefer the angry one?"

"Because I can fix the angry one. I can't be sure that I can fix the troubled one."

"That's because you are usually the cause of the angry frown," she quipped.

"That's true enough," he chuckled.

They walked in silence for another minute until they arrived at the parsonage.

"Well, Pastor Albright, we have arrived at your humble abode and you have yet to tell me what is troubling you," he said as he tied his horse to the post.

Phoebe took a deep breath. She folded her hands in front of her and turned to face him. "I wanted to discuss you – and me."

Will's eyebrows shot up. "Really? Well, my dear, you have my full attention now."

"This needs to stop."

Will stared at her. When she did not continue, he lifted his eyebrows in question. "What needs to stop?"

"This," she said waving between her and Will. "People will begin to talk."

"What?" A look of shock slowly turned to anger. "What are people saying?"

"Nothing yet, I don't suppose."

"And what are you afraid they will say?"

"Well, after your display tonight at the boarding house, I'm sure they will say that you are courting me."

Will's face turned from anger to confusion to mirth. "I suppose I could have let the Bigley boy sit next to you, but I don't like the way he looks at you."

"It's none of your business how he looks at me."

"You like the way the Bigley boy looks at you?"

"No! Of course not, but I don't see how it is any of your concern! After tonight, I'm certain that every boy at Mrs. Smith's thinks you are my intended!"

"What's wrong with people thinking that?" he said, scowling.

"Because – well, because...." she stammered. She really wished she'd had more time to think about her choice of words. "I know God has called me into ministry, and I know that it's not an easy path to choose, especially as a single woman. It was my hope – is still my hope – that God will send me a partner, a man with the same calling. But just because he hasn't chosen that for me yet doesn't mean that I am not called."

"I agree."

His statement startled her, but she continued. "You have been very kind to me, and I would be lying if I said that I wasn't flattered, but you must understand that my calling comes first."

"As it should. I understand that."

"You do?" She hadn't expected this to go so well. "Good. Well, then, you must understand why I must ask you to stop pursuing me."

"Now, that I don't understand."

"Surely you can see that if you continue to – to, well pursue me, others will notice and will begin to think of me as, well, as your girl."

"Yes, I see how that will be perceived."

"And what if a proper preacher gets called to Iron Falls, and if he is single, then he would not consider me a proper candidate for wife, because he will think me taken by you."

Will removed his hat and raked his fingers through his hair. "So, let me get this straight... You don't want to be courted by me because you think that God might send you a preacher husband, here in Iron Falls?"

"Well, yes, I suppose that is what I believe."

"A man like Gregory Parker?"

The angry tone of his voice only added to her indignation. "Not that it is any of your business who I choose! If God has called me to ministry, then I believe he will send me a helpmate to fulfill that calling."

"That's the only thing you've said that makes any sense!" Will said, his voice beginning to rise and the muscles in his jaw flexing angrily.

He sighed and again ran his fingers through his hair. "Seriously, Phoebe, I swear I will never understand you."

Phoebe crossed her arms. "I don't know what you are getting upset about, and I don't see what there is to understand. I am dedicated to God and His calling on my life. Why can't you see that?"

"Oh, I see it. I see it very clearly. It's you who are blind!" He placed his hat on his head. "Why do you keep looking for something that isn't coming?" He stepped off the porch and untied his horse. "It isn't that God hasn't answered your prayers. It's that he has answered in a way you never expected. Look around this town. According to the locals, there's never been more people in attendance in that little church, and more keep coming. The people trust you and rely on your spiritual guidance. You're meeting their needs, inside and out of that little church building. This town doesn't need a new preacher," he said, mounting his horse. "It already has one." And with that, he'd ridden away.

"I nearly forgot!" Wendell said, interrupting her replay of the other evening's events. "Stay here. I'll be right back."

Wendell left the parsonage and returned in minutes lugging a heavy wooden piece of furniture. "Will asked me to bring this to ya. Where would you like it?"

It wasn't until he had set it in the middle of her room that Phoebe recognized it.

She stared in wonder at the beautiful, dark mahogany bookshelf - a far cry from the broken down, moldy piece it had been when her father had thrown it into the brush pile. How many hours must Will have spent working on the piece – sanding and repairing, oiling and finishing?

She wanted it placed under the window, so Wendell moved the empty trunk out of the way and positioned the shelf in its place. Phoebe stood there, running her hand over the carvings along the face of the bookshelf. This was different than buying a mirror. This was a sacrifice of time and labor. And something else – something she didn't deserve.

After Wendell left, she couldn't keep her thoughts from trailing to Will. In the days since their argument, she hadn't seen him at all. She thought he'd just needed a few days to cool off, but a few days had melted into over a week, which had left her feeling an entirely different emotion. Now, with the delivery of this gift, she had the perfect opportunity to make things right.

She donned her coat and hat, for the early November days had grown quite cold. It was nearing nightfall, but not so close that she worried about another run-in with the local wildlife. What she was hoping for, however, was a run-in with a certain Michigan State Trooper.

She glanced up toward the constabulary but knew she couldn't go there. She could weather his anger alone, but she wasn't sure she could do so with an audience. She needed to thank him in private, not in front of a group of fellow officers.

The wind picked up, slicing through her wool overcoat, proving how foolhardy her plan had been. She turned to retrace her steps back down Commonwealth when her thoughts were interrupted by the sound of a car speeding down the road. It came to a halt next to where she stood.

"I didn't dare to hope that I would actually run into you on my way through town," Gregory Parker shouted out the passenger window. "But it seems that fate is on my side this evening."

"Mr. Parker!" Phoebe exclaimed. "What are you doing here?"

"Just passing through on my way to Marquette."

"This late? Surely you won't make it there this evening?"

"I'll do my best. C'mon," he said, leaning over and opening the passenger door. "Hop in. I'll drive you home."

Phoebe hesitated. "That's alright. It's not a long walk."

"Nonsense. It's freezing out there."

She wanted to decline but could see no plausible excuse. She slid into the seat next to the handsome evangelist.

"What church are you holding meetings at this week?" she asked politely.

"Oh, a little town along Lake Superior," he said with a wave of his hand. "Nothing to concern your pretty little head with."

The hair on the back of her neck stood on end. "This 'pretty little head' has more than enough capacity to understand geography, Mr. Parker. I can assure you I am anything but dull. What town?" she asked him crossly.

"Phoebe, by now I would think you would know that I find you anything but dull." His features softened as he gazed at her. "I just meant you would find my work boring."

He leaned closer and the comfort he had in being so familiar with her was a bit unsettling.

"I — I never find God's work boring," she said, shakily.

The corner of his mouth twitched, as if he were enjoying her discomfort. He straightened again and put the car into drive.

Once at the parsonage, he made no move to step out and around the automobile to open her door. She opened it herself, at least grateful that the ride was at an end.

"Thank you, Mr. Parker. I hope you have a successful evangelism meeting."

"Oh, I intend to. If my meetings wrap up early enough this week, maybe I'll swing by for dinner," he said with a wink and sped off.

Phoebe never understood men like Gregory Parker. He was handsome, to be sure, but his manners and ego were enough to send a woman off a cliff. How a man like that could become a successful evangelist, she just couldn't figure out. But, she reasoned, in this world, looks and charm can get you far, even in the church.

She had barely enough time to take her coat and hat off before there was a knock at the door. She opened it, hoping Mr. Parker hadn't returned. But it wasn't the smooth-talking evangelist standing on the other side. It was Will.

"May I come in?" he asked rather gruffly.

"Of course," she answered in shock. After several days with no contact, having Will suddenly in her home - and in a sour mood - caught her off guard.

"What did Parker want with you?"

"Pardon me?" she asked.

"You heard me. What did he want?" Will stood, feet slightly apart, hands behind his back. He appeared completely at ease, yet every muscle was pulled tight, and although his face was void of any emotion, he had an intenseness about him that confused Phoebe. She felt as if he were interrogating her, and she didn't like it.

"I don't see how that is any of your business," she said curtly.

"I believe that it is my business. Why do you refuse to answer the question?"

"Because it is a ridiculous question."

"Ridiculous? How about we continue this conversation at the post with the other state troopers? Maybe you won't find it so ridiculous then."

"Hand me my coat," she said, calling his bluff.

The two stood there, staring one another down. Will's face did not betray any feelings, but Phoebe was sure that hers was red with anger. How dare he intrude in her personal business as if he had a right? And to do so as if on official business! How on earth did he even know...

"Wait one minute...how do you even know that I was with Mr. Parker? Were you spying on me? I've been looking everywhere for you and saw no sign of —"

"You were looking for me?" he asked, his face softening.

Phoebe was caught. "No – no, of course not. I just meant that I was out and about, and I never saw you." As soon as she had said the words, she regretted them. Why was she lying? She despised lying, and to hear it come out of her own mouth was a shock to her system. She tried again. "Listen, Will..."

"Stay away from him," he said, placing his hat on his head and opening the door. Phoebe watched as he slammed it behind him.

The Holy Spirit convicted her so strongly and so swiftly that she ran to the door. The force of it opening so quickly must have shocked him, and he turned to look at her with concern.

"Will, I – I need to tell you something. I – I..." her voice trailed off as he stepped back onto her porch and came to stand very close to her.

"I'm listening," he said, still rather gruffly.

"I wasn't completely honest with you. No, that's not right. I must admit – I lied to you."

Will's eyebrows shot up in surprise, but he said nothing.

"I told you that I wasn't looking for you, and that was a lie. I don't know why I lied. Maybe because you were already so angry with me. I was afraid of what you would say to me if I admitted that I went out tonight with the sole purpose of running into you. Or maybe it was just my own silly pride. I don't know, but my reason doesn't matter. What matters is that I lied, and for that I am sorry."

Will's expression had lost all its hardness and she couldn't stand to gaze into those intense blue eyes any longer. She looked away and searched for something to say that would break the awkward silence.

"Why were you looking for me?" His tender tone sent a wave of shock through her system that made her almost quiver.

"I – I wanted to thank you – for the bookshelf."

"Oh." His expression returned to its emotionless state.

"You don't understand," she tried. "It means so much to me. You have no idea the happiness…"

"So, the bookshelf – that is the only reason you were looking for me?"

"Well, yes, but I…"

"I'm glad you like the bookshelf, Miss Albright," he interrupted, "but if that is all, I need to get back to the post. I'm still on duty."

She hadn't expected her gratitude to make everything better, but she had hoped that things would improve – even if slightly. But it appeared that she had somehow made things worse.

"I'm sorry for having wasted your time," she said quietly.

He said nothing further. He nodded and left her standing there, wondering if she would ever again be friends with Will Caffey.

28

BIRTHDAY SURPRISE

The sun was well past the horizon before Phoebe was finally drawn from sleep. She had spent a fitful night, thanks to her altercation with Will. But, as she stretched her limbs in the unusually bright November morning, she determined that her day would not be controlled by thoughts of that State Trooper. It was Wendell's birthday, and she decided a visit with Mrs. Smith was in order.

"Birthday?" Her ever-present frown deepened slightly. "He didn't say a word to me about it."

"I didn't imagine he would," Phoebe said. "That's why I wanted to stop by. I thought I might bake him a cake."

She nodded. "Well, since you've got nothing better to do, you might as well."

Phoebe ignored the barb. "I could bring it by after the evening supper, if that's agreeable to you?"

"Nonsense. You might as well eat with us. I'll make a roast." Mrs. Smith ran her hands down the front of her apron. "You know, I've grown quite attached to that boy."

"I think we all have," Phoebe said, smiling.

"But I'm not much for celebrations, so it will be just a plain roast dinner. And your cake. Nothing more," she said as she ushered Phoebe out the door.

Phoebe knew full well that a roast dinner was itself a special occasion at the boarding house, despite Mrs. Smith's argument.

"I'm sure he will appreciate whatever you make."

"He won't appreciate nothin' if you don't leave me be and get to baking that cake."

Before Phoebe could respond, a commotion at the constabulary interrupted them. Men – all the state troopers it seemed - were running to the barn for their horses. Jack Simmons came rumbling down the street in his buckboard.

As he passed them, he slowed and hollered. "There's been a collapse – at one of the old mine sites. I'm going to grab all the rope we have at the store," he yelled. He stared hard at Phoebe. "Pastor – it's Will and Wendell."

29

SINKING

*T*he ground around Phoebe began reeling. What had Jack said? Will and Wendell? *But why would they be at an abandoned mine? He must be mistaken.*

She tried to move, but her knees wouldn't allow it. Blackness encircled her vision. But then Mrs. Smith was in her line of vision, shaking her.

"Snap out of it, girl!" the older woman shouted. "There isn't time to lose. We must go now!"

Mrs. Smith drug Phoebe behind her toward a carriage house behind the boarding house and threw open the large doors.

"You – you have a car?" Phoebe asked, still in shock.

"It was my husband's. Don't take it out much. Too much hassle if you ask me. But it will be faster than hitchin' the horses. You know how to crank one of these?"

Phoebe nodded; the car was almost the exact model as her father's. They got the car started and Mrs. Smith sped in the direction the officers had just raced.

Phoebe's mind was a whirl of emotions. What had Jack meant? Were Will and Wendell helping someone in the collapsed mine? Were they injured, or even trapped themselves? What if – if they... she couldn't bear to imagine the other possibilities.

Mrs. Smith stopped at the bottom of a hill just as Jack was pulling up in his rig. They watched him jump out, arms full of heavy rope, and run to the troopers that covered the hill. Phoebe jumped out and followed. She didn't know what she was running toward, but whatever it was, she knew it would lead to Will.

The ground leveled off and Phoebe could see an officer grab the rope from Jack and yell at him to get back.

"I want to help," he yelled back. "They are my friends!"

Phoebe's stomach lurched. His friends – Will and Wendell.

"You can help by keeping those women back," the officer replied, running toward the group of officers. Jack turned around to see who the officer was referring to. When he saw Phoebe, he ran to her.

"Jack!" she said, her voice cracking. "What's going on? Where are they?"

Jack's face looked so grave, she thought she was going to be sick. She had asked the question but was afraid for the answer. She felt the ground spinning again. Jack grabbed her by the shoulders.

"It's a cave-in. A sinkhole over an old mine shaft. This is an old tunnel, not used anymore, so no one noticed the decay."

She was absorbing the information, but the real question still had not been answered.

"But what about Wendell and – and Will..." her voiced cracked.

Jack seemed unable to answer. With one swift motion, Phoebe pushed herself away from him and ran in the direction of the State Troopers. She tried busting through the line of men, but one of them caught her and held her in place. He wasn't a very tall man and Phoebe was able to see over his shoulder. Several yards past the men, lying face down, was Will. The lower part of his body was spread eagle, not moving. She couldn't see most of his upper body. He lay so still.

"Is he – is Will – oh please no, please tell me he's not..." she begged the officer.

Just then, Will moved enough for his head to poke above the surface of the ground.

"GET ME THAT ROPE NOW!" he yelled frantically.

Phoebe's heart soared at the sound of his voice. Relief flooded her body, but the sensation did not last long.

"What's going on? Why doesn't someone give him a rope?"

"Calm down, Pastor. We are trying to figure out a way to do just that, ma'am."

She didn't understand. Why didn't someone just walk it over to him...

Just then, she heard Will grunt and watched in horror as the ground around him moved. It was collapsing slowly.

"Will!" she screamed.

"Phoebe?" he yelled back. "Keep her back! Don't let her near here!"

She was shaking uncontrollably. Never in her entire life had she been so frightened.

She watched as they tried throwing the rope to Will, but they couldn't get it close enough for him to grab it. They tried tying the end into a lasso, but still it fell several feet short.

"I can't get it there," the officer throwing the rope hollered back. "And if I try getting any closer, my weight's gonna cause it to collapse more."

As he spoke, small pieces of turf surrounding Will's prostrate body continued to break away.

The men near Phoebe discussed options, but none of which were feasible. They were running out of ideas.

"Let me do it." The words were out before they had even formed in her mind. "Let me get the rope closer to him."

The entire group of men looked at her incredulously.

"It's the only option you have," she argued. "I weigh far less than any of you. I'm the only reasonable choice."

"I'm sorry, Miss Albright," an older officer answered her, "but we can't risk your life. Besides, if it worked and we saved Caffey's life, he'd kill each one of us for putting you in danger."

The ground heaved again. "HURRY!" Will screamed.

"There isn't any time to argue with me!" Phoebe cried as she threw off her coat. "Tie one rope around my waist and give me another one for Will and Wendell. When I get close enough, I'll throw it to him. If the ground caves beneath me, you can pull me up."

Another officer grabbed a rope. "We haven't a choice, men. Little – come secure this around the pastor's waist."

Frank Little ran to Phoebe and expertly tied a knot unlike any she had ever seen. As she watched him test it - even in the midst of this turmoil - she still wondered at the vast talents of the Michigan State Troopers. Another officer handed her the end of a long rope. She looked at it and handed it to Officer Little.

"Tie a knot at the end – a good one. It will make it easier for them to grip."

The young officer nodded in agreement and secured a sturdy knot at the end of the rope. Phoebe turned toward the hole and prayed.

'Lord, please help me. Help me to save them.'

She walked toward Will slowly, testing each step before placing her entire weight on the foot. She had moved several feet before one of her steps seemed unsteady. She felt the ground move slightly but was still too far to throw the rope to him.

"Please, God, please!" she begged, closing her eyes. "Please help me!"

"Naw, Pheebs, like this," Will said, dropping to the ground on his belly. "Ya gotta keep your whole body flat and crawl with your arms and legs."

Phoebe rolled her eyes as she dropped to the ground. The last thing she wanted to do was get her dress dirty, but mama had said to play with Will outside, so she guessed she had no choice.

"Why do we have to do it like this?"

"Cuz, that's how they do it in the army. Keeps you safe from bullets."

"There ain't no bullets in my momma's garden."

"Maybe not now, but you never know. Besides, you don't know what dangers you'll face out there in the world. Someday you'll be glad I taught ya this," young Will said with a wink.

Her eyes flew open. Phoebe slowly dropped to the ground and lay on her belly. If her weight was distributed evenly across a greater surface area, not concentrated over her feet, maybe she would disturb the ground less and be able to get much closer.

She began moving forward, army crawl style, toward the hole. To her great relief, it appeared to work. Slowly and methodically, she crept across the ground, inch by inch, until she was nearly close enough to reach Will with the rope. She could hear him speaking into the sinkhole.

"Stop talking like that," Will was saying. She couldn't hear Wendell's response. "We are going to get out of this, you just have to trust me."

She was nearly close enough when she felt the sickening feeling of the ground giving way. Everything was sinking around them.

"No, Wendell, no!" Will was begging. "NOOOO!" he screamed one last time.

Phoebe looked up and could see that everything was caving,

beginning around the hole and moving outward. Within seconds, Will would be swallowed. Frantically, she said one last prayer and swung the rope, praying it would reach him. The last thing she saw was the rope hit Will in the back, and then she was being jerked back out of the sinking hole by her waist, crushing her breath away. She felt herself being lifted, she saw Jack's face, and then everything went black.

30

THE SAVED AND THE LOST

*W*hen Phoebe regained consciousness, Jack was there, wrapping her coat around her shoulders.

"Are you alright? Are you hurt?"

"I'm fine. I – I just need to breathe a little."

"Sit," he insisted when she tried to rise. "And button your coat. It's freezing out here."

She did as instructed, even though she wasn't cold – just numb. She shook her head, trying to remember. She remembered crawling, and a rope, and...

"Will! Where is Will? Jack? What's going on?" She looked up at her friend, but he wasn't listening. He was looking intently at the scene unfolding behind Phoebe. She rose and turned. The rope she had carried was hanging over the edge of the now much larger hole.

"Jack!" she yelled, shaking him. "Tell me! Where is Will?"

He turned to her, fear in his eyes. "I don't know, Phoebe. I don't know."

She ran toward the troopers, most of whom were holding the other end of the rope, as if they were involved in some sort of one-sided tug of war competition. Realization finally sunk in.

Will was at the other end of the rope. He was dangling from a rope, but he was alive.

"Miss Albright, we need you to keep back," one officer said sternly as he pushed her away.

She leaned around the officer to watch the rope. They dug their feet in the ground, leaned back and strained to pull it up. She watched intently, and her heart soared when she saw one of Will's hands reach out of the hole and grasp at dirt, but her heart sank just as quickly as the ground around the rope gave way and he fell out of sight again.

"He will hit solid ground eventually, right? The sinkhole can't go on forever, can it?"

"Yes," the officer blocking her said, "if he can hang on that long."

Phoebe gasped. She hadn't thought of that and seeing how the rope had jerked when the ground gave way, losing grip was a very real possibility.

"Shut up, Rogers!" Officer Little yelled at him. "Have a heart when speakin' to her!"

"Sorry, ma'am. I wasn't thinking," the officer named Rogers apologized, but she didn't really hear him. She was mesmerized by the rope – she couldn't look away from it, knowing Will's very life hung from the unseen end of it. She was oblivious to everything and everyone around her. It was just her, the rope, and Will...and God. She fell to her knees before her Lord.

"Please, dear God, please. Don't let him die. We need him – I – I need him. Please God, save him. Please save him!" she sobbed.

"Harder boys!" someone yelled. "Almost there!"

The officers heaved. One officer lay on his belly, another two clasping his ankles. He was stretching toward the hole, reaching for an unseen hand. Then, suddenly, Phoebe saw something. Was she imagining, or could she actually see fingertips? Yes! Yes, it was Will's hand.

She watched without breathing while he grasped for something - anything - to hold tightly to. The officers pulled the rope one last time and in one quick motion, the officer on his belly grabbed Will's hand. The rope was pulled, the officer on his belly was pulled, then, suddenly, Will was above ground and rolling down the incline, away from the sinkhole.

He stood bent over, hands resting on his knees and breathing heavily as the other officers patted him on the back and spoke encouragement. Phoebe watched it all unfold, cemented in place. She didn't know whether to laugh, to cry or to pass out. It was over, and Will was alive.

Will stood upright, still out of breath, and his eyes locked with Phoebe's. Unconsciously, she took a step toward him. Then, he took a step toward her, and suddenly she was running into his arms. She was sobbing uncontrollably, but she didn't care. All that mattered was that he was alive. Will was alive!

He held her, stroking her hair and whispering, "It's ok, Pheebs. I'm ok." His voice soothed her with unbelievable swiftness. Her racing heart slowed, and she was able to breathe more regularly. Her mind began to clear. It was then that she had another horrifying thought.

"Wendell! Will, they need to save Wendell!"

Will took a deep, ragged breath, but said nothing.

"Will! What about Wendell?"

"He fell," Will whispered.

Phoebe's mind could not process what Will was saying. "Then, they must go in after him. Tell them, Will! They will listen to you!"

Will shook his head. His eyes were closed tight - his lips, a thin line.

"Will! They must hurry! Before it's too late!" she shrieked. Tears began to plummet down her face again, her slender body trembling. "Before it's too late!"

"It's already too late!" he cried, his voice cracking. "It's too late. Wendell fell, Phoebe. A long, hard fall. It's too late. He's gone."

His words sliced her heart in half like a dull butcher knife, ripping and shredding along the way. She felt her knees crumple beneath her as the truth of his words finally broke through the foggy barrier of her mind. Will's arm tightened around her as the sobbing overtook her body. As she crumpled into a heap of mourning, Will knelt, wrapping her in his arms, as the tears consumed her completely.

CONSOLING WILL

y late afternoon, they still had been unable to retrieve Wendell's body from the mine. Mr. Speer and Mr. Wiggins had been summoned for their expertise in the matter, as well as some of the more veteran mine workers. There was talk of leaving his body in the shaft until the tunnel could be tested properly, a thought that horrified Phoebe. Blessedly, Mr. Speer and Mr. Wiggins argued emphatically against the idea. They said that he wasn't that far in, and with proper preparation, they could have him out by nightfall.

Several times, different townsfolk encouraged Phoebe to leave, to rest, to eat something, but she turned each person down. It didn't seem right to leave until her friend Wendell had been recovered.

Will was there and appeared to be refusing rest and nourishment as well. Wendell's first two friends would be there until the last, Phoebe realized. She took a deep breath and turned away from the commotion for a moment. It was then that she noticed her – Mrs. Smith. She was still there as well, although Phoebe had forgotten her long ago. She approached the old woman, not certain what to say or do.

Mrs. Smith broke the silence. "I had begun to think that God was no longer angry with me." She looked older, more tired than she had that morning. "I was never sure as to why the Lord was so upset with me that he would punish me by takin' my husband and my two boys..."

"Oh, Mrs. Smith, God doesn't work that way..."

"You say that, but my life says otherwise." Some of the sharp edge returned as she muttered the last, but she continued in the same melancholic tone in which she'd begun. "But I had begun to think that God was happy with me again, that he was sending me – well, another life. That boy – he was somethin' special. Before I realized what was happenin', he had gotten under my skin and grown into my heart. I loved him like he was my own," she stopped when her words caught in her throat. "An' now, the Lord has taken him, too."

Phoebe knew she should say something, but she had no words. She felt like the most miserable excuse for a pastor.

"Well," Mrs. Smith said, "the other boys will be expectin' supper. You think you can catch a ride with Simmons?"

When Phoebe walked back up the incline, Will was standing at the top, watching her.

"You alright?" he asked as she neared.

"No," she answered honestly. "Are you alright?"

"No," he answered, offering his hand to help her to the plateau. It was then that she noticed the fresh bandages wrapped around them.

"Rope burns," he answered simply.

She remembered the sight of the jerking rope. "I was so afraid you would lose your grip."

"I did a couple of times - I never would've been able to hold on for that long, but the rope had a knot at the end that I was able to steady my feet on."

The knot. God's wisdom in the midst of chaos.

They stood in silence, looking at nothing, but just being in

Will's presence comforted her. He had spent most of the time since the accident speaking to other officers who in turn were writing everything he said down in notebooks – reports, Phoebe assumed. But that seemed to have concluded, and he appeared to be as comfortable with their silent companionship as she was.

Phoebe noticed some state troopers coming down from farther up the hill. They had a large branch of some sort on their shoulders. Hanging from the wood was a doe. Phoebe looked at Will.

"It's Wendell's deer. We were tracking it up this hill when the ground..." Will didn't finish his sentence. His eyes followed the two men down the hill.

Phoebe's temper flared. "Why are they bringing it down? Who cares about that silly deer now, after what has happened?"

"Wendell told both Jack and me that he wanted to get a deer today so he could split the meat between you and Mrs. Smith. He said it would help feed you through the winter." Will looked at her. "Jack is insisting on seeing that Wendell's wishes are completed."

"For...for Mrs. Smith? For me?" Was Will saying what she thought he was - that Wendell had died in an effort to keep her alive?

Greater love hath no man...

"No," she uttered weakly. "That can't be."

She shook her head pathetically as the tears began anew, coursing down her cheeks in a torrent of misery. Over-whelming grief ravaged her once again and she felt her knees begin to wobble. "I'm sorry," she cried again and again, her heaving sobs distorting her words. "I'm so sorry."

Will pulled her tight against his chest. "You aren't to blame, Pheebs. How on earth could you think this is your fault? It just happened. It was an accident."

There in Will's arms, she was transported to the past. She

could smell her mother's roses, feel the adult-sized despair of two children. But they were no longer children. And this time, it was Will who comforted her.

"They're coming out with him."

The words of the State Trooper broke through the fog of misery that had overtaken Phoebe.

Will bent his head toward her. "What do you want to do?"

Phoebe took a couple of ragged breaths and pushed away from him. "I want to be there."

"Are you certain?"

"I am his pastor...and his friend. I will be there when they bring him out."

Will nodded and led her down the hill. They walked around the side of the incline to an opening in the hillside that Phoebe hadn't noticed on her way in.

Before long, the shuffling of feet could be heard from within the tunnel and soon the miners were emerging, carrying a stretcher. Will still held her hand, but she made no protest - glad for the strength it gave her.

On that stretcher, under a sheet, was the body of their friend, Wendell Jackson.

Several state troopers relieved the miners of their burden and moved toward the waiting wagon. Everyone present stood in silence as the young man was carried past. As the stretcher moved past her, Phoebe noticed Wendell's limp arm dangling over the side.

"Stop!" she commanded. She did not yell, but she did speak with an authority. Everyone stopped.

Phoebe slowly walked to her dear friend's side, gently lifted his arm back onto his chest, smoothed the sheet back into place, allowing her hand to come to rest on top of his body as she prayed aloud.

"Dear Father in Heaven, we thank you for the short time you gave us with this special young man. Please comfort us as we mourn his passing but remind us that this is not the end – it is only the beginning of eternity. We may cry over our loss, but may we find solace in the fact that Wendell is rejoicing with you in Heaven today. In Jesus name, Amen."

In unison, all present repeated 'Amen.'

She watched as the officers loaded Wendell into the wagon. When they had finished, she turned to the miners.

"Thank you for all you have done today. You'll never know what it means to me that you were willing to sacrifice your time, effort, and quite possibly your own safety in order to retrieve his body."

"He was one of our own, Pastor Albright," Mr. Wiggins responded. The big, quiet man dropped his head and let the tears freely flow, seeming not to care if anyone saw him. "He was one of our own."

PHOEBE STOOD at the bottom of her porch for several minutes after Jack had dropped her off. It had been a long day, lengthened by her stop at the store to send her father a telegram and Mary's subsequent forcing of food and drink before she would let Jack take Phoebe home. Although she felt exhaustion seeping into her bones, she dreaded walking into her tiny home where she would be all alone. She thought of all the things that would greet her – the basket that had held the lunch she'd shared with Wendell and her father at the train station those many months ago, the table where they'd sat together as he had learned to read, her box of stationery with which only yesterday she had helped him compose a letter. Wood he had chopped. Books he had borrowed. A bookshelf he had carried. Wendell had left an imprint all over her life, physically and emotionally.

Phoebe was about to step onto her porch when she heard a sound. She wasn't certain, but she thought it was coming from behind the church. She stepped off the stairs and headed for the flower garden behind the building. As she drew closer, she thought it sounded like – crying?

She walked around the back of the building and there, crouched between the rose bushes, was Will. She ran to him and knelt by his side. He never looked up, but leaned into her, lying his head on her lap.

"I couldn't save him," Will sobbed. "I tried. I tried so hard, but I couldn't. He died. I didn't save him."

"Oh Will," Phoebe uttered, stroking his hair. "You did everything humanly possible. There's nothing more you could have done."

"I'm the one sworn to protect others. Me. But it was him. *He* wanted to protect *me*," he cried.

His wide shoulders quaked with sobs and his face was buried in Phoebe's skirt, so she wasn't sure if she had heard him correctly.

"What do you mean, Will? How did Wendell protect you?"

He shook his head, unable to speak. Phoebe bent over and laid her head on his back. She continued to stroke his hair and pat his back.

"Will, I don't understand…"

"The ground started to cave," he choked out. "We both knew it was giving away completely. He told me that he knew I couldn't save both of us. Even if they got us a rope, I couldn't hold the rope tight enough with only one hand. I tried arguing with him, but he kept saying that his time had come, that he was ready. I told him no, but he wouldn't listen. He said I still had a purpose, a reason to live – that I needed to survive for …" his voice cracked. He tried to finish. "He wouldn't listen to me. He just smiled and said it was time, then he – he – let go. He sacrificed himself so I could live."

Now Phoebe was crying as well, imagining the scene that

had haunted Will all day. She knew the feelings, had been there herself, and Will had been so strong for her.

"It isn't fair, Phoebe. It isn't fair."

"I know," she agreed through her tears. Wendell, in one last act of love, gave up himself so the man he admired so much could live. "It's not fair at all." She paused for just a moment, then took a deep breath and added, "But Will, can you honestly say that if God were to open the heavens right now and allowed you, would you pluck Wendell from paradise? Would you bring him back, just so he can finish the life that we feel was cut short for him here?"

Will shook his head. "Of course not."

"We are crying for ourselves, not for Wendell. He's rejoicing right now. We cry because of the empty hole in our lives left by his absence. But you can't blame yourself or feel guilty about a choice Wendell made."

Will had spoken these same words, in soothing tones, only hours before, back when the whirl of her mind had barely been able to grasp at the truth of them. They were words Phoebe had clung to.

"He did it out of love. Find solace in that, Will. Wendell loved you so much, he was willing to lay his life down for you. And he did love you, Will. I wish you could have seen how his face lit up every time he spoke about you. You were like the big brother he never had."

Will's crying slowed as Phoebe continued to touch his hair. He slowly sat up and looked at her. She reached out and wiped the tears from his cheeks, offering him a weak smile. He did the same to her, and they both chuckled. The full moon illuminated the flower garden and cast a bluish light across Will's face. She smelled red roses, once again, but this time, the grief was abated, replaced by another sensation her senses could not readily identify. Her hand fell from his cheek and rested on his chest. Even through the thick wool coat, she could feel the strength of his chest muscles as they raised and lowered with each ragged breath. She couldn't remember ever having touched him like this and her body trembled. Her eyes lifted and she found him staring at her. Even in the semi-darkness, when their color could not be detected, his eyes pierced her with a staggering intensity. He was so close. She leaned in but hesitated for a moment. She could feel his breath on her face, but he didn't pull away. She was out of her mind, but she wanted to – needed to…

She leaned in again and her lips touched his. It was the gentlest of touches, but it sent a wave of fire through Phoebe as if she had been hit by lightning. Will's hand came up to cup her face as he began kissing her back. Her senses were reeling as his lips moved across hers, activating some inert, instinctual drive deep within her. Her lips moved in unison with his, as if they spoke a common language known only to them.

A coyote howled in the distance and the eerie sound of its cry brought Phoebe back to reality. She quickly pushed away.

"Oh, my goodness. I'm sorry – I – I shouldn't have," she stammered, stumbling to her feet. Tears started coursing down her cheeks. "I'm sorry. I'm – I —…"

Horrified, Phoebe ran off to the parsonage, leaving Will alone in the flower garden.

GOING HOME

"She's going with you?"

Will looked over his shoulder at Phoebe who waited patiently for him at the end of the platform. "I didn't even try to convince her otherwise," he said.

"Would've been a waste of breath. After yesterday, don't think there's a trooper in town that would try arguing that woman out of anything."

"What do you mean?" Will asked, but before Frank could answer, Captain Reynold's walked up. He had arrived in the middle of the night and spent the last several hours interviewing the troopers involved in Will's rescue.

"Take these with you," he said, shoving a thick, sealed envelope into Will's hands.

"Sir?"

"It's my report. When you arrive in Lansing, after you have delivered the boy's body, you are to immediately report to headquarters. Colonel Vandercook is waiting for that report. Then he will tell you what decision they've made."

"Decision?"

"Son, a man has died. On your watch. There had to be an

investigation. I tried to show the facts as clearly as possible, but your fate doesn't rest in my hands. I wish it did."

Will nodded and picked up his haversack. He should have seen this coming.

"Why's she here?" Reynolds asked, flicking his head in Phoebe's direction.

"She's the pastor, sir," Frank intervened. "She's going for the family's sake."

Captain Reynolds' scowl didn't change. His eyes flicked between Will and Phoebe, then settled back on Will. "Report immediately. Do you understand?"

"Yes, sir."

'A man has died. On your watch.'

Captain Reynolds' words echoed repeatedly through Will's mind as he and Phoebe traveled. He couldn't shake them. Nor could he shake the feeling of failure and loss that blanketed him, smothering him.

"Will, where's Wendell?"

Phoebe's small voice broke through his torrent of thoughts, a wave of fresh air to his suffocating soul. He turned to look at her. She sat, head down, twisting her handkerchief in her hands. His heart sank even further. He had been so engrossed in his own thoughts and anguish that he hadn't even considered the turmoil she was experiencing.

"In a special freight car. The train company has a system for transporting..." he trailed off. She didn't need to know all the details. "I made sure his casket was loaded into the car and secured before coming to get you."

She nodded, but the hankie twisting did not diminish. In fact, it seemed to increase in intensity. Without thinking, he reached out and took her hand in his.

As soon as he did, he realized his mistake and braced himself for a rebuke. But there was no rejection, no sharp words. Will leaned back and rested his head against the seat, grateful that, at least for the moment, he could draw strength from her.

After several moments, she finally spoke.

"Will?"

"Yes," he said. He continued staring straight ahead at nothing.

"Will, I need to speak with you."

Her tone was serious, yet she still didn't pull her hand away.

"Go ahead. I'm listening."

"I need to apologize to you. I want you to know how truly sorry I am for wronging you so."

Thoroughly confused, Will turned to face her. "Wrong me? How have you wronged me?"

She looked up at him, her brown eyes pleading. "Please, Will. Don't make me say it out loud."

"I'm sorry Phoebe, but I have no idea what you are talking about."

"I am trying to apologize for what happened last night – behind the church."

For the life of him, he couldn't recall a single thing from the previous evening behind the church that he would label 'wrong.'

"Are you really going to make me say it?" she asked incredulously.

"I'm sorry Pheebs, but I'm afraid you must, because I haven't a clue what you're trying to apologize for," he answered sincerely.

Phoebe looked at her hands as they nervously fumbled with her handkerchief. "I'm talking about the kiss," she said quietly without looking up.

Will was silent for a moment. He had the urge to laugh, but the distress on her beautiful features, coupled with the absolute sincerity of her voice wrapped around his heart in a way no other woman's words or actions ever could.

"Phoebe, why on earth would you need to apologize for that?"

"I shouldn't have done that. I had no right," she insisted. "I don't know why you're confused. It wasn't that long ago that you apologized to me for doing the very same thing."

"That was different," he argued.

"I disagree. It's the same exact situation," she insisted. "If anything, this is worse, because I'm not a child."

"It is completely different. When I kissed you, I didn't have permission. Your heart didn't belong to me. But you – well, my heart – mine is completely yours."

She raised her eyes to his, her perfectly formed lips struggling to form words themselves. He longed to put action behind the words he had just expressed. Instead, he said, "And you have my permission to repeat that kiss whenever you wish."

Flame rose to her cheeks and indignation returned to her voice. "How can you joke about this?"

Because if I don't, I'll kiss you. "It's not a joke to me," he answered, shrugging his shoulders. "Listen, Phoebe, now is probably not the time to discuss such matters, but you have to know how I feel. I haven't exactly been secretive about the affection I have for you."

Phoebe started to protest, but Will put up his hand to stop her.

"You can't tell me that I'm wrong about my feelings. They're my feelings."

Phoebe dropped her head, avoiding eye contact with him.

"Like I said," he continued, settling back into the seat. "Now is not the time. But I don't want you to feel guilty about that kiss. For me, at least, it was a ray of hope in an otherwise very dark day."

That ray of hope continued to blossom as she continued to hold his hand. He knew he was in uniform and shouldn't behave so informally, but the train car was nearly empty, and he was willing to risk his professional reputation for even a few moments longer of her touch. Besides, he had no idea what would happen once they arrived in Lansing, so maybe he didn't need to be concerned about being a Michigan State Trooper for much longer.

With his free hand, he tapped the envelope that held his future against his knee. He didn't know what the report within said, but no matter how scathing, it couldn't compare to the brutal judgment his own mind was unleashing upon him.

"Will," Phoebe whispered. "What's wrong?"

Will breathed deeply. "It's nothing," he answered lamely.

"It's something. You were frowning so severely just now. I know something is wrong. If you can't talk to me, who will you talk to?"

Will took another deep breath. "I was just thinking that I should have been the one to die."

Phoebe gasped. "Oh Will! Don't say such a thing!"

"You don't know what it's like, Phoebe – being called by God to serve and protect others, then to fail at that calling. How would you feel if the tables were turned?"

"I've failed in lots of ways, Will."

"But not with Wendell. You didn't fail him."

"You did everything in your power to save him."

"Did I?" he asked. "Wasn't there something more I could have done?"

"You said yourself that it wasn't anyone's fault. It was an accident."

I said it wasn't your fault, he thought.

But in his heart, he felt responsible for Wendell's death, and the envelope in his hand might just confirm that suspicion.

He fell into a brooding silence, knowing that she too was sensitive about the subject of the hunt. It was ridiculous for Phoebe to feel any sort of responsibility. But Will - that was another matter. It had been his foolhardy idea to go hunting in the first place.

"I'd never seen him happier," Phoebe said, interrupting his thoughts.

"What's that?" he asked.

"I've never seen Wendell happier than when he told me that you were taking him deer hunting for his birthday."

Will blinked. "When did you speak with him?"

"Friday evening – the night before..." her voice trailed off. She cleared her throat and continued. "He had received a horrible letter from home – his girlfriend back in Lansing broke off their relationship and he wanted my help in composing a response."

Will's head flopped miserably back onto his seat. "You've got to be kidding me! How awful!"

"Oh no, Will, it wasn't like that. He wasn't upset. He trusted God, showed the girl immense grace, and then talked cheerfully of his upcoming hunting adventure with you the next day. Will, that trip meant the world to him – you meant the world to him."

With his head still resting on the seat, Will closed his eyes. Wendell had meant the world to him as well, and now he was gone. Will wondered...would he be able to protect Phoebe if the time came?

Phoebe withdrew her hand and reluctantly, Will released his grip. He tried to hide his disappointment, but his disappointment was soon replaced with delight when, after a few minutes, he noticed the slow, steady rhythm of her breath. He was happy she was able to find rest after all they had been through. He was even happier when her slumbering head began lowering toward his shoulder. With a slight adjustment of his position, he was able to angle himself beneath her bobbing head. After a few more bumps of the train, Phoebe's head lay nestled against his shoulder. Will couldn't think of a more delightful way to travel.

MRS. JACKSON

*P*hoebe took Will's offered hand as she exited the train. As she did, she couldn't help but notice how different his face, and his demeanor, appeared. Where he had looked exhausted and defeated most of the trip south, he now looked determined and serious. And she thought she knew why.

Standing on the train station platform, next to Phoebe's father, surrounded by a group of Michigan State Troopers, stood a woman dressed in black. Wendell's mother.

Will walked straight to her and removed his hat.

"I'm so sorry — "

"Thank you so much for coming all this way to bring my son home to me, Constable..."

"Caffey, ma'am. Will Caffey."

Mrs. Jackson's face lit with a huge smile. "Will!" she nearly shouted, "I had hoped it would be you!"

Wendell's mother threw her arms around his neck, nearly toppling him with her embrace.

Phoebe thought she saw a tear slide down Will's face as shock turned to relief.

"Now, let me take a look at ya," Mrs. Jackson said as she

released her grip on him and held him at arm's length. "I can see why my Wendell thought so much of ya – so strong and handsome – what every young boy wishes to become, eh?"

He blushed and Phoebe had to bite her lip to not laugh at the irony of him falling victim to teasing. Had it been any other circumstance, she would have laughed straight in his face.

"Officer Caffey, you will never know how grateful I am for all ya did for my boy. He loved ya like family, that he did."

Will's head dropped. "I loved him too, ma'am."

"You loved him enough to put your life on the line for him, from what I've been told."

Will shook his head. "I did love him that much, Mrs. Jackson, but he saved my life, not the other way around."

Tears poured down the woman's cheeks as she wrapped Will in another embrace. Phoebe couldn't hear what she was saying, her words lost in the puddle she was making on Will's shoulder, but Will nodded in response.

She pulled back once more and turned her puffy, tear-stained face to Phoebe.

"Now, you must be that Pastor. My, my, Miss Albright, you're even prettier than his letters said." She winked. "I could tell which letters dear Will here helped him write, because they were all about you, just like your letters were all about Will."

Phoebe blushed. "I just wrote what Wendell asked me to."

"Oh, I know it. I just meant that based on the letters, I knew he was well loved up there in the U.P."

"That he was, Mrs. Jackson. Very well loved."

The round woman's eyes misted again. "You know, Miss Albright, I've been askin' God as to why he had to move my Wendell so far away from me, then take him away – why I couldn't have him nearer in his last days. But then God showed me that if he hadn't left – hadn't gone north, well, he wouldn't have given his life to the Lord. And because of that, I get to see my boy again someday on the other side of eternity. And for that, I have you to thank, missy!"

Mrs. Jackson grabbed Phoebe in her chubby arms, crying unabashedly. And despite Phoebe's belief that she had cried herself out, she found herself joining the woman.

"It's time, Mrs. Jackson," Reverend Albright interrupted.

The party turned toward the train just in time to see the group of Michigan State Troopers, including Will, walking out of the last boxcar, carrying the casket. Phoebe stood near Wendell's mother, holding the dear woman's hand, as the men transferred Wendell to the waiting hearse.

Phoebe's father spoke quietly to Mrs. Jackson, making arrangements for the funeral, but Phoebe's thoughts were distracted by the officers. They stood talking to Will, who stood very tall, she thought, and very resolute. He reached inside his coat and pulled out the envelope that she had seen him holding on the train. He handed it to one of the officers.

"If that's agreeable with you, Pastor Albright."

The conversation halted and Phoebe turned to find that Mrs. Jackson was talking to her, not her father.

"I'm sorry. What did you say?"

"Mrs. Jackson would like you to give the eulogy," her father said.

"Oh, but I'm not ordained. I couldn't possibly…

Rev. Albright held up his hand. "Just deliver the eulogy. I'll officiate the funeral."

Phoebe hadn't considered the possibility that this would be asked of her, and the thought petrified her. But she couldn't deny this request to honor her friend, so she silently nodded and forced a smile on her face.

"You'll be fine," Will whispered next to her. "It's what Wendell would have wanted."

Phoebe wasn't certain how long Will had been standing there, but she appreciated his encouraging words.

Phoebe's father extended his hand toward Will. "Are you still on duty?" Reverend Albright asked.

A sad smile curled the corner of his mouth. "No, sir. I thought I had to report to headquarters, but they said they'll contact me if they need me."

"Good, because there's a mess of people at my house that will have my head on a platter if I don't bring you by, even if for just a moment."

And a mess it was. The car had no sooner pulled to a stop when Phoebe's mother, followed by her sisters and brother-in-law, poured out of the parsonage, and descended upon them.

Mrs. Albright yanked open the car door and pulled Phoebe into her arms. Before Phoebe had a chance to breathe, Sarah attached herself around her waist, then, whirling her around, Esther pulled her from both and crushed her in a hug.

"I have missed you so much!" Esther whispered in her ear.

Phoebe was trying hard not to cry, so overwhelmed by a feeling of homesickness like she had never known, that she just nodded in agreement against her sister's hair. As she hugged her tighter, she realized she was able to wrap her arms completely around Esther's midsection.

"The baby! Where's my nephew!"

"Over there," Esther pointed.

Phoebe turned to find John slapping Will on the shoulder. Will stood holding a precious little bundle – William James Ward. Will's face was alive again and Phoebe couldn't help but notice what a fine picture he was with an infant in his arms.

"How is it that you get to hold my nephew before I do?" Phoebe teased.

"Because he's my namesake, so naturally, I come first," he teased back, never taking his eyes from the baby.

"Enjoy it while you can, Officer Caffey, because when that boy is old enough to decide for himself, I'll be his favorite visitor from the north."

"We'll see about that, Miss Albright. I intend to spoil this boy until he is rotten to the core."

"Rotten to the core? That's fitting – since his name is William."

Will chuckled at that but appeared too preoccupied with the sleeping newborn to retaliate. "Perfect. He truly is – absolutely perfect," he said in a near whisper.

Phoebe stood next to him and looked down at her nephew. Will was right. Perfect was exactly the right word to describe him. His round, cherubic face, nestled softly against Will's chest, was topped with a full head of sand-colored hair – just like his father's. Long, thick eyelashes rested against his chubby cheeks and fluttered a bit as if he were about to wake. Phoebe held her breath, afraid the angelic sleep was about to be interrupted, but the little guy just took a deep breath and sighed, snuggling deeper into Will's arms. Phoebe reached out and placed her finger into his tiny grasp and her heart fluttered as baby William's chubby little fingers curled around hers.

"Never in my life have I felt such instantaneous love for another human being," she said in awe.

"I know," Will agreed. "I didn't realize I had a hole in my heart until now – now that he's here to fill it."

"Yes! That's what it feels like," she said, smiling at Will. He smiled back and their eyes locked for a moment. A hole – one she never felt before – was filling with a love she couldn't put into words.

Someone in the room cleared his throat and Phoebe realized everyone was watching the two of them.

"As much as I hate to let you go, little man, there's someone else here that would like a turn meeting you." He kissed the baby on the forehead then placed him in Phoebe's arms. "But remember," he whispered, "I'll always be your favorite."

"I know he's a boy," she said, "but he is the prettiest thing I have ever seen!"

John laughed. "Your sister is always saying that!"

"Because it's true!" Esther quipped. "Come, Phoebe. Let's sit in the parlor with him. You must be exhausted, coming all that way in one day."

Phoebe followed the women into the parlor while Will, John and Reverend Albright stayed behind in the entry to talk. She settled onto the settee next to Esther who plied her with questions about her life in Iron Falls. The conversation was upbeat, and Phoebe was grateful that no one brought up the subject of Wendell or the accident. It was good to be with family. She'd needed it so much.

Mrs. Albright shooed Sarah off to bed and went to the kitchen to brew some coffee for the men. As soon as they were alone, Esther moved closer and spoke to Phoebe quietly.

"Enough about all that, I want to know everything about you and Will," she smiled wickedly.

"Me and Will?" Phoebe asked in shock. "There is no 'Me and Will', Esther."

"Come now, you can trust me. I've never betrayed your confidence before. Tell me – has he proposed yet?"

"My goodness, Esther! Of course not! We aren't courting."

"Well, why on earth not?"

"Because I don't have feelings for him – not like that."

Esther frowned at her sister, then looked at her suspiciously. "I find that hard to believe. He's handsome, charming, intelligent, has a great faith in God, and he is obviously insanely in love with you – or hasn't he confessed his love yet?"

"No – well, not in so many words…"

"But he has feelings for you?"

"Yes," Phoebe swallowed hard. "Yes, I believe that he does."

"And yet, you don't return his affections?"

"I – I just don't think he is God's plan for me."

Esther sat back into the cushions, a look of pain on her face.

She was silent for a moment, and when she turned back to Phoebe, the pain was replaced with anger.

"And yet, you still lead him on..."

"Not true!" Phoebe protested. "I have been very clear with Will about my feelings."

"Are you certain, because that display of flirting a moment ago would argue otherwise."

"We weren't flirting! We were – we – it was just teasing."

"Yep. Teasing between two single people...flirting."

"You're being ridiculous. Will Caffey and I have been friends since we were small children."

"Yes, and the majority of that time he has been in love with you."

"How would you know that?"

"I'm married to his best friend, remember?"

Will looked up from his conversation with the men and caught Phoebe looking at him from across the room. He smiled a devilish grin and winked at her.

"Oh yes," Esther whispered in her ear. "You aren't leading him on one bit."

Phoebe dropped her gaze and blushed. She didn't know what to say to her sister. She needed time to think.

"I'm very tired," she said, handing the baby to her sister. "I think I should retire. It's been a long two days."

Esther reached for her hand. "I know it has, and I'm sorry for what you've been through, but I must say this before you go. Will has been through a lot as well, and I can't bear to see him hurt further. If you honestly do not harbor any love for the man, then you need to make it very clear to him so he can move on. It's not fair for you to keep him hanging on like this. He deserves a chance to find someone who will love him with the same devotion and intensity that he – well, that he shows you. If you continue to toy with him and break his heart, well, I just have to say it would take a long time, and an act of God, for me to forgive you, Phoebe Albright."

Phoebe was speechless. Of course, they were sisters, and nothing could destroy that bond, but the anguish in Esther's voice and Phoebe's knowledge of her entire family's love for Will drove the message home. She was grateful when the men interrupted their conversation.

"I hate to rush off, but it has been a long day and I need to get to headquarters and procure a bunk for myself," Will said.

"A bunk? Nonsense," Esther scoffed. "We have plenty of room. You can stay with us."

"I wouldn't want to impose. Besides, I will be spending a lot of time at headquarters anyway. I'm sure they'll need to question me during the investigation."

"Investigation?" Phoebe asked.

All eyes in the room settled on Will.

He nodded slowly. "Yes, into Wendell's death."

"But why? Why would there need to be an investigation?"

"Because there was a death, and a State Trooper was involved."

Phoebe gasped. "You mean – *you* are under investigation?"

"There's nothing to worry about. It's only a formality. I'm sure that once they speak with me and read the reports I brought from the officers on duty, the whole thing will be dismissed."

Reports, Phoebe thought. *That's what had been in the envelope Will had carried.*

"Well, what do the reports say?" Esther asked.

"I don't know. They were sealed. But honestly, I'm sure there's nothing to worry about."

"Too late," Mrs. Albright spoke up. "I'm already worried."

"Now, Mother Albright, I'm sure that everything will be fine," John reassured. "But why don't we spend some time praying over Will. That will do more for our peace of mind than worry ever will."

John pulled Reverend Albright's chair to the middle of the room and had Will sit in it. The family gathered around him, everyone placing their hands on him for prayer. Phoebe, on the settee, placed her hand on his right arm. When all heads were bowed and John began praying, Phoebe felt Will gently place his left hand over hers.

When John finished praying, they both quickly pulled their hands apart. However, the icy stare she received from Esther let her know that Phoebe had not been quick enough.

BABY WILL

*A*lthough Esther had been successful in convincing Will to stay with her and John – by using her adorable son as bait – Will had been correct when he predicted that he would be busy at headquarters. Phoebe had visited her nephew several times and had never run into him.

On her third day home – the day before Wendell's funeral – Phoebe once again stopped by Esther's home, but this time to borrow a dress. Esther had nearly had a heart attack when Phoebe had mentioned wearing one of her deaconess skirts to the funeral. She'd insisted she had an 'absolutely appropriate' dress that wasn't the least bit hideous, as Esther insisted all of Phoebe's 'church attire' was. But when Phoebe arrived, it was John who answered the door, not Esther.

"She went to the mission to help a new girl settle in, so I took the morning off to watch William. She should be back shortly – and she told me to not let you leave before she returns."

"This is where my nephew is...I'm not going anywhere!" Phoebe said, scooping up the cooing baby from the blanket he was resting on. She sat down with him, covering his plump cheeks with kisses.

John laughed and sat in his chair across the room.

"So, Esther tells me you had no idea Will's been in love with you his whole life."

Phoebe jumped as if she had been slapped. She was grateful that William was resting on her lap while she played with him, otherwise he may have been thrown in the air.

"She told – I mean – I, I – I can't believe she told you that!" Phoebe stammered.

"Don't be upset. You're my sister now, too."

Phoebe's gaze dropped to the floor and she blushed brightly. She liked her brother-in-law, but she couldn't help but feel betrayed by Esther.

"How do you even know – I mean, about Will's feelings for me."

"He told me."

"Honestly? You mean, he just matter-of-factly told you he has been in love with me for years?"

"Well, yes, I guess so. But it wasn't as simple as that. We were friends, you know, in the war, and I used to watch him in the trench - when times were quieter - play with this marble. He'd roll it around in his hand, back and forth, and his eyes would get this glassy, far off look. I was curious, so eventually I asked him about it. That's when he started telling me all about you."

"What – what did he say about me?"

"Well, I don't remember everything, and I'm not sure I would tell you everything even if I did, since I don't want to lose his friendship."

"Don't you think he would be upset if he knew you were telling me any of this?"

John chuckled. "You may be right, but I think it's important you hear it. Anyway, he spoke of you often after that, about your smile and your laugh; he said his favorite thing to do when you were young was to get you to laugh in class, then watch you blush when the teacher got after you. He talked about winning your prized aggie from you and how he had never been without it since. He also talked about his first kiss with you."

She could feel heat instantly in her ears and knew she must be blushing the deepest of reds.

"I don't know if I would have had the guts to tell your father like Will did, especially knowing he might lose his respect. Anyway, he spoke often of your father and mother, of the church he grew up in, but mostly, he spoke about you and about how he prayed that if God brought him out of the war, he was going to spend, well, the rest of his life if it took that long, winning your heart.

"I had never felt anything close to that kind of adoration for anyone in my life, so when my injury brought me back to the states, I applied for work at the Lansing State Journal. I don't know why. I had no ties in Lansing, that I knew of at the time. I guess curiosity just got the better of me. I wanted to meet this Reverend Albright that had been so influential in Will's life, see if he was as real as Will said, wanted to meet his charming wife...but most of all, I wanted to meet the woman that owned the heart of my best friend.

"But meeting that woman was nearly my undoing. The minute I saw her, I knew exactly why Will was so in love with her. She captivated me and ruined me all at once. I'm telling you, Phoebe, never in all my life had I felt such despair, because I knew in an instant that the daughter of Reverend Albright was the only woman I would ever love, and it was a wretched feeling since she was also the woman my best friend – and the man who saved my life – loved as well."

Phoebe sat perfectly still, horrified at what she was hearing. Surely, her sister's husband was not saying...

John continued. "For weeks, although I avoided her at all costs out of respect for Will, my thoughts were captivated by that wavy blonde hair and those piercing green eyes..."

"Esther!" Phoebe smiled, relieved. "You thought Esther was me."

"Yes. As far as I knew, there was only one Albright sister of marrying age. Can you imagine my heartbreak?" he chuckled.

"How long was it before you realized your mistake?"

"Months! It wasn't until Will returned for his mother's funeral that I found out the truth."

Phoebe laughed heartily. She had never heard this story.

"So, it may have taken months for me to figure out my folly, but it only took minutes to decide I needed to correct it. Unfortunately, in my earnestness to keep a respectful distance between your sister and myself, I had done a lot of damage to her opinion of me. I found myself in the position of a man who had to work hard to win the love of a woman. But, as you well know, I succeeded in the end."

"I'm so happy that you discovered Esther's true identity. I can't imagine our family without you. I can't imagine you two loving anyone else."

John grew serious. "Yes, we do love each other. And that's what we want for you – and for Will. Phoebe, Esther has told me that she's concerned about your relationship with him."

Phoebe dropped her eyes again. "Yes. She thinks I am stringing Will along, but I tried to explain to her that I have been very clear with Will about my feelings – or lack of feelings, I suppose."

John nodded. "I see. Well, like I tried to tell Esther, Will is a grown man who can make his own choices. But Phoebe, please be careful. Even strong men like Will can have fragile hearts. They can sustain a chip easily and even a crack, but when that kind of heart is broken completely, even the sincerest apology won't be able to repair it."

35

REVELATIONS

*P*hoebe stood between her two sisters as six officers of the Michigan State Constabulary carried Wendell's casket to the open grave. She watched Will, at the head of the casket, and wondered at his quiet strength. All the constables performed the duty with the dignity and respect due any fallen comrade, but no one knew as well as Phoebe how difficult the task must be for Will. This truly was his fallen comrade – his friend, adopted sibling, brother in Christ – that he was laying to rest.

Still, the other officers seemed to take on the task with more earnestness than one would expect. They didn't appear to be merely performing a ceremonial duty for a stranger. There seemed a brotherhood shared with the deceased, a total stranger, yet a member of a fraternal group – not earned by military training or by admittance through initiation – but by his final act of sacrifice to save the life of one of their own. They were honoring Wendell as if he were one of them, as if they now claimed him to be so.

As she watched the faces of the officers, many not much older than Wendell himself, she couldn't help mourning what

261

could have become of the young man. He was so young, so full of promise, yet God had destined that his time in this world was complete. Complete? But what about his mission to win the other young miners for Christ? Or his continuing education now that he could read? There was so much he could have accomplished. What about love?

Sarah shifted her weight and leaned her head against Phoebe's shoulder. How many times had Phoebe thought of Sarah when she'd been with Wendell? He was only slightly older. They would have liked one another, she mused. So much so that she had even hoped that someday, if she could convince Sarah to visit for the summer, maybe the two would...

This last thought of what could have been was too much for Phoebe. She had tried so hard to maintain her composure, and had been successful throughout the funeral, but she could control her emotions no longer. She felt a shudder from deep within, like the vibration of distant thunder within her soul. Her body shook once, then twice – a silent sobbing, before the actual tears appeared. She couldn't control the weeping any more than she could control the shaking that had taken over her body. She was lost in a wave of sorrow and felt as if she would be sucked into the tide had the arms of her brother-in-law not kept her afloat. John held her tight against his side as she sobbed quietly.

"It's alright. You're going to be alright," he said above the top of her head.

Phoebe could hear her father's deep voice somewhere in the distance.

"To everything there is a season, and a time to every purpose under the heaven: A time to be born, and a time to die; a time to plant, and a time to pluck up that which is planted..."

'But why him, Lord? Why now? Didn't he have so much to offer? To others? Wasn't there work left undone for you?'

"Phoebe," came John's voice in answer. "Don't be sad. Wendell is with Jesus. He isn't crying. He is rejoicing."

"A time to weep, and a time to laugh; a time to mourn, and a time to dance..."

"Mourn for your loss, for the emptiness you feel without him," John continued. "But don't mourn for Wendell. He is where we all yearn to be – at the feet of our Savior. And even if you could, you wouldn't take him away from that just to come back to us, would you?"

Hadn't she said nearly the same words to Will?

'But they were so much easier to say than they are to hear, Lord.'

WILL STOOD in formation with the other officers, but his mind was far away, in the Upper Peninsula, fixated over the gaping opening of the sinkhole. Try as he might, he could not stop himself from playing the scene over and over again in his mind. He looked for details, missed opportunities, anything he might have done that might have changed the outcome. He knew it was useless, but he couldn't stop himself. The guilt he felt about Wendell's death hung over him like a shroud.

'Cast your cares on me,' came a voice within Will's spirit.

Will trembled. *'I can't, Lord. I can't forget.'*

'Give me your burden.'

Will closed his eyes. *'I want to. I want to give it to you. But I can't stop thinking about it.'*

It didn't help that Will was also worrying about the meeting with his superiors planned for the upcoming afternoon. They would question him, probably go over every single detail, and make him relive that horrible day. But it couldn't be avoided.

'Lord, please give me strength.'

'The Lord will give strength unto his people; the Lord will bless his people with peace.'

Will took a deep breath, finally laying his burdens at the feet of Jesus. He wasn't certain how, but he would try his hardest to leave them there and to finally let go of the guilt he had been carrying for the past week. Will felt a stirring within him and a renewed spirit rise up in his soul. He opened his eyes hoping for a new peace, but his eyes rested on the sight of Phoebe sobbing in John's arms.

Phoebe. How he longed to comfort her right then. His stomach lurched at the sight of her weeping. She had sought to comfort him – the night of the accident, on the train, and in her prayers, he was certain – but now that she needed him, he was helpless. Well, not completely helpless.

'Dear Father, hold her in your arms. Soothe her spirit. Take her burdens,' Will prayed.

The committal service ended, and Will shook hands and thanked the officers who had served as pallbearers for Wendell.

"Glad to do it, sir. He deserved the honor, considering his sacrifice."

Will nodded and dismissed the junior officers. He turned to look for Phoebe. She was still standing with John's arm around her, although her crying had stopped. Will started for her, but a soft touch on his arm stopped him. He turned and found Esther looking at him sympathetically.

"Leave her be, Will."

"Esther," he said, laying his hand on hers. "I know you're concerned, but I am fully aware of what I am doing."

"Are you?" she asked, eyebrows raised. "And has 'what you are doing' brought Phoebe any closer to loving you?"

Will wanted to answer yes, but he wasn't completely certain that was true. Yes, they had grown closer. Phoebe no longer looked on him with disdain, but did she ever look at him with affection? He couldn't say that was true, no matter how desperately he wished it to be so.

"Even a friend would want to comfort her right now."

"She has John to comfort her. And mother and father. No, Will, if you were honest with yourself you would realize that you want to comfort her for *you* just as much as you want to for her."

Will swallowed hard, watching Phoebe smile weakly at an elderly couple from Lansing First Church as they spoke to her. Esther was right. There was a churning, empty feeling in the pit of his stomach that only Phoebe's touch could fill right now.

"Is that such a bad thing?" he asked, never taking his eyes off Phoebe.

"No, I can't say that it is. But Will, I know how you feel about her. Even if she is too daft to realize it, the rest of the human race can see it all over your face. You are in love with her."

"Completely," he admitted easily.

"Then leave her be."

Will finally turned to look at Esther. Why would she say something like that when he had just admitted his feelings for Phoebe to her?

"I know you don't understand," she answered his unasked question, "but I know my sister. She is very independent and headstrong. If mother and father ever told her she had to do something, she would do everything in her power to do anything but what was expected of her. If, on the other hand, they let her come to her own conclusions, she generally chose the right path – the path they wanted her to take in the first place."

Will considered this. He knew very well how stubborn Phoebe could be. It was something he loved about her.

Esther continued. "If you want Phoebe to love you, you must let her love you on her own terms, in her own time. The more you pursue her, the farther you may end up pushing her away. I genuinely believe that if you back away, she will come to you on her own."

"Back away," he said. "Easier said than done, Esther."

"It's your decision – you back away or she will. It's just the truth of the situation."

Will watched as John escorted Phoebe from the cemetery to her father's waiting car. Maybe Esther was right, he thought, but he sure wasn't looking forward to finding out.

～

IT HAD BEEN A LONG, emotionally exhausting day and Phoebe had decided to go to bed early. She and Will would be leaving out on the first train in the morning, so one last good night's sleep in her bed would do her good. She was about to say so when someone knocked at the front door.

"Who in the world would come knocking at this hour?" Mrs. Albright wondered.

Reverend Albright opened the door and found Will, still in uniform, on the other side.

"I'm sorry to bother you so late, but would it be possible to speak with Phoebe?"

Shocked, she rose from her seat in the parlor and met the two men at the door.

"Could I take her for a walk, sir? I won't keep her long."

Any other man would have received a stiff 'Absolutely not,' from her father, but Phoebe knew her father trusted Will implicitly. He agreed. Will helped her with her coat and opened the door.

They were quite a way down the street and Will had said nothing. Phoebe glanced at him out of the corner of her eye.

"I thought you wanted to talk, Officer Caffey. Words must come out of your mouth if you are to accomplish that," she teased, but when she looked at him in the gleam of the street-light, she realized he wasn't laughing. Will was angry.

"What were you thinking!" he nearly shouted.

She was so caught off guard that she stumbled back a step or two and gasped. "I – I don't know what you are…"

"Are you crazy? I have a mind to shake you right now, woman. I don't think I have ever been so angry in all my life!" He stood, fists clenched. She could see veins popping out on his forehead. She had been shocked at first, but his anger had brought her back to reality and she felt her own ire rising to meet his.

"Excuse me, William Caffey, but I won't be spoken to in this manner. If I have done something to anger you, then you will have to enlighten me. If you want to continue ranting like a lunatic, you can do it alone. I refuse to stand here and be subject to it."

She attempted to walk away, but he grabbed her elbow and swung her back around to face him. He held her firmly, but not painfully.

"I'm talking about that day – the sinkhole. I just came from an afternoon of questioning. I had answers for everything they asked, until they brought up your name. I, looking like a fool, asked why you were even mentioned in the reports. That's when my superiors informed me that it had been you – not another officer – that had risked death to get that rope to me! It was you that crawled across the sinking ground, you that put your life on the line. It took every ounce of self-control I had to not bolt out of that office right that minute to come looking for you. Do you realize you could have died?"

"Of course, I do," she spat back. "Do you realize you would have died had I not acted?"

"I would rather have died than to have you endangered. Do you understand? That's my job – saving you, not the other way around!"

"I couldn't let you die," Phoebe said, her voice cracking. "I – I couldn't bear to…" her voice trailed off.

Will grabbed her other elbow and jerked her close to him. His angry scowl was mere inches from her face.

"I couldn't endure it if I lost you," he said, his voice husky, though still angry.

"Had you died, I would have lost you," she whispered. Without permission, a lone tear fell from the corner of her eye.

Will's eyes grew large at her admission and the hardened lines of his face turned from anger to something else. His breathing slowed, and Phoebe felt her breathing fall into the same, slow rhythm as his. His eyelids lowered to a slit as his eyes skimmed her face, searching for something. They traveled from her eyes to her lips for several moments, then back to her eyes. His breathing became ragged, and he swallowed hard.

"I told myself I would never again kiss you without permission," he said in a low groan.

Phoebe's heart began beating so hard she truly believed that it had crawled into her neck and was throbbing against her throat. As if sensing it there, Will's lips floated over her cheek and down her slender neck, never once actually touching her, only hovering there, caressing her with his breath. He slowly made his way back up, leaving a trail of chills along Phoebe's skin as he did, and returned to lock eyes with her. His lips were so close to hers, but he did not break his promise.

"May I?" he asked, his breath hot against her lips.

Phoebe could feel her blood pulsing through her veins like a river of molten liquid.

"Please," he begged huskily.

"Yes," she answered breathlessly.

In an instant, his lips were on hers, hungrily devouring her. She returned his kiss with the same passion and found her senses reeling in the heady sensation he was stirring within her.

He released her elbows and wrapped his arms around her waist to pull her nearer to him. She slid her arms up around his neck and let her mind spin as Will's lips left hers only to forge a path down her neck where his breath had teased only moments earlier. A small moan escaped her lips and, as if searching for the sound, his lips were on hers again, tasting, teasing, devouring.

Just when Phoebe thought she could take no more of this onslaught without going mad, Will quickly pulled away from her. They stood there, breathing heavily, staring at one another for several moments. Then, without a word, he grabbed her hand and began leading her back to her house. Once there, he stopped outside, not opening the door.

"I'm still angry," he said firmly.

"I know," she answered just as firmly.

"But I'm also grateful," he said, locking eyes with her once again. "I'll never forget what you have done. Never."

And with that, he bounded down the stairs and disappeared into the night, leaving Phoebe trembling in his wake.

36

THE TRIP HOME

"*D*o you think all these rumors about a railroad strike are true?" Reverend Albright asked John.

"Seems they'll turn from rumor to fact any day now. At least, that's how it appears down at the paper. "

The pastor shook his head, his frown deepening. Phoebe watched him rub the back of his neck as they stood on the boarding platform waiting for Will.

"Are you concerned that we'll have difficulty returning to Iron Falls today?" she asked.

"No, dear. I'm concerned you'll be unable to return home for Christmas."

Now it was Phoebe's turn to frown. She had not been able to get home for the holidays last year and was already looking forward to spending this year's Christmas with her entire family – especially baby William.

"Now, no use worrying over something that hasn't happened yet," John said, giving Phoebe's shoulder a squeeze. "And even if they do strike, chances are they'll have it all patched up in time for Christmas. We'll just have to wait and see."

Phoebe agreed. After all, worrying about something she had

no control over was a waste of energy. Besides, she was currently too busy worrying about something else – or more like someone else. Their train was to leave soon, and Will still hadn't arrived. He had been so angry with her last night, she began to worry that he would refuse to travel with her.

Last night. Just the thought of it caused her heart to race and her cheeks to warm. She could still feel his lips on hers, on her cheek, her neck. His mere touch had awakened something in her that she never knew was there - and she longed to feel it again.

"What are you thinking about?" Esther whispered.

Phoebe looked up and found Esther staring at her. Her eyes were so probing, Phoebe felt as if her sister could read her mind. She looked away, avoiding Esther's gaze.

"I see," Esther answered, sitting down next to Phoebe on the bench. Baby William slept peacefully in his mother's arms as she shook her head at her younger sister.

"I don't know why you just don't allow yourself to love him. We both know he would make you happy – or die trying."

"It's not God's will for my life," Phoebe answered her, still averting her eyes. Although she knew it was irrational, she feared that if she were to make eye contact with her sister, Esther would discover exactly what she was blushing about.

Esther let out a long, tired sigh. "Well, if that is truly what you believe, then you need to let him go – completely. It's the right thing to do, Phoebe."

"Are you ready, Pheebs?" Will asked, placing his hand on her shoulder. He had arrived without her noticing and his touch made her jump. She wasn't sure if it was the residual effect from the previous night's rendezvous, or the icy stare she was receiving from her sister, but when he touched her, every hair on her body stood on end. Did he notice, she wondered, how he was affecting her?

Will was not in uniform and Phoebe felt as if his attitude

seemed to reflect his attire – relaxed. The platform became a flurry of hugs and goodbye tears. Phoebe saved her last goodbye for baby William but discovered she would have to fight Will for the honor, who had already taken the baby into his arms.

"Alright, little man; don't grow up too much while we're gone," he whispered as he nuzzled the baby, kissing him on the forehead. He handed little William to Phoebe who also took her turn cuddling the infant.

Their final goodbyes said, Reverend Albright said a quick prayer and the two boarded the train. Unlike their train south, this one was very crowded. Private seating would be difficult to find, and Phoebe wasn't sure if she were relieved or disappointed.

They searched the entire car for two seats together but found none.

"We'll probably have to sit separate," Phoebe said to him, but an elderly woman grabbed Phoebe's hand as she walked by.

"Here dear, you two sit here," she said, rising from her seat and crossing to the opposite side, where a portly man was sleeping across the entire bench. The woman tried to wake him, but his snores barely paused. Phoebe was about to tell the woman that she needn't worry about them when the woman swung her purse and smacked the man right upside the head.

"Oh my!" Phoebe gasped. She heard Will laugh out loud behind her, but her eyes were on the formerly sleeping man, wondering how he would respond to the woman, who, as if oblivious to her own actions, spoke sweetly to him.

"Excuse me, young man, but could you make room for an old woman?"

Still in shock, the man nodded and straightened himself into only one spot, leaving the woman the other. She settled herself in, then looked up at Will and Phoebe, motioning to the now vacant seats.

"Come on, now. Have a seat. We'll be pulling out soon."

They sat down and Phoebe thanked the woman.

"Oh, don't mention it dear. If he were my beau, I wouldn't want to be separated from him, either." She accentuated her remark with a wink at Will.

Phoebe started to protest, but Will spoke first.

"Well, ma'am, I can't imagine your beau would want to be separated from you either," he said, returning the wink.

"Aw, go on wit' ya," the old woman said, waving her hand at him and dropping her gaze.

'Amazing,' Phoebe thought. *'He can even make a granny blush.'*

As the train pulled out of the station, Phoebe let out a small sigh and waved to her family. If the strike rumors were true, it could be a long time before she got to see any of them again.

"It must be very hard for you, every time you have to say goodbye," Will said.

Phoebe nodded. "Yes. I miss them very much. But I'm sure you understand."

Will was pensive for a moment. "Yes, in a way, but it's not the same for me. I love your family like they were my own, and John is my best friend, but – well, my life is in Iron Falls now. Everything I need is there."

Phoebe felt awful. For a moment, she had forgotten that Will was alone now, with no family. But her family was very much his, so of course he would miss them. But he didn't seem sad. She believed him when he said his life was in Iron Falls, and somehow, she knew that to Will, that included her.

"But I have to admit," he continued, "it's much harder this time. That baby back there holds a chunk of my heart in his tiny fist."

"I know," Phoebe agreed. "I miss him already!" They smiled at each other and she found herself lost in the intenseness of those blue eyes. Her heart began thumping uncontrollably, and she looked away, afraid he would be able to read her thoughts.

"I think we should talk," Will said in a hushed tone. "I don't want us to spend the day sitting this closely, wondering what the other is thinking."

She couldn't bring herself to look at him. "I don't know if now is the right time," she argued. "It's so crowded, and others can hear..."

"I'm not concerned about Rip Van Winkle over there, and our new friend doesn't appear to hear what we are saying anyway."

Phoebe looked at the pair across from them. The portly gentleman was indeed already fast asleep, and the elderly woman had busied herself with some crochet work she had brought on the train.

"Besides," Will continued. "I can't go a minute longer without getting this off my chest." He turned in his seat so he could look at her.

"I think I know what you are thinking, Phoebe, so let me speak first. I know you aren't ready for – well, for anything with me, and I can respect that. I have trusted God this long. I can wait a while longer. But if last night did anything, it taught me one thing – I don't have a lot of self-control when it comes to you. You have no idea what you do to me – how you affect me. And I can tell that I have an effect on you."

Even without looking at him, she knew his eyes were on her and that he could see the red creeping across her cheeks.

"Don't try to deny it."

"I wasn't going to," she whispered.

"You weren't? That's a shame."

This was enough to bring her eyes back to his. "What do you mean – a shame?"

"Well, if you denied it, I had half a mind to prove you wrong right here on this train," he answered, the corners of his lips curling into a smirk. Before she could answer, he threw his head back against the seat and groaned.

"There I go again – no self-control. I'm sorry. Let me start again. Until you are ready – completely ready – then we can't keep doing that. I should never have asked to kiss you. It wasn't right, no matter how badly I wanted to. And I do want you Phoebe, but not like this – an occasional stolen kiss here or there, then acting like nothing is going on the rest of the time. I want you, all of you, as my wife, when the time is right – in God's perfect timing, not mine."

"But Will," she argued, "I'm not sure I'll ever be ready."

"You will."

"What makes you so confident?"

"Because my dear Pheebs, you aren't the only one who speaks with God. I trust Him – with my life and with yours."

Phoebe pondered that. It had never occurred to her that Will had been praying about the two of them.

"So, what do you say? Do you think we can turn back time a bit and return to being just friends? Then let things progress naturally, according to God's will?"

"I'd like that," she lied, because already she was experiencing a growing ache in the pit of her stomach over the realization that she would not be kissing Will Caffey again.

37

MEMORIAL

*P*hoebe was praying when she heard a light knock on her door.

"Good morning, dear," Mrs. Speer said kindly when Phoebe opened it. "I know you've had a difficult week and you've only just returned yesterday, so I was just stopping by to see if you were up to giving the sermon this morning."

Phoebe looked at her watch. "I'm sorry. I guess I lost track of time during my morning prayers. I'll be right over."

"You take your time, dear. Thomas and I will greet for you this morning. You just come along when you are ready." Mrs. Speer reached out and squeezed Phoebe's hand before leaving.

Phoebe sat again at her Bible and picked up her notes for the morning's service. It was a solid sermon, she was certain, but her heart just wasn't in it. So much had happened in the past eight days, and she couldn't seem to settle back into her old schedule. Everything felt different. She felt different.

It was several minutes before Phoebe entered the church. Mrs. Speer had already begun to lead the congregation in "How Great Thou Art." It had been the hymn played at Wendell's funeral and Phoebe had to pause in order to control her emotions.

She opened the door, but her way was blocked by a few men. They parted for her to enter, and when they did, Phoebe gasped. From where she stood, she could see that every pew was full, and men were lining the back and sides of the church. There were well over a hundred people in attendance – the most she had ever seen in the tiny building.

Phoebe carefully navigated her way to her chair on the platform. From this vantage point she could see the entire congregation. Mrs. Smith was in her usual spot. Phoebe had feared that without Wendell's bribery, Tommy and Lester would have deserted the boarding house matron this morning. However, to Phoebe's great surprise, not only were those boys sitting next to her, it appeared as if all of the boys from the house were in attendance.

She looked around at all the faces. Some she knew, others were strangers, but all had one thing in common. They carried a sadness with them – it was evident in the furrowed brows, the slumped shoulders. This is why she'd had difficulty concentrating on her sermon, she realized; God didn't intend for her to preach it today. The people weren't there for a normal Sunday morning lesson. They'd come looking for solace, for peace, for understanding. They were here for a memorial service.

Phoebe thought back to how nervous she had been to participate in Wendell's funeral in Lansing, and she only had to share a scripture and say a small prayer before her father's message. That was nerve-racking for her, but for some reason, she felt no anxiety now. Even as she approached the pulpit, completely unprepared for what she was about to do, she was at total peace. Then she realized, as the sun broke through the clouds and a ray of sun shone through those tall glass windows, why she wasn't afraid or concerned in this moment. These were her people, and she was their pastor. And God was in control of this service.

Just as Phoebe was about to speak, the door opened, and a very late and obviously abashed Will entered. Phoebe watched his face as he looked around the room. He looked at her wide-eyed, questioning, but when she smiled at him, realization of what was happening must have set in and a slow, somber smile spread across his face, as well.

Phoebe opened her Bible to John 11 and read aloud the first half of the account of Jesus' resurrection of Lazarus from the dead.

"I feel now, more than ever in my life, I understand the grief that Martha was experiencing. She had just lost her beloved brother and she wanted desperately for Jesus to do something about it." Phoebe looked around the room. "I have felt this way as well. Oh, how I wish I could have Wendell back, even for a few moments, just to let him know what he meant to me. But I don't believe that I am the only one in this room to feel this way. Wendell was a special person that meant a lot to so many people, which is apparent by the number of you who have shown up today to honor him.

"I think it is only fitting that we take a few moments this morning to allow anyone who would like to come forward to say a few words about our friend, Wendell Jackson."

Phoebe sat down, not knowing if anyone would accept the invitation. She didn't have to wonder for long, though, as Russell Weaver, a fellow miner, wasted no time walking to the podium.

"Wendell was the first person to believe in me," the tall miner said, his large hands shaking as he spoke. "I have spent most of my life being told that I would never amount to anything, and I guess, well, I guess I believed it too. But, one night, I came back to the boardin' house from a night of gamblin' and drinkin' – sorry pastor," he said nervously, looking at Phoebe quickly then turning back to the congregation. "I came in all drunk and Wendell was waiting for me. I don't know why, he just was.

Anyway, he says to me, 'Russ, why do you keep doin' this to yourself? Don't you know God has a better plan for ya?' He went on to tell me that I could be a better man. He said that I could be a better husband and a better father than my own pa, and that I didn't have to follow in his footsteps. You could have knocked me over with a feather, 'cause I never told Wendell anything about my pa – and he didn't know anything about Emily and the baby yet. That was God speakin' through him, that's what that was. I knew Wendell had somethin' special, and I wanted it, too. If Wendell had never been my friend, I never would have talked with Pastor Albright and I never would have accepted Jesus, and I never would have made things right with Emily. My life is changed because of Wendell, and I wish I would have told him before..." Russell's voice trailed off. He stood there for a moment, shook his head, left the podium, and sat back down next to his new wife, tears falling down his cheeks.

Russell's speech started a flood of other men's testimonies. One by one, miners of all ages and backgrounds came forward to share stories – some humorous, some heart-wrenching – of how Wendell Jackson had touched their lives. The sharing went on for over an hour, and there wasn't a dry eye in the church.

When the speeches ended, and all hearts appeared to be clear, Phoebe walked to the pulpit again. She looked at her watch and frowned. The sharing had been such a good time of healing for all those hurting, but there was still so much to say. She worried that the congregation would get restless if the service went much longer, but her thoughts were interrupted by a voice in the back.

"Go on, Pastor. You got a message for us that we need to hear. Ain't none of us goin' nowhere."

The voice came from Mr. Wiggins. Big, gruff, usually quiet Mr. Wiggins. Phoebe smiled at the old miner, grateful for his interjection. There wasn't a miner in the room that would complain now that he had given his blessing.

Phoebe opened her Bible once again. "John 11:25… 'Jesus said unto her, I am the resurrection, and the life: he that believeth in me, though he were dead, yet shall he live: And whosoever liveth and believeth in me shall never die.'

"When someone as dearly loved as Wendell is lost, we mourn just like Martha and Mary, and even as Jesus, who mourned the passing of his friend. Like theirs, our hearts are broken, and we weep for the loss of our friend. But God does not intend for us to remain lost in our sadness. In fact, it is out of this deep moment of sorrow that Jesus encourages us with his statement about life after our earthly death. He is the resurrection. He is the life. Through him, we experience eternal life.

"Wendell has been resurrected through Jesus, and, as Paul says in 1 Thessalonians 4:17, we will forever be with the Lord. You too can have the assurance of eternal life – if only you would believe."

As the altars filled that Sunday morning and as Phoebe watched Mrs. Smith's smiling and tear-soaked face praising God, she remembered something Wendell had said to her when he walked her home one evening.

'I just feel like I'm here to make a difference for God," he had said. *"I know God's got something big for me to do. And somehow I just know it has to do with all them at the boarding house.'*

He had been right. God did have a big plan for him, and although Phoebe had spent the majority of the last week asking God why he had cut Wendell's life short, she could now see that Wendell had lived the life God intended. He had accomplished his mission and God had called him home, greeting him at the gate with "Well done, good and faithful servant."

38

THE LETTER

*W*ill had just as many faults as the next man, but reliability was not one of them. Faithful to his promise, Will backed off from pursuing Phoebe. But after a week of just being Will's friend, she was beginning to wish that the man was just a little less constant.

Sure, she saw him just as much as she had before but gone was the intimacy. And despite her best efforts to act like she preferred it this way, she didn't. She missed the way he used to stand near her. She missed the way he used to look at her. She even missed his teasing. But most of all, she missed kissing him.

"Good morning, Pastor."

Phoebe swung around, and quickly dropped the hand that had been absentmindedly tracing her own lips as she thought of Will.

"Mary! What a pleasant surprise."

Mary Simmons stared at her intently. "Are you all right, Phoebe? You are positively flush. You aren't coming down with something, are you?"

"No, no. Of course not."

"You've been through so much lately, the tragedy then the long trip, you've probably overextended yourself."

"Nonsense. I was probably just standing too close to the stove."

Mary continued to frown at her. "I have some chamomile tea that just arrived. I'll bring some down later. Say, after dinner? We can have a late-night chat before you retire."

"That would be lovely." It was useless to argue with Mary, Phoebe had already learned, and the thought of tea with her friend sounded delightful.

"Great. I'll see you then."

"Mary? Was there anything you needed?"

Her friend looked confused for a moment. "Needed?"

"Yes. Did you come here for anything?"

"Oh, dear. I nearly forgot. This letter came for you."

"A letter from home? But I've only just returned from there."

But as she took the letter, she could see that it was not from home. It was from Rev. Berger.

She thanked Mary as she left, then took a seat in the back pew. She'd had no correspondence at all from Rev. Berger since taking the pastorate in Iron Falls and had no idea why he would be writing now.

Dear Miss Albright,

Let me begin with a thank you. I am so very appreciative to you for taking the church in Iron Falls. I had been desperate to fill that pastorate for some time, and at the time, you seemed the perfect solution. I now see the error of my decision.

The story of the tragedy in Iron Falls has made it to my desk. Had I known how dangerous the area to which I was sending you, I never would have considered you, a single woman, for the job. I can't imagine the hardships you have endured. Please accept my apologies.

Fortunately, I have found a replacement for you. Rev. Hudspeth and his wife have ministered in the Upper Peninsula in the past and know the dangers. They need only a couple of weeks to get their affairs in order before they can relieve you of your duties.

I understand that I have not spoken to you personally. It is very well possible that you already have a suitor and a pending marriage that I am unaware of. If this be the case, I would gladly allow you to continue your ministry in Iron Falls.

I await your response as to whether or not there is a pending marriage. Please respond as soon as possible so I may get word to the Hudspeths if need be.

Sincerely,

Rev. Berger

Phoebe's chest began to burn, and she realized she had been holding her breath. Slowly, jaggedly, she inhaled.

A new pastor. A man. A married man, at that - precisely what she'd thought this town needed from the very beginning. So, why did this letter break something deep within her? Why did it hurt so much?

Will's words echoed through her memories. *"This town doesn't need a new preacher. It already has one."*

She dropped her head into her hands and wept.

IT HAD BEEN A TORTUROUS WEEK. Why had he promised to give her space? Hadn't he already learned that keeping his distance from Phoebe Albright was about the loneliest feeling he'd ever experienced? That had been after he had first made himself known to her here in Iron Falls, and it nearly did him in. But this time, he had volunteered. What kind of fool offers to stay clear of the woman he loves?

Will had scarcely finished the thought when, off in the distance, like an apparition of his dreams, Phoebe appeared. Will took this sighting as a sign from God to go to her. To be fair, it wasn't that unusual for him to see her. Iron Falls was a small town, and he was constantly looking for her, even a glimpse in the distance. But no matter. This time, he decided, was from God. He tapped his heels into Tolly's flank and set him into motion.

Phoebe lifted her head when he neared, but he couldn't read her expression. He dismounted and fell into step beside her. She gave him a weak smile but said nothing.

They walked in silence for a bit, but he could tell something was amiss.

"Something is bothering you. I can tell."

"You can? she asked.

"You have a special frown when you're troubled. Remember? I prefer the angry frown – the one I'm more accustomed to seeing."

He laughed, but his attempt at humor fell short with her. He tied Tolly to the hitching post in front of the church and turned back to her. "What's going on, Pheebs?"

Without a word, she produced a letter from her pocket and handed it to him.

Will read the contents, then read them again. "They want to replace you?"

"Yes."

"Unless you marry."

She lifted her eyes to his, a hint of moisture pooling in the corners of her brown eyes.

Will grabbed a hold of her hand and led her into the church. She didn't withdraw her hand, but instead held tightly as he led her up the steps of the church and into the sanctuary.

Will removed his hat, then waited for Phoebe to do the same. He waited until she had laid both her coat and her hat on the back pew then he took both of her hands in his.

"Do you want to leave Iron Falls?"

She shook her head. "No."

"Then there's only one solution."

Will unbuttoned the top two buttons of his uniform and pulled out the necklace hanging around his neck. He unclasped the chain and, holding one end of it in his right hand, lifted it to allow his mother's ring to fall into his left. He knelt on one knee in front of her.

"Phoebe Albright, since I took my first breath on earth, you have been God's plan for me. I have loved you since I was a precocious little boy who had no idea how to show his affections properly, into a foolish teenager who couldn't resist stealing a kiss from you while you were blindfolded. And that affection has only grown deeper in adulthood. I love your spirit, your determination, your love for God and his people."

Her beautiful lips parted, and her hand traveled up to rest on her chest.

Will continued. "I have dreamed of how I would do this so many times, and I wanted it to be so much more romantic than this, but in the end, all that matters is that I love you, and I want to spend the rest of my life with you. Phoebe, will you marry me?"

"No."

It took a moment for him to process what she had said. One word. No. She had said no.

"What do you mean, no?"

"Will, please stand up."

He didn't. He stayed on his knee, shaking his head. "Don't do this, Phoebe. I know you love me. God has a plan for us."

Phoebe nodded. "Yes, He does, Will. But you are not God's plan for me."

A wave of nausea swept over him as he slowly rose. This couldn't be happening. He couldn't have misread God. Not after all this time, all this prayer. "I love you, Phoebe. Don't you believe that?"

"I'm not denying that — "

"You're just denying that you love me?"

"I'm sorry, Will."

"You can't say that you don't love me. I see it in your eyes. I've felt it in your kiss."

"I should never have... I never meant to mislead you. But regardless of the way I have allowed myself to respond to you physically, I could never allow myself to love you."

"And why in the world not?"

"Because you aren't the kind of man I need."

"And what kind of man is that?"

"I've prayed that God would send me someone called to God's purpose. Someone who has answered God's call for their life."

"You don't think I've answered God's call for my life?"

"No, of course you have. But it isn't the same."

"It is," he protested. "God has called me to be exactly who I am, a Michigan State Trooper in love with a woman of God. Don't you see that God created me to be his servant as well? Just because I don't stand behind a pulpit doesn't mean I'm not doing His work!"

"Of course, but it's not the same. I wish you could understand."

Will sighed. "Then explain it to me."

"If he has called me to ministry, then I believe he will send me a helpmate to fulfill that calling."

"Why can't you see that I am that helpmate? Have you lacked for anything since accepting your calling here? Have I stood in your way in the least bit?"

"No." She spoke the single word, barely above a whisper.

"No. Not only that, but I have done everything in my power to support your ministry. Can't you see that?"

"But marriage, to you or any man not in the ministry, would mean I would have to give up my calling."

"Why?"

She was momentarily silenced. He watched her perfectly

shaped lips form words, but none came out. She blinked several times, then said, "A husband would expect me to be in the home, not working outside of the home, especially in a job usually reserved for men."

"Who told you that?"

"I - I don't —"

"Not me. I've never said such foolishness because I've never felt that way. I would never expect you to give up your work because you chose to marry me."

"But what of children? What then? Surely you would expect your wife to be home with the children."

"If children are in God's plan for us."

Will had never thought about that possibility. Hearing his own words was as shocking to him as they had obviously been to Phoebe. She stared at him, eyes wide, her delicate mouth hanging open.

"Listen, Phoebe. Neither of us knows what the future holds. We only know Who holds that future." He reached for her hands, and she didn't pull away. "I love you. Of that I am certain. And I trust God for the rest. Please say that you will, too, and accept my hand in marriage."

"Well, there you are Miss Albright! Did you forget about our afternoon outing?"

Both Will and Phoebe turned to the door where Gregory Parker now stood.

Phoebe quickly pulled her hands from Will's and stepped back from him quickly. As she did, realization dawned on him. She had said that Will wasn't God's plan, and Parker was the reason why.

Something began to stir deep within him, something he was not often the bearer of...anger.

"I didn't realize you had plans," he spat out at her.

Her head whipped back in his direction. "Will, I —"

"Save it. It all makes sense now," he said. "You already said

I'm not part of the plan." He grabbed his hat off the pew and stormed past Gregory Parker.

"Good to see you again, Sarge."

Will skidded to a halt and his hand went to his holster instinctively.

Do you trust Me? a still small voice spoke within him.

Did he? Could he still trust? He had trusted the Lord in every way for every part of his life. But trusting had given him nothing but heartache.

Will tore open the door and bound down the stairs before he did something foolish.

Grabbing Tolly's reins, he hoisted himself into the saddle. Anger was quickly being replaced by numbness, everywhere except for the stinging he felt in his right palm. He looked down at the hand he hadn't realized he had been clenching and uncurled his fingers. The ring lay there, in a deep, purpled imprint of the same size. He slid his mother's ring back onto the chain he wore around his neck and dug his heels into the gelding's flank, wishing to get as far away from Phoebe Albright and his shattered hopes as quickly as possible.

39

GREGORY PARKER

*P*hoebe listened to the sound of Will's horse galloping away, but the echo of his words rang louder than anything she had ever heard.

"Neither of us knows what the future holds. We only know Who holds that future."

She had spent her entire life trying to orchestrate her every move in order to fulfill God's calling. The foolishness of it was so apparent now. Did she think that she was bigger than God? That, somehow, if she took one misstep, she would destroy His plans? God and His plans were so much greater than hers, were they not?

Will had also made something else very clear. He had never stepped in the way of her calling. In fact, he was far more supportive than any of the men she had met at Bible College. How many of them had married educated women from the school, only to resign those women to the status of helpmate rather than ministry partners? In contrast, Will Caffey had at every turn worked to help her accomplish her ministry. How many times had he woken early to get the stove running so the church would be warm by the time she arrived? She couldn't count the times, nor could she count the numerous chores he had done in secret that gave her more freedom and time.

And what had she done in response to his support and kindness? Jilt him at every turn. Accept his aid, but not his love. And he did love her. She knew that with all her heart, because she now realized what true love felt like. It felt like this. She was in love with Will Caffey as much as he was in love with her.

"Now, don't go and cry. Wouldn't want to mar that pretty face by making it all red and puffy."

She quickly swiped at a tear that had silently escaped down her cheek.

"Mr. Parker." Phoebe had completely forgotten that the evangelist was standing there, and seeing his smug face reminded her that he was the reason Will had left. "To my knowledge, we had no plans for this afternoon."

"I know. I just wasn't willing to lose you that easily to that Keystone cop."

Phoebe gasped. "You were eavesdropping. You knew what he was doing, didn't you?"

"Proposing? Yes, and you said no."

Phoebe felt the heat rush to her cheeks. "I — I spoke rashly. He caught me off guard..."

Gregory Parker continued to smile at her, but the twinkle in his eyes had left and this change was not lost on Phoebe. "Come now, my dear, don't back down from your true feelings. You gave the boy your answer. Just because you feel sorry for him —"

"I feel no pity for him, I assure you, Mr. Parker. What I feel for Will —"

"Is juvenile," he said, taking a step closer to her. "It is nothing like what you and I feel for one another."

He no longer smiled as he continued toward her. In its place, his face held a severity like she had never seen before, and it frightened her.

Phoebe took a step back. "I think it is time you left, Mr. Parker."

A sinister grin twitched at the corner of his mouth. "No, my dear pastor, I'm not going anywhere without proving to you that I am more of a man than that boy that's been chasing you."

Phoebe quickened her backward movement. She knocked into the altar, and, before she could right herself, Parker was there. He snaked one arm around her waist and the other wrapped around the back of her neck.

She pushed against him, but within seconds he had her trapped in his arms, her body pressed against his. As his lips came toward hers, Phoebe let out a terrified scream.

"What's going on in here?"

Both Phoebe and Gregory turned to the door. Dressed in plain clothes, Thomas Rogers stood staring at them.

"Officer Rogers!" Phoebe screamed. "Help me!"

Gregory swore repeatedly but did not release his grip. "I told you to stay in the car!"

"Yeah, but you also said you'd only be a couple of minutes," Rogers replied. "And if Caffey comes back, the whole operation is blown."

Phoebe looked back and forth between the two men. "He's hurting me," she said to Rogers, struggling in vain to pull free. "Aren't you going to do something?"

Thomas Rogers looked at her sympathetically. "I'm sorry, ma'am. Really, I am." He then turned his attention back to Parker. "What are you going to do with her? She's seen me."

"And whose fault is that?" Parker yelled. "If you would have stayed where I told you to stay —"

"Well, I didn't. Now we have a problem with only one solution, as I see it."

"Keep quiet," Gregory grumbled.

Phoebe's heart began to race. How did Gregory Parker and Thomas Rogers know one another, and, although she was quite certain that she was the 'problem' Rogers spoke of, she couldn't process what the solution was that he was suggesting.

"I'll keep quiet once this batch of hooch is delivered and we get our money. You're wastin' precious time."

Hooch. Phoebe may have led a sheltered life compared to most, but she knew that word. Liquor.

All these months, Phoebe had sensed something was never quite right about Gregory Parker, the evangelist. And now it made sense. He was no man of God. It was all a front.

Gregory released another stream of obscenities. "YOU IMBECILE! You've gone and blown my cover!"

"Like I said," Rogers said, opening his coat and resting his hand on his revolver. "Only one solution."

Gregory ran his fingers through his hair and swore again. Slowly, he lifted his eyes to Phoebe. Gone was the angry, volatile man she faced moments ago, replaced with the charming, slick smile of the gentleman he had always previously presented. She wasn't certain which was more frightening.

He reached inside his coat, pulled out a gun and aimed it at Phoebe. "Well, my dear, it seems our plans have changed."

"Steady, boy."

Will couldn't relax his bearing any more than he could remove the anger from his voice. The words, meant to calm Tolly, did little to stop the nervous stamping of the horse's hooves. Tolly could sense the tension of his owner, and was ready to bolt the minute Will gave the word. Will did not intend to race away from this spot; he forced himself to take several deep breaths. As Will calmed, so did the horse.

Their location was a familiar one to them both. Will had discovered early on that this small copse of trees on the far end of Iron Falls was the perfect location to observe without being seen. It had been an indispensable location during that first week after Phoebe's arrival, when he had needed to keep himself hidden, but he had continued to use it quite regularly. It not only gave him a clear view of the church and parsonage, but from this location, you could see pretty much the entire town, an advantage for an officer of the law. He knew he should share the location with the other troopers. But if he did that, how would he explain his presence there while not on duty?

It was foolish to continue to watch her. She had made her decision. She didn't want him. She never would. It was finally time to give up. That was the logical choice, but his heart didn't want to admit it.

Continuing to keep a watchful eye on her was not making it any easier to walk away. Healing would take action, and the first action he should take would be to leave his hiding spot for good. But he wasn't certain he had the strength to do it on his own.

"Lord, I need you," he prayed.

I am with thee, be not dismayed. I am thy God. I will strengthen thee.

He pulled the reins and tapped Tolly's flank to move him out of the copse. He chanced one more glance at the church. As he did, he saw a man stepping out of Parker's car and running up the stairs of the church. Why hadn't Will noticed him before? Because he had been too emotional to notice anything but his aching chest, too enraged to see anything but red. He had let his emotions dictate far too many of his actions since returning from the war. It was time to stop that as well. He looked away from the church.

He led Tolly back toward the center of town. His horse, out of instinct, started down Commonwealth - toward the church.

"Not this time, boy," Will said as he pulled the reins in the direction of the constabulary.

As he passed the store, he saw Mary Simmons walking out. He nodded to her. "Mrs. Simmons."

"Oh, hello Officer Caffey! How are you this fine evening?"

Broken. Aching. Completely lost. "As well as the good Lord sees fit." It wasn't a lie. God was still God. Will would not let his broken heart doubt that.

"I'm so glad to hear it. Are you just beginning your shift or ending it?"

"I'm off duty, ma'am. Just heading back to turn in. Why? Was there something you needed?"

"No, just thought you might like to join the Pastor and I for some chamomile tea. I made homemade shortbread," she said, lifting the tin she held in front of her.

"I'm afraid the pastor has other plans." He hoped his words did not sound as angry as he felt saying them.

"Oh, I'm certain she doesn't. I just spoke with her a short while ago and made plans for after dinner."

The hair on the back of his neck stood on end. "Are you certain?"

"Absolutely. Why?"

"She must have forgotten," he said as nonchalantly as he could muster. He didn't want to alarm Mrs. Simmons. Phoebe never forgot anything, certainly not plans she made only a short time ago. "It seems she has made plans with someone else."

"That doesn't sound like her," Mary said.

"I agree." He smiled. "Tell you what, I'll see if I can find her for you."

He tapped his heels into Tolly's belly and turned the horse back toward Commonwealth Street. Something wasn't right.

As he rounded the corner, he could see that Parker's car was no longer parked in front of the church, its only remains were a cloud of dust far off toward the outskirts of town.

He didn't bother tying the horse as he slid off the saddle and bolted up the stairs. He threw open the door, calling her name, but the sanctuary was empty. Maybe she was already back at the parsonage. That would make sense if what Mary said was true and she was expecting her.

He turned to leave, but something caught his eye. Lying on the back pew, right where he had seen her put them, were Phoebe's coat and hat.

40

LOST TRAIL

*I*t had been an unusually dry November for the Upper Peninsula, which made tracking the car even more difficult than usual. Had there been more snow this month, the ground would have been wetter, softer, making obvious tire imprints inevitable.

Trying to follow such a ghostly trail was most likely a fool's errand, Will told himself. Phoebe was safe. She had to be. She had simply made her decision - she had chosen Parker. Hadn't she? Will's misgivings about him were probably just jealousy, he knew.

But still...

Will couldn't shake the memory of the creepy feeling he'd had the first time he'd seen the way that snake looked at Phoebe. True, she hadn't argued with Parker when he'd said they had plans, but what about the plans Phoebe had made with Mary?

Phoebe never forgot her appointments, as Mary had confirmed. And why leave behind her coat and hat in this weather?

But what if she did go with him willingly? Will asked himself. What would Phoebe say to him when he finally tracked them down? She'd say he was meddling in her life, among other things, he was sure. He should just turn around and head back to town. Shouldn't he?

Will bowed his head. "Lord, I don't know up from down right now. I think I should turn around and head back. If you want me to continue, you're going to have to throw me a bone."

A cold wind blew down the tree lined road. Will flipped the collar of his coat up to cover his neck. "One more mile, then I'm giving up."

As he finished speaking, something cold and wet fell on his hand. He lifted his eyes toward heaven. Snow. A thick, heavy snow that was quickly covering what trail might have been left.

"Well, I guess that's your answer." He turned Tolly back toward town.

One more mile.

Will stopped. He had made that commitment, but that was before the snow promised to make his search even less fruitful than before. However, he had learned not to question God's still, small voice. He turned his horse again.

The wind blew hard against him, making it hard to see at times, but he pressed on. One mile wasn't much, even in a storm like this.

Then, as quickly as the giant flakes had appeared, they vanished, along with the wind, leaving a light dusting on every-thing. Even Tolly's mane was covered, making him look oddly camouflaged amongst the snow blanketed cedar and fir trees that flanked the road.

Will tapped his horse into a trot to cover the distance quicker since he was no longer searching for a trail. He had just about covered the promised mile when something caught his eye down the road. He pushed a little further past the mile he had planned, and there they were...tire tracks. The car must have still been traveling when the squall hit.

He followed the tracks in the snow until they turned down a

narrow path in the woods. Will might have missed the turn off in the dense woods, especially with nightfall quickly approaching, had it not been for the tracks left in the fresh snow.

He had asked for a bone, and the Lord had given him the entire cow. This was no fool's errand.

⁓

GREGORY PARKER roughly shoved Phoebe through the door of the old, run-down cabin. The building was larger than Phoebe's own home, but the thick layer of dust on everything made it far less appealing.

"Get a fire going," Parker barked at Rogers. "It's freezing in here."

He finally released the grip that he had maintained on her arm the entire car ride from Iron Falls to this cabin in the woods. Phoebe had tried desperately to keep her eyes on the passing scenery so as to find her way home, but the cold barrel of the pistol Gregory kept shoved against her neck coupled with the dwindling daylight made it impossible to keep track of all the twists and turns the car made along the heavily wooded journey. But, if she could get away, she'd take her chances of getting lost over whatever Gregory Parker had planned for her.

She rubbed her arm where he had held her. Gregory holstered his gun back under his coat and reached for her.

"Dearest, have I hurt you?" He slid his hands gently up and down her sleeves.

Caught so off guard by his sudden change in demeanor, she found herself momentarily speechless.

"Here," he said, guiding her to the only cushioned chair in the room. "You should rest."

He dropped to one knee in front of her and leaned in, his face only inches from hers. "You know, I could have loved you," he said, his right hand coming up to play with one of the tendrils that had come loose from her bun. "I still could." His eyes grew soft as he ran his knuckles along the line of her jaw and down her neck, stopping just short of the top of her breast. "I really could, Phoebe. I could love you so much more than that constable of yours." He let his fingertips trail a little lower.

Phoebe jerked her body away from his touch and her movement broke his trance. Fury once again burned in his steel-colored eyes.

"Your choice," he said, standing up. "But I'll have you either way. I do think you would have enjoyed it much better had you been willing, but to be honest, I think I'll enjoy it better this way."

Before she could respond, his fist came down with thunder against her cheek. The blow sent her flying out of the chair as the pain of a thousand knives exploded behind her eyes. She rolled to her hands and knees in an attempt to rise but slid prostrate on the wooden planks as darkness closed in around her. As she lost consciousness, the sound of laughing men swam in the circles of her mind.

WILL TIED TOLLY to a tree deep into the woods then crept behind the log cabin to peer through the window. Why hadn't he gone for backup before heading out? Because he thought he was acting on jealousy rather than instinct, that's why. But there wasn't time to go back now. If Phoebe truly were in trouble, time would be of the essence.

The window was filthy, but the firelight from within was enough to make out at least two men, Parker and another, standing bent over a table near the hearth. Unfortunately, the fire wasn't bright enough to illuminate the entire room. Will couldn't be certain that there weren't more men, but more concerning to him was that he couldn't see Phoebe.

He crouched down and leaned his back against the building's exterior. The blanket of snow that had led him here also covered heavy tarps flung over something piled behind the building. Carefully, Will inched his way to the piles, careful to stay out of the moonlight. He lifted one tarp corner. Crates full of bottles were stacked under the tarp.

Rum runners.

He left the window and kept low as he edged himself toward Parker's car. He quietly opened the door. Phoebe wasn't there. He saw no sign of blood, but that brought him little comfort.

He hid behind the car as he weighed his options. He could disable the vehicle, maybe by slitting the tires, then return to town for help. But what if they had Phoebe somewhere else? He would need to be able to follow them to her, so slitting the tires was out of the question, for now at least.

He could break down the door and bank on the element of surprise being in his favor, but without knowing exactly where Phoebe was, or how many men were inside, that didn't seem like a logical plan, either.

As he contemplated his options, he heard another vehicle approaching. He quickly slid back into the woods to where Tolly waited.

Through the pines, he saw a second car pull to a stop and a hulking figure step out. This man entered the cabin as well. That made three men, as far as Will could tell.

He kept low as he headed back to the window. He slid behind the second car, and as he did, he looked at the back tires. One was nearly bald. The other three were brand new.

Will's gut twisted. This was the car that had left tracks at the scene of the Richardson boy's murder. That meant that the murderer was now inside the cabin with Parker. But the only piece of information he truly cared about was the one piece of the puzzle that was still missing. Where was Phoebe?

He crept back to the window. Parker and the other man still

stood over the table, but he couldn't see the third man he knew to be there. This only confirmed Will's fear; there could be any number of men hiding within the dark corners of the cabin. There was only one thing to do. He would take care of the tires of the two vehicles then ride as fast as he could to Iron Falls to get help. He only prayed Phoebe was somewhere safe.

He was about to turn when a movement inside the cabin caught his eye. As he tried to focus through the dirt covered window, something... no, someone, was moving on the floor. He watched in horror as the figure sat up. Despite the poor lighting, he would have recognized that figure anywhere. His blood ran cold with dread and his heart thumped hard against his chest.

Phoebe.

～

COLD. Hard and cold. It's strange the things that you think when first waking. Phoebe didn't know where she was or why, but she knew it was hard and cold. The mist clogging her mind began to fade and she noticed other details. The musky scent of sweat and unwashed bodies. Hushed whispering and the crackling of a fire. The taste of dirt. The drums pounding in her temples.

Gingerly, she lifted her head and wiped the dirt from her face and mouth. From her vantage point, she could see the floor was covered in filth, much like the rest of the cabin. She looked at her two captors, hunched over the table discussing something spread in front of them. As engrossed as they were, they took no notice of Phoebe's consciousness or her movements.

She had no plan but realized this may be her only opportunity. Slowly and quietly, she stood. Inching her way away from the men, she kept her eyes on Gregory and Rogers. Only a few more feet, and she would be at the door.

"Were you going somewhere, miss?" came a voice from the shadows.

Startled, Phoebe ran toward the door only to find her arm gripped in man-sized talons. She shrieked as she found herself once again a captive, this time by a man nearly twice the size of the other two.

"Miss Albright, meet Mr. Karch," Gregory said without lifting his eyes from the papers on the table.

Mr. Karch smiled down at her through crooked teeth lost in a dirty, unkept beard. She now knew where the smell in the room was emanating from.

"Mr. Karch, it appears our guest needs another taste of what she can expect if she tries to escape again. My fist must not have done the trick."

The horror of his words seeped into the very depths of her stomach. Surely this man could cause more harm than Parker, and Phoebe was still feeling the effects of his punch.

"But she's a priest."

Parker turned to look at the brute. His confusion turned to mirth.

"Close," he chuckled, "but not quite."

"Don't matter. I ain't hittin' a woman of the cloth."

"You superstitious fool. I swear you're more afraid of the leaders of the church than you are of God himself."

Karch didn't respond, but he didn't make any attempts to injure Phoebe either.

Maybe he is my path to safety, she thought. "Please," she whispered. "Please help me get away from here."

"Now, why would I do that?"

"Parker is going to harm me, or worse. Surely you can see that."

"Sure, I can."

"But you won't help me?"

"Just 'cause I won't touch ya, doesn't mean I care one bit what he does wit' ya. He'll answer to God for that, not me."

"But you'll answer to God for letting it happen," she pleaded in desperation.

The man muttered something about Mary and Grace. Phoebe realized it was useless; this man wasn't concerned about her at all. She turned back to her original captors.

"This time will be more dangerous, what with you draggin' around dead weight," Rogers said with a jerk of his head in her direction.

Parker's eyes met with Phoebe's. He smiled, a slow, casual smile. How had she ever thought he was handsome? She shivered under his stare.

"That weight's not dead...yet."

Her stomach lurched. He couldn't be serious. He stood, feet apart and arms crossed, his lean body and expression completely relaxed. He acted as if he were discussing the weather, not holding her hostage, and discussing killing her. Over what?

Liquor? Shipments?

Bits of conversations from the car ride and fragments she must have heard while on the floor were beginning to come back to her slowly.

"You gotta take care of her, and now. We gotta get on the road."

Fury furrowed Parker's brow as he looked at Rogers.

"You don't tell me what to do. I'll take care of her when I'm good and ready."

"You can't be thinkin' of takin' her with us?"

Parker appeared to ponder that. His gaze slid down her body, and back up to meet hers.

"I'm not done with her yet," he answered, a slow smirk spreading across his face. "And as you pointed out, we are in a hurry right now. But I plan on taking my time with that one."

Phoebe fought back the tears she felt burning behind her eyes. She would not let him see her cry. Why hadn't she listened to Will's warnings about this man?

Will. She choked back a sob. How could she have been so foolish? If she hadn't been so prideful, if she had only seen what God had placed in front of her all this time, she would be celebrating her engagement right now. Instead, she was here with three dangerous men and no escape in sight. Despite her best efforts, a single tear escaped down her cheek.

Parker smiled. An arrogant, self-satisfied smile as he pulled her from the large brute's grip with one hand and wiped the tear with the other.

"Don't cry, my dear. I won't make you wait long."

He crushed her against his chest and brought his lips down to hers. But Phoebe hadn't lost all of her fight yet. She didn't have much time left, if these men's words were to be taken seriously, and there was no way she would allow Gregory Parker's kiss to be her last memory. If she was going to die, she would die knowing only the taste of Will Caffey's lips.

She turned her face away, but that didn't slow him down. His lips, hot and slimy, slithered a path across her cheek and down her neck. She tried pulling away from his embrace, but that only seemed to entertain him. He laughed, a low, throaty laugh, then bit her sharply on the neck.

Phoebe cried out in pain.

"I told you I'd enjoy it more this way," he laughed again.

"We ain't got time," Rogers growled.

Parker rolled his eyes and sighed. "Then let's get this over with." He dug his fingers into her arm and pushed her through the door and into the darkness.

'Please, God. I need a miracle.'

A pack of coyotes howled not too far away, reminding her that she was nowhere near civilization. She was in the woods. And she was alone.

"I don't like that," Rogers complained. "Never heard 'em that close before."

"Then get to the car, you fool, so we can get out of here."

Phoebe fought hard against her captor, digging her heels into the ground and pulling away with all her might.

Parker shoved Phoebe hard. "Quit stalling!"

Then, out of the darkness, a deep, strong voice called out. "Now, is that any way to treat a lady?"

41

RUM RUNNERS

"*W*ill!" Phoebe shouted. He was here. She didn't know how he had found her, but he had, and her relief caused a flood of tears.

He stepped out of the shadows and into the moonlight, his gun aimed at Gregory Parker.

"Well, well, well...if it isn't the constant constable reporting for duty." Parker tightened his grip slightly but appeared for the most part unaffected by Will's arrival. "How'd you find us, Sarge? Stalking the young lady again? Yeah, we know all about your obsession with the girl. Seems like everyone but Miss Albright here knew how closely you watched over her. How's it feel, Caffey, knowing that after all of your pursuing and wooing, she still chose me?"

"Doesn't seem as if you are giving her much of a choice. Why don't we try it now? Let her go and we'll see who she chooses."

"Well, that doesn't seem to be in my best interest, now does it?"

Will held the gun steady. No one moved. "Let her go, Parker."

Parker laughed and pulled Phoebe's back tight against his chest.

"Come now, Sarge, surely you can see that you don't have the upper hand in this situation." While Parker's left arm held her shoulders immobilized against his chest, his right hand began moving up her side. "No, no you don't have the upper hand. Seems I have all the hands," he said, bringing his up to cup her right bosom.

Phoebe whimpered at his touch, which only seemed to please him. She squeezed her eyes shut as his hand moved, roughly fondling her breast. His hand slid from her breast toward the buttons of her blouse. He fumbled for a moment, then angrily ripped two buttons off and slid his hand inside to her other breast.

"Get your filthy hands off her."

Phoebe's eyes flew open at the rage in Will's voice. His eyes never leaving her assailant, Will stood rigid, every muscle seemingly ready to pounce, but Phoebe couldn't tell in what direction. His cat-like stance, poised and steady, gave her the impression that he was keenly aware of even the smallest movement around him. He boiled with anger, yet he controlled every muscle in his body.

"I have spent all these months being teased by this woman, just waiting for the time when all my work would pay off. And it will pay off, you mark my words. This little broad owes me, and before this night's up, I'll get what I'm owed."

"I said take your hands off her!" Will said, raising his voice.

"Drop your gun, and I'll at least let go of her chest."

Will was silent for a moment, then conceded and lowered his arm.

"I meant drop it to the ground."

"I'm not releasing my weapon until you release her."

"You don't get it! You aren't in control here – your uniform means nothing to us! You are just another man – one man – with one gun. You are no match for three armed men."

"I can take out at least one of you," Will quipped with a smirk.

Parker laughed, then leaned in to rub his cheek against Phoebe's.

"Probably, but I'm willing to bet that it won't be me," he said, kissing Phoebe on the cheek.

Will was silent. Phoebe watched him as Parker's statement settled in. Parker had the upper hand, and they all knew it.

~

'WHAT NOW, LORD?' Will prayed.

He sized up the situation. Out of the corner of his eye, he saw the man on the left – the largest of the three – slide his hand beneath his jacket. The man in the middle, who kept his hat pulled low over his face, started to do the same. Parker, although undoubtedly carrying a weapon, held Phoebe in front of him, blocking easy access to the gun. It wasn't impossible, though. He had to think quickly, because one of these men was going to be the first to shoot, and his best chance at survival – and Phoebe's – was if he were that man.

Parker was partially correct. The other two men were more likely to taste the lead from his weapon – first. But Will had no intention of letting any man walk away from this confrontation – least of all Parker. But he held Phoebe so close and kept his head close to hers. Will was a good shot, but Parker, or Phoebe for that matter, would only have to move slightly and... no, he couldn't chance it. If only she could somehow break away...

'Dear Jesus, I need a miracle.'

"I can see that reality is starting to sink in," Parker smiled smugly. "Here's how this is going to play out. You are going to drop your gun – to the ground. Then me and my friends here – including the beautiful Miss Albright – are going to walk gracefully into the moonlight to my waiting car. Do you understand?"

An unexplainable calm came over Will as he realized what he was going to do. A smile spread across his face.

Thank you, Lord.

"Your plan for a graceful exit will never work," Will stated matter-of-factly.

Parker laughed. "What makes you say that?"

"Well, because you've picked the wrong girl as hostage," Will answered, smirking. "Walking gracefully isn't one of her talents. She's much better suited at tripping and falling."

The look of outrage on Phoebe's face was obvious, even in the moonlight. But she was more than angry, Will could see. She was hurt. She was hurt because she thought Will was making fun of her in a time when her life was in danger. But he wasn't teasing. For the first time tonight, Will looked at her. His eyes were steady, locked with hers, willing her to understand what he meant. And somehow, she did. Slowly, her furrowed brows softened, and she nodded her head slightly.

Immediately, Will lifted his gun.

42

WOUNDED

The instant she saw Will lift his gun, Phoebe let her legs collapse beneath her like a disobedient toddler. She felt the sleeve of her dress rip as her own weight pulled her out of Parker's grip. She heard gunfire as she dropped to the ground – four shots. Then silence.

Phoebe lay in a heap on the ground, hands over her head, crying. She heard nothing more, only her sobs in the stillness. She feared looking up, feared she would see Will, lying on the ground. She feared she would see the rum runners standing over his body.

She heard rustling. She had to get away before her captors grabbed her again. But before she could move, a hand grabbed hers.

"Phoebe, are you hurt? Please tell me you're ok," came Will's quiet, searching voice.

She looked up in shock. Quickly looking around, she saw three bodies lying in awkward positions on the ground around her. Their guns were no longer in their hands, but in Will's.

"It's ok," Will whispered as he looked into her eyes, concern for her still evident on his face.

"Oh Will!" she exclaimed and threw her arms around his neck. He seemed to wince for a second, but instantly drew her close to him. They held each other, Phoebe still crying softly, Will burying his face in her hair. She could have stayed there forever, wrapped in his arms. She had never felt so safe in her entire life.

But then she felt it. A warmth on her arm. A wet warmth.

In the darkness, Phoebe instinctively felt for the blood. Will's shoulder was drenched with it.

"You've been shot!" she exclaimed.

"Just a flesh wound, I'm sure," he said. "When you dropped, I got two shots out on the first two men – Parker and the one in the middle. But the one on his right was able to get one in on me before I got him."

Will helped Phoebe to her feet with his good arm. She looked at the men on the ground.

"You shot them all?"

"Yes."

"Parker too?"

Will grunted. "He 'got what he was owed.'"

"And Rogers?"

Will stopped. "Rogers?"

Phoebe nodded slowly. "Will, one of them was Thomas Rogers."

Will let go of her hand. He slipped his boot under the body closest to the cabin and rolled him over.

"Rogers?" he said, shaking his head. "All of this time, it was him?"

Phoebe leaned around Will uncertainly. "Should we get the doctor?"

"No," Will said, leading her away from the bodies. "They are all dead. I made sure of it."

Phoebe gasped. Will grabbed her hand gently.

"I was aiming to kill, Phoebe. I wasn't going to give them any opportunity to hurt you further."

Phoebe shuddered at the thought of what might have happened had he, had Will not... she couldn't bear the thought.

"We need to get back to town, so the doc can tend to this wound. We can alert the other officers as to the location of the bodies."

Will led Phoebe to his horse. He emptied the shells of the men's guns onto the ground then placed them in his saddle bag.

"Should we take one of the cars? Wouldn't they be faster?"

"Yes, if I hadn't punctured the tires. I wanted to make sure they couldn't get away with you."

With a wince, he helped her onto his horse, then hoisted himself up behind her. Then he reached his arms around her to grab the reins. She was pressed closely to Will, but she wasn't embarrassed or uncomfortable. She allowed her back to relax into his chest, reveling in the comfort Will Caffey brought her.

Will turned the horse toward town. He kept a steady pace, not too fast, for which Phoebe was grateful. Her head was still spinning from the ordeal. She was also enjoying this closeness and didn't want to see it come to an end. In fact, if she had her way, she would have slowed the horse even more.

When she did in fact feel his horse begin to slow, she thought Will had read her mind. She turned to look at him. In the moonlight he looked so pale, like a fragile china doll. His eyes fluttered shut and his body weight shifted. It was then that she realized that he was falling off the horse.

With all the strength she could muster, Phoebe grabbed his khaki jacket and tried to right him without toppling herself.

"Stay with me, Will!" she shouted at him, but it was too late. He had passed out. How on earth would she ever get him back to town like this. She thought about throwing him across the saddle and walking beside the horse, but time was of the essence, so walking would not do. Besides, she would never be able to lift his body in order to position him properly. She would just have to find a way to keep both of them astride the horse and get back to Iron Falls as quickly as possible.

Phoebe scanned his body looking for some sort of idea. By this point, the entire front of his jacket was soaked. He was losing a lot of blood, and he was losing it fast. She noticed his gun strap that crossed his body from shoulder to waist. She slid her right arm through the leather strap and with her other hand clung to the opposite side of his jacket. She grabbed the reins with her right hand and urged the horse forward. It was an awkward pose, and Phoebe wasn't sure if she had the strength to continue it for very long, but she willed every muscle in her body to cooperate.

She urged the horse forward. She wanted to go faster, but anytime the horse went anything above a trot, the jostling made it too difficult to hold Will steady, and she almost lost both of them a couple of times. She kept talking to Will, urging him to stay with her. She kept telling him they were almost there, but in truth, the trip seemed to Phoebe to take a lifetime.

Eventually she could make out the outline of the little town in the moonlight. She passed by some of the small farmhouses, but all were dark. She thought momentarily about shouting for help but getting Will to the doctor seemed her best option. Stopping seemed like a waste of time. No, she had to continue on to the doctor's, even though it was clear to the other side of Iron Falls.

They trotted past her little parsonage. Her muscles ached and her hand was numb from holding tightly to Will's jacket, but she had to get to the doctor. She tapped her heels into the horse's side, urging him forward.

"We'll be there soon," she said to him.

Will let out a grunt of pain and jerked a little, causing Phoebe to lose her grip. Her other arm was still caught in the leather strap on his chest, but it was no use. She could not keep him, or herself, on the horse any longer. They both started to slip.

"Please, God, please. Help me!" she cried out loud. The only hope she had left was in God, for there was no one near to hear her words.

"Pastor? Is that you?"

Before she could answer, someone was catching her. And someone else was pulling Will down as well.

"What happened, Pastor?" the other voice asked.

"Help me get Constable Caffey into the parsonage!"

The two men lifted Will and followed Phoebe as she ran ahead to the house. Once inside, she lit a lamp and motioned for them to place Will on the bed. It was then that she realized that the two men weren't men at all, but boys – Lester O'Grady and Tommy Fuller.

"We need the doctor, now!" Phoebe yelled.

"You fetch Doc," said Lester. "I'll stay and help Miss Albright."

Phoebe was already by the bed, ripping Will's shirt off. To her relief, the wound had started to clot. But he was so pale, and his breathing was only getting worse.

"Miss Albright? You hurt too?" asked Lester.

"No, Lester. I'm fine."

"But all the blood... on your back?"

She turned in shock. In the mirror above the bureau, Will's mirror, she could see that her back was completely red. So much blood. How could anyone survive after losing that much?

"I'm fine, Lester. It isn't my blood. Listen to me. I know you are concerned, but I am alright. I need you to get to the State Constabulary. Get other officers. Tell them Constable Caffey has been shot. Can you do that for me?"

"Yes ma'am!" Lester said, running out the door.

She turned back to Will. He was barely breathing. He had saved her life and she had no idea what to do for him. There was only one thing she could do. Phoebe knelt next to him and began to pray.

"Please God. Don't take him. Not now. Not now that I – that I..." she couldn't finish the sentence. She remained on her knees, praying an indiscernible prayer until the door flew open and in walked Doctor Langley followed by two constables.

"What happened?" asked the doctor.

"Rum runners. Will was shot."

"And the rum runners?" asked one constable.

"Dead. All three of them."

The constable took Phoebe by the elbow and led her to a chair at her table. He and the other officer crowded around the bed with the doctor. They spoke in hushed tones, occasionally glancing back at her.

"Officer Moore, would you please take Miss Albright outside?"

The constable named Moore came to her side. "I think that's probably best, pastor."

"No. I can't," Phoebe argued. "Will may need me."

"The doctor will take care of him. And you don't need to be in here seeing what the doc has to do."

"What do you mean?"

"That bullet's gotta come out. If not, then lead poisoning will surely get him. But it isn't a pretty sight. You're better off outside."

Phoebe tried to protest, but he cut her off. "C'mon. Outside."

When they stepped onto her front porch, she saw that Lester and Tommy were still there, leaning against a post. The constable led her to a bench then turned his attention to the boys.

"So, tell me how it came to be that you two were out in the middle of the night like this."

The boys told the officer about the coyote problem that Widow Allen had been having and that she had offered to pay them if they would come coyote hunting a couple nights a week. They were just on their way home when they saw Miss Albright and heard her cry for help.

"Well, it was quite lucky that you boys were here to help."

"Weren't luck, sir. It was God. He caused all the coyotes to stay away from town tonight. Otherwise, we wouldn't a been here when she cried out to Him for help. We'd still been huntin'."

The coyotes. Phoebe knew exactly where God had sent them that evening. The boys were right. The events of the past few hours had nothing to do with luck.

As the boys finished their tale, three more officers rode up, but didn't dismount. Officer Little handed a bottle to Lester and told him to take it to the doctor. Constable Moore greeted them, then they all turned to Phoebe.

"Ma'am, it would appear that you've been through a lot this evening, but it would be mighty helpful if you could tell us as much as possible. And if you could tell us where this all happened."

Phoebe began, keenly aware that so many eyes were on her. "Gregory Parker kidnapped me from the church —"

"Parker?" Moore asked. "The preacher?"

"He is no preacher."

"Hmmph. Caffey was right about him after all."

"Parker wasn't alone. Thomas Rogers was with him."

All the officers stopped and stared at her.

Moore spoke first. "Officer Thomas Rogers? You must be mistaken."

"I wish I were, but I am certain. Will identified his body as well."

"Rogers is dead?" Frank Little asked in disbelief.

They all looked at her for answers she knew she didn't have. "I know it's hard to fathom, but yes. He was one of my captors. And from what I overheard, he was deeply involved with these bootleggers."

They all shook their heads in disbelief. "Well, I guess you never know a man," Frank finally said.

"How'd Officer Caffey find you?" Officer Moore continued.

"I don't really know," she began. "He must have followed us somehow."

"Good thing Caffey kept a close eye on ya, eh?" Officer Little smiled.

Grateful for the darkness, Phoebe stared at the ground as she felt her cheeks grow warm.

Moore cleared his throat. "So, after the altercation, you rode with him on his horse back to town? You sat in front of him?"

Phoebe's cheeks grew even hotter, realizing these men were now imagining the proximity in which she and Will rode. "Well, yes. Will had already ruined the tires of both vehicles, so we had no other choice."

"We aren't judging you, Pastor. Just looking for an explanation. That would explain all the blood on your back. Is that right, ma'am?" asked another officer.

Blood. She was covered in blood. Will's blood. "Yes. That's right," she finally choked out.

"And then he passed out. How did you get back to town?"

Phoebe explained how she used his gun harness and jacket to keep him upright. Moore was silent for a moment.

"Well, ma'am. I'm right impressed. Not sure how a little bit of a thing like you were able to keep a grown man like that upright and control a horse. Right impressive, it is."

Suddenly, agonizing screams came from within the tiny parsonage. Phoebe let out a whimper as tears flooded her eyes. She started to rise, but Constable Moore laid a reassuring hand on her shoulder.

"There's nothing you can do for him right now, except pray."

Phoebe did continue to stand, but only for a moment and only to turn herself around so she could kneel at the bench. She heard Moore speak quietly, presumably to the other officers, because the clap of horse hooves could be heard shortly afterward. It was very quiet, except for the occasional scream from inside. When she finished praying, Phoebe lifted her eyes. She discovered that she was not alone at the bench. Both Lester and Tommy had joined her on their knees, as did Constable Moore as well.

43

AFTERMATH

*H*ours later, Phoebe sat quietly outside her cabin waiting for news of Will. Constable Moore remained with her, although he did not try to engage her in conversation. She was grateful for this because she had no strength left for anything other than prayer. Or, maybe more accurately, what little strength she had at the moment was because of prayer.

When Doctor Langley finally opened the door and motioned for them to enter, she was hesitant. The doctor looked so grave, so weary, that although she had waited anxiously all this time for answers, she now feared what those answers would be.

"He's lost a lot of blood."

She heard the doctor speak as she walked by him, but didn't really comprehend what he was saying, so intent was her focus on Will. He lay on the bed, motionless, and looked, if possible, even more pale. She stopped short and stared at his chest, looking, praying for movement.

"But we did get the bullet out, all of it I'm certain," Dr. Langley continued. "It's just a waiting game now."

And then she saw it. Slowly, raggedly, Will's chest, bare except for the bloodied bandage wrapped around it, lifted, and settled. One breath. Then a second.

Phoebe's own chest began to burn, and she realized she had been holding her own breath in anticipation of seeing his. She inhaled just as raggedly as Will.

"How soon before we can move him out of here?" asked Moore.

"You aren't moving him anywhere. If he's to survive, he needs rest."

"Alright. Alderson," Moore said to the officer who'd assisted the doctor and was now drying his hands over the basin of bloody water. "You stay here with him. Miss Albright, do you have somewhere you can stay?"

Phoebe gathered her wits. "I'm not going anywhere," she said. "I'm staying to keep watch over him."

"But ma'am, it isn't exactly proper for my man to stay here with you. I don't want the town talking."

"Neither do I, so your man can leave." Phoebe crossed her arms. "There is no need for anyone to stay. I am completely capable of seeing to his needs and summoning the doctor if need be."

"But Miss Albright, you're a single woman and Constable Caffey is a man…"

"A man who is on his death bed," interrupted Doctor Langley. "I seriously doubt any member of this community will think that anything inappropriate is happening while Miss Albright cares for the constable. Now, it's late and we need to leave both Constable Caffey and Miss Albright to rest," said the doctor, leading the men toward the door. Phoebe noticed that the officer named Alderson was carrying Will's bloody coat and shirt.

"Wait," she called after them. "What are you going to do with his coat?"

"It's evidence, ma'am. But we will probably just destroy it. It's ruined now, even if you could get the blood out. It has the bullet hole in it."

"May I – may I see it, please? Just for a moment?"

Alderson looked at Moore, who shrugged his shoulders. He handed it to Phoebe.

She held his bloodied jacket in her hands and moved it around until she found the bullet hole, noticing that in some spots, the blood was still wet. She stared at it, wishing she had listened to Will's warnings. Seeing the hole in the light, she thought about what a tiny thing a bullet is that can do such enormous damage to a man. She unbuttoned the chest pocket and dug inside for the aggie. It was right where she knew it would be.

"What's that?" Moore asked when he saw her pull something from the shirt.

"It's a marble," she said handing the coat back to the officer. "He'll want it when he wakes."

After the two troopers left, Doctor Langley returned to the bedside and began gathering his things. Will shifted a little in his slumber and began to speak.

"Phoebe. Phoebe – wait!" he called out. He thrashed slightly. "Phoebe, my love." He calmed then and fell back asleep.

Phoebe felt her cheeks grow warm. "He must have a fever. He - he is delirious," she stammered.

The doctor chuckled. "Not delirious, just drunk."

Phoebe gasped. It was then that she noticed the bottle that Frank Little had brought.

"Whiskey?"

"Yes ma'am."

"But shouldn't you have used ether instead?"

"I would have if I had any. Used up the last of my supply when I fixed up those miners from the cart crash last week," replied the doctor.

"I don't understand. Where did you find the whiskey?"

"It's from my medicinal stash. I don't advertise that I have any – wouldn't want it to come up missing when I'm away from the office. But it's completely legal for a doctor to own a supply. Don't you worry about that, Miss Albright," the doctor said with a smile. "No laws were broken here."

Phoebe couldn't miss the irony that it was liquor that got that bullet in his shoulder, and liquor that helped get it out.

"The Constable here was passed out until we started digging for that bullet. The whiskey was to help with the pain. And, seeing as how Mr. Caffey isn't a drinking man, it did the job faster than with most men. But, if he wakes in the morning, he'll have one heck of a hangover. May even make him forget his shoulder."

"'If' he wakes up? You said 'if'." She held back the tears that threatened behind her eyes.

The doctor set his bag on the chair. "I wish I could promise you that he's going to be alright, but I can't. His life is in God's hands now." He reached for something on her bedside table. "Here."

Dr. Langley handed her a necklace with a ring on it. Phoebe took it and looked at the ring that only hours ago Will had offered to her. "Put this with that marble. It was around his neck and he'll probably be looking for it when he comes to."

The doctor patted Phoebe's shoulder and headed for the door. "Come get me if his condition worsens. I'll check back tomorrow. Try to get some rest."

Rest. She knew that's what she needed, but so much had happened, she wasn't sure she would ever sleep again.

She wanted to change out of the bloody clothes, but where could she change? There were no walls separating the sleeping quarters from the rest of the tiny parsonage. But she couldn't stay in this dress. She looked around in vain, but eventually made the decision to change in the shadows.

After placing the aggie and necklace in her dresser and lowering the wick on the lamps, she backed into the corner across the room from the bed. She quickly dropped the bloody dress to the floor and swiftly replaced it with a clean frock. She would have much rather slipped into her night clothes, but that was impossible with Will here. Another dress would just have to do. She touched her hair. Blood was caked there also, but her water had been used up in the caring for Will, and she didn't want to fetch more. The hair would just have to wait until morning.

Phoebe walked back to the bedside. *'If*. Never had one word sounded so miserable. She knelt and began to pray again.

"Dear God. I know I have asked you for so much recently, but if it is your will, please save him. I can't – I can't do this without him. I couldn't bear..."

She began to sob. Why had she been such a fool? Will had done nothing but show tenderness for her, protection, kindness. And what had she shown him? Disdain? Indifference? Just because he didn't fit the ideal that Phoebe had built up in her own mind for the kind of man she expected God to provide for her. Will was an even better man than she deserved. Why had she denied her feelings for him for so long? And now, now that she realized her folly, he might be gone forever.

He had saved her life, and possibly sacrificed his own for hers.

"Please, God. Please don't take him."

Without thought of propriety, Phoebe lay on the bed next to Will. If he were to die tonight, she wanted to be able to know what it felt like to hold him, even if he couldn't hold her. He never woke, but the minute she lay her head on his shoulder, he wrapped his arm around her and drew her near, as if he had done it a thousand times. He pressed a kiss into her forehead.

"I love you Phoebe Albright," he whispered before falling back into complete oblivion.

Phoebe cuddled into his arm and whispered back, "I love you too, William Caffey."

ROOM TO HEAL

*H*e was in pain. Searing pain. And although a slight repositioning might have relieved some of that pain, he refused to move. He would endure any pain if it meant holding her in his arms for just a while longer.

Will had awoken close to an hour ago and thought he was dreaming. In fact, he was still feeling the effects of the whiskey the doctor had insisted on last night. But even in his slightly inebriated state, her body was too warm, her hair too soft against his neck to be a dream. This was real. Phoebe was lying in his arms and he refused to give up the moment.

She stirred slightly in the small bed and he had to pull her closer against him to keep her from falling off the edge. He shuddered slightly. This is how it was supposed to be, could have been, or at least that's what he had thought. But he had been a fool.

A loud banging on the door brought him out of his musings.

"Miss Albright?" a voice from outside yelled. "It's Constable Jesse Moore, ma'am."

In a flash, Phoebe sprang from the bed. Will had to suppress a snicker as she quickly checked her appearance in the mirror.

She was a mess - her dress wrinkled, and her hair tangled around her face.

"I'll be right there," she hollered.

When Phoebe opened the door, Jesse Moore and Frank Little entered, Captain Reynolds close on their heels. The appearance of Will's superior officer wasn't a complete surprise, but the appearance of the fourth Michigan State Trooper was. The first three troopers were followed by none other than Colonel Roy C. Vandercook, commanding officer of the Michigan State Constabulary. Close behind the officers walked Dr. Langley.

"How is Caffey doing this morning?" Captain Reynolds asked Phoebe.

"I...well, I'm not sure..." Phoebe sputtered.

"I'm fine, but my headache would do much better without all the pounding and yelling."

Phoebe twirled around and Will had to stifle a laugh at the look of shock on her face. A deep blush traveled up her neck to her cheeks. "I'll be out back if you need me," she said, quickly picking up the basin of bloody water and scooting out the back door.

It was then that Will noticed something about her hair that he had missed earlier. The back of her head was caked with dried blood. He winced as he tried to sit up to take a better look, but she was out the door too quickly.

"Hold on there," Dr. Langley said, placing his hand on Will's chest. "Where do you think you're going?"

"Did you see all that blood? Is she alright?" he asked him.

"I noticed the dried blood, too," Captain Reynolds said, eyeing the door she had exited through. "But her shirt was clean."

All the officers, including Will, scanned the room. Their gazes came to rest on the pile of woman's clothing in the far corner.

Dr. Langley cleared his throat. "I examined her. Save for some bruising under her eye and the back of her head, she is fine."

"But all that blood?" Will insisted.

"Is yours," Moore interrupted. "The pastor kept you atop your horse by weaving herself into your gun strap. She was covered in your blood by the time she got you back to town."

"I don't remember much past getting onto my horse."

"You gave us quite a scare. By Moore's report, I didn't expect you to be awake so soon," Reynolds said.

"Well, I was taken very good care of, I suppose, Captain."

"I suppose you were," Captain Reynolds said, looking once more at the pile of clothes in the corner. "So, tell me, son. What happened?"

"Bootleggers, sir."

Reynolds nodded. "Just like you thought. None of us believed you, but you knew all along."

"I only had a hunch, sir. If I had known for certain, I wouldn't have been caught out there alone against them while they had a hostage."

Colonel Vandercook nodded. "Pretty impressive detective work, Caffey. How did you find their hideout?"

"Pastor Albright went missing. I had been speaking with her at the church and when I left her, there was a car and two men." Again, he was reminded of his own stupidity for leaving her alone with Parker. But he was also reminded as to why he left her. "It was the only lead I had, so I just followed their trail. I didn't expect that she was in that much danger when I set out."

"Why didn't you grab another officer or two before heading out?"

Because I was led by my heart, not my head. "I should have. I made a mistake."

The Colonel looked at him again. "I wouldn't call it a mistake. Misjudgment, maybe. But I suppose in the heat of the moment, you can't always expect to make the right call. Fortunately for you and the pastor, you were able to handle the situation."

He continued to question Will about the events of the previous evening. Will explained, in detail, how he had found the trail that led to the cabin deep in the woods, and the hidden crates of liquor. He then told about confronting the bootleggers and how he had taken all three of them down, including Officer Rogers.

"I still can't believe Rogers was messed up in all of this," Captain Reynolds said, shaking his head.

"That would explain how they evaded us for so long," Moore said. "They knew our every move from the inside. If Will hadn't taken him out, no telling how many more lives like Jimmy Richardson's would have been lost."

Will nodded. "The tires."

"Yep. That car belonged to Lucky Dombrowski, the third man you took down. He has a long rap sheet as 'muscle' for a major gang in Detroit."

Will frowned. "I don't get it. Why would Detroit bootleggers need to throw their weight around a little town like Iron Falls?"

"Iron Falls was just a gateway to Marquette and other bigger areas. But I guess they didn't like anyone stepping in their way, and they saw even the local moonshiners as invading their territory. Ain't that right, Little?"

Frank nodded. "I spoke with Henry Lambecker. He confirmed that it was the Detroit mob that burned down his still. He also said that Dombrowski had threatened him just days before poor Jimmy was found dead."

Colonel Vandercook pulled a kitchen chair close to the bed and sat down. "These weren't simple rum runners you tangled with, son. And to think, you did all this on your own. You're lucky you're alive."

"I had no choice but to do it alone, sir. I couldn't chance losing them. Not when they had a hostage."

"No. I don't suppose you could." Colonel Vandercook turned to the other officers. "Once he's had ample time to rest, I'd like a more detailed account of how he took down three armed men with only one bullet hole in return."

"Rest is exactly what he needs," Doctor Langley agreed. "And this powder will help." He pulled a small envelope out of his pocket.

Will shook his head. "No, thank you. I'm still trying to sober up from last night's *medicine*."

"I'm afraid I'm going to have to insist. This will help you sleep, which will get you healed up faster."

Reluctantly, Will agreed.

"Well, I know you need to rest now," the colonel said. "But there's still a few matters I need to discuss with you."

"Matters?"

"Yes, son. Namely, the matter of your future with the force."

Even the pain in his shoulder couldn't distract him from the headache those words caused. Will had known he had acted foolishly, but he didn't think he had been so foolish as for it to affect his future as a Michigan State Trooper. But he had escaped unscathed from the disaster that ended in Wendell's death. The force couldn't overlook two major incidents. He closed his eyes and pushed his head back against the pillow. "You've already decided the disciplinary action, then?"

"Disciplinary action?" Colonel Vandercook asked.

"Isn't that what you meant by my 'future with the force'?"

"I'm not planning to discipline you, son. I want to promote you."

Will's eyes flew open. "Promote me?"

"We need more men like you protecting our fine state, influencing and training future recruits. In Detroit, you could really make an impact on the force."

"Detroit?"

"I know Lansing is where your heart is, son, as is mine, but Detroit is where we have the biggest crime problem, if you ask me. Last winter, bootleggers drove their cars right across the frozen Detroit River, right in front of my men. And the preliminary investigation of that hideout you discovered last night proves me right. Maps and letters, amongst other evidence, directly connects that ring you broke up to the Purple Gang in Detroit. In fact, we may have gathered enough to bring that bunch of criminals down once and for all, and I'd like you to be the one to lead that effort. You'll need to heal up first, of course. But as soon as you can travel, I'll have you on the first train south."

"It's a lot to consider."

Vandercook frowned. "Consider? The promotion isn't a lateral move, Caffey. It comes with a raise in rank as well. You might want to consider that."

"Yes, sir. It isn't that it isn't a generous offer – "

"It's more than generous. You'd be the youngest man to reach that rank. I'm offering you opportunities that you will never see hidden away way up here in the U.P."

"Yes, sir."

"But obviously you have some healing to do. And once your head is cleared up from the doc's medicine, you'll see what a great opportunity this is for you." Colonel Vandercook stood and placed his hat on his head. "Doors like this don't open every day."

Just then, the back door opened, and Phoebe entered carrying a bucket of fresh water.

Open doors. It was a great opportunity that Will knew he should seriously consider, not only for his career, but for his heart as well. Phoebe had shut any doors that Will had hoped to someday open in her life. What doors did he have left in Iron Falls?

But God had called him, hadn't he? And hadn't He called him to be Phoebe's protector? Or had Will misread God's plan all along. Maybe Will's calling as protector was only meant to extend to Phoebe for a short time. And maybe that time had come to an end.

Walk worthy of the vocation wherewith ye are called, with all lowliness and meekness, with longsuffering, forbearing one another in love.

Will pushed the thought aside as the doctor's medication began to take effect. The pain in his shoulder began to subside, but in its wake, the pain in his heart increased. Yes, he should go to Detroit, if for no other reason than to give his heart room to heal.

Will's eyes grew heavy. Yes. Room to heal.

"Well, Caffey, I bet when you volunteered for this post you weren't expecting excitement like this from a sleepy town like Iron Falls."

Will's eyes shot to Phoebe. She stared back at him, her mouth slowly falling open. She now knew the truth. Iron Falls had been his choice. "That is true, sir. I didn't expect this."

"We don't get many volunteers in the troops wanting to come to the U.P., especially one that graduated top of his class. You could have had your pick of posts."

Will hadn't lied to her. But he also never told her exactly how he came to be in Iron Falls. Yes, he had other posts available to choose from, but when one of them happened to be the same as where Phoebe was being called, then it seemed that God's hand had been in this from the beginning. "Yes, sir. But I felt like this is where God was calling me."

"You probably were hoping for a quieter assignment. Hope all this excitement hasn't disappointed you."

"No sir, but, if you please, I'll let some of the rest of you chase the rum runners for a bit while I rest up from this adventure."

45

THE AGGIE

"He is doing much better than I had expected, thank God. I had very low expectations when I left last night."

Phoebe turned, a little surprised at the doctor's voice. The other men had left so abruptly at her return, she'd barely noticed that Dr. Langley remained.

"His color is much better, I believe," she said. In truth, his coloring could have been improved by the natural light that poured in through the tiny window above the bed. Oil lamps did little to help a person's coloring - but there was more. His breathing was much less labored, and he slept far more peacefully now than he had all night long.

"Yes, I agree." Dr. Langley held his stethoscope to Will's chest and listened quietly. He nodded and smiled. "Our constable here is a fighter, that's for certain. But he still has a long way to go. He needs rest, time for his blood to build back up. The others are already talking about moving him back to the Constabulary barracks, but I told them I wouldn't allow it. He needs to stay put, until he's a little better." He looked up at Phoebe. "However, if you aren't comfortable with keeping him..."

Phoebe shook her head vigorously. "No sir, I'm not uncomfortable. I want to do whatever is necessary to help him back to full health." Her voice cracked as she choked back tears. "He saved my life."

Dr. Langley picked up his bag and hat. "Well, madam, from what I can tell, it seems you have also saved his."

Once the doctor had left, Phoebe quickly washed her hair and braided it. She then spent the remainder of the day alternating between scrubbing on her bloody dress and checking on Will. Will fitfully slept the day away, except for a few moments to eat some of the broth and bread Mrs. Speer had brought over. He no longer talked in his sleep, but occasionally grunted and winced when he moved. Phoebe felt helpless, wishing she could do something to make him more comfortable.

By the time Mrs. Speer brought the evening meal, Will's condition had not changed, but her dress had improved.

"How did that soap work out?" Mrs. Speer asked her quietly as the two women sat at the table.

"As good as I think is possible," Phoebe answered. "There is still a small area on the upper back that won't seem to budge, but there was a lot of blood..." Phoebe choked on those last words. The thought of Will's blood pouring down her back was still hard for her to think about.

Mrs. Speer patted her hand. "Would you like me to take it home and work on the stain?"

"No," Phoebe answered. "No, I think I will leave it. If I wear my hair down, it won't be noticeable. Besides, I think it will be a reminder of what he sacrificed to...to save me." Tears flowed freely down her cheeks, but she didn't care.

The older woman only stayed a few minutes more but promised to check on Phoebe the next day. When thinking back to her first encounter with Mrs. Speer, Phoebe couldn't help but marvel at what a difference a few months could make. So many things had changed. She had made many friends, grown confident as a pastor, and had fallen in ...

She looked at Will. She wondered if she should wake him. He seemed to be sleeping peacefully now, but he had eaten little today. He needed nourishment, she knew, but did he need rest more? She sat in the chair next to the bed and looked at him. In his restlessness, he had shed the blankets, leaving the upper half of his body exposed. He wore nothing on his torso, except for the bandage wrapped around his left shoulder. She reached out and gently touched the bandage, intending to pray for his healing, when like a bolt of lightning, Will grabbed her wrist and sat upright. Phoebe was so startled that a small scream escaped her lips.

"What are you doing?" he asked, frowning at her.

"I – I was just going to pray."

Will loosened his grip on her wrist but didn't let go. They sat there, looking into each other's eyes, not moving or saying a word. Will still frowned, and Phoebe thought that his eyes looked even more blue, if that were possible, when he was upset. Phoebe was the first to break the trance.

"Mrs. Speer brought dinner," she said, pulling her hand away and walking to the table.

"I'm not hungry."

She scooped some food on a plate and placed it on the bedside table. She grabbed the pillows and folded them behind his back.

"I said I'm not hungry," Will repeated, sounding annoyed.

"Hungry or not, you need to feed your body so it can heal. Now, would you like me to help you?"

"I don't need anyone to feed me. I still have complete use of my right arm," he answered gruffly.

Phoebe handed him the plate and returned to the table. Will's curt attitude was evidence that the effect of the whiskey had worn off. He was still angry with her, and she knew he had every right to be. She wanted to tell him everything, tell him how blind she had been, tell him how she truly felt, but now was not the time. What was important was Will's health. There would be plenty of time for petitions for forgiveness.

She dished herself some stew and ate silently at the table. She didn't look at him, wanting to give him whatever space he desired. But when she heard him grunt in pain, she couldn't keep her distance.

Phoebe bolted to the bed just in time to catch the plate before it toppled off. It was true that he had use of his right arm, but with a left arm completely immobilized, he had been balancing the plate on his lap with great difficulty. Phoebe sat down and held the plate so he could finish eating.

"I don't need your help," he grumbled, trying to take the plate from her.

She held it out of his reach and answered him gently. "Please, Will. Please allow me. It's the least I can do."

Will's stiff posture relaxed somewhat. He relented but said nothing. With her assistance, he finished the meal without speaking. But when he tried lying down again, it caused him so much pain that he couldn't keep quiet. He moaned so loudly Phoebe was concerned that he had hurt himself badly.

"Are you alright?"

"No, I'm not alright!" he shouted.

"Should I get the doctor?"

"No," he calmed down. "No. There's no need for that."

"But he could give you something for the pain."

"I don't want any more pain medication. I need to keep my wits about me."

Phoebe wasn't sure what he meant by that but decided that it was better not to question him. She took the plate and started cleaning the supper dishes. She was washing, lost in prayer, asking God to help Will heal. She wanted desperately to help him, to alleviate his discomfort, but she only seemed to be making him feel worse. She turned to glance at him, and to her surprise he was watching her. He looked away quickly. What had happened to the man that reveled in being caught staring at her? What had happened to the man that enjoyed making her uncomfortable with a smirk or a wink? She knew what had happened to him - she had broken his heart.

"I've changed my mind," he said, interrupting her thoughts. He spoke tenderly to her. "I would like to see the doctor. Would you mind fetching him for me?"

Phoebe found Dr. Langley at his home just beginning his evening meal. He promised to head over as soon as he had finished. Phoebe thanked him and hurried back to the parsonage, concerned to leave Will for too long unattended.

When she returned, she found Will sitting on the side of the bed attempting to dress himself.

"What on earth are you trying to do?"

He didn't stop what he was doing or look at her. "It's time I returned to the barracks and let you have your bed back."

"Dr. Langley said you shouldn't be moved if you are to heal properly."

"Well, he told me that I am healing much faster than expected, so I think it's time I get out of your way."

"You aren't in my way," she protested.

Will lifted his eyebrows over emotionless eyes. "Is that so? Where do you plan on sleeping tonight?"

Phoebe flushed. "I can sleep on the floor. I have plenty of blankets," she stammered nervously.

"I'm not letting you sleep on the floor, so that's not an option. So, is your plan to repeat last night's sleeping arrangement?"

Phoebe's face was hot with embarrassment. "Will, I am so sorry. Truly, I am. I should never have taken advantage of the situation like that. I can't explain it, I just – I don't know. I guess

I just needed to hold you in that moment. Not knowing if I would ever have another chance to..."

"Stop. Just stop," he said, dropping his head and clutching his shoulder, his face contorted in pain.

She came near to him, not certain what to do. She wanted to touch him but was afraid. Timidly, she sat on the bed next to him, but to her surprise he did not object. Despite her best resolve, she couldn't stop herself from reaching out and touching his arm. His hand left the bandage and clasped hers, drawing her hand to the middle of his chest. He held it there, embracing it against him tenderly. Phoebe drew closer to him and placed her right hand on his back. She leaned against him, resting her cheek gently on his arm, not wanting to hurt his injured shoulder. He seemed oblivious to the pain, though, as he pushed back against her, resting his cheek on her head.

"Please," she whispered, "don't go."

Without breaking contact, Will moved his head to face her. The motion caused her head to tilt toward his, forehead touching forehead. His lips were so close she could feel his ragged breath against her mouth. She had only to move slightly, and her lips would be on his. She remembered the taste of his kiss, the feel of his mouth against hers. She knew that he might reject her, but the urge was too much. She leaned forward, and to her relief, he met her kiss with a passion matching her own. His lips sought hers, hungrily drawing them between his own. Her heart pounded wildly, and she felt as if he were stealing her every breath yet felt at the same time as if he and he alone gave her breath to breathe.

"Will," she gasped against his lips, and the sound of her voice intensified Will's efforts. He kissed her deeper, harder. And she kissed him back with equal intensity. A moan escaped his throat as Phoebe's right arm slid around his waist and pulled him closer to her.

The sound of footsteps on the front porch broke the spell.

Will immediately released his grip and dropped her left hand. He sat upright and moved away from her. Stunned, Phoebe rose quickly and returned to the basin where she had been washing dishes. Doctor Langley knocked once then entered the tiny home.

"Well, Officer Caffey. I am surprised. Your color seems to have returned," the doctor said as he approached Will. He pulled the chair close to his patient and his brow furrowed. "In fact, you look quite flushed. You haven't been overexerting yourself, have you?"

Phoebe was grateful that the doctor's back was to her, because had he caught sight of her face, he would have noticed that she was far more flushed. She looked at Will, but he did not look at her. She excused herself to fetch more water.

Once outside, she splashed her face with the cold water from the pump. The temperature was still cool outside, and she prayed that the water and the weather would be enough to reverse the effects of what had just happened with Will. After only a minute, she felt confident and returned to the house. When she entered, though, she was met with the sight of Dr. Langley helping Will out of the parsonage.

"You're leaving?" was all she could say.

Dr. Langley answered. "He says that he thinks he will heal better in his own bed. I'll take him in my buggy and see that he gets properly settled."

Phoebe stood there, speechless, watching the two men slowly walk out.

Will never once looked back at her. As the doctor reached back in to shut the door, Will partially glanced over his shoulder. "Thank you for your hospitality, Miss Albright." Then he was gone.

Phoebe stood looking at the door, dazed. She hadn't planned to kiss Will, but once it happened, she had assumed it would change things, change his demeanor toward her. But it hadn't, and she was left with a strange, empty feeling. She had been the one to initiate the kiss. Still, he had kissed her back, heartily in fact. How could that not have changed things for him? Could he not see the truth? Didn't Will understand that she was desperately and absolutely in love with him?

As she stood, still staring at the closed door, someone knocked on the other side. Still caught in her daze, she opened it. Will stood there. Her heart began to pound wildly again.

"I am missing something," he said. "My mother's wedding ring. I was wearing it on a chain. Do you know what happened to it?"

Without a word, she walked to her dresser, opened the top drawer and pulled out his items. She returned to him, held the necklace dangling from her left hand and he grabbed it from her. He was about to leave, but she stopped him.

"You forgot something else."

He looked at her inquisitively. She grabbed his hand with her left and with her right, she placed the aggie in his palm. He took a deep breath and looked at it for several moments, and she thought he was about to say something. But he didn't. He nodded without looking at her then slowly wrapped his fingers around the marble. He pulled his hand away from hers and left.

4 6

COUNTING TO TEN

*O*ne day passed, then another and another with no word from Will. Phoebe wanted desperately to check on him, but short of barging into the barracks and demanding to see him, she had no way of doing so. Besides, her last visit to the constabulary had been humiliating enough to last a lifetime.

She took many walks around the center of town, hoping to see him sitting outside, getting fresh air or maybe going for a short walk, but no matter how many excuses she made to visit Mary at the store, she saw no sign of Will.

Although she saw nothing of Will, there was no lack of Michigan State Troopers around Iron Falls. Every time she left her house, she saw a different officer, most of whom she had never seen before. With no familiar faces near, she wasn't even able to ask another officer about Will. So, it was to her great relief when on the third day she did in fact see a familiar face. She waved at Jesse Moore as he rode by the church.

Moore guided his horse toward her. "Good afternoon, Pastor. What can I do for you?"

"I was just wondering if you had any news about Officer Caffey – about his health?"

Moore looked confused. "He hasn't been in contact with you?"

Phoebe felt her cheeks grow warm. "No, he hasn't."

"Well, I'm sure he will be soon. He's been real busy with all of the state officials in town."

"I had noticed a lot of new officers. They're here for Will?"

"Yep, that's right ma'am. Anyone who is anyone has come here this week. You saw for yourself that Vandercook was here and I'll tell you, that was pretty exciting. That beau of yours – he's being hailed as a hero across the entire state!"

"A hero? Yes, that is exactly what he is," Phoebe said. "And all of these people are here, just to congratulate him?"

"No, not exactly. I mean, yes, there's been a lot of accolades, to be sure, but they're actually all meeting here to go over the crime scene. There was plenty of incriminating evidence to link those men with a gang that's been giving our troopers in Detroit a run for their money. And our men have been setting up traps all around this area for other runners based on that evidence as well. Our jail is jam-packed with offenders right now."

"Do you mean to say that Will has been out in the field already? He has healed that much?"

"No ma'am, I'm sorry. Getting ahead of myself. No, the other officers you have seen around town, them along with me and Officer Little. But your original question was about Caffey's health. He's mending up quite well, but he's still in a lot of pain. The doctor still has him on bed rest, although he's snuck out a few times in the evening for a walk. I believe he's getting a little stir crazy being cooped up like that."

"I'm sure he is," Phoebe said. "Officer Moore, can I bother you with one more question?"

"Of course, Pastor. Anything."

"That night, the night that Officer Caffey," she swallowed hard. "The night he saved my life. The next morning, I overheard one of the men mention that Will volunteered for the post here in Iron Falls. Is that true?"

"Yes ma'am. It was a big deal at the time. You knew that he was the top of his class, right?"

"I hadn't, until it was mentioned the other day."

"Yep, and highly respected there in Lansing. He's not only real smart, but very skilled, but I guess you got to see his skills firsthand."

"What do you mean?"

"Well, that night, I mean. I've never met another man alive that can do what he did, facing three armed men with a hostage, dropping all three of them with one clean shot each, and surviving with only a scar on his shoulder as proof. And in the dark, no less! It's downright amazing."

Phoebe hadn't thought about the skill level needed to accomplish what Will had done.

"Well, if he had his pick of posts, why on earth did he choose Iron Falls?"

"That's what none of us could ever figure out. To be honest, I wasn't very happy about his arrival. I expected him to be an arrogant son of a — pardon me, ma'am. Let's just say, I was a bit jealous of him. But I gotta admit that he was the right man for the job. None of us realized how much liquor was running through the woods surrounding this area. But somehow Caffey figured it out."

There was a sound behind Phoebe, and both she and Moore looked up to see Mary come out of the store.

"Well, I must be going," said Jesse Moore. "Good day Mrs. Simmons. Good day Pastor Albright. And I'll be sure to let Caffey know you were wondering about him."

Phoebe tried to protest, but he had already ridden off. She sighed and dropped her shoulders. How would Will react if he knew she was speaking to other State Troopers about him? She heard Mary laughing behind her.

"What's the matter? Why don't you want your Will to know that he fills your every thought?" Mary teased.

Phoebe looked up at her friend. With tears forming in her eyes, she said quietly, "Oh, Mary. I've been so wrong. And I think I have damaged Will's feelings for me beyond repair."

Mary's eyes grew wide. She stuck her head back through the door.

"Jack, mind the store please. I'll be back in an hour or so," she said and rushed down the stairs. They walked to the parsonage, arm in arm, Phoebe crying and lamenting her story of turning down Will's declaration of love and of all that had happened since, Mary listening and consoling her. Once inside, Mary made a pot of tea.

"And then we kissed…"

"What? Did you say you kissed?" she said, seating herself next to Phoebe at the table.

"Yes. Well, I kissed him."

"You kissed him?" Mary's eyes were wide. "Did he kiss you back?"

"Yes," Phoebe said, looking straight at Mary. "Very much so."

"Well, then, it can't be as bad as you say. He must still have feelings for you if he kissed you."

"That's what I thought at first, but he still left. And he wouldn't look at me. He was so cold."

"Oh Phoebe, I wish I knew what to tell you. I can't begin to understand what Will is thinking. There are still times that I don't understand my own husband's mind. But what I do know is that if a man makes himself vulnerable to a woman like Will did to you, and is rejected, it can be very devastating to his heart. It may take a long time to heal. But dear, isn't it better that it happened now so that Will can move on and learn to forget about you. That is, unless you have discovered what I've thought all along – that you actually do have feelings for Will Caffey?"

At this, Phoebe's tears turned to sobs. Mary pulled her chair close and hugged her friend.

"That's what I was afraid of. Oh my, you are in a difficult spot, aren't you?"

∽

ANOTHER WEEK PASSED, and still no word from Will. He had even avoided attending church service, the one place she thought for certain she would be able to approach him. Phoebe knew he was hurt, both physically and emotionally, and tried to be patient. However, patience had never been her strongest trait, and her nerves were wearing very thin.

Mary had encouraged Phoebe to write her feelings out in a letter to Will.

"John will deliver it," Mary had said. "You mustn't wait a moment longer."

But Phoebe hesitated. That isn't how she wanted to tell Will of her change of heart. He had been honest about his feelings from the start and had never shied away from verbalizing those feelings. And he deserved nothing less from her.

But after another week with no contact, she felt her options were limited. So, she found herself opening her box of stationery, the box that hadn't been opened since Wendell's letter had been written and attempted to put the truth of her heart down on paper.

She was several drafts in before she crumpled her last piece of stationery and dropped her head on the table. How does one put into words not only the depth of foolishness they have exhibited, but also the intensity of love that they now feel without it sounding trite? Phoebe surely did not know, and that fact made her heart ache even more.

Someone knocked at her door and Phoebe looked at her watch. Mary was early for tea, and Phoebe could not be happier.

Maybe Mary could help her with the letter, and hopefully, some fresh stationery.

But when she opened the door, it wasn't Mary standing on the other side.

"Will!"

As if out of a dream, he stood in uniform, clean and crisp, hair meticulously combed back. His hat, held steadily in his hands, looked oddly intrusive the way it separated her from throwing herself into his arms.

"Hello, Phoebe." Will stared at her for several moments with a look she didn't quite recognize, and she wondered if he was still experiencing pain from his injury. "May I come in?"

"Oh!" she said, backing up hurriedly. "Yes, of course. Please." She motioned for him to join her at the table.

Will's eyes darted around the pile of crumpled stationery.

"I — I was just writing you a letter," she stuttered, quickly sweeping the balls of paper out of the way.

"Me?"

"Yes," she answered easily. No blushing. No stammering. The time had come to tell Will everything. "I have much to say."

"So do I," he began.

Phoebe took a step toward Will. "You were right, Will." She took another step. "You were right about so many things." She reached her hand toward him.

"I'm leaving Iron Falls."

It was said so quickly and with so little emotion, Phoebe thought for certain that she had misheard him. "Leaving?"

"Yes," Will answered. "I've been offered a post in Detroit. I leave immediately."

"But — but what about —?" *me*, she thought.

"Jesse Moore has been promoted to Sergeant. He is a fine officer. I have no doubt Iron Falls is in good hands."

"I'm… I'm sorry Will…"

He stared at her, eyes void of any affection, and it chilled her.

It occurred to her that for as long as she could remember, Will had looked upon her with affection...no, he had always looked upon her with love. The chilling reality of the present situation reminded her of John's words at Wendell's funeral.

"Even strong men like Will can have fragile hearts. They can sustain a chip easily and even a crack, but when broken completely, even the sincerest apology won't be able to repair it."

"There's no need for an apology. This is an amazing opportunity for me," Will interrupted. "Opportunities like this don't come around every day."

She had done it. She had broken Will's heart irrevocably. And sorry wasn't going to fix it. Not this time.

"I don't know what to say," she said, her own soft words sounding petty to her own ears.

She watched Will swallow hard and felt the vice around her heart squeeze tighter. She had never seen him this distant before. The anger he must feel for her...

"Say you wish me well," he finally answered. "Say you will pray for me."

She didn't want to wish him well. She didn't want him to leave. She wanted to throw herself into his arms, beg him for forgiveness, ask him to stay. But she didn't. Once upon a time, Will had quietly supported her as she followed her dreams. Will had set his own dreams aside and had given up far better opportunities to come to Iron Falls just so he could ensure that Phoebe's calling was fulfilled. He had done nothing to deserve what he had endured. It was Phoebe's own fault, her own selfish desires that had caused her to lose this man's love. But she refused to be so selfish as to keep him from answering his own calling. It was Will's turn to follow his heart. Even if it meant that hers would be broken in the process.

"I wish you well, Will," she said. "And you will be in my prayers. Every day."

Will nodded once, picked up his haversack, and left the

parsonage.

Phoebe slowly counted to ten, begging God to return Will to her, begging Him to urge Will to turn back. But the longer she stared at the closed doors, the weaker her knees became until, all at once, they gave out beneath her, landing her in a sobbing puddle in the middle of the room.

WILL STOOD outside of the parsonage for several moments. He stood completely still, waiting for some sort of sign, some sort of reason to not go.

Every fiber in his being said to turn around. Walk back into that cabin and wrap her in his arms. Tell her that he loves her.

But he didn't. Because his loving her had never been the issue. After all these years, after everything they had been through, Phoebe still did not love him. And there was nothing he could do to change that.

Leaving was the right thing to do, the right thing for both of them. Will knew that was the truth.

Then why was it so difficult?

Just move, he told himself. *Take one step, then another, until you step onto that train.*

It was that simple. And it was that difficult.

"Dear God, please help me."

But he heard no answer. He felt nothing from God. He only felt the constricting pain in his chest each time he breathed, each time his heart beat.

"Just move," he said.

Will took one step, then another. He walked away, from the cabin, from his hopes, from what he had thought God had called him to.

And he walked away from the only woman he knew he would ever love.

MEETING THE COMMANDING OFFICER

DECEMBER 1919

a brisk winter wind hit Phoebe hard as she stepped out of Simmons' store. She buttoned the top of her coat tightly around her neck and hurried toward the train depot. She was too impatient to wait until she reached home to read the letter she had just received, so she took refuge in the partition on the empty platform that had been erected to block the wind for waiting passengers. The platform was empty now and would offer her all the privacy, and shelter, she needed.

Phoebe ripped open the envelope and began to read.

Dear Miss Albright,

I must admit that your letter was a bit of a shock, not only in content, but also in attitude, and it took me a few days to digest the full weight of it entirely...

Phoebe squeezed her eyes tightly, afraid to read on. Unlike the letter to her father when she had first arrived in Iron Falls, which she had written hastily and with anger in her heart, her letter to Dr. Berger had been written with intention, each word chosen carefully and prayed over. Her future in Iron Falls depended on it. If Dr. Berger's response was negative, she had no other recourse but to abandon her ministry in the Upper Peninsula and return home, having failed at not only love, but God's work as well.

She took a deep breath and continued.

Now that I have taken the time to pray and to consider your words carefully, I have an answer for you.

Never in all of my career have I been taken to task by a subordinate the way that you did in your letter. My first inclination was to travel to Iron Falls post haste and relieve you of your position immediately. However, that was before my wife got a hold of your letter.

You see, although I have never been taken to task by a subordinate in the church, I am well practiced in the art by my wife. It has been with her guidance that I can now see the error of my ways. As you so eloquently pointed out, the only fault I found in your ministry was the fact of your singleness. In every other sense, your work has been exemplary. To remove a successful pastor from a pastorate just because he or she is unmarried is ridiculous and I am embarrassed to admit that you are correct...if you were a man, I never would have considered this.

Please understand, I never meant to insult you. But, as my very wise wife has pointed out, just because I would not be where I am today without her by my side does not mean that somehow you are unable to complete God's calling on your life just because God has not chosen a mate for you.

I pray that you can find it in your heart to forgive this old, ignorant man. I pray that God will continue to bless your ministry in the Upper Peninsula.

Sincerely,

Dr. Francis Berger

"Well, good morning to you, Pastor Albright."

Phoebe jumped, nearly dropping the letter. "Officer Moore! I'm sorry. I was so engrossed in my letter that I didn't see you."

He smiled and nodded toward the papers in her hand. "Good news, I hope?"

Phoebe smiled as she refolded it and placed it back in the envelope. "The best."

Jesse Moore smiled. "Glad to hear it. I was hoping I would get a chance to see you before I shipped out."

Phoebe had not noticed the bag on his shoulder before now. "Shipped out? Are you traveling somewhere?"

"Yes, ma'am. Detroit."

Detroit.

Will.

"Oh, how long will you be there?" she asked, trying to sound far more nonchalant than she felt.

"Well, forever, I hope. Detroit is my new assignment."

Jealousy swelled within her at the thought of this man being able to see Will on a daily basis. "This is sad news for Iron Falls, Officer Moore, but I do hope that it is happy news for you."

"It sure is, ma'am. I'm finally gonna take a swing at big city living."

Phoebe smiled. "Then I am very happy for you."

Moore's mouth opened, but any words he might have wanted to say would have been drowned out by the incoming train that screeched into the station. He nodded and smiled, then turned to the slowing train that would be his exit from the Upper Peninsula and the transport to his waiting future.

Since Will's departure, Jesse Moore had been Phoebe's only connection to the Michigan State Constabulary. Many of the officers she had become acquainted with had moved on, some returning home, some receiving promotions and new assignments in the wake of the Parker incident and ensuing arrests. Only Moore had remained, along with a slew of new officers that Phoebe did not know. With Moore's departure, so left any news of Will Phoebe could receive. Up until this point, she had been afraid to ask, but now it felt as if it were her last opportunity.

"Wait!" she yelled above the scream of iron scraping against iron as the train came to a stop.

Moore turned a questioning look to her. "Yes?"

Phoebe clasped her hands, willing them to stop shaking. "Officer Moore, have you —" the words caught in her throat.

"Have I what, ma'am?"

This was it. This was her last opportunity to ask for news of Will, and she couldn't form the words in her own mouth. How many nights had she sat at her window, wishing to see the silhouette form of a trooper on horseback ride by her parsonage? How many Sundays had she stood before her congregation, hoping to see Will standing in the back, offering his encouraging smile? How many times had she collected mail, begging God for a letter from him? She had lost count. But Will had not returned for her. He had sent no communication. He did not want her in his life. And she needed to respect that.

Phoebe forced a weak smile. "Never mind. It's nothing."

Moore's face softened as if reading her mind and Phoebe felt an all too familiar feeling of misery rising in her throat. She choked it back and offered him her best smile possible.

"Do write and let us all know how you are doing in Detroit."

"I sure will."

Phoebe nodded and turned to leave.

"One more thing," Moore said, drawing her attention back. "I want you to know that I'm leaving you in good hands. When Caffey left, I promised him I'd keep an eye on you, make sure you were kept safe."

It was too much for Phoebe. Hearing the one name she so

desperately wanted to ask Moore about and hearing that he had thought about her before leaving Iron Falls was too much to bear. She wiped in vain at the tear that fell down her cheek, only to find another following quickly behind.

"That's awfully kind of you," she said as she continued to wipe away the tears.

At the sight of her crying, Moore seemed to grow uncomfortable. "I have to get goin', but before I leave, I'll make sure the new Commanding Officer makes that same promise as well."

Panic seized her. "Oh, no. That isn't necessary —"

"A promise is a promise. I can't leave 'til I know you'll be looked after." Moore looked over her shoulder. "There he is now, gettin' off the train. I'll introduce ya."

Before she could protest, Moore passed her and headed toward the train.

Grateful that her back was to the platform, Phoebe's swipes at her face became much more purposeful as the horror of meeting the new officer with a tear-soaked face brought her crying to an end. Never in her life had she been so thankful for the crisp, December winds of Michigan. She only hoped it would be enough to erase any evidence of her tears, because as quickly as he left, Jesse Moore returned.

"I can leave in good conscience now." Moore smiled and nodded joyfully at her. "Good luck to ya, Pastor Albright," he said before picking up his haversack and rushing back to the train.

"Wait! Aren't you going to introduce —" but he didn't hear her. He had already jumped onto the train as the whistle blew.

Phoebe took a deep breath then slowly turned.

The platform was empty save for the Michigan State police officer that stood there, knapsack in hand. He wore the familiar khaki uniform and khaki Montana campaign hat.

He also bore the mesmerizing blue eyes that had become so familiar to her as well.

"Will," she breathed.

Will Caffey dropped his haversack and slowly made his way to her.

Phoebe's hand started shaking and she felt her knees knocking beneath her. Was this real? He'd felt so real in the dreams that had haunted her since he'd left.

The closer he came, the more real it became. This was Will. And he'd come back.

"What — what are you doing here?" she asked, shakily.

"Iron Falls needed a new commanding officer."

He hadn't come back for her. He'd been assigned.

"I'm so sorry, I thought they were going to give you your pick of assignments. This must be very disappointing for you."

"I was given my pick. I chose Iron Falls."

Phoebe's heart began to beat rapidly. *Will chose Iron Falls?*

He dropped his bag and moved closer. "No more lies. No more deceptions, Phoebe. From now on, only the whole truth. I asked for this post. I asked to return to Iron Falls."

"But why?" She hoped that she knew the answer but didn't dare believe that it could actually be true.

"I think it rather obvious." He stepped closer to her. "These past two weeks have been torture."

Phoebe nodded, tears welling in her eyes. "I'm so sorry, Will. I never meant to hurt you."

"I'm the one to apologize. You have been very clear where your heart stood. God had called me to wait for you, and I got impatient. And when your life was on the line, I lost my mind. All that time spent on the battlefield, my own life on the line, never once did I worry about my own safety. Then when I thought I would lose you? My whole world fell apart. And I didn't know how to handle that. I thought if I left, it would make not having you as mine easier to handle. What I've learned is that without you, Phoebe Albright, my life isn't worth living. So even if I can't have you, even if you never love me, just being near you will have to be enough."

"No," Phoebe said her voice quivering.

"Please don't argue with me Phoebe. I give you my word. I will respect your wishes. I will keep my distance. But please don't exclude me from your life entirely."

"No," she repeated. "That will never work."

Will exhaled and his shoulders dropped. "Don't tell me that. Please. I've come all this way. You have no idea the sacrifices I've made in my career in order to —"

"It will never work," Phoebe interrupted, "because I cannot be near you, day after day, and not love you."

Will's mouth opened and quivered, as if looking for words he could not find, until it finally decided to curl into one of the handsomest smiles Phoebe had ever seen.

"Really, Pheebs? Do you mean it?"

A laugh escaped her. "I've never meant anything more in my entire life."

Without hesitation, Will wrapped his arms around her and pulled her to him. She wrapped her arms around his neck as he buried his face in her hair.

"I am the most blessed man in the world," he whispered. "I only wish we weren't in the middle of town for all to see, because there is something I would like to do right now."

"Do you mean give me something that belongs to me?"

Will pulled back and looked at her quizzically. He lifted a brow. "I'd like to give you something. And, yes, I do suppose my lips have always belonged to you."

She swatted at him playfully. "What I'm talking about is hanging from your neck, not plastered on your face."

Will's face grew solemn as her words sunk in. He removed his hands from her waist and reached up to pull the necklace out from his shirt collar. As he unclasped the chain, he knelt in front of her, tears streaming down his cheeks.

"Phoebe Renee Albright. You were my first love, and you will always be my forever love. Would you make me complete and become my wife?"

With tears streaming down her face, she said, "William Harrison Caffey, it is I who is completed by you. You were always, and will always be, God's best for me. Yes, I will marry you."

Will placed his mother's ring on her finger, stood, and wrapped her in his arms again, and this time, neither of them cared who saw as he gave her the kiss that had always belonged to her.

- THE END -

<<<<>>>>

Forgiving Sarah

CHAPTER ONE

Of all the situations Sarah had gotten herself into in her life, this could possibly be the worst one yet. But could she really be to blame? It wasn't her idea to pack her up and ship her off to Bible College. It was her parents' idea, and it had been a terrible one at that. How could they expect her to breathe in such a suffocating confinement masquerading as an educational institution. It was insufferable and she could no longer bear it. So yes, she was about to do something terrible, something that would likely humiliate her parents and bring her father's wrath upon her in a way far greater than she had ever experienced, but her mother and father only had themselves to blame. It was, after all, their fault that she was in this situation in the first place.

Vindication did little to calm Sarah's queasy stomach. She was confident this was the only way out of her situation, but the longer she waited, the less confident she became. She pressed her back against the wall and melted into the darkness of the hallway. They should have been here by now. She knew the letters had been delivered. Why hadn't they acted on them yet?

Maybe she was being overly foolish. *She who hurries her footsteps errs.* Sarah sighed. Now she was beginning to think like her mother.

Her mother. Would she ever be able to forgive Sarah? Doubt began to creep into Sarah's bones, inching its way up her spine, and for the first time since conceiving the idea, Sarah wondered if maybe it wasn't such a great one. Footsteps sounding down the distant hall ended her doubts, however. They were coming. Time to finish what she had set into motion.

She carefully turned the handle of the door and quickly slipped into the classroom. A man sat bent over a desk, completely oblivious to her presence. She peered over her shoulder, very much aware of the presences approaching the room.

Sarah cleared her throat. "Professor Foley?"

The man jumped. "Miss Albright! You startled me."

"I – I'm so sorry," she said, lowering her head. "I didn't mean to..." her voice cracked as tears began flowing down her cheeks.

Professor Foley rushed from his seat and crossed the room. "Miss Albright? What is the matter?"

Sarah shook her head, allowing the tears to fall freely. The professor pulled out a handkerchief and offered it to her. She wiped her cheeks, but kept her head bowed.

He placed his hands on her shoulders. "Chin up. Whatever it is, I'll do my best to help," the man said kindly.

She looked up then and nodded. "Yes. I'm certain that you can." Immediately, Sarah threw her body against his, wrapped her arms around his neck and kissed him.

~

CHAPTER TWO

Grant Foley paced back and forth outside the office of his administrator, the dean of students. He was waiting for his turn, whatever that meant. He paused and stared at the paneled wood door, wishing he knew what was being said on the other side, yet not wanting to know at the same time.

How could he have gotten caught in such a compromising situation? He had always been so careful not to let any hint of impropriety enter into his relationships with his students. He kept his distance, remaining aloof and detached, often erring on the side of being rude to the women in his classes. He never dreamed any of the young women he taught would find him the least bit desirable, let alone throw themselves at him.

That poor girl. He had heard of young women developing crushes on their professors. He had read about it in an academic journal, but had laughed it off. Grant had never been one to turn many women's heads in the past, so he hadn't worried about it happening to him. There had been only one woman who had ever noticed him, and that had ended with Grant's heart torn in two.

But apparently this student-love complex was a real thing, and the poor Albright girl had somehow found herself wrapped up in some sort of fantasy involving him. He felt for her, really he did. He just hoped that the dean was kind to her. She had acted impulsively, of course, but she was young and probably didn't realize the consequences of her actions.

Did you consider the consequences of your actions?

Grant stuffed his hands in his pockets and began pacing again. He was caught off guard, of course. Any man would have reacted similarly in his situation. Wouldn't he?

Grant shook his head and continued pacing. What man wouldn't lose himself in a kiss to a beautiful woman? That's all it was, a temporary loss of reason. He had been caught off guard, that's all. Otherwise he would have pushed her away the second her lips touched his. Naturally, he had done nothing wrong.

But if that were true, why did he feel like he had something to apologize for?

The door opened suddenly, light flooding the dimly lit corridor of Grant's pacing.

"Professor Foley," the dean said solemnly. "Would you please join us?"

Miss Albright sat in a leather chair across from the dean's desk. The dean motioned for Grant to take the seat next to her.

Dean Baker sat down at his desk. "I have spoken at length with Miss Albright about her actions and the road that a life of sin can lead a person down."

Just as he thought. The man was shaming the girl. "Sir, I don't think Miss Albright had any malicious intent – "

"Malicious or not, there are consequences. We all must answer for our sins."

Grant nodded. "And Jesus paid the ultimate sacrifice so we could be washed clean of our transgressions."

The dean drummed his fingers on the leather blotter. "Of course. We will someday reap the rewards in heaven."

Grant couldn't help but notice that the sour expression on the man's face did not match the joy of the words he spoke.

"But," Dean Baker said. "On this side of paradise, there are consequences."

Grant didn't like where the conversation was headed. "Consequences? Surely, you aren't considering expelling the girl?"

His eyebrows shot up. "Do you think sin should go unpunished, Mr. Foley?"

"Of course not – "

"Good. I'm glad we understand each other." The dean stood. "Miss Albright, I will contact your parents immediately, but until such time as they can retrieve you from this institution, I expect you to remain in your room, and you will tell no one of what has transpired here this evening, do I make myself clear?"

Grant turned to look at the girl, expecting some sort of teary outburst. But she only nodded, a slight twitching playing at the corners of her mouth.

He turned back to the dean. "Don't you think that is harsh for – "

"And I expect you to be gone by morning, Mr. Foley."

Grant stopped breathing. "Excuse me?"

"If you leave discreetly, the college will let this scandal die quietly. However, there will, of course, be no letter of recommendation."

Grant jumped to his feet. "You can't be serious! I've done nothing wrong!"

"This college cannot be associated with a disgrace such as yours."

"Disgrace? What have I done?"

"You've led a young woman down the path of unrighteousness. It cannot be tolerated by this college."

"No, you can't fire Professor Foley! I kissed him. He holds no fault in this!"

Grant looked at the girl. The twitching lips were gone, replaced with a look of horror.

"I'm sorry, but you have made your bed. Now you both shall lie in it." The dean grabbed his coat and left Grant and his student staring after him.

A piercing throb began to beat in his temples. Was he dreaming? He couldn't possibly have just been fired, could he? Somewhere deep in his mind, he knew he should say something to the girl, offer her some sort of comfort, but he couldn't move. A coldness swept down his spine, making him certain he was frozen in this moment in time. Miss Albright's voice finally broke through the icy silence.

"It wasn't supposed to happen this way. They were only supposed to send me home."

Grant slowly turned to look at her. "What did you just say?"

She jumped, as if she had forgotten he was there. "I – I'm sorry. I didn't mean for this to...I never thought they would fire you."

Realization broke through the ice that had gathered in his brain. Swift heat flooded his system as her words sank in. "You planned this?"

"No! I mean, I didn't plan for you to get fired."

"But, you did plan this! You deliberately set out to ruin me!"

"It wasn't supposed to happen like this."

"Then how was it supposed to happen, Miss Albright? A reprimand? A campus-wide shaming? Is that it? Was your intent to publicly humiliate me?"

Perfectly arched eyebrows knitted above her green eyes. "I admit that I acted rashly, but you have to believe me when I say that I never intended to injure you."

"What I believe, Miss Albright, is that you are a spoiled little girl that thinks of no one but herself. You are a disgrace and an embarrassment to yourself and your parents. You should be ashamed of yourself."

The girl bit her bottom lip and squared her shoulders. "Trust me, I am well aware of that fact. I've known it my entire life." She pushed past him and ran out the door.

Grant stood staring at the empty doorway for several moments before numbly heading to his classroom, or what used to be his classroom.

The room was dark, save for the moonlight that filtered through the tall windows. But even in the dim light, Grant could make out every corner of the room. The large, scratched blackboard that spanned the front wall still displayed the notes from the day's classes. It was in desperate need of repair, maybe even replacement, but Grant's maintenance repair requests had gone unanswered for weeks. The rows of desks, half of which wobbled underneath the students that occupied them daily, sat askew, begging to be straightened. The small, chipped teacher's desk, much too small for a man of Grant's stature, sat in the corner, his Bible and notes still scattered across it where he had left them. All in all, it was a miserable excuse for a classroom, but as a first year professor, he hadn't expected grand accommodations. Still, it had been his classroom, an answer to not only his dreams, but also his prayers. And now it was all gone...his dreams and his future. No other Christian college would employ a man fired for misconduct with a female student.

Grant returned to his desk and began gathering his notes. As he did, his eyes fell on the last thing he had written... "God is God, no matter what your circumstances. If he is God in the good times, he has to be God in the bad."

He dropped into the chair and cradled his head in his hands. "I know you're still God, but it doesn't feel like you're here right now." A breeze blew through the open window, cooling the tears that coursed down his cheeks. Never in all his life had he felt so rejected. But he knew the truth of the lesson he had just prepared. God was still God, even though Grant's life was falling apart around him.

He wiped his eyes with the back of his sleeve. He stood and stuffed the contents of his desk into his attache. Then he walked up and down the rows of desks, slowly straightening each one as he went. Finally, he picked up the large, tufted felt eraser and began the work of cleaning the blackboard. He started with the terms for his Homiletics class and moved across the board, clearing each class's notes one subject at a time. He was just wiping the notes from Systematic Theology, Miss Albright's class, and his hands stopped. His face grew hot at the memory of the conniving blonde. She had ruined him and his future with her impulsive behavior, and she had deserved every harsh word he had spat at her. He knew she deserved it. He pushed back the guilty twisting that rumbled in his stomach.

When the room was sufficiently cleaned and prepped for the next day and for whomever took over his classes, he grabbed his case and left the classroom, and his dreams, behind.

～

A MESSAGE FROM JEN

~

Here it is. Finally. The story that launched my writing journey.

Years ago, when I first decided that it was time to finally commit to writing a novel, this is the novel I began writing. At the time, I thought God was giving me this one story, so I threw myself totally into the writing of Phoebe and Will's tale. The problem was, I jumped in without any thought to story structure or plot. 130,000 words in, and I had a mess on my hands. It didn't help that I put this novel aside to write Anna and Esther's books first. But, after *a lot* of editing and prayer and work...A Calling for Phoebe is finally finished.

As you may already know, my youngest daughter's name is Phoebe. However, the heroine of this story is not named after my daughter and is in no way patterned after her. But the origins of Phoebe Albright did begin during my pregnancy. When trying to agree on a name, both my husband and I quickly agreed on Phoebe. We liked it, and I knew it was a Biblical name (as are my other two daughters' names) but I knew nothing about Phoebe in the Bible. So, I did a little research.

Not much is said about Phoebe, but what is said tells us a lot. You will find her account in the Book of Romans, chapter 16 verses 1 and 2. There is so much that I could unpack right now about these two verses, but in favor of brevity, I will just point out two words that are important: *diakonos* and *prostatis*. With these two words, along with the fact that Paul trusted her enough to give her the responsibility of delivering his letter to Rome on his behalf, we can see that not only was Phoebe a well-respected benefactor, but she was also a minister as well! (If you are interested in reading more on this, I wrote an entire blog post on it that you can read here...)

Much later, I came across an article that shared the statistics of female pastors over the years within the denomination of which I am a member. In the statistics, I discovered that there were several hundred women pastors around the time of World War 1, but by World War 2, there were less than fifty. What had changed? I still don't know, but I was intrigued. What would it be like to be a woman in the ministry during the time following The Great War? What kind of woman would choose the life of a pastor? These questions led me to the Phoebe of this novel.

But you can't have a romance without the handsome hero, right? So, what kind of man would be the perfect foil for my confident, independent pastor? Exactly what she thinks she doesn't need...someone obsessed with protecting her. Thus, Will Caffey was born. The name William means "protector" and Will certainly fits that description...to a fault, because you can't have a hero who is perfect, right?

I truly hope you enjoyed reading Phoebe and Will's love story. They are two of my favorite characters, and to be honest, I'm kind of sad to be finished with their romance. Maybe I should write a sequel that follows their romance into marriage...

But first, Sarah gets her love story!

ACKNOWLEDGMENTS

~

As always, first gratitude goes to the Lord. I'll never understand why You chose someone as undeserving as me to share these stories, but I am grateful for this journey.

To my family. We are a team, and without your day-to-day help, I would never have been able to finish this novel. You make life amazing. I love you 3,000.

To parents, my greatest cheerleaders and helpers. Thank you for every minute of babysitting, every phone call, and every bit of behind-the-scenes help you have given me over the years. I am the woman I am today because of the two of you. I love you both very much.

To my friend and editor, Jamie Hershberger. This book was rough, and the amount of time and energy you put into editing it was proof of that. Thank you for not giving up on me or this novel. Great things are happening, and much of that is due to you and the love you show me. I appreciate you more than you will ever realize.

To the ladies of the Christian Indie Writers' podcast, Tina, Rhonda and Jamie. You are my writing partners, my accountability keepers, and my friends. I love and appreciate you knuckleheads!

To Jennifer McNab, thank you not only for your meticulous attention to detail that made this book shine, but for your enthusiastic support of all my books! Thank you for being my friend!

And finally, to my Phoebe. May you always answer God's call on your life and may you find your own Will to support and protect you as you do. *Love, Mommy*

ABOUT THE AUTHOR

Jenifer Carll-Tong is the author of historical Christian romances. She is a graduate of Boston University's College of Communication. Searching for Anna is her debut novel.

Jenifer lives in Michigan with her handsome husband, three beautiful daughters and two lazy dogs. She also has three adult stepchildren who have left the nest, but not her heart. When she isn't writing kissing scenes between devilishly handsome heroes and strong, independent heroines, you might find her napping or wearing sandals in the snow. You probably won't find her cleaning her house. Unless company is coming over.

Learn more about Jenifer and her books HERE .

And don't forget to sign up for her newsletter to stay up to date on the latest news and releases. Visit https://goo.gl/Qur2sU and you will also receive the *Avoiding Esther* ebook absolutely free for signing up!

facebook.com/jenifercarlltongauthor
instagram.com/jencarlltong

ALSO BY JENIFER CARLL-TONG

Love in Lansing Series

Book One

Searching for Anna

Book Two

Avoiding Esther

CPSIA information can be obtained
at www.ICGtesting.com
Printed in the USA
LVHW032319210721
693313LV00005B/780

9 781733 682244